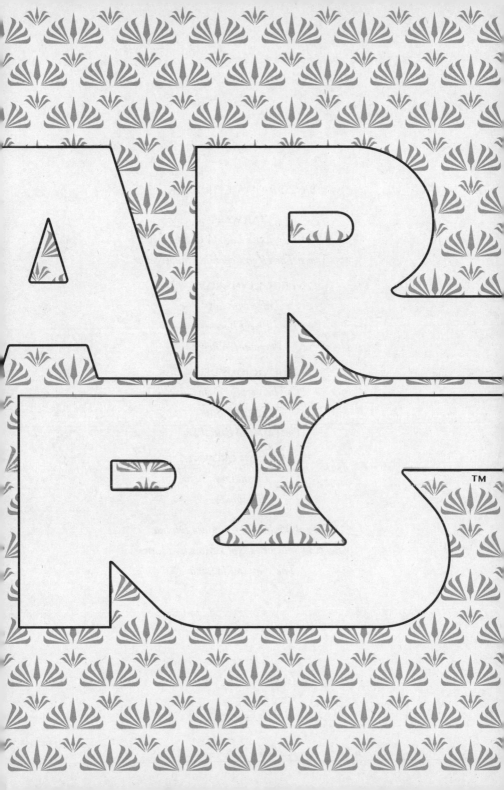

BY ZORAIDA CÓRDOVA

STAR WARS
Star Wars: Galaxy's Edge: A Crash of Fate
Star Wars: The High Republic: Convergence

BROOKLYN BRUJAS
Labyrinth Lost
Bruja Born
Wayward Witch

THE VICIOUS DEEP
The Vicious Deep
The Savage Blue
The Vast and Brutal Sea

HOLLOW CROWN
Incendiary
Illusionary

The Inheritance of Orquídea Divina
Valentina Salazar Is Not a Monster Hunter
The Way to Rio Luna

CONVERGENCE

STAR WARS

THE HIGH REPUBLIC

CONVERGENCE

Zoraida Córdova

RANDOM HOUSE

WORLDS

NEW YORK

2023 Random House Worlds Trade Paperback Edition

Copyright © 2022 by Lucasfilm Ltd. & ® or ™ where indicated.
All rights reserved.
Excerpt from *Star Wars: The High Republic: Cataclysm*
by Lydia Kang copyright © 2023 by Lucasfilm Ltd.
& ® or ™ where indicated. All rights reserved.

Published in the United States by Random House Worlds,
an imprint of Random House, a division of
Penguin Random House LLC, New York.

RANDOM HOUSE is a registered trademark, and
RANDOM HOUSE WORLDS and colophon are
trademarks of Penguin Random House LLC.

Originally published in hardcover in the United States
by Del Rey, an imprint of Random House,
a division of Penguin Random House LLC, in 2022.

This book contains an excerpt from the book
Star Wars: The High Republic: Cataclysm by Lydia Kang.
This excerpt has been set for this edition only and may
not reflect the final content of the forthcoming edition.

ISBN 978-0-593-35865-8
Ebook ISBN 978-0-593-35864-1

Printed in the United States of America on acid-free paper

randomhousebooks.com

2 4 6 8 9 7 5 3 1

For Alexis Daria and Adriana Herrera.
You literally got me through this book.

Que la Fuerza las acompañe.

THE HIGH REPUBLIC

Convergence
The Battle of Jedha
Cataclysm

Light of the Jedi
The Rising Storm
Tempest Runner
The Fallen Star

Dooku: Jedi Lost
Master and Apprentice

I   THE PHANTOM MENACE

II   ATTACK OF THE CLONES

Brotherhood
The Thrawn Ascendancy Trilogy
Dark Disciple: A Clone Wars Novel

III   REVENGE OF THE SITH

Inquisitor: Rise of the Red Blade
Catalyst: A Rogue One Novel
Lords of the Sith
Tarkin
Jedi: Battle Scars

SOLO

Thrawn
A New Dawn: A Rebels Novel
Thrawn: Alliances
Thrawn: Treason

ROGUE ONE

IV   A NEW HOPE

Battlefront II: Inferno Squad
Heir to the Jedi
Doctor Aphra
Battlefront: Twilight Company

V   THE EMPIRE STRIKES BACK

VI   RETURN OF THE JEDI

The Princess and the Scoundrel
The Alphabet Squadron Trilogy
The Aftermath Trilogy
Last Shot

Shadow of the Sith
Bloodline
Phasma
Canto Bight

VII   THE FORCE AWAKENS

VIII   THE LAST JEDI

Resistance Reborn
Galaxy's Edge: Black Spire

IX   THE RISE OF SKYWALKER

A long time ago in a galaxy far, far away. . . .

It is a time of great exploration. In an effort to unite the galaxy, the chancellors of the Republic, working alongside the courageous and wise Jedi Knights, have dispatched dozens of PATHFINDER TEAMS into the farthest reaches of the Outer Rim.

But it is also a time of great uncertainty. Communication is unreliable, and tall tales of mysterious planets and monstrous creatures abound. Prospectors and pirates roam the frontier, and the worlds of Eiram and E'ronoh are locked in a FOREVER WAR.

And on the far-off planet of DALNA, a new threat to the galaxy is beginning to emerge. . . .

PART ONE

THE BARGAIN

Chapter One

THE ROOK, E'RONOH

For the first time in five years, the sky over E'ronoh's capital was clear of fighting ships. When errant debris pierced the atmosphere, it was little more than ash by the time it settled over the stone arches dotting the landscape like great giants of the planet's dawn, frozen against the red morning.

The war was not over, but life went on as life always does. Though parts of the city still smoldered, mourners hurried to inter their dead. As news of the latest cease-fire attempt with Eiram spread, the market of the Rook, E'ronoh's capital, flooded with citizens anticipating the promise of the day's water shipment.

Among them, Serrena, a slender figure dressed in a gray cloak, slipped through the haggling crowds. *Tip-yip ten pezz a kilo! Thirty per barrel! Bargain asterpuff—dream the dream of the dead!*

A mother bargained for a carton of eggs while keeping an eye on the sky. A girl, days short of the draft, shouldered her hungry baby brother on one side and cheap fatty cuts from the butcher on the other. A beggar waved an empty cup. A vendor shooed flies away from his spoiled fruit. A palace guard jumped at the resounding crunch of metal—only to turn and find that a speeder hauling scrap had overturned.

Serrena tugged at the hood of her cloak, but nothing, save for a breath mask, could stop anyone on the forsaken planet from eating a mouthful of dust, even when the winds were still. Snaking through the market and down a narrow underpass, she stopped at the fringe of the hangar bay. Here the canyon's natural archways made it the perfect architecture for the royal launch pad. Locals liked to say the cavernous opening was the petrified yawning mouth of an old god. To Serrena it was just another place, another opportunity to serve the only entity truly committed to keeping the galaxy in balance.

As crewmembers flitted back and forth, readying a squadron of starships for flight, Serrena crept along the undulating walls of the canyon, invisible as the pilots huddled almost protectively around their captain. The young woman's face was half cast in the canyon's shadow, but Serrena could just make out the calm intensity on her regal features. The promise in her fist she pounded over her heart. Words that cut through the cacophony like E'roni gems as they all shouted—"For E'ronoh!"

"Thanks for the rousing pep talk, Captain A'lbaran," Serrena muttered as she crouched behind one of the astromech droids and inserted a slender program chip into its front panel. A sharp thrill of victory coursed through her, but the moment was short-lived.

A soldier with an eye patch rounded the corner and halted. Confusion, then alarm twisted his face as he closed their distance in long, swift strides. "You're not authorized to be here!"

Serrena cowered, let herself sink toward the floor, but he yanked her upright and shoved her against a stack of crates. There was the hard *plunk* of an empty canteen hitting stone. Dust, *always* so much dust, lodged between her teeth, the back of her throat.

"What are you—"

"Please," Serrena whimpered and coughed. "Spare a pezz for a poor farmer? Some water . . ."

"There's a ration distribution at high noon," the soldier said, releasing her with a frustrated huff. His medals boasted the rank of lieutenant, though she hadn't noticed him at his captain's side. Pity, then frustration flitted across his scarred face as he reached into his pocket and fished out a bronze coin. "Now get out of my sight."

Serrena clasped the coin then sprinted away from the launch pad, merging back into the sea of dusty cloaks in the market where a fight was breaking out. The desperate citizens of E'ronoh shoved one another to secure a better place in the queue for water rations, which had doubled in size in the time it took her to fullfill her mission. Serrena pushed harder, shielding her face against the current of sweaty bodies, until she broke through the throng. Tossing the bronze pezz into a beggar's tin cup, Serrena straightened and made for the road leading out of town.

"It is done," she spoke into a short-range comlink.

A worried voice crackled back, "Are you sure . . . it was . . . the right . . ."

"*Yes,* yes, I'm certain." She bit back the ire at being questioned. *She* had been chosen for this mission.

"Hurry back. Got a . . . perfect spot to see . . . the fireworks."

As Serrena broke into a jog, thirty starfighters rocketed into the sky. Serrena let her hood fall, welcomed the heat of the rising sun, and smiled in anticipation of the will of the Force—because if the Force willed it, none of those starfighters would return.

Chapter Two

BEYOND E'RONOH'S GRAVITY WELL

Captain Xiri A'lbaran was tired of waiting. For the ice hauler to drop out of hyperspace. For the enemy to break their tenuous cease-fire and attack. For her world to go up in flames again and again, and know that this time, despite everything she'd fought for, it would be all her fault. And yet Xiri waited, because in the outer reaches of the galaxy, the dregs of better-known worlds and sectors, waiting was all she could do. The helplessness of it all tore through her, though she kept her chin up, eyes locked on the chasm of space. She was the captain of E'ronoh's fleet. She had to set an example for the batch of new recruits, every wave of them younger and younger than the last.

Xiri's Thylefire Squadron had held sentry over the planet's atmosphere since daybreak. Before the war, E'ronoh's monarch might not have deployed a naval squadron for what was supposed to be a simple escort mission. But as drought ravaged her world, and hyperlanes crawled with pirates, the safety of the cargo was a matter of life and death.

Under different circumstances, Xiri would have marveled at the awe-inspiring view of their curious pocket of the galaxy. Her world, with its red mountains and sleek canyons, and neighboring Eiram's turquoise seas mottled by constant storms. Locked between them were a belt of debris—remnants from years of battle that cluttered the corridor like asteroids—and the Timekeeper moon. Her own grandmother used to say that, billions of years before, E'ronoh and Eiram were two cosmic beings that emerged from stardust, and the moon was their shared heart, vital to E'ronoh's winds and Eiram's tides. Xiri had loved that story once. Whether in peace or war, the planets and their moon were irrevocably bound, not simply by the pull of their gravity, but by a long past and an ever-murky future. A future Xiri would dedicate her life to making right.

Now the restlessness among the young pilots was beginning to show as one of them nudged out of formation, then back.

Captain A'lbaran and Lieutenant Segaru had selected an unprecedented thirty pilots for the mission: safely escort an arriving ice hauler to the capital's docking bay and ready the ice for immediate distribution. A hauler that was late. The previous shipment had been destroyed amid the most recent clash with Eiram. The one prior had mysteriously disappeared in the maze of new hyperspace lanes. The one before that—or what was left of it—had been found, likely ravaged by pirates and stripped to the wires, half the crew drifting dead in space. No, the only way to secure this haul was to intercept and escort it the instant it dropped out of hyperspace.

"Captain, we can't stay out here much longer," Lieutenant Segaru said, the steady tenor of his voice fringed by the hum of their private channel's static.

"It'll come," she clipped back.

"Captain—"

"It *will* come." She worked her tongue against the dry roof of her mouth. She'd given her water canteen that morning to a child begging in the market and tried not to think of her own thirst. "It has to."

Xiri turned to her left where he always was in their chain-link formation, his bronze helmet obscuring most of his bearded face. She imagined the scrutiny in his storm gray eye, the way the scars under his eyepatch turned red when he was frustrated and angry. She also knew that he was likely squeezing the pommel of the ceremonial bane blade every E'roni soldier had strapped at the hip, a habit she shared. That a part of him would never forgive her for being promoted instead of him. That he resented her, even as he turned in her direction, like he could feel her stare.

"Captain." Then softer. "Xiri."

"Don't." She snapped her attention straight ahead, past the blue of Eiram, and at the pinpricks of distant stars. "We're lucky to have secured this shipment after Merokia reneged on their promise of relief."

Merokia was the latest on their list of former allies. What could she or the Monarch have expected? With every passing year, every broken cease-fire, every failed attempt at peace, even their closest trading partners had turned their backs on E'ronoh. Few dared to intervene in the conflict, and most simply waited for a victor to arise to choose a side.

"I am aware of our predicament, Captain A'lbaran. It's . . ." He paused for so long, Xiri moved to toggle her channel to see if her comm had fritzed again. "We agreed to clear the corridor between the two planets for Eiram's military escort. They could take our prolonged presence here as a breach of the terms. I'm always ready for a fight, but this cease-fire, clearing the corridor—all of it was *your* plan."

Your plan. Jerrod Segaru always knew how to get under her skin.

It had taken years off her life to convince her father to agree to this in the first place. He'd been convinced the circumstance was an elaborate plan for the enemy to catch E'ronoh with their guard down and attack, hence the thirty starfighters. The conditions were simple—Xiri would lead an escort mission in at daybreak and clear the space for Eiram in the afternoon. No weapons would be engaged. Previous ceasefires had been broken over less, but she counted on Eiram being equally desperate for relief, so they would understand.

Xiri knew quite well where the blame would fall when—if—something went wrong.

"Thank you for reminding me, Lieutenant. But we can't go home empty-handed, and I won't have another one of our shipments destroyed or raided because our backs were turned fighting a war. I'll handle Eiram. We're staying."

"I hope Eiram's general is as—understanding—as you would be," he said, then switched his comm channel.

She followed suit, the restless chatter from the pilots filling the time. Every moment they remained in open space, they seemed to forget their captain was listening. She didn't mind. It was how she got to know them, during rare moments of stillness, listening to the rhythms of their voices.

"Look at all this *junk*," Thylefire Ten said.

"That's not junk," Thylefire Nine piped up, his voice breaking on the last word. The youngest of them all, Thylefire Nine had been dubbed Blitz on his first day of training.

The fresh recruits were mostly a result of the draft, but Blitz had begged for permission to enlist early, in honor of his fallen sister, Lina. He'd been weeks away from the conscription age. Xiri had done the same after her brother's death, and perhaps that was why she had signed off on the request.

Xiri had seen hundreds of soldiers fall, but Lina's death had been a turning point for E'ronoh. What should have been a routine recon mission to Eiram's western isles ended in destruction when her starfighter's thruster malfunctioned moments after lift-off, and she plummeted from the sky—the third malfunction in consecutive days, but the first to result in a casualty. It felt like everyone in the Rook collectively held their breath as they watched the ship crash into the Ramshead Gorge.

It was Lina's tragic end that had sent civilians rioting into the streets. How many others had they lost, not to Eiram, but to their own fleet of outdated starships? What would the Monarch do to ensure it didn't happen again? What would he do to finally win this war? Where were the food and water rations promised? Xiri couldn't—wouldn't—fight her own people and Eiram at the same time, but the dissidents propelled the Monarch to lease a plot of the mountains in the southern hemisphere to Corellia in exchange for three dozen devilfighters. Xiri had cursed the bargain. But she knew it was the most strategic solution. Their fleet was stretched too thin. E'ronoh was stretched too thin. But what would the Monarch sell off next? What would be enough? Questioning the decision, especially during a time of war, and especially by one of E'ronoh's own captains, would have been treason. Even for the Monarch's own daughter.

Xiri's only form of rebellion had been giving one of the new ships—assigned to her—to Blitz, fresh out of basic combat training. She'd opted to remain in the ancient clunker she'd been flying since she enlisted. Besides, no matter what the ship, she'd get where she needed to go.

"It's *not* junk," Blitz repeated. His ship wavered, likely toggling his controls with trembling fists.

"*Easy*, Thylefire Nine," Lieutenant Segaru growled low into the comm. "Get ahold of your ship."

Blitz stilled and whimpered an apology.

"I didn't mean anything by it," Thylefire Ten muttered. "It's just—look at it."

The belt of debris was unavoidable. Remnants of starships and people floated in a river of scorched metal and frost-covered limbs. At first, Xiri had run salvo missions and turned cargo holds into reaper barges, if only to give closure to those waiting on the ground. Now it was nearly impossible to tell the wreckage apart. If the cease-fire held, she would try again.

People just want something to bury, Lieutenant Segaru liked to remind her. They might never be friends again, but she could never call into question his loyalty and ability to get his hands dirty for the cause.

"No, he's right. It's not junk. It's a graveyard," Thylefire Six said, his somber words followed by a strange yowl.

"Is that your stomach?" someone asked.

"Ah, he's just nervous," Lieutenant Segaru said amiably. "It's his first flight."

Or he's hungry, you giant fool, Xiri thought. The words were on the tip of her tongue. But Lieutenant Segaru had a way of smoothing out the moods of their soldiers. *Take it easy, kid. It's just a tiny explosion, kid. There're casualties in war, kid. We will make Eiram pay for their crimes and sink their glass palaces to the bottom of the seas, kid.* Segaru could be their friendly lieutenant, while Xiri was the one who made them run drills until their bodies ached. The one who had to worry about whether or not they had the rations promised to the new recruits and their starving families. The one to fight with her father about prioritizing water over fuel, which was why that ice shipment needed to appear and it needed to appear intact and it needed to appear now because after five years of fighting, their homeworld had decided it had had enough.

The old gods are angry, cried the temple elders. *The old gods are angry at the Monarch's war and have stopped the rain.*

Xiri couldn't blame the old gods or new for the worst drought in her recent memory. All she could believe in was herself and do everything in her power to get aid to her people. E'ronoh would require every fiber of her being, and she would give until there was nothing left of her.

As the planets crept along the moon's orbit, Xiri scanned Eiram for movement, but saw only swirls of clouds over turquoise oceans. No escort ships, but there would be.

"My wife's going to kill me for missing supper again," Thylefire Three murmured. The woman she knew as Kinni was among the eldest members of Xiri's squadron and had been a retired mechanic when she'd reenlisted a couple of years prior.

"I miss my mum's pilafa stew," Blitz added.

Kinni chuckled softly. "You're all welcome, of course."

"Now that the war's over—" Thylefire Six began but was cut off by a grunt.

"Don't let your guard down," Thylefire Thirteen snapped. "*Nothing's* over. Not until they return everything they've taken. Our colony, our prince, our *lives.* Eiram should never know peace."

Thylefire Thirteen was Rev Ferrol, son of Viceroy Ferrol, one of Xiri's father's most trusted advisers. Rev was repeating the same acidic words the Monarch spoke from his balcony whenever he felt morale was low. There was a mutter of assent, and Xiri tried to swallow the knot in her throat, but her mouth was dry. She could feel Lieutenant Segaru's stare on her, but she only gave a shake of her head. Her people were frustrated, and she would be failing them as not just their captain, but their princess, if she shut off her comm simply because of her own guilt.

"We're just catching our breath is all. The barnacles are, too," Lieutenant Segaru added.

"M-my gran used to say when *she* was small, they measured time not by the moon, but by when Eiram's ships flew over the city." Blitz chuckled nervously. "I—I think she was exaggerating but it was *ages* ago."

"Was it now?" Kinni scoffed. "Then I'm ages old."

There was a string of laughter.

"Well, when it's over," said Blitz in his boisterous way, "I'm taking a pleasure barge to one of them resort planets."

"There's no pleasure barge coming out here," Rev muttered.

"I hear that on some worlds you can pay to have simultaneous—"

"Simultaneous what, Ten?" Xiri spoke into the comm, crackling as others snickered at the embarrassed pilot.

The younger boy swallowed his words, then stuttered, "P-princess! I mean, Captain. Captain A'lbaran."

"All right, Thylefire, stay sharp," Lieutenant Segaru commanded in his easy drawl.

Xiri allowed herself a small smile. She *liked* when they spoke of their dreams, their plans. That they imagined a *when* and an *after.* Their hope was a fragile thing, but it was there, and she couldn't allow herself to forget it, not for a second.

A sensor blinked on her control panel. A dozen of Eiram's ships emerged from their cloudy atmosphere. Their starships had a bulbous quality, outfitted for underwater submersion first and spaceflight second.

"They're here!" Blitz said. His ship lurched forward, then staggered to a stop.

"Easy does it," Lieutenant Segaru warned.

"I-it's these new ships," Blitz stuttered, his breathing heavy. "The controls are too sensitive."

"*Riiiight,*" Thirteen muttered, and the others took the easy shot and laughed at their nervous friend.

"Remember," Xiri said, commanding silence, "Eiram is receiving cargo, too. We're both escorting deliveries home. Wait for my orders."

"Captain," Lieutenant Segaru said. "They're hailing you."

Xiri licked her front teeth. She tried not to think of her thirst, her own pounding heart. Her squadron needed her to lead. E'ronoh would need her to lead.

"This is Captain Xiri A'lbaran." Her words were steadier than she felt.

"Captain, this is General Nhivan Lao." His clipped voice came in warbled through her ancient starfighter's comm. She punched the panel hard to clear it. "We agreed the corridor between planets would be clear. Those were your terms, I believe."

"I understand that, General," Xiri said. "But our shipment is delayed. We would afford you the same courtesy in the same position."

"Would you?" the general all but scoffed.

Xiri wouldn't take the bait, and so their silence stretched heavy in the space between until the general cleared his throat and said, "Very well. See that you don't cross your side of the corridor."

"Wouldn't dream of it." She switched over the comm.

Xiri updated her squadron, then squeezed her controls and watched the empty field of space as if she could split open a black hole and wrench out the ice hauler from hyperspace.

"We should take whatever cargo they have, plus ours," Rev growled. "I bet they're planning the same thing. I bet—"

"I wouldn't trust the Eirami, even if I had two good eyes," Lieutenant Segaru interrupted. "But we stay put for now."

"Didn't you lose your eye in the first battle, sir?" Blitz asked.

"Precisely."

"I want this channel clear," Xiri said. "Is that understood?"

One by one, they signed off that they did.

Her sensor suite blinked. A coil of anticipation tightened in her gut as she said, "A ship's coming out of hyperspace."

Hidden among the pinpricks of light that surrounded them was the exit zone for the hyperspace lane the Republic had opened a few years back. It turned out that E'ronoh and Eiram were in the middle of nowhere, but on the way to everywhere.

When the ship emerged from hyperspace, Xiri stopped breathing. She had taken her squadron flying over the glittering spires of the Modine Valley, seen the first desert roses bloom, and yet, right now, nothing had ever been as beautiful as that rusty old ice hauler.

She sat forward in anticipation, smiled so hard her chapped lips cracked and bled. Even as she watched the hauler glide through the corridor between E'ronoh and Eiram, Xiri made a mental note that every bit of ice aboard was already spoken for, and they'd have to figure out a way to get more even before the last drop was distributed. It was a worry for later that night.

Xiri was a breath away from hailing the hauler when her fighter's sensor suite chirped, this time flagging an anomaly.

"Captain," Segaru said, worry and confusion in the single word. "There are *two* more ships dropping out of hyperspace. We must clear—"

Segaru's words were lost as one gargantuan ship blinked into dead space after the other, narrowly missing a deadly impact. Xiri had only ever seen their likeness from newsfeeds on the holonet, and by the chatter instantly filling the comm channel, so had her squadron.

"Is that an *Alif*-class Longbeam?"

"Aren't those Republic ships?"

"Dank farrik, what's the *Republic* doing here?"

The Longbeams had narrow bodies ending in tapered noses. Xiri tracked the path they were on, and it ended in a double collision course with the ice hauler. To prevent a crash, the hauler listed, careening toward Eiram. If it got pulled into the ocean planet's gravity, E'ronoh could kiss their water supply goodbye. Eiram could claim the ice hauler on the mere grounds that it had entered their space, and everything Xiri had worked for—this tender wound that was their temporary peace—would rupture all over again.

But if she accelerated to claim it, she'd cross the corridor of space and into Eiram's territory and they would be clear to fire.

"General Lao," Xiri said. "Come in!"

A crackle of static swallowed his response.

"Captain . . ." Lieutenant Segaru said urgently on their private channel.

Xiri's fingers trembled on her panel. "I'm trying to flag them!"

A garbled voice came through from one of the Longbeams. "This is the *Paxion* of the Republic. Who is responsible for hyperlane traffic?"

Xiri couldn't help but return the question with a bitter laugh. "Pull back, *Paxion*. You are not authorized to enter E'roni space."

"Who is this?" asked the affronted party.

Xiri did not answer. The river of debris was moving, picking up speed as the *Paxion* barreled into the space between worlds. Wreckage pelted her squadron. Something that looked like a helmet smashed against her viewport and left behind a tendril across the transparisteel. The second, unidentified Longbeam broke away from the *Paxion* and headed toward the moon. But because Eiram and E'ronoh were so close together, the corridor of space was unusually narrow, and ships

16

unaccustomed to navigating their system could easily fall into either planet's gravity well. The *Paxion* pilot clearly wasn't used to such tight maneuvering and was being pulled toward E'ronoh. When attempts to make contact failed, Xiri knew she couldn't sit here. She had to move and hope that Eiram understood it was to avoid the Longbeam and not an act of aggression.

"Thylefire Squadron, on me," Xiri said, flying higher and higher. "Get clear of the *Paxion*, and do not, I repeat, do not cross the corridor."

"But the ice hauler is still going the wrong way!" Blitz came in, panicked. She could see his devilfighter deviating from their cluster.

"Thylefire Nine, stay in formation," Xiri ordered. "Lieutenant Segaru, keep hailing the ice hauler and get them to reroute. I'll deal with the general."

But Xiri wouldn't get the opportunity. The rogue devilfighter completely broke formation and sailed through space in sweeping dips and dives.

"Thylefire Nine, if you weren't endangering the mission, I'd congratulate you on the best flying of your class," Lieutenant Segaru said. "Now get your ass back here!"

"It's not me!" Blitz shouted. "The ship's out of control. I can't—"

"Nine, that's an order! Do you copy?" Xiri said, the channel crackling with the sharp note of feedback. Every ship was trying to communicate and unable to get their messages out as a green blur blasted through the debris field and at Eiram's forces. It didn't matter that it didn't make contact. It was a shot fired from Thylefire Nine's starfighter, from E'ronoh.

A single shot was all it took.

Xiri's pulse roared in her ears. She tasted the blood on her cracked lips, choked on the helpless cry no one could hear. For a heartbeat, there was finally silence as the comm went dead and every one of Eiram's forces fired back.

Chapter Three

Moments before the collision, Jedi Knight Gella Nattai was safely aboard the *Valiant*'s cargo hold, walking on air.

The relief crates of medical supplies destined for Eiram nearly reached the Longbeam's ceiling, but Gella always made do with the space she had. Stripped down to her sand-colored tunic and leggings, she concentrated on taking one step at a time. The Aerialwalk, which she'd seen performed by a priestess of the Singing Mountain during her last pilgrimage to Jedha City, took every bit of her concentration. Gella's heartbeat slowed to the rhythm of her deep breaths. Every bit of her body was buoyed by the Force, a contradiction of sensations— adrift yet anchored, steady yet in motion. She was a moment and somehow infinite.

She took another step, now standing completely sideways. Slowly, she extended her arms outward, keeping her palms up, and felt the first tremble in her muscles. *Focus,* she reminded herself. She kept her eyes trained on the marbled blue and white light from the viewport. Her travels with the Order had taken her to oceanic worlds, across mountain valleys, and into cities hovering in the clouds. But there was something about hyperspace that humbled her like nothing else. Meditating while in hyperspace was like being buried within light, within the Force itself. There, and then gone. A blink of an eye, a star, a life.

She inhaled once more, then felt the presence before the door to the cargo hold hissed open.

"That can't possibly be comfortable," said Master Roy's Padawan, Enya Keen.

Gella grasped at the air, but her concentration snapped. She fell hard on her side, pain ricocheting up her arm and shoulder.

"That looks even *less* comfortable," Enya added, plunking down on the crate where Gella had set aside her lightsabers and the rest of her robes.

Gella grunted, pushing herself to her feet. "It was perfectly comfortable before I was rudely interrupted."

Enya offered an apologetic smile but showed no signs of moving. She tucked one leg under her thigh, absently twirling the tuft of her Padawan braid. She must have been sleeping, because there were creases under her eyes on her deep-brown skin, and her dark hair was coming undone from the two braided knots that ran perpendicular to her spine.

"I've never seen anyone meditate standing up," she said, "or floating upside down. You looked like a Loth-bat."

"There are many ways to meditate, you know that." Gella yanked on her brown tabard and holstered her twin lightsabers on either side of her hips, then quickly tugged on her socks and scuffed boots.

"But what's the function for a Jedi?" Enya pressed in her lilting soprano.

Gella hadn't exactly thought about the *function* a Jedi might have for the Singing Mountain's sacred ritual. She'd simply been eager to understand it. To challenge herself to see if she *could*.

Enya, however, did not let her explain before continuing, "Can you teach me?"

"I clearly have yet to master the Aerialwalk myself." Gella didn't mean to be curt, but she'd hidden in the cargo hold because she'd wanted to be alone, and her room didn't have a view of hyperspace. She half considered excusing herself and hiding in one of the stationed *Alpha*-class ships parked in the hangar.

"Right. Weren't you supposed to be on your way to Jedha before you got in trouble with the Council?" Enya sucked in a sharp gasp. "Oh, I probably wasn't supposed to overhear the masters talking about that."

Gella bristled. "Likely not."

"Well, I'm sure what happened on your expedition to Orvax won't happen here! I also overheard that Jedi Neverez only bruised his tail-bone and the rest are going to make a full recovery."

Gella pinched the bridge of her nose. Two weeks and the reminder of her failure on her first mission as a Pathfinder team leader was still fresh. At the time of the accident, she'd requested permission from the Council to return to Jedha where she could train with one of the many orders studying the mystical ways of the Force. To center herself. To regain equilibrium and perspective about where her choices had gone wrong. Instead, she'd been reassigned deeper and deeper into the Outer Rim, aboard the *Valiant* with Masters Sun and Roy, and Padawan Enya Keen. It was hard not to feel like she was being punished.

She might as well know everything Enya had heard. "Is that *all* Master Sun said?"

"He also said that you are impulsive, but that you've got the skills to be a great master one day if you just apply yourself."

Gella returned Enya's wide smile with a scowl, though it didn't last long. She couldn't remember ever having the Padawan's levels of energy even though at thirty standard years Gella was only a decade her senior. Still, there was something about Enya that wore anyone down, with her sunny, eager smiles and innocent hope. Even if it was exhausting on long journeys such as these.

"Very well," Gella said. "I will teach you when we get to Eiram. I need the practice."

"See? I'm going to tell Aida Forte that you *are* friendly," Enya said, touching her finger to her chin. "I wonder how long we'll be on Eiram. Lately it seems like we're never in the same place for long."

"Long enough to get them medical supplies, I suppose." Gella pulled on her robe and combed her fingers through her long black hair.

"For as long as they need our help." Master Creighton Sun rounded the corner. He was a stoic man of imposing height; Gella had caught glimpses of him over the years at various summits, but he never seemed to change. She was nearly certain Master Sun was now about forty standard years, but even when he'd been a young Jedi Knight, he'd had the same patches of silver hair at his temples, and fine lines around his eyes, like someone born to be wiser and older. Perhaps that appearance was why Gella always felt the need to correct her posture when he entered the room.

He glanced around the cargo hold like he was expecting to find it set on fire or destroyed. Honestly, that had only happened once, and it hadn't been Gella's fault.

Gella and Enya stood to attention.

"Of course, Master Sun," Gella said.

Creighton Sun's bushy dark brows knitted together as his gaze settled on Gella. He scratched his freshly shaved jawline and gave a long-suffering sigh. "As I'm sure Enya came here to tell you, we're approaching the coordinates."

The Padawan rushed out the cargo hold ahead of them. Gella would have, too, if not for the beat of hesitation she sensed from Master Sun.

"I heard what Enya said."

Gella dispelled his words with a shake of her head. "It's all right, Master Sun. But it is bolstering to know you believe I might make a great master one day. I had hoped to have time to further my training in light of my last assignment."

She liked the way he listened, the permanent furrows of his brows deepening. "And you believe you should do that on Jedha?"

"It seems the obvious choice," she said. "What better way to learn about the Force, and my place in it, than to train with all the religions and groups who live their lives by it? Perhaps it's safer to learn and train that way . . ."

"Safer?" Master Sun asked softly. "From whom? Or what?"

Gella met his kind eyes, the brown of forests. The first reply that came to mind was *Myself, apparently.* But when she went to speak, she could not say it out loud.

"I know how deeply you believe in our cause," he said, noting her silence. "To be a guardian of peace and justice in the galaxy, we must first experience the galaxy. Better understand all the living beings that are connected through the Force. The Council didn't send you on this mission so you could help deliver medical supplies. They sent you to learn to be part of a team."

As a Padawan, Gella had done everything she was told. She leapt off a cliff and trusted the Force to stop her fall. She trained at temples across worlds. On Jedha, she learned about the wide spectrum of Force wielders and believers. She trained. For hours. Days months years. She tuned in to the very makeup of her body, meditated until she didn't know where her physical being began and the Force ended. She'd done everything she was supposed to, but when she was called on for her most important mission as a team leader—she'd failed.

"Perhaps I'm better off serving the Order on my own," she mused.

Master Sun raised his brows sympathetically. "There are many paths, and I trust, in time, you will find yours, Gella Nattai. But it seems to me that you are only scratching at the surface of what you might be capable of. You must have—"

"Patience," she finished for him.

"Exactly," he said, turning to leave the cargo hold. "You have the ability to connect in ways that are not obvious to the rest of us. We will all work in tandem."

"I appreciate that, Master Sun," Gella said. She would not fail again.

"Now let's hurry and buckle in. Our last trip to Eiram was a bumpy drop out of hyperspace."

She followed Master Sun through the corridor and up to the

cockpit, where Master Char-Ryl-Roy was at the helm. Even sitting, the Cerean man towered over the others. He acknowledged Gella with a quick nod, the yellow and white cabin lights gleaming off his smooth, oval head.

"You've been to Eiram before, is that right?" Gella asked Master Sun as she strapped herself into the seat behind Enya.

"Oh yes," Enya said, eagerly cracking her knuckles. "Though last time we evacuated before we could even dock."

Master Sun's lips flattened slightly, then he said, "This will be our third time in the last year. Eiram and E'ronoh have been embroiled in a conflict for going on half a decade now. Though I remember hearing about their squabbling when I was a Padawan. I fear the opening of the hyperspace lane in their sector and the tragic circumstance behind the death of E'ronoh's prince stirred old wounds."

"Is it wise to still get involved, then?" Gella asked.

Master Sun's brown eyes were shadowed in deep consideration. "It is our duty to aid those who ask for help. Eiram has asked for aid several times, but E'ronoh has never called on us. Their monarch is wary of outsiders."

Gella considered this. "And Eiram's queen is not?"

"Oh, she is," Master Sun said grimly. "The recent destruction of a military hospital left Eiram desperate. We convinced them the only way to safely get more medical relief was to agree to the cease-fire proposed by E'ronoh's princess. I do believe it's been the longest cease-fire since the fighting started."

"A victory indeed," Master Roy added from the pilot's seat.

"How long is that?" Gella asked.

"Three days," he answered with a pleased smile.

Three days! Gella thought. That was nearly as long as it took them to get to the Eiram-E'ronoh system within the Dalnan sector.

"Speak your mind, Gella Nattai," Master Sun encouraged her. "I know you have joined us by *suggestion* of the Council, but I want you to feel like you are part of our team. I can sense you are holding back."

Gella had never felt particularly eloquent when asked to voice her thoughts. Still, she cleared her throat and said, "To be honest, I don't think three days is much of a victory."

Enya snapped her attention to Gella, her large eyes nearly bugging out of her head.

"Perhaps. But it is a start," Master Sun said confidently. "It is a delicate time for Eiram and E'ronoh. The wounds between these planets go deep, but I am hopeful they will find a way toward true, lasting peace."

"A start," Gella repeated. Is that what this mission was for her? A new start after so much trouble? "Right."

Then the ship jerked in the hyperspace tunnel.

"Hold on to your backsides!" Enya shouted, white-knuckling her harness. Master Sun shut his eyes and grabbed hold of the handlebar above him.

Gella felt oddly steady, moving with the ship as they entered realspace and the blue glow faded to star-speckled black. Master Roy grunted as his head slammed into his headrest. There was a hard thud, and the entire ship trembled.

"What the kriff?" Enya blurted out.

Gella hadn't heard the Padawan curse in front of her master before, but the situation called for it. Emergency lights blinked and alarms blared as the ship took a hit. At first, she couldn't understand what they were colliding against. Straight ahead was what looked like some kind of old cargo hauler careening through a field of debris and toward the turquoise planet. Gella knew to expect Eiram's military escort, but E'ronoh's forces remained stationed in the narrow gap between worlds. She would have thought it impossible to divide something intangible like space, but these warring planets had found a way.

"Pull back!" Enya shouted.

Emerging from their blindspot was a second Longbeam cruiser. Gella's insides churned as Master Roy strained to avoid the Republic ship attempting to right its course, but the nose of the *Valiant* ground into the tail of the other ship.

"It's the *Paxion,*" Enya said, reading the control panel.

"Are you sure?" Master Sun asked.

Gella knew that ship's name by reputation alone. "What's Chancellor Mollo's ship doing out here?"

Before anyone could speculate, a green blast shot through the dark. It impacted a bit of wreckage, but the source seemed to be a lone Corellian devilfighter charging through the debris.

"I guess the cease-fire is over," Gella said, holding on to the copilot's headrest.

Master Sun's lips flattened into a scowl, then braced as they took another hit.

"This is Master Char-Ryl-Roy with the Jedi Council," the Cerean male thundered into the comm. "We are a medical relief transport en route to Eiram. I repeat. We are a medical relief transport. Halt your fire."

The cockpit's lights flickered, and everything rattled as laserfire and debris rammed into them from all sides.

"Redirecting auxiliary power to the shields," Enya said, punching in the directive.

"Erasmus Capital City, come in," Master Roy roared, but only garbled comm feedback answered. "Eiram, come in!"

"I was trying to respond to the *Paxion*'s hail, but I think"—Enya's pointer finger tracked a dish spinning into the debris field—"we took out their receiver."

"Head toward Eiram," Master Sun shouted over the alarms. "We can't wait for the escort."

"I have good news and bad news," Enya said over the din. "The good news is that now they're shooting at each other instead of us."

"Interesting idea of good news, but go on," Master Roy said.

"I can't get in touch with Erasmus to give them our landing clearance. Without that, the city's defenses might shoot us down as soon as we enter the atmosphere."

"Well, we can't stay *here,*" Master Sun argued.

He had said that it was a fragile time for Eiram and E'ronoh, but what had been enough to trigger an attack when both planets were urgently waiting for much-needed relief?

Gella gripped the armrests of her seat, itching to do *something*. She could sense Master Sun's frustration, too. "We should get out there."

"We can't," he said, lament thick in his words.

"We can't choose sides," Master Roy agreed. "Our mission is to deliver the requested aid to Eiram, not fight their war. For now we'll head for the moon before we get pulled into E'ronoh's gravity."

Gella kept her eyes trained on the dogfighting in dead space. She reached out through the Force to the destruction ahead. Anger and fear tinged every pilot, but one radiated brighter among the rest. A vessel that was out of control. The Corellian model, an older class by the looks of it, red paint splattered over the gray metal in haphazard violent stripes, and a laser cannon protruding from each wing. She watched as the fighter pilot tried, but failed, to regain control of the ship. She could sense the pilot's absolute fear and panic. It left an acrid taste on her tongue.

Gella pointed at the rogue devilfighter. "There."

"I feel it, too," Enya said. "The pilot has lost control and is scared."

"There's nothing we can do. We must get to safety first," Master Char-Ryl-Roy said as the ship took another hit.

They could make it to the moon's surface, and Gella would have to convince the masters to let her take one of the Alpha-3 Jedi starfighters and help the pilot who seemed to be in distress. But by then it would be too late.

Before the plan had fully formed in her mind, Gella Nattai unbuckled her harness and hurried to the back of the ship, descended the ladder, and boarded one of the two starfighters. The thought of flying alone made the pit of her stomach squeeze unpleasantly, but she steadied her breath. Her own feelings didn't matter, not when someone was crying out for help. After all, wasn't that what they were there to do? Help. She punched in the controls to release the magnetic clamps, let the cockpit canopy pressurize shut.

As Gella descended into the fray, her nerves vanished, and her goal was clear. She wasn't the best pilot in the Order, but she had the Force on her side. Darting past red blurs, Gella pierced into the heart of the battle. Blue metallic ships with rounded tops zigzagged between the larger chunks of debris, chasing down red-streaked starfighters. Chunks of charred metal and what looked like the remnants of a boot were deflected by her shield, the green crackle of energy a momentary comfort as she raced toward the pilot in need.

"Come in, Alpha One," Master Roy said. He did *not* sound pleased with her. "Return to the *Valiant,* at once, that's an order!"

"I'm sorry, master. But this pilot is in too much distress. They won't make it out here much longer."

There was a grunt of disapproval followed by, "We'll clear your path."

Gella stayed on course toward the Corellian devilfighter. Up closer, she could see a number painted on its wing. Nine. The pilot was locked in trajectory toward Eiram, forward-facing rapid-fire cannons blasting a path. Eiram's defenses were engaged with E'ronoh's forces in an attempt to obliterate the threat.

Gella considered the angle she'd have to fire to clip the pilot's wing and glide the ship safely. She was certain she had to steer the pilot *away* from Eiram—landing there would cause another planetary incident.

"One thing at a time," Gella reminded herself.

Her sensors detected two ships fast approaching her flanks. She took evasive maneuvers and pulled up on the controls to shake them. They sailed in an upward arc, barreling clear of the debris.

An urgent voice spoke through her comm. "This is Captain Xiri A'lbaran. Back off, Alpha, or I will fire. This is your only warning."

"Oh, Captain," came the second, bitter voice. "We should have known you were up to something. A liar, just like your father."

"This is a misunderstanding, General," Captain A'lbaran said, her words interspersed with static and immeasurable restraint. "I am willing to uphold and resume the cease-fire, just let my pilots reach the hauler safely."

"You think I care about ice when an enemy ship is bound for my capital?"

"He's not in control!" the captain shouted.

Gella could sense the situation called for action, not words. By the Force, she truly hated flying, but there was no place for fear in her heart. She gunned her controls hard, jerking against her safety harness as she flew in a diagonal loop, cleaving the space between the enemy ships close enough to drag the edges of her ship's wings against their flanks. The grind of metal grated against her ears, but now their focus was on her.

"Now," Gella said, heart pounding, "General, Captain, I'm trying to help you, dammit."

"Help?" Captain A'lbaran scoffed, still flying in lockstep, trailing after the rogue pilot.

"*Yes,* help. My name is Jedi Knight Gella Nattai."

"Jedi," came a hiccup of surprise from one of the other pilots. It seemed no matter where she went in the galaxy, the word was voiced with the same tone of surprise. Gella focused on that, on the recognition, the weight of it. Nothing as selfish as pride but bolstered by a sense of rightness she could never truly put into words.

"Call off your fighters," Gella said.

"There is an enemy starship flying toward Erasmus Capital City," the general spat. "Absolutely not."

"Eiram called for our help, General," Gella said. "I can keep them calm while they reset their control systems. Please, trust me."

There was a beat of silence, the maddening growl of dead air, and then a begrudging, "Do it."

"I'm coming with you," Captain A'lbaran said.

Gella wasted no time. She took off, accelerating at maximum speed to catch up with the rogue E'roni devilfighter. One by one Eiram's forces pulled back, while E'ronoh's squadron surrounded the cargo hauler. The *Valiant* and the *Paxion* coasted along the corridor toward the silver moon between worlds. Gella exhaled a pent-up breath of relief, but she couldn't celebrate yet.

"Nine, come in," Gella said, racing at its side as it approached the giant blue planet. "What's your name?"

She nudged into the ship from the right side, pushing it up and away from the capital city's trajectory.

"I can't stop! I don't know—"

"Listen to my voice." Gella's voice was a smooth alto that seemed to cut through the comm and right into his thoughts. "What's your name?"

"Who are you?" he asked, and Gella heard just how young and scared he was.

"It's okay. Talk to her, Blitz," Captain A'lbaran encouraged.

"Bly," he said, panting. "Bly Tevin, but everyone calls me Blitz."

"All right, Blitz, I want you to listen to your captain."

His devilfighter veered into hers again, a flare of automatic beams blasting from its forward cannons. It was trying to redirect, to get back toward Eiram. Captain A'lbaran squeezed in from the other side, the three of them locked together in a crunch of metal and sparks. Gella reached out through the Force, letting the weight of it envelop the pilot. If she had time with him, perhaps she could better understand him. Ease the riot of emotions clouding his actions. This would have to do.

"Blitz," Captain Xiri urged. "Shut it down."

"I can't, I don't—!"

"You can, you will," Gella said, letting the calm vibrations of her voice reach him. "It'll be for a moment."

She felt him spark with anxiety, losing control of himself and the ship again. It rattled against them, and together, Gella and Xiri redoubled their efforts to keep him in place.

"It's not working," Blitz shouted. "It's running an autopilot program. I'm locked out of the controls. You're—you're going to have to shoot me down."

"That is not an option, Thylefire Nine," Captain Xiri shot back. "I don't care if you have to open up that panel with your bare hands, find a way to shut it down."

If Blitz responded, they didn't hear it. Gella turned her controls as far as they'd go. The Alpha-3 was lighter than the old E'roni starfighter and devilfighter. Gella could fly faster, more gracefully with the Force, but the effort it was taking for her to keep Blitz aloft would physically and mentally split her at the seams. Her grasp on their already tenuous connection frayed as a new guttural voice interrupted their comms.

"Many apologies, Princess," the stranger said. "But we did not sign up for this. Releasing cargo."

Gella caught the flash of the hauler blinking out of the sector, the massive crate plummeting toward the debris, as the princess blared a string of curses. In that moment of uncertainty, Blitz broke free, his ship diving back down to its intended target of Eiram. "They dumped the ice and bolted! Lieutenant Segaru, do *not* lose that haul."

Then, all at once, the out-of-control devilfighter powered down, drifting into a spin. "I did it. I got it!"

Gella sensed Blitz's relief, the bitter tinge of his fear scraping against her skin like gravel.

"General Lao . . . Please . . ." Captain A'lbaran began. Blitz was still on a collision course with Eiram, but at least he wasn't armed.

"I understand," General Lao said with reluctance. "I'll personally make sure you both get home."

"Thank you, Gella," Captain A'lbaran said, as Gella maneuvered her ship away from the trio, and made for the *Valiant.*

"Captain," Blitz's voice rang with fear. Gella turned to see the captain and general still flying side by side with the pilot. Something was wrong. "There's a problem. I—"

Before he could finish, before Gella could go back, red-and-white fire bloomed from Bly Tevin's exploding devilfighter.

BEYOND EIRAM'S GRAVITY WELL

Bly Tevin had always wanted to see the blue waters of Eiram up close, even if it was a place he was supposed to hate. But the boy they called Blitz couldn't hate anyone, not really. Not the way some of his fellow pilots did, with an anger so deep it was branded into their skin. That day's mission should have been the first day of a long military career. An opportunity to finish what his sister had started, what his grandfather had fought for as a young man. For E'ronoh. Always for E'ronoh.

When he'd been reassigned to one of the new vessels, he'd reveled in the sensation of breaching the atmosphere into infinite space. It was something no simulator and no practice runs in the Ramshead Gorge could replicate. He'd prove himself. Not Blitz, the fumbling pilot. Bly Tevin, hero of E'ronoh.

But he hadn't been the hero he'd set out to be. The moment he'd lost control, he'd attempted to steer the devilfighter off course, even if at first sight he could have been branded a deserter. He didn't want anyone to get hurt, but the controls wouldn't respond. They were programmed to fire and his ship was set on a collision course with Eiram's capital.

It felt like he'd been out of control for hours, screaming into his own sick, before he heard her voice. Felt a pressure against his chest, clearing the clouds of fear until he knew what to do. He remembered the ceremonial bane blade at his hip. Sweaty, shaking fingers worked at the clasp until he freed it from its sheath. Passed down from his grandfather, it wasn't sharp enough to slice skin on a first try but it would do the trick. He rammed it into the port. A current shorted the navigation and powered down his ship.

"I did it. I got it!"

He could manually restart the ship. He had clearing to land on *Eiram* of all places. He thought of his mother, sitting in their apartment. She'd promised to make a fresh batch of pilafa stew when he got leave, if the cease-fire held. That's why he was up there, so far and so close to home. He thought of her then, smiling as he played with other children on the narrow, dusty streets outside the palace. A woman who could stretch a ration for days. A miracle, he thought once, until he realized how thin and sad she was stirring their pot of thin soup. Together they'd watched his sister fall out of the sky, and he thanked his lucky stars she never got to see him struggle during training, struggle as he crashed one simulation after the next until he was branded Blitz. Blitz Tevin. A name he laughed at with everyone else even though he hated it.

When he stopped shaking, and the manual restart began, he shut his eyes and thanked the old gods. The ones his mother still prayed to. Even then, he was certain she was waiting, climbing onto the watchtower where all the families waited for the ships to come home. Because she was why he did this. For her.

As his ship whirled back to life, and a countdown began, he called for help that wouldn't come. Bly Tevin's last thought was of his mother. She always wanted to see the turquoise seas of the enemy, too.

Chapter Four

When stars fell over Eiram, no one looked up. The citizens of the capital knew there was nothing particularly interesting in hunks of rock from space, not when there were bellies to feed and dwindling rations being distributed. And so, as two objects pierced the mountainous clouds that perpetually clung to the planet's skies, there was no panic. No fear. No spare wishes or awe. Soon the city's defense missile towers would lock in on their targets, and in the event the missiles malfunctioned, the electrostatic domes that encased so many of Eiram's major cities would shield the citizens beneath.

Phan-tu Zenn was the first person to spot the ships entering Eiram's atmosphere. But the boy who'd come from nothing had a habit of gazing toward the clouds.

He had been distributing relief to the people in the Rayes Canal, a narrow waterway that emptied out into the Erasmus Sea. In this sector of the city, squat buildings leaned into each other like rows of rotten, crooked teeth. Drying seaweed and barnacles dotted the walls and waterline, breadcrumbs anyone could follow to the piers. Skinny saltwater birds that flew too close to the dome received a conk on the head and a shock. Though transparent, the protective shield around the city was visible across white electric bands tracing the patterns of cresting waves, marking entry points for ships to come and go, and the steady hum of the shield was ever-present.

Phan-tu shouldn't have been in the Rayes Canal in the first place, but over the years he'd learned to shirk his security detail. He'd hopped on the back of an agopie and guided the water horse to his favorite pier.

Within moments, he'd been swarmed by people—those born and raised in the Rayes and the refugees coming in droves from the western islands, the latest to be attacked by E'ronoh's forces. Phan-tu should have felt fortunate that the war with E'ronoh had yet to reach the capital, but the destruction of nearby towns meant the infrastructure of Erasmus was eroding as quickly as their coastlines during monsoon season. And it was those at the very bottom who felt that strain the most.

Even as he handed out rations of food, hydration pellets, and anything else he could salvage from the palace's waste, he knew it was not enough. His cart had emptied and he'd only just started distributing. Pain wedged between his ribs as parents and elders walked away empty-handed. He'd gone as far as to offer the linenfiber tunic off his back, the gold-stitched slippers that made him feel positively ridiculous. But they never accepted. They never cursed him, never let their desperation turn into anger, not toward him.

Phan-tu was, after all, one of them.

He should have been on his way back to the palace. His mothers worried. But his muscle memory carried him to the pier. He made a mental note of how many people had left with nothing. More than he could count. The helplessness of it all was suffocating, and he sought solace from the sight of the sea.

At the southernmost edge of the canal a pale blue scorpion, the size of a pebble, crept along the cracked pier, too young to be poisonous yet and small enough it must have slipped through the dome. He toed it off the ledge.

Along the coast, tiny square houses crowded the shore. White stone washed in bright blues, greens, and yellows. Canvas awnings provided little shade at the height of the sun, but it was home. Once, before the worst monsoon in his lifetime, he'd lived there with his biological mother and Talla, his little sister. Once, when the electrostatic dome hadn't been strong enough against the waves of a storm, they'd all been carried out to sea. Only Phan-tu had swum back.

As the crowds dispersed, a girl with short brown curls and a dress stitched of some sort of recycled canvas tugged at his pant leg. She looked so much like his sister once had, and so he got down on his knee and pointed to her closed fist.

"What have you got there?" he asked.

She seemed to lose her nerve, but Phan-tu only smiled patiently. The little girl had his same coloring, tawny brown skin, pale-green eyes, and a dusting of green freckles, the distinctive marking of Eirami who had settled on the planet generations before.

"For the queen," she peeped, unfurling her tiny fingers to reveal a cluster of mud-flecked pearls.

"I know she will love them," Phan-tu said, pocketing the gift.

As he stood, he caught the first flash of light in the sky and used the flat of his hand to shield his eyes from the sun. No one else looked up at first, used to the safety that the missiles and dome provided—in times of peace only used for storms.

Phan-tu watched the pair of ships falling from orbit, too obscured to be recognizable. He searched the sky for others, but these two were anomalies. The defenses should have been engaged by now, yet the vessels kept free-falling. He had the sinking realization that something must have gone terribly wrong with the escort mission of the Jedi transport.

One of the incoming ships bore the telltale metallic blue of Eiram's fleet. Its wings were on fire, and in the moment he blinked, it released its cockpit bubble. The transparisteel was snatched up in the breeze and rammed into the dome. A prismatic shimmer rippled from the hit and spread. Someone screamed as the Eirami ship exploded on impact. He couldn't tell if the pilot had ejected or not, and there was still the second starship obscured by the glare of the sun.

Phan-tu reached for his comm, then cursed himself for having left it at the palace.

The little girl tugged at his pant leg and asked, "Is that a shooting star?"

"No, dear heart," he said, trying to keep his voice even so as not to scare her. He nudged her back up the pier. "Why don't you go inside?"

As she took off in a sprint, the city's alarms wailed to life and every Eirami in the streets finally looked up. They pointed fingers, clapped palms over their mouths. As it got closer, Phan-tu could make out the streaks across its hull like red wounds. An E'roni starfighter.

"All of you, inside," Phan-tu shouted. "Now, please!"

To make matters worse, his security detail had spotted him and were running down the narrow canal street.

"My lord, this is not the place for you. We must hurry back," said the leader. His distaste for the Rayes Canal was evident in the sneer of his thin lips.

"Not until everyone is safe inside," Phan-tu muttered, pushing past the guards to help an elder climb the steps into her home.

"That is not your job, *my lord,*" the guard said, exasperated.

"You're right, Vigo, it's yours." Phan-tu sidestepped the tall man and picked up a toddler, nose dripping as his cries put the alarms to shame. He scanned the crowd searching for the mother, but there were still too many bodies clustering to get a view of the crash. People climbed onto rooftops and clustered in doorways and windows. Terrible cries came from the refugee camps at the edge of the pier.

"Why aren't the anti-missile cannons firing?" Phan-tu asked.

"All we know is there's been some sort of accident and General Lao gave an order to stand down. But that was before—"

Phan-tu handed the baby over to a frantic young mother. She bowed low to him, and he ignored the feeling of discomfort at the deference.

"My lord," Vigo tried again, clenching his gloved fist. "Might I remind you that you are my charge. The city's defenses will hold."

With his arms free, he whirled on his guard, pressing a finger on the man's decorated vest. "I have been there when the dome failed. Have you?"

"No, my lord." Vigo's freckled nose wrinkled as he looked down to find his boots covered in mud. So far from the palace, and even with exploding ships in the sky, Phan-tu's *armed guard* cared more about his boots. "But there isn't anything you can do from here. Put Her Majesty at ease and come home."

Phan-tu kept his feet squarely on the muddy ground, confusion and uncertainty thick in the air. He fixed his gaze on the remaining starfighter. Black smoke trailed from the wings. The canopy launched, along with a parachute, but the pilot must have been stuck in the cockpit. One of the wings sparked against the dome following the curve of the sphere. Then one of the dome's panels directly over the Rayes Canal opened. A malfunction? An order? There was no way to tell. A prism of light refracted against the sun. Birds shot out into the clouds as the enemy ship came through the gap in the dome, barreling straight for the sea.

"How unfortunate that we can't drown them all," Vigo said with uncanny calm.

Phan-tu imagined the horror of falling from such a great height, helpless and stuck. Alone. No matter who was in there, he could never wish another being such a fate. Perhaps that's why he ran.

"My lord!" the royal guard blustered. "Where are you going?"

But Phan-tu had already stripped off his sheer shawl and tunic, kicked off his ridiculous bejeweled slippers, and leapt off the pier. The tide was low, so he couldn't dive. He splashed through the sandy muck of the canal, broken shells digging into the soles of his feet. He thanked the great sea gods for the calluses he'd earned from a lifetime of running barefoot through the streets.

Phan-tu was grateful for the life he'd had, the home he was given after the storm that changed everything. But in his heart, he was still a little boy from the poorest slum in the capital. The people of the Rayes Canal helped one another. His mother had, and it had led to her demise. Even now, fifteen years after her death, after the monsoon, he still heard her voice. Still knew that in the worst moments, in the face of war and death and drought, she would say that there was always someone in need of help. If he could do it, he should.

So it didn't matter that the plummeting ship was from the planet across a corridor of space. It didn't matter. If it was a life he could save, he had to.

When he was far enough out, the ship breached the turquoise sea. A huge wave followed and Phan-tu dived. He could hear shouting from the distant shore, and then the pounding of his pulse as he kicked. His eyes burned against the salty brine, but his limbs welcomed the sensation of being enveloped by the warm sea. Like generations of Eirami, Phan-tu could hold his breath for long periods of time. It was a trait that had come about from eras of diving for food. But even his strong lungs had a limit, and he swam for the wreck as hard and fast as he could.

The water was hazy with disturbed silt, though farther out there was less pollution than at the shoreline. For the briefest moment, he was ten years old again, sinking to the bottom of the ocean after that terrible storm.

He wasn't helpless now.

He spotted the sinking vessel, dragging against the Erasmus Sea. It hit the shelf of a cliff and teetered at the mouth of the trench. If it tipped over, he wouldn't be able to follow. Phan-tu cut through the water like a krel shark, with only the first signs of pressure on his lungs as he reached the open cockpit.

Phan-tu was startled at the sight of her. Red hair, dark as copper. Fear and distrust in her amber eyes as she struggled to get free of her harness. Streams of bubbles escaped her nose. She was losing too much air, and still she raised her arms as if to block his attack. As if he'd come all this way to hurt her.

He held up his palms and gave a slight shake of his head. Then she pointed to the floor, where she couldn't reach. There was a glint of metal. A blade. He seized it, yanked it free of its sheath, and cut through the safety straps of the harness. There was a terrible crunch of stone giving way. He felt the shift in the water as the cliff ledge began to crumble under the weight of the ship.

As they sank, he grabbed hold of the second strap and sliced and tore through the fabric. There wasn't time for her distrust, her fear of him as he grabbed the front of her red uniform. She clung to him as her vessel tumbled into the dark pit of the trench. Pain laced her features, but he tugged on her arm, and they kicked up toward the beams of light refracting under the sea. His insides screamed for oxygen, jaw trembling as he gritted his teeth and fought to not open his mouth wide and inhale.

The E'roni woman admirably kept pace with him, though when he looked back, he could see a trail of blood unspooling like a ribbon. He couldn't tell which one of them was injured.

He'd swum his entire life, but the final meters put his mettle to the test, thrashing and kicking until he could feel the light on the surface, the fire in his lungs, and then the humid kiss of air as they broke the surface and choked on the ragged intake of oxygen.

The sea, which was never calm during the summer, steered them on rolling waves to the pier. They dragged themselves onto the muck of the canal, and up rickety wooden steps. Phan-tu dropped the dagger and flopped onto his back, coughing the salt water he'd swallowed.

"Are you all right?" He regretted the question the moment he voiced it. Because when he sat up, she was looming over him, water dripping from her hair, a bruise blooming on her forehead, and her dagger resting under his throat.

Chapter Five

LEVEL 2623, CORUSCANT

If there was one certainty in Axel Greylark's life, it was that he could always bet on himself. Quite literally. Deep in the back room of Raik's Parlor, Axel was one of five players hunched over a roulette wheel that the eponymous proprietor of the gambling den had created as a true game of chance. Illuminated by a low-hanging lamp, the chrome-and-gold pit spun, and each player tossed their cues into the fray. Axel kept his eyes trained on the shimmering carapace of his cue. He'd chosen the violet-and-emerald one because they were his family's colors, and since he was gambling with his family fortune, the correlation seemed apt.

As the spinning slowed and each tiny sphere rattled into one of the forty slots, several players threw up their hands in disgust and disappointment. Axel squeezed his trembling knee as his cue teetered on the rusty line between two divots. He'd bet his last stack of credits, plus the chit Raik herself had backed him, on account of him being such a good regular and all.

The cue finally tumbled into the golden jackpot.

Axel blinked sleep-deprived eyes.

He'd won.

He'd finally won and it had only taken—Axel glanced at his chrono. Damn it all to hell, had he *really* been here for ten hours?

One losing player smacked the lamp overhead, causing it to swing and strike the dealer. Two hulking enforcers removed the poor loser, leaving those accusing Raik of fixing the games utterly silent. Axel eased back into his seat. His fingers had come away sticky from the armrest. He didn't want to know what the secretion was, but he was certain it hadn't come from him.

Axel's droid, QN-1, nudged his pant leg below the table. Quin beeped something that sounded like disapproval of Axel's choices, then opened the triangular panel on its chest. It offered up a small silver flask, which Axel accepted with a gracious smile. He unscrewed the top and took a quick nip. Smoky whiskey burned pleasantly all the way down as he carefully watched the patrons of the gambling hall thin out. Some headed to find better fortunes in the rat-infested dens lining the pleasure district. Others might clean up and head to the upper levels for the start of the workday. Axel gave no sign of moving, and neither did the Mirialan woman or a tipsy Rodian who tapped a credit on the lip of the table.

"What?" the Mirialan woman sitting beside him all night asked. He'd rather liked the black diamond marks on her cheeks, and she'd rather liked taking his credits. Until now. "The cheap stuff's not good enough for you?"

The Rodian chortled, and Axel drank again, a drop landing on his thousand-thread-count shimmersilk tunic.

"How do you know this isn't the cheap stuff?" he asked.

"Don't mind him." Raik spoke in her scratchy, whistling voice. "Coruscant's little prince don't trust no one to pour him a drink, isn't that right?"

Raik was an Utai with a wrinkled, pinched mouth that gave her the appearance of sucking on a sourdrop. Her bulbous, protruding eyes were affixed on Axel as she slipped between the roulette and sabacc tables. She relieved the dealer and plunked into his seat. A pink drink appeared at her side from the many-armed bartender.

"Raik, darling, I mean no offense," Axel said, taking another sip of the Chandrilan whiskey, a gift from the senator's daughter on his last visit. "But this was a very good year."

And it was true. That batch was a thousand credits a bottle. A tragic shipping accident had made it the rarest batch in the galaxy, with only three hundred bottles left in existence. But what Axel Greylark wasn't saying was that he'd seen far too many people poisoned in his day to trust a drink from a dank hole in the wall in the steaming bowels of the city, even one as—*nice*—as Raik's Parlor.

"Why would I poison you, my best, most handsomest customer?" Raik asked. The ring of her mouth took on the drink's pink tinge. "Besides, you owe me too much money. If anyone wants you dead, it's that heiress. What's her name?"

The Mirialan snapped her fingers. "Lady Lulu Faradaisy? Something ridiculous like that."

Quin bleeped what might pass for a chortle among droids. Axel shoved the flask back into its chest compartment.

"Lady Lu-reen Faraday," he corrected. Even going down as far as the entrails of Coruscant wasn't enough to get away from the gossip of his very public split from the Chandrilan heiress of Faraday Spirits, now shipping all over the galaxy. The only reason he remembered the Faraday family business's slogan was because it was the first thing Lu-reen had said to introduce herself, followed by her father's title of senator. "And don't believe everything you watch in the holos."

Raik reset the roulette table and re-racked the selection of cues. "So you *didn't* break up with her by standing her up at the spaceport?"

"No, that's right," he admitted. "There's just more to the story."

Axel bit down on his back teeth and frowned at his warped reflection on the side of the lamp. The yellow overhead light made his complexion sallow, and emphasized dark circles that hadn't been there three days before. His dark hair was rumpled, and his eyes were bleary, but he had looked worse.

In his pocket, his comlink buzzed. Likely his mother. Again. He silenced it because he knew what she wanted. His mother wanted what everyone else did: an answer as to why he'd done what he'd done. Instead of making the decision to settle down, start to get serious, he'd taken his favorite speeder and a stack of credits, and wound up at whatever gambling den, club, or cantina would give him entry. He didn't need to explain himself. Why bother? The HoloNet, his "friends," and his family had already made up their minds. The only place to hide from another one of his family's interventions was at Raik's. Which was why he was determined to let his good luck take him as far as it would go. His talent for silencing any voice of doubt allowed him to ignore his comm.

"Besides, you're all much better company," Axel said, never letting his smile falter. A lifetime of the very best schooling, from private tutors to the royal academy, had given him pretty manners. Raik ate it up. "And because you've been so good to me and extended me a chit to keep playing, I'd never leave you in the lurch."

"'Cause you don't want to end up in a ditch," the Mirialan woman murmured.

He leaned forward on his elbow and grinned. "Darling, don't threaten me with a good time."

"Losing to you is not my idea of a good time," she purred, walking slender fingers across the top of his hand. He angled himself slightly toward her. "But now things have turned. You sure you're not secretly a Jedi?"

The sniveling orange Rodian honked a laugh. "If he was Jedi, he wouldn't be losing all day and night!"

A cold, ugly sensation spread from the apex of Axel's chest. He brushed her slender green fingers away, his voice like flint as he said, "Don't insult me, darling."

Confused, the Mirialan backed off and snatched a drink off a passing serving droid's tray. She knocked it back.

"Are we going to flirt all night or are we going to play?" asked the Rodian.

"You've had enough, friend. Buy-in's a lot more than that," Raik said benevolently.

The Rodian got up abruptly, muttering in the language Axel barely understood from accompanying his parents on ambassadorial visits to the swamp world. Something about his husband killing him? Whatever it was, the Rodian was out.

The Mirialan stacked her winnings into neat towers. The two of them had been trading the same credits back and forth for hours.

"You keep having your fun, little prince. The rest of us must go *earn* our fortunes." She raised her hand to caress his face, but he leaned away.

What bores. He wasn't going to let her or anyone ruin his new streak. He sat up and reached for the tray of cues.

"You too," Raik added, gesturing at him. "Go home, Greylark. I already run the risk of angering your mother."

"Leave my mother out of this," Axel said, a hard edge clipping his voice, one he did his best to keep buried.

Quin hovered into the air, the droid's triangle chest panel backlit with pulsing red light, as happened when Axel's temper flared. Stragglers in the den turned to glare at him, to see if he'd cause a scene, if he'd join the unfortunate moof-milkers tossed out into the gutter outside. He couldn't help but feel he'd done the very thing Raik had wanted him to do: let himself be baited. Because of his mother, the admirable, glorious, magnanimous Chancellor Greylark, he had been denied entry into most of the clubs on every other level, but not here.

This was a place where he could have fun, forget. Buried so deep in the belly of Coruscant, in a place that smelled like acrid sewers and musty, recycled air. A place of shadows where he didn't have to be Axel Greylark, son of the most important woman in the galaxy. He could just be his wretched self.

"Come on, Raik, darling," Axel said, resting his arms behind his head. "After all we've been through? You, who give refuge to many, would deny me one more parlor game?"

"Ah, but I give refuge to those victims of your mother's policies," Raik said, then glanced around the quiet room, the band at the center of the room merely stretching aching fingers and tentacles. "Who told you to stop playing? *Never* stop playing, is that understood?"

The band kicked into a cover of the irritatingly popular "Your Love Sends Me to Level 9."

Axel smiled at the Utai. His best Greylark smile. "One more. Please?"

When she made no show of moving, a tightness wrapped around his chest at the thought of stepping out those doors with nothing to show but a few hundred credits. He'd already lost so much. His accounts had been frozen, and he was certain the chancellor's security detail was searching for him. He *could* go home. Explain himself to his mother, issue a statement, and perform an act of community service as penance for his behaviors. Or he could stay because his luck had finally turned on that last hand.

"And what are you going to bet with?" Raik grinned as she played with the house's stack of chips.

Axel undid the sash of his cape and folded it neatly onto the pile. "The shimmersilk count alone is worth seven hundred."

"Keep your garments," Raik sneered. "I want something precious. Something the galaxy covets from you."

Axel tried not to grimace. The price of his upbringing was that he'd been on the holofeeds since the day he was born. Despite his penchant for getting into trouble, he was coveted as one of the galaxy's most eligible bachelors.

"You flatter me," Axel said, and Quin gave a warning beep.

"If you win this round, I will clear your debt to me."

Axel did his best to keep the thrill of that possibility from showing on his face. He glanced at the wall of trophies behind the bar, then the tank where Raik housed neon carnivorous piirayas that were all mandibles and tiny fins. He cleared his throat. "And if I lose?"

"All I want is a lock of hair from your pretty head."

Axel's bloodshot eyes traced the wall of trophies proudly displayed behind the bar. The horns of a Devaronian male. An upper row of teeth from a Karkarodon. Preserved Togruta montrals encased in glass. The shriveled hands of unfortunate thieves and cheats. Rumors were that she'd been exiled from her clan and from Utapau itself because of her affinity for such vicious trophies. She ended up on Coruscant, running the tables for the Romero Cartel until they set her up with her own gambling den in exchange for their protection fee and information. Axel threaded his fingers through the thick black strands of his hair.

Hair grew back.

His debt to Raik would keep growing, too.

QN-1 made a deflating *beepboop* sound Axel knew quite well. It was his droid's way of telling him to go home.

"What say you, little prince?" Raik ran her fingers across the box containing the cues, strange tiny reptiles that some believed had evolved in the gutters of Coruscant from rats and lizards. When light hit them, they curled into compact little balls no bigger than a roulette cue. Axel picked up his lucky purple cue and brought it into the shadows of the den. The critter unspooled, its pointed face and beady eyes moving in the air. Axel snagged a piece of the rind from a discarded drink on the table and let the ugly little beastie feast.

"A tempting offer," Axel said, deliberating on the odds. Raik's roulette was a true game of chance, not skill. There were forty slots—thirty-seven numbers, one golden jackpot, and two black house slots. He'd alternated his bets, inside, outside, doubles, and triples across evens and odds. Sometimes, when he was reckless and bold, he bet on a single number—eighteen. Now he had one shot. For Axel, possibility itself was like an electric charge. The sleepless aches, the bloodshot eyes, the worries of his uncertain future—it all zapped away and there was nothing but the thrill of chance.

He stacked his remaining credits across four numbers for a split bet. Two odds, two evens. One included eighteen, naturally.

"What are we waiting for?" He flashed a smile at Raik, who returned it, revealing tiny yellow teeth.

Axel moved his palm into the light, and his cue clamped up, its shimmering violet-and-emerald carapace ready to roll.

Raik's Parlor, nearly empty, had attracted the remaining patrons to their table. QN-1, never one to be left behind, hovered at Axel's shoulder. He tapped his droid's domed head for luck.

"Such pretty hair," Raik said, and set the roulette to spin.

Axel let his cue drop with a turn of his palm. Raik's red house cue bounced as the gold-and-chrome pit whirled, blurring the metal and numbers as it picked up speed. The Utai woman seemed unusually calm, like she knew something Axel didn't. Like she'd already foreseen the outcome.

For a fleeting moment, as the roulette slowed and the cues bounced from black to chrome to gold, Axel raked his hair back. He could hear his mother's voice, soft, low, and defeated. *Oh, Axel.* He'd deal with the inevitable confrontation when it came. For now, he had a game to win and a ledger of debt to clear.

"Come on," he whispered, the creak of the table, the rattle of the carapaces reverberating. His cue bouncing from slot to slot, edging so close, so very close to the jackpot gold. "Come on, come on."

The roulette stopped completely. Raik's cue rattled into the double zero belonging to the house, while his landed one fraction to the left of the jackpot and away from any number he'd bet. There was a winded sigh from everyone around him, like they'd all felt the gut-punch of his loss.

Raik chuckled, reaching to hoard the credits on the board toward her bosom. "Don't worry. I'll—"

Then his iridescent cue, his lucky strange little critter mutated in the gutter, did something impossible. It made a tiny gurgling sound and bounced into the jackpot as the wheel gave a final nudge.

"I won." He said it so he could believe it himself, and then said it again with his usual confidence. "I won."

A cheer went up around him. Hands pounding his back. Quin head-butted his thigh in victory, its front panel pulsing an array of colors.

"You deserve a name," Axel said, cupping the creature between his palms. It unfurled enough to waggle beady eyes.

"That didn't count!" Raik snarled. "You—you tampered with the cues."

"I did no such thing." Axel fed his cue the pith from a discarded cocktail fruit, then stood. His thighs ached from disuse. He needed to get to the bathhouses and get the crick in his lower back worked out. "Don't be a sore loser."

A thick, grubby hand wrenched the violet cue from his grip. The critter made a whistling cry, then was silenced by the crunch of Raik's teeth. Axel was still staring at the Utai masticating on the creature that had helped him win when all at once there were hands on him. He groaned as his face was shoved onto a sabacc table. QN-1 whirred and flew to his side. Axel threw his arms back but pain wrenched up his forearm as he was pinned harder. All he could see was Raik's slimy teeth and Quin crashing hard to the floor.

"This is between you and me, Raik!" No one touched his droid. No one.

The Utai approached, large golden eyes with dark blinking slits narrowed on him. He wanted to gag from the whiff of her breath. "The last person who insulted me I fed to my piirayas."

Axel heard the knife before he saw it. The soft clang of metal being unsheathed. Sticky hands fisted around a lock of his hair and yanked. He tried to pry his pinned arm toward his attacker's holstered blaster. He would get out of this. He always got out of this.

"You know, I usually expect a nice dinner before getting in this predicament," he said.

"Always so glib," Raik said. "Perhaps I'll send a second lock to your mommy."

"I'm sure she'll frame it." Axel wheezed as the pressure doubled against his back and his arm felt like it was going to be wrenched off his shoulder. Enough fear worked its way through to him that he felt cold from the inside. He shouted and tried to wrestle out of the grip but there were too many of them and the cold kiss of metal pressed against his hairline. He should have listened to QN-1's warning. But he'd been greedy. And if he was honest, he simply hadn't wanted to go home. To the tower above the world, to the empty halls. This was the ultimate price to pay to feed nightmares he couldn't quite shake.

"Wait, wait!" Axel shouted, his voice ragged. "I'll make you a new deal."

"You have no credits. Even the chancellor won't bail you out. What do you have to offer me when I can take what I am owed?"

Axel saw the blinking red light of his droid, which was slowly getting back up.

"The chancellor herself would owe you a favor. That's got to be worth more than a bit of my hair, doesn't it?"

"Your mother doesn't rule alone, and she isn't here to speak for herself."

"Right, but I just needed your attention a little longer. *Now, Q,* what are you waiting for?"

Quin flew out of Axel's view, but he heard the electric shock that felled Raik and her enforcer. The droid bounced in a short-lived victory.

As Axel picked himself up, along with the remains of his dignity, he was faced with three figures—a muscular Twi'lek, a hulking human, and a Hassk that screeched loud enough to scatter everyone except the band, who kept playing under Raik's earlier command.

"Looks like we've overstayed our welcome, Quin."

The little droid made a sound that likely translated to "I told you that *hours* ago."

"I know!" Axel raised one palm to stop the trio ready to smash him into smaller pieces that would likely go on Raik's wall of trophies. "Wait, let's just settle this like old friends. Have a drink with me."

The three of them glanced at one another in confusion, and for a wild moment seemed to consider it. Axel gestured to his droid. All night, everyone had seen Axel reach into the droid's panel for his flask. Quin's sensors blinked red as Axel retrieved not his rare whiskey, but a silver blaster.

Axel only got one moment of surprise, and he took it. He shot the biggest of the three in the thigh, then knocked over the sabacc table. He propped himself against it, turning to Quin, its front panel still blinking a disapproving red. It whirred a suggestion.

"No, *I'll* take the Twi'lek, you take the ugly hairy one."

Quin beeped. As he prepared to attack, blasterfire was returned. Glass crashed around them, but the band played on, only missing a few notes before the music died. No screams, no blasters, no shouting patrons. A grunt came from Raik, who was slowly rousing from her shock.

"See?" he said, even though he knew something was wrong. "They're no match for us."

QN-1 made a deflating sound, then peeked over the edge of their cover, trilling a response.

"What do you mean, backup is here?" Axel shot to his feet, blaster pistol leveled, and came face-to-face with a troop of Coruscant Guards. He blinked, relieved.

Axel holstered his pistol and offered his most charming smile. "Thank *goodness* you're here. I've been looking all over for you."

"Sorry, sir," one guard said, raising his blaster. "Chancellor Greylark's orders."

"No, no, wait!"

The last thing Axel Greylark saw was a ring of blue light.

Chapter Six

ERASMUS CAPITAL CITY, EIRAM

Xiri couldn't be here. Not on Eiram, not on this pier, and not with this stranger. Even if he had rescued her. She rubbed her chapped lips together, her tongue aching for water even if the salt would make her sick.

"Please," he said, raising his hands to show he was unarmed. Salt water clung to his soft brown curls and to the heavy lashes that fringed wide, steady green eyes. "If I wanted to hurt you, why would I have saved you from drowning?"

Xiri took a step back but did not lower her bane blade. The sun was bright on E'ronoh, but here on Eiram it was different. Refracted against the mottled blues and greens of the sea, light gave the effect of a dream, though the situation felt like a nightmare. Breathing heavily, her throat burned with the ocean she'd swallowed. She hadn't screamed as she'd lost control of her starfighter when the explosion of Blitz's ship had sent her careening into Eiram's atmosphere. Her fear had never been of falling. It was worse than that. She'd been afraid of the encroaching sea. The same waters had stolen her brother from her.

At the sound of heavy boots, Xiri leveled her blade at the

approaching guards. Eight of them. From what she'd studied of Eiram, the brocaded vests and sashes designated them of the palace. *His* retinue then.

She made a terrible sound—half laughter, half whimper—as she took several steps back to the edge of the pier. "Why let me drown when you could have a prisoner?"

His lips twisted with frustration as he stood, glancing back at the retinue of guards flanking him, raising thin staffs, threads of electricity crackling around the metal ends.

Xiri used to dream about a moment like this. Strategized about what she would do. How she would fight in the event she was captured. She could not let herself become a prize of war dangled over her father. She was born of E'ronoh. A child of the thylefire scorpion, the creature that survived in the scalding heat of the desert. When she came of age, she was dropped into the canyons that would devour lesser beings with nothing but her bane blade, and she found her way back home. Her abilities as a warrior were not in question.

She could shove the unarmed man aside. Tackle the biggest of the guards, then use his electrostaff on the others. She'd plow through two, perhaps three, before she could make a run for it. Her heart thundered at the idea of being lost in the maze of the city streets. And then what? If she got out of Erasmus, would someone give her shelter while she wore the uniform of their enemy? Would she have done the same if it was Eiram's prince at her door?

That's when she looked up and saw the people peeking out from their windows, was hit with the stench of dried seaweed and waste. Noticed the tents lining the lower level of the slum. Gaunt faces, hungry faces. Without the strange sea-green eyes and freckles of most Eirami, she might be looking at her own people.

Xiri bit down on the side of her lip. She needed pain to focus on what she had to do. A numbing calm spread through her limbs. She stopped shaking as the resolve set in. Eiram did not take prisoners because any warrior of E'ronoh would rather take a dagger to the heart than be a captive. She looked down at her bane blade, a gift from her brother when she'd been sent into the desert for her rite of passage. The hilt was dotted with rubies. *Like your hair,* he'd told her.

She turned her blade on herself. A hard jab through her solar plexus would require her total resolve.

"Please," begged the stranger who'd saved her. He took one step forward, his voice like an anchor. "Please, don't."

Indecision sliced through her. She turned her face to the sky. The shadow of the Timekeeper moon and her homeworld were there. She briefly shut her eyes and hoped Lieutenant Segura had managed to salvage the haul.

"Please," the stranger said again. It was the softness in the word that made her look at him differently. Who was he, dressed like a royal in a slum like this? "I won't let anyone harm you. I swear it."

"What good is your word?" She blinked, taking in the fine linen-fiber of his open vest, the gold pendant resting over the bare skin of his torso. She recognized the sigil of the queen's household.

"Then do not take me by my words. Take me by my actions." He raised a stern hand toward the encroaching guards. "Stand down, Vigo."

"But, my lord—"

"Stand. Down." He did not spare the guards another moment before returning his attention to her, one arm still outstretched like a lifeline. "You're Captain A'lbaran."

Xiri squared her shoulders. "You know my name. I demand to know yours."

The corner of his lip twitched. Did he think she was *funny*? "I'm Phan-tu Zenn. Now, you can either go with them to a holding cell. Or you can come with me for an audience with the queen."

"And who are you to the queen?"

When he frowned, he looked boyish, though she guessed they were the same age. "Well, she is my mother."

So this was Queen Adrialla's adopted heir.

It's a trick, Viceroy Ferrol's voice echoed in her ear.

Is that all you've got? Lieutenant Segaru, the man who had taught her everything she knew.

Your brother would have known what to do. Her father's voice then.

Her father. There had been a moment as she was falling into Eiram, when Xiri had wondered, not about her own survival, but about the way her father would retaliate. He'd doubled down on the war after Niko's death, even though no evidence ever existed that proved it was anything but a tragic accident. If the Monarch lost his last living heir to the enemy, everything Xiri would have fought for, and everything she wanted to do, would end with her. She'd be nothing but a memory, a cause, a vicious cycle.

What would the Monarch do if Xiri drove the blade through her heart? The answer came in a cold realization. She relived every battle she'd fought in a fury of memories. She imagined drill ships raining merciless destruction on these people. Without her, all he'd have left would be his poisonous counsel. Xiri had to stay alive, captured or not. General Lao had been willing to listen, but she didn't know if he'd survived the fall. No. Xiri was alone and she had to trust this stranger.

For E'ronoh.

Then Xiri A'lbaran tossed the dagger up in the air, catching it by its metal tip. She offered him the hilt. It was the highest gesture of trust from an E'roni warrior she could give.

He removed the thin gold chain from around his neck, the pendant spinning between them like the eye of fortune. She didn't soften, but snatched his offering at the same time he took hers.

The princess of E'ronoh put one foot in front of the other and began the winding road into the heart of Eiram's capital.

Chapter Seven

THE MOON BETWEEN E'RONOH AND EIRAM

The *Valiant* came down hard on the moon's landing pad. Master Creighton Sun did not unstrap the harness right away. Instead, he shut his eyes and centered himself in the Force. For Creighton, it was like standing at the center of a green field, beneath a blanket of gray sky. There was a moment when the clouds parted and a beacon of light illuminated everything. He needed to be sharp in order to understand the circumstances they'd waded into.

The steady voice of his old friend Master Char-Ryl-Roy grounded Creighton back to the ship, to the moon between worlds.

"The waystation and refueling depot are still functioning," Enya Keen said, "though there are no signs of life."

"Status on Jedi Nattai?" the Cerean asked his Padawan.

Enya toggled a switch on the control panel. "She's on her way here but her comm might be down."

"It's not our receiver?" Master Roy asked.

Enya shook her head. "I'm checking the systems, but I can't pinpoint the damage."

Creighton asked, "And the chancellor's ship?"

"The *Paxion* is docking now," Master Roy replied, tugging on the neat tuft of his dark brown beard. His blue gaze flicked toward the Republic Longbeam.

Over the years, the two Jedi Masters had traveled together so often that Creighton felt he could understand his friend's intentions without so much as a word of explanation, which was why he removed the safety harness and stood.

"Enya, meet us on the launch pad when you're finished," Char-Ryl-Roy ordered, and caught up with Creighton in a few long strides.

"I was under the impression Chancellor Mollo was on the other side of the galaxy," Creighton said, lowering the boarding ramp. He felt a needle of frustration pierce his otherwise calm disposition.

"I know what you're thinking," Char-Ryl-Roy said, the deep register of his voice louder than the pressurized hiss of the ramp. "And no, we do not know how events would have unfolded if the *Paxion* had arrived earlier or later. We don't even know why it was called or who called the ship here, or if the chancellor is aboard. First, we must find out all the facts. Then we can plan anew."

"You know I hate it when you do that," he said, though there was no actual malice in the words. Creighton trusted his friend implicitly.

Char-Ryl-Roy's lips quirked. "Only because you know I'm usually right."

Creighton walked ahead into the cool air of the moon, his boots crunching on strewn gravel. A repair crew from the *Paxion* wasted no time in patching up the damage. The way station appeared to have been abandoned for years. Overturned empty crates were piled at a stripped refueling station. Faint dusty footprints tracked paths from the row of destroyed storefronts, though there was no way to tell how recent the damage was. He crouched and touched the layer of sediment, rubbed it between his fingers, then brought it to his nose. There was no odor, but he tasted salt.

"What is it?" Char-Ryl-Roy asked.

He wasn't sure yet, but as a cohort from the *Paxion* disembarked and approached, he quickly dusted his palms and rose to his feet.

Two young aides, a golden-haired human and a Nautolan, trailed behind Chancellor Orlen Mollo's blue, fluttering cape. The Quarren stomped through the gravel in mud-flecked boots, and outstretched his arms as he bellowed, "Master Jedi! It's been an age."

Creighton exchanged a confused look with his fellow Master Jedi, because the Quarren was clearly not surprised by their presence, and neither were the two aides. The last time they'd seen the Republic leader, he had successfully negotiated a territory dispute on his world of Mon Cala, but that had been nearly a decade ago.

"Chancellor, how unexpected it is to see you," Creighton said, bowing in greeting. "Though I wish it were under better circumstances."

He'd often been told the deep register of his voice was commanding but comforting enough to put most at ease. He didn't have to reach out to the Force to sense Mollo's distress. His wriggling face-tentacles gave him away.

Mollo's turquoise eyes took in the abandoned way station and the sprawling view of Eiram and E'ronoh beyond the swell of the horizon. Both sides had retreated, but the belt of debris orbited the moon like the rings of ice on Coto-Xana.

"Yes, well, I came as soon as the Office of the Frontier alerted me of your mission to Eiram. We sent you a tightbeam transmission, but when I did not hear back, I did what I thought best. I'm sure Chancellor Greylark will agree that we had to seize this opportunity. In our haste to intercept you, I was unable to update her of my change of plans." He chuckled nervously. "Not that I require her permission, of course."

Creighton nodded but thought it better not to comment on the last part. As far as he'd witnessed, both Republic leaders worked in harmony, with Chancellor Greylark most comfortable operating from Coruscant and the Senate, and Chancellor Mollo often traveling the Outer Rim to better serve the frontier expansion. But what did it mean that Mollo had come all this way without initially telling Chancellor Greylark? The Jedi would have to nagivate that carefully.

"Unfortunately, we never received your message," Master Roy said somberly.

Creighton added, "Queen Adrialla of Eiram appealed to the Jedi Council through the Office of the Frontier. We were given a precise arrival time, as we understand were terms of the current cease-fire."

"I hope you're not suggesting this accident was my fault," Chancellor Mollo said, tenting the tips of his wide fingers.

Creighton took a deep breath to smooth out the bite of frustration. He sensed the Quarren's vulnerable emotions, but nowhere was there malice. Still, he couldn't deny the *Paxion*'s traffic collision didn't *help*. "Of course not, Chancellor Mollo."

"I sense there was more at work here," Master Roy said, radiating a well of tranquility. "After all your travels, you know that better than anyone. Isn't that right, Chancellor Mollo?"

The Quarren man eased and admitted, "That I do."

Creighton bristled slightly at having to placate politicians, but he understood that their situation would require more than their Jedi cohort. "Please, Chancellor Mollo. To what opportunity are you referring?"

"For the Republic and the Jedi to bring peace to this system and beyond!" Mollo said with fervor. "We've received several requests for aid from Sump and Shuraden. We've gotten word Merokia has cut off all ties to E'ronoh. This war is now affecting the trade routes in the Koradin sector."

"And the Lipsec Run," the young Nautolan aide added.

Mollo nodded. "Entire worlds dependent on imported food are starving. Twice now we've had to undertake extensive remapping to keep the hyperlanes functioning and clear of the scourge of pirates picking off the spoils of war. Enough is enough. Eiram and E'ronoh can divide their worlds, their space, delivery schedules, but they cannot divide the galaxy. It is time, for the good of the Republic, to settle this matter. And I need your help to do it."

Creighton Sun knew in his bones that there was a reason the Force kept bringing them back to the Eiram-E'ronoh system. True, Queen Adrialla had beseeched their help, but in the previous instances, they'd only been able to drop relief shipments. The Jedi couldn't fight a war for them, but they could be a neutral party. He could feel a brush of encouragement from Master Roy.

"We will have to discuss it further, but from what we know of E'ronoh," Char-Ryl-Roy said, "the Monarch is wary of outsiders. But perhaps there is a way to bring the leaders of both worlds together."

Creighton agreed and added, "We will get in touch with Eiram's capital as soon as our repairs are finished."

"Katrana," Chancellor Mollo addressed his golden-haired aide. "Be sure to dispatch any mechanics that can be spared to speed up the process."

"Yes, Chancellor," the young woman said.

"We thank you. That is very generous," Creighton said, bowing his head slightly.

The deep green Nautolan cleared his throat. Creighton sensed he was working up the courage to speak. "Chancellor, are you ready for me to update Chancellor Greylark now? We can use an EX droid."

"Thank you, Wix, but I'd like to have a full report first," the chancellor said tightly, before turning his intense turquoise stare on the Jedi. "I understand one of your starfighters was in the thick of the fight. We will need that report."

Creighton caught Char-Ryl-Roy's slight frown. Gella Nattai *had* disobeyed orders, but now they needed her testimony. Everything happened as the Force willed it. As he caught a glance of the approaching *Alpha*-class starfighter, he felt a sense of relief that Gella was safe. "There she is now."

Gella Nattai landed her Jedi starfighter beside the *Paxion* and the *Valiant*. Repair crews and astromech droids worked quickly on the Republic ship's hull. Even with their presence, there was a stillness to the solitary moon, cold and distant.

Opening her canopy hatch, Gella inhaled the whiff of salt carried in the cold air as she disembarked. She turned toward the horizon, and the startling view of the moon's salt-strewn ground, and then the expanse of space beyond. E'ronoh, like a red welt among the stars. Eiram, spinning blue and green seas with storms visible even from as far away as she stood. New wreckage left behind was only distinguishable from past waste because it was still smoldering.

Gella cast out into the Force. What was she hoping to find? Someone alive. Someone crying for help. The pilot—the boy really—Bly Tevin was gone. She'd felt his passing in the senseless explosion, like a final gasp. She took a moment of silence for the lives lost, comforted by knowing they were in the Force. But the fate of E'ronoh's captain and Eiram's general was elusive. Her last glimpse of the two vessels was when they spiraled toward the ocean planet's surface.

"Gella!" Enya's sharp voice cut across from the *Valiant*'s ramp.

The young Padawan waited for Gella to catch up before joining the Jedi Masters and the being she recognized as one of the chancellors of the Republic, Orlen Mollo, and two of his aides.

Striding toward them, Gella passed the ruins of an abandoned refueling station. Crates had been left scattered and broken. A storefront with a sign that read PEDRA'S PICKLES & PROVISIONS sported a shattered window, but the neon glowing sign buzzed to life at off intervals.

"You must be our intrepid pilot," Chancellor Mollo said, clapping Gella on the back so hard she'd have fallen forward if not for her quick reflexes. It was most peculiar behavior, both for a Quarren and for a chancellor of the Republic.

Gella had only ever seen him on the HoloNet, which often reported that Mollo trekked through the galaxy to the beat of his own string drum, and on well-worn muddy boots, but he was exactly as lively as he presented himself. She was sure she'd have to wait until the Jedi were alone to understand why the chancellor was in the system.

"Intrepid indeed," Master Char-Ryl-Roy said with only a hint of disapproval.

Gella remained deferential but winked at Enya, who offered a friendly smile.

The chancellor continued, tangling his thick fingers through his face-tentacles in the same way Master Roy tugged at his short beard. "Jedi Nattai, please give us a report on what you saw out there. Be our eyes and ears."

Gella looked to the masters. She'd never been given a direct command from a representative of the Republic, and even if he was one of the leaders of the Republic, she was not about to break protocol. Again.

The Cerean Jedi gave an almost imperceptible nod, likely not to offend Mollo. She felt him reach out through the Force with encouragement, and so she told them everything, though she did not retrace the moment she went rogue. One of the chancellor's aides took furious notes while the Quarren clung to her account—how they'd done everything to stop the E'ronoh ship from crashing into Eiram, and it still hadn't been enough.

When she was finished, Gella turned her gaze to the red and turquoise planets. "I'm almost certain the captain and the general were alive when their ships went down." There had even been a moment when Gella had wanted to follow, but she knew her best course was to rendezvous with her fellow Jedi.

"Captain A'lbaran is E'ronoh's princess and the Monarch's last living heir," Enya said, radiating worry.

When the pilot of the ice hauler had said, *"Many apologies, Princess,"* she'd assumed he was being patronizing as he dropped the cargo to get clear of the melee. The severity of the situation stretched the silence between them.

"Katrana, what's the status on repairs?" Chancellor Mollo asked.

The human aide looked up from her tablet. Her hair was in the elaborate braids Gella had seen on representatives from Alderaan. The young woman gave a small shake of her head. "A couple more hours at least."

"My diagnostics test turned up nothing unusual," Enya said. "What if we're being jammed?"

"We haven't detected anything coming from either planet," Katrana said.

"Master Sun," Gella said. "I'd like to volunteer to take the Alpha-3 on a recon mission to learn Captain A'lbaran's whereabouts."

The Jedi Master was deep in thought before he said, "The path is not clear. We shouldn't separate. And if we can't communicate with them, I don't want to risk the city defenses perceiving foreign vessels as a threat."

Enya grimaced. "That wouldn't bode well for the princess, then."

Gella believed Captain A'lbaran was alive. She had no proof, and had only briefly known the young woman, but it was a feeling she needed to explore. She needed a moment alone.

Gella took steady breaths and opened herself up to the Force. The sensation, here on the salt-strewn moon, felt like traversing along the edge of the horizon, as if at any moment she could launch herself into the endless sky and know she'd be safe in the blanket of night. She might not always follow orders, but she did follow her intuition, even when it got her in trouble.

Letting that sensation guide her, Gella broke from the cohort. She took careful steps across the launch pad. She wasn't certain of what she was looking for, but she was certain she would know it when she came upon it. There was no breeze, just salt crunching under her boots, and bits of glass from the front of an abandoned shop. Partial footprints were still imprinted in the sediment. She wished she had the skill to touch objects and see the impressions through the Force. She breathed through the knot of frustration building in her core, untangled it like a spool of thread, and kept going.

Her master, who passed into the Force years before, had commended Gella's intuition, her desire to devour knowledge, to question everything around her. One of Gella's most treasured memories was of the wise old Jedi saying, "Curiosity is your strength, my Padawan. It is your next step on your Jedi path." At times she wanted her strength to be some special ability like psychometry or healing, but then she remembered that every Jedi's connection to the Force was as unique as the stars in the galaxy. Hers still felt distant, though bright.

It was there, in the rubble of overturned crates and the remnants of the refueling station, that she noticed something she hadn't registered at first glance. Faint rings of disturbed salt, blast marks as if from turbo engines. Perhaps a small, single-pilot ship.

"Gella." Master Sun's voice was low, concerned. He approached carefully, his brown robes rustling in his wake. "What is it?"

"I think I found something," she said, even if she couldn't put a name to the thing she'd found. Only that the Force had guided her to this spot, this stack of scavenged crates, arranged almost too carefully. She reached inside one crate and found it wasn't empty.

Master Sun got on one knee to examine the cylindrical object that had metal pipes and the flat dome of an astromech droid. He scratched the graying spot on his left temple and let his fingers drag across his jaw in consternation. "If I didn't know any better, I'd think someone cobbled together a jamming beacon out of salvage yard finds."

Gella unholstered one of her lightsabers, the black moonstone hilt cool against her palms. She thumbed on the violet plasma blade, felt the familiar hum of its kyber core.

"Wait, no!" Master Sun began, drawing up a blocking blow with the Force. It knocked the trajectory of her downward swing off by a hair, though she still decapitated the beacon.

Gella disengaged her lightsaber and turned in confusion to the Jedi Master. "What was that for?"

He pinched the bridge of his nose, then loosed a long-suffering sigh. "We could have traced it back to whoever cobbled this together."

"Oh," she said, wincing at the canopy of space above. "Right. Perhaps we still can?"

Master Sun stood, still holding a severed piece of the homemade jamming beacon. There was no time for apologies as moments later the others began running toward them.

Katrana waved her datapad.

"She's alive. The princess is alive!"

"Whatever you did, a message from Eiram came through on every frequency," Enya added.

Gella turned her sights on Eiram's turquoise surface. She whispered, "Thank the Force."

"The princess is the answer," Master Roy said with certainty. "Arranging safe passage home for Captain A'lbaran is how we can invite the Monarch and the queen to a peace summit."

"Coruscant, perhaps?" the Nautolan aide asked.

Master Sun shook his head thoughtfully. "We should keep this summit here."

"*Here*, here?" Enya asked, gesturing around at the moon.

A reminder of a scavenged, abandoned place would not have been Gella's first choice. To her understanding, each world had a different name for it. The *Valiant* was a neutral place. Though not exactly equipped for royalty and still packed with medical relief for Eiram. But Chancellor Mollo was used to traveling with senators and world leaders.

"What about the *Paxion*?" Gella asked.

The Quarren's blue eyes burned with pride as he turned to his ship. "I was going to suggest it myself, my intrepid Jedi."

When the Master Jedi agreed, Chancellor Mollo wasted no time in ordering his aides. "Dispatch messages to both capitals at once. The *Paxion* will be stationed in the corridor between worlds. A stepping-stone on the route to lasting peace."

THE ROOK, E'RONOH

It was happening again.

Not Lieutenant Segaru's report of the day's skirmish. Not another lost cargo. Not the riots he could hear despite the servants shutting the glass panes of his war room. For the Monarch of E'ronoh, war was inevitable. A guarantee. A promise to defend the might and honor of his great house and lineage against any and all who would threaten them.

None of that mattered when his daughter was—

He swallowed the foreign emotion that wedged itself in his throat as he watched, then rewatched the holorecording of the clash that broke the cease-fire and ended with the explosion of Thylefire Nine's ship. It would have been an instant death, thank the old gods. But Xiri—Xiri's starfighter had been too close to the explosion, and she'd plummeted into enemy territory. There was no word of her whereabouts. No word if the enemy across the corridor of space had taken her hostage. If she'd been lost to those terrible waters.

"Monarch," Lieutenant Segaru said, with the impatience of someone who had to repeat themself.

The Monarch adjusted the cuffs of his tunic. Balled his fingers into a fist as he was unable to stop his hands from trembling. He had to pull himself together. It was time to act. His council and his lieutenant were waiting for an answer he did not have because all he could think of was that it was happening again. He'd lost his boy, his first son and heir, to those waters. If something had happened to Xiri—

Well.

He'd rip Eiram apart, pollute their oceans, blacken their clouds. He'd find a way. He'd do anything and everything in his power to destroy them.

"Yes, Lieutenant?" the Monarch said, leaning against the bronze head of his cane.

Jerrod Segaru's broad frame moved around the table. He'd come straight to the palace the moment he landed, judging by the haphazard way his flight suit was rolled down to the waist, exposing the sweaty shirt underneath. "I heard General Lao's last order. If, and that's a very big if, the barnacles powered down their anti-missile cannons like he ordered, there's a chance Xiri's still alive."

"A cunning girl," Viceroy Ferrol said. "Thank the old gods Princess Xiri was stubborn enough to reject your *gift* of a new ship."

Lieutenant Segaru cocked a brow. "Tevin wasn't as lucky."

"Though surely happy to give his life for E'ronoh." The viceroy smiled with yellow teeth. "My son also flew under Xiri's squadron, and he's still in the medbay. I am certain he feels the same way."

The Monarch nodded absently, then used his cane to point. "What triggered the explosion?"

"Sabotage," the viceroy supplied eagerly. "From Eiram, naturally. They've done nothing but cower against our attacks, and they've finally struck at our heart."

His adviser was right. Hailing from one of the founding families of E'ronoh, the man had been at the Monarch's side for decades. He was a constant in the sea of death that surrounded him. The only thing that had changed in Viceroy Ferrol was threads of gray in his auburn coif.

"Of course," the Monarch said.

Lieutenant Segaru cleared his throat. "My monarch, if I may?"

Viceroy Ferrol's lip curled with a barely perceptible snarl. But the Monarch motioned for the boy to proceed.

"Our ports are secure. Entry codes are routed to the capital's traffic tower. Anyone suspected of sympathy for Eiram is under surveillance. Whoever is responsible would have to have had knowledge of our hangar bays, and I simply cannot give the barnacles that much credit."

"Are you saying there's a traitor among us?" the viceroy asked.

"I'm saying," Segaru said, straightening to make himself a fraction taller than the other man, "that this is a distraction. Our eyes should be on Eiram."

"In that, we agree. We must strike," the viceroy said.

"That's not what I meant. We must get Xiri—Captain A'lbaran—back. The Republic and the Jedi have arrived in our sector," Lieutenant Segaru argued, pointing at the ceiling. "*In* our orbit. It would be unwise to move against them."

Viceroy Ferrol turned his cheek to the younger man. "If they have come to choose sides, then they *deserve* to be shot down. You must learn to make tough decisions, Jerrod."

Lieutenant Segaru had the nerve to smile, though there was no humor in the way he bared his teeth. He took a step, and the viceroy flinched as the soldier removed his eyepatch, exposing the brutally scarred tissue that had been mended shut. "Talk to me when you can make the call to send our soldiers to their deaths. Better yet, talk to me when you can look someone in their eyes and watch the light leave them. You've grown too comfortable, *Viceroy,* while our people starve." He tapped the flat of his hand against the older man's suit.

The viceroy balked, wrapping a hand around the bane blade at his hip. "You insolent—" He blubbered. "My *son—*"

"Do not hide behind your son," Segaru shot back, securing the eyepatch back in place. "His sprained wrist will heal."

The Monarch had had enough. He raised his cane and slammed it onto the marble floor, hearing the satisfying crack of metal on stone. The two men stood at immediate attention. In their restrained silence, the roar of unrest in the streets slipped through the cracks. The Monarch's tremors returned, more and more prominent with every step he took to the windows. Wrenching them open, he let in the evening dust. Opened his mouth and let it coat his tongue. Dust of his world, of E'ronoh. It was in his veins. In the long line of Monarchs that came before him. His family stewarding the safety and endurance of their planet, unchallenged for more than a century.

All that power and it granted him everything but peace. Now his enemies surrounded him. Eirami who had stolen his land, his son's life. Viceroy Ferrol was right. If the Republic and the Jedi were adamant about getting involved, he would make enemies of them, too.

His daughter would caution reason, diplomacy. She'd talked him into a cease-fire, and this was the result.

He knew, whether Xiri was alive or not, that he needed to show strength.

"*Captain* Segaru," the Monarch said. The young man's storm-gray eye widened with surprise before he lowered himself into a reverent bow. "Prepare to attack."

Chapter Eight

Gella Nattai raced to the communications center aboard the *Paxion* with Enya Keen at her side. The Republic Longbeam ship was cavernous compared to her starfighter, and it felt more so with only a skeleton crew keeping the ship operational in the "late night" shift.

"It should be right here," Enya said, turning into a dimly lit corridor that emptied out into an—aquarium. "Or not."

Gella absently touched her pocket as if the datacard Master Sun had entrusted them with had vanished since the previous second she'd checked. She glanced back in the direction of the meeting parlor and frowned. "Chancellor Mollo certainly modified the ship to his tastes."

Though the Jedi traveled in the same class ship, this one had a briefing room where he recorded his *Holos from Mollo* segment for the HoloNet, a room entirely dedicated to artifacts and gifts given to the Republic from the worlds he'd visited, a training room (though it seemed entirely unused), and apparently an aquarium.

"*Real* glowing plankton from Mon Cala," the Padawan marveled. "I wonder if he gets homesick."

Gella hadn't considered that a chancellor of the Republic, a being whose position was to lead a huge portion of the galaxy, *could* get homesick. As a youngling, she'd felt a longing for a place she no longer could recall except in flashes. But that longing had vanished over time.

Enya, who had a penchant for getting sidetracked, began to step into the pale-blue light of the room, but Gella tugged the Padawan by the hem of her tabard. The doors slid shut, and they resumed heading down the corridor.

"Let's retrace our steps before we get even more lost," Gella suggested.

"A Jedi is never lost," Enya said, taking on the severe baritone of her master, Char-Ryl-Roy. "As long as the Force is on their side."

Though she realized Enya was only half joking, Gella did, in fact, reach into the Force and found a very anxious, very worried someone nearby.

"This way." Gella took off in that direction, the network of corridors dimly lit, likely to redirect power to repairs and conserve fuel. When she heard a groan of frustration, followed by a fist pounding a screen, Gella knew they had the right place.

The communications room buzzed with Republic officials. Several beings made quick work of piecing back together an astromech droid while a human woman tinkered with the wiry guts of a control panel, her riot of curls falling into her eyes every time she reached for her tool belt.

Enya cleared her throat, but no one looked up.

Gella approached the nearest Republic official, sensing the anxiety radiating from them. The green Mirialan had black markings on their chin, like Master Roy's beard, and wore large goggles that made their dark eyes appear magnified.

"Excuse me," Gella began.

"You're excused," they said, punching several buttons on a control table all at once.

Gella tried again. "Hello, I am Jedi Knight Gella Nattai. Chancellor Mollo said you could help us send a message."

Then Enya added brightly, "Please."

"Well, I am tech supervisor Oshi Karmo, and I'm sorry to tell you that no one is sending any messages anytime soon."

Gella reached into her pocket and traced the datacard. "But Chancellor Mollo said—"

Oshi rubbed their face in frustration. "I'm sorry. It's been—"

"Rough day?" Enya offered, tacking on a smile to her empathetic question.

"Yes." The fellow nodded. Finally, they looked up, deflating into the swiveling chair. "Yes, it has been *a day*."

"Perhaps we can help."

Oshi returned Enya's infectious smile. "Is either of you a mechanical engineer?"

Enya thought on it very briefly before saying, "No."

"Then, no, you can't help." Oshi spun on their chair and pointed at the datacard in Gella's hand. "Transmissions are down."

Gella felt the pinch of anger, then noticed how weary the young Mirialan looked. Their entire ship had dropped into a war zone, and from what the Jedi had told her in their private quarters, Chancellor Mollo's venture to Eiram and E'ronoh was a bit rogue. Gella had been prepared to join the fray, Oshi wasn't. She wasn't used to smiling at everyone and everything like Enya, but she tried.

"What's your face doing?" Oshi asked.

"Nothing," she muttered, flattening her lips. "The chancellor said we could use one of the Ee-Ex comm droids."

"Oh, why didn't you say so?" Oshi thumbed to the right without sparing the Jedi another glance. "Down the hall."

"Come, on," Gella said, tugging at Enya by her sleeve. "We have to update the Jedi Council."

Gella wondered how much of Master Sun's report would be about her, and an uneasy feeling weighed down on her shoulders. Her impulsive move to jump into the fight had led to E'ronoh's princess getting stranded in enemy territory, and she'd destroyed evidence that could have given them answers. Her intentions were good, but intentions were not the same as results.

"Have you ever used one of these?" Enya asked.

The droids were docked in individual ports, with a row of capsules lined like escape pods. In remote parts of the galaxy, where transmission beacons were few and far between or were often damaged by wars, like in Eiram and E'ronoh, the EX droids were vital for shepherding messages safely between Pathfinder teams.

"When we were on Orvax, yes," she said, her voice tight as she hoped Enya wouldn't pry into the ordeal once again. Gella powered up the nearest EX droid. With its flat top and spindly mechanical legs, it reminded her of spiders. She inserted the datacard into the narrow slot. "That should do it. Turn on one of those thruster pods so it doesn't disintegrate in Coruscant's atmosphere."

Enya knelt in front of the capsule, its outer panels covered in dings and scrapes. It wouldn't open, so she moved on to the next. "Do you want to talk about it?"

"Talk about what?"

Enya shrugged as if it were obvious. "Your mission with the Republic Pathfinder team. *On Orvax.*"

Gella crossed her arms over her chest, a musing smile on her face. "Didn't you overhear everything from Master Roy already?"

A blush darkened Enya's brown skin, but she likely sensed the walls Gella was putting up. "You're part of our team now. I can sense your guilt from a hyperspace jump away."

"That is impossible," Gella noted, but the Padawan was wise.

"As impossible as the gravitational anomaly that keeps a moon perfectly locked between two warring planets?"

Gella shook her head, tapped open the next available pod. For days since she'd been reassigned from her Pathfinder team, she'd gone over their mission from every angle. After three days of being unable to make contact with the sentient species of the planet, their equipment began to vanish. Then GT-3 never made it back from mapping the surrounding forest. And then . . .

"I made the wrong call. My team got hurt and we never made contact. I was reassigned here. There's nothing more to tell." Gella locked the EX droid in place and the capsule pressurized shut. "There is no sense in lingering on the past, you know that."

Enya's dark gaze was understanding, but disappointed. "It's only lingering if it eats away at you."

"I know that," Gella said solemnly.

"It's not so bad, is it?" Enya asked. "Being assigned with us?"

Gella felt a pang of guilt. She'd admired Master Sun and Master Roy since she was a Padawan. She wanted to understand how Enya could always find a reason to smile. "On the contrary. Our education as Jedi is never over. Before I got my orders, I even considered making a petition to the Council to become a Wayseeker."

Enya raised her brows. "That makes sense."

"It does?"

"From what I've heard, Wayseekers are solitary, and you spend most of your downtime aboard the *Valiant* on your own. No offense."

Gella shook her head ruefully. There was more to being a Wayseeker than being solitary. Yes, she could travel on her own, but she could also choose wherever in the galaxy she wanted to explore. She could follow the calling of the Force, the threads that bound every being together. She could learn on her own.

"I've only ever known one Wayseeker," Gella said, remembering the pink-skinned Zeltron girl she'd grown up with. "Jedi Meli Day. Even when we were younglings she talked about going out on her own. She always got caught vanishing into the forests around the temple."

"To do what?"

"To listen to the Force, she used to say." Gella kept her hands busy by punching in the coordinates to the Jedi Temple on Coruscant. "I never thought we were anything alike. And I know not all Wayseekers are the same, just as not all Jedi are the same. But Meli was so certain."

"Is that why you didn't go through with it?" Enya asked tentatively.

Gella knew the answer. She'd changed her mind because at the time it had felt like running away. If she couldn't be certain, as certain as Meli Day had always been, then perhaps it wasn't her path after all. Not yet at least. Why couldn't she admit all of that to Enya?

"It wasn't right, in the end," Gella said, then turned the release valve.

There was a satisfying *swoosh* as the pod was ejected into space, its thruster igniting as it sailed through the junk field and toward the hyperspace point.

Enya pressed her hands on the small viewport, watching the pod, and said, "Thank you. You're the most helpful being we've met on this ship."

Gella couldn't help but chuckle as they headed back through the comms room on their way out.

Oshi pushed their goggles up so they rested atop their head. The spheres had left behind indentations around their eyes.

"The first couple of pods don't work," Enya let them know.

"These things need constant repairs—pretty much like everything out here," Oshi said with a note of defeat.

"That's the way of the galaxy," the same curly-haired repair tech said, before jumping back as the wire she'd been working on sparked. "You patch up one thing and find a break somewhere else."

"Maybe if everyone helped," Enya said thoughtfully, "there would be fewer things to patch up."

"Wait." Oshi raised a hand. "Are we talking about the galaxy or a ship?"

Enya didn't miss a beat as she decided on "Both."

"At this rate, we might have to ask Chancellor Greylark for a new ship," the repair tech muttered.

Oshi shut their eyes. Gella had seen many Jedi Masters make that face, especially when dealing with younglings, as if they were summoning all the patience the Force would grant them. "Don't. Don't even say that in front of Chancellor Mollo."

"I thought—" Enya began, but Gella rested a palm on the Padawan's shoulder. There was something between the chancellors that the Jedi were not privy to, and she sensed it was best not to pry.

Instead Gella redirected their attention and asked, "Has E'ronoh responded to the peace summons?"

"Not since they blew up the protocol droid envoy." Oshi sighed.

Gella raised her brows in surprise. "That doesn't bode well for the summit."

"That's why everything is chaos here. Our deflector shield took a hit during the drop from hyperspace and collision with your ship. We didn't notice until we returned to the corridor and got pelted by the debris."

"And we can't dock again because we're running out of fuel—" the repair tech said.

"And yes," Oshi added, noting Enya readying to make a suggestion, "we sent astromechs to fix it, but they keep getting beheaded and we can't damage any more."

The repair tech whistled in agreement. "Yup. Pretty sure those things cost more than my salary."

Gella saw the solution with utmost clarity, then turned to their Republic allies. "Then it's a good thing you have Jedi on board."

Enya nodded emphatically. "Send out another droid."

Oshi eyed them from head to toe. Enya with her robes, always a little slouchy, as if she'd gotten dressed in a hurry because she was simply that excited to begin her day. Gella with her arms crossed and her lips set in challenge.

"We've tried everything else," Oshi said though didn't seem convinced.

The repair tech set down her tools and came closer. "I've always wanted to see Jedi in action and up close."

While they readied another astromech, Gella and Enya positioned themselves in the middle of the viewport. Starboard side, they had a view of the red bruise that was E'ronoh's atmosphere, and the river of debris left behind by their war.

"So much destruction," Enya lamented. "I've never seen anything like it."

Gella took Enya's hand, still soft against Gella's own calluses. Though she wasn't always great with words, she was certain she could offer this comfort. "That's what we're here for."

Gella raised her free hand and extended it forward. She calmed her mind of the events that day—the moon, the dogfight, the long travel through hyperspace. And beyond that, hidden in the recesses of her heart, the doubt and fear that tested every Jedi. Mistakes that lingered like smoke long after a fire had been snuffed out. Choices she could not take back. All of it was set aside to fix the problem in front of her.

She felt Enya's bright aura through the Force, a heady feeling that reminded her of the first ray of sun after a storm. Together they guided the debris field away from the silver astromech rolling its way across the ship's panels. Gella shut her eyes, slowed her breathing. There was resistance as the objects in motion fought against her. She was among them. She was weightless. She was strong enough to do this.

"Well, I'll be damned," Oshi murmured.

It was the awe in their voice that made her look.

The astromech was already returning toward the air lock, task completed.

When Gella and Enya let go, the metal scraps rushed back in, only pelting the deflector shield before drifting back into the space corridor.

Gella smiled, truly smiled, at her fellow Jedi, then caught a movement at the corner of her eye. She shuffled closer to the viewport.

Where E'ronoh's atmosphere had been still moments before, it was shifting. White whorls of clouds ruptured like bloody cysts as six massive ships emerged into orbit. Hulking metal beasts nothing like the starfighters she'd seen upon their arrival. These were drill ships with twisted steep noses capable of cracking through slabs of marble or splitting an asteroid in two—or the hull of a Longbeam. Master Sun had described the weapons in E'ronoh's arsenal on the way to the Dalnan sector, but seeing them for herself, she was finally able to imagine the damage they could wreak.

"Sound the alarm," Gella said, already reaching for her comlink to alert Master Sun.

E'ronoh had answered the peace summons.

ERASMUS CAPITAL CITY, EIRAM

Xiri had never seen so much water in her entire life. The Erasmus Sea was a great expanse of impossible blues and greens refracting a lazy sun and lazier clouds that skimmed the coast. Xiri could have opened her mouth to quench her thirst with the humidity.

Eiram. She couldn't stop repeating the word again and again as she paced across the balcony of the great palace nestled on a cliffside with the city sprawled beneath. She had been prepared for the man who had rescued her to betray his word. It was what Viceroy Ferrol would have ordered if the situations were reversed, and an Eirami ship had crashed on E'ronoh. She could admit that to herself with great shame. Instead, they'd offered her food, water, a room, and a bath.

She had refused.

First she needed to understand. To see. Xiri gripped the iron railings of the balcony and leaned forward as far as she could.

Thousands of people gathered at the gates below while harried guards shoved small bundles into skinny hands and moved on to the next. Phan-tu Zenn, as her savior had called himself, had said that each parcel contained three rations of round loaves, a week's supply of hydration pellets, and protein squares made of kelp and salt worms. She'd wanted to raise her nose in the air and grimace at how revolting it sounded. But what did she have to give her people? On E'ronoh, the stores of grain were empty and the fields were suffering from drought.

She should have reveled in the certain fact that her enemy's world was suffering as much as hers, but it only left her hollow. Uncertain. Now was not the time for uncertainty.

Here was Eiram's capital with nothing but seas and canals that cut through the city like great arteries in a messy, beating heart trying to stay alive. What a cruel fate to be surrounded by oceans and not be able to cup water in your hands and drink deep. Not without getting sick from the salt.

She hated Eiram. She hated Eiram for everything they had put her family and her world through. She hated Eiram because it would have been easier if they'd beaten her, hurt her, shoved her in a cell. Most of all she hated Eiram because she had never seen a place so beautiful and admitting it felt like a betrayal to everything she had ever known.

"Is it everything you've been told?" A soft, pretty voice spoke behind her.

Xiri whirled around to find Queen Adrialla of Eiram, regal and swathed in a blue shimmersilk dress that gave her the effect of floating. The brown skin of her shoulders was dusted in a gilded powder. Though Xiri knew the queen was nearing her mid-sixties in standard years, she had only the faintest traces of winkles around her eyes and the corners of her full mouth.

At her side was Phan-tu Zenn. His soft black curls were still damp, but he'd changed into a long silk blouse, trousers, and slippers. Behind him, she spotted two armed guards flanking the open doors to her room, grips tight on their electrospears.

"It is certainly different," Xiri answered honestly. She nodded to the queen but did not bow. Her father said they would never bow to Eiram.

"How is it different?" Phan-tu asked. He'd been silent nearly the entire ride to the palace, and when they'd arrived, he'd instructed a group of young attendants to treat the princess as a guest. He'd stressed the word *guest* several times.

Xiri didn't care for their small talk or attempts to put her at ease, but her nerves betrayed her. "I thought all people of Eiram have green birthmarks. But you do not, unlike your—ward?"

"My son," the queen said patiently, taking a seat facing the wide-open balcony. She gestured to the one beside her, but Xiri stood, as did Phan-tu. "And no, not all people of Eiram have green markings."

"It's the kelp," Phan-tu explained. When he smiled, his eyes crinkled at the corners. His light brown skin had a cluster of green freckles across his nose and the tops of his cheekbones. It was a startling effect when doubled with the rings of blue and green in his eyes. "It's in all our food. Well, most of our food."

"I'm sure your merchant class or the palace aren't dining on it," Xiri said with a pointed smile.

Queen Adrialla did not take Xiri's bait. She merely sat back and gestured at the open sky behind them. "My dear, your father is launching an attack to come and rescue you. It is one thing to refuse our hospitality. But do you truly want to waste an audience with me making petty remarks?"

"My father—" Xiri couldn't form the rest of the words. She ran back out to the balcony and was relieved that there were no ships visible behind the clouds. The white bands of the domed shield were intact, and the city's alarms hadn't been engaged. "What has he done?"

"After we sent word of your state of well-being, he has decided that we are holding you hostage. We have brought you his message." Queen Adrialla spoke every word with a calm Xiri did not feel. At least Phan-tu Zenn frowned at the news.

The queen nodded to her son, who placed the holoprojector at the center of the table. A flickering rendering of her father appeared.

"This is Monarch A'lbaran of E'ronoh. I know my daughter is alive and I know she has been taken prisoner by the callous queen of Eiram. First, I require proof that Princess Xiri is alive and unharmed. Then, if she is not returned to me by sunrise, I will unleash the full might of E'ronoh's forces until there is nothing left of your planet but salt."

Her father's holo cut out, and the three of them sat in silence for a moment. The shouting and haggling of the capital's markets drifted in with the brine of the breeze. Xiri placed a hand over her heart; her mouth was dry as the Ramshead Gorge. She found herself taking up the empty seat beside the queen after all.

Phan-tu Zenn filled a goblet with water and placed it in her hand. "Rainwater. Please, drink."

Please. He'd said that to her over and over when she'd held a knife to his throat and when she'd turned it on herself. Xiri remembered what it was like to be falling through that warm ocean. On E'ronoh, there were no great wide seas. There was rock and heat and dust storms that could leave you buried and blind, mere steps from the door of your own home.

Rain was precious. Here she held it in her hand, and when she drank it, she could hardly breathe as she gulped it down. Thirst over-powering her, she tilted the goblet higher, but she did not dare waste a single drop. When she was finished, she cleared her throat, cheeks burning that they were seeing her in such a state. She set the empty cup on the table and sat forward with the remains of her dignity.

"We should send word right away," Xiri said. "Can you prepare a ship to leave immediately? We will cover the cost of fuel—"

The queen waved her hand in the air. "We will prepare to leave at once, but we aren't going to E'ronoh."

"We're not?" Xiri tensed, searching the queen's face for trickery.

She couldn't forget that she wasn't home. She wasn't with allies or friends. She was in the world that had caused every suffering on her planet, not just for the last five years, but before that as well. She was picking up the war her grandparents had fought. It was a cycle of never-ending war and violence. *War* was her inheritance. *War* was con-stant, not peace. Not this Eirami hospitality.

"Immediately after the Monarch's holo, we received this message from the Republic and the Jedi."

Xiri remembered the Longbeams that had created discord in the space corridor, and the Jedi starfighter that dived into the middle of the fight trying to help Blitz. The Monarch believed the Republic had no business meddling in the Outer Rim, and he'd refused aid from the Jedi Order at the start of the war on account of them helping Eiram as well. She could not imagine her father was reacting well to any of this.

When Phan-tu played the second holo, two forms flickered to life, one Cerean and one Quarren. She noted the Jedi by his robes and the lightsaber at his hip. The other, she recognized as one of the Republic's two chancellors, Orlen Mollo.

"This is Master Char-Ryl-Roy of the Jedi Order," the tall Cerean said in a deep, calming voice. "Chancellor Mollo and I come to you at this urgent hour to invite your great worlds to a peace summit aboard the *Paxion*. The ship will remain in the corridor between E'ronoh and Eiram, along with Eiram's medical shipment."

"If representatives from your planets do not arrive by sunrise," Chancellor Mollo interjected, his face-tentacles wriggling as his voice boomed, "the Republic will be forced to place sanctions and carry out an investigation into who was responsible for damage sustained to the Jedi and Republic ships, and the destruction of Republic droid envoys. It is our hope that you choose peace."

Xiri watched the images dissolve. "My father will never agree to it."

Queen Adrialla's brown gaze slid toward Xiri. "He doesn't have to. You are the captain of the fleet, and the princess of E'ronoh, a daughter of thylefire. Are you not?"

"Yes, I am," Xiri said, emphasizing each word. "But the Monarch is still the Monarch."

She flicked her wrist, as if that would dispel Xiri's worry. "The Republic and the Jedi have always conspired to meddle in our system. My own parents dealt with it, and now it is my turn. I am certain, when the time comes, Phan-tu and his consort will as well."

Phan-tu blinked hard at her response. "My queen, I don't need to remind you that they have our medical shipment, and we did *ask* the Jedi to get involved."

"But not the Republic," Queen Adrialla clarified. "And I assume E'ronoh would never. Yet, they are here now and we must deal with it."

Xiri blanched. If she'd talked to her father that way, she would have felt the cool sting of his rings across her face. She and Niko had learned from a young age to choose their words carefully. In response to her son, the queen merely pursed her lips. There was even a touch of humor there. Was this for show? Was this to lull Xiri into some sort of false sense of camaraderie?

"We asked for their aid. Meddling is entirely different. I do not like having the terms of a deal altered, and I do not like my hand being forced. Especially"—she looked pointedly at Xiri—"when I am told Eiram did not initiate the conflict."

Xiri had the sense to look away. Yes, it had been Blitz who sparked the chain of events that led her to this predicament. But there was something she was missing. Ships didn't simply explode, and she was too far from home to speculate.

Could she voice those concerns among the enemy?

Surely not.

She needed to get to the Rook, to confer with Lieutenant Segaru and her father.

"I want answers, too, Queen Adrialla," Xiri said. "And I thank Phantu Zenn for his assistance earlier."

The queen reached out and brushed his cheekbone with the affection only a mother knew. They had little in common, but the adoration was there. It made something stir inside Xiri, like the stitches of an old wound becoming undone.

"Assistance?" the queen repeated. "Is that what you call saving your life, Princess? You haven't even asked about General Lao. He is alive, thank the seas, though barely."

Xiri pressed her lips together to keep them from trembling. The general. She'd hoped the old gods would keep him safe. But still, she deflected because this was not her queen, and this was not her planet. "Captain. It's still Captain A'lbaran."

"As you wish it," Queen Adrialla said. "You may attend the summit and give your people hope, or you may stay there to be collected like a war prize, but either way, we are leaving for the *Paxion* tonight."

"Tonight?"

"There has been so much loss we both have to answer for. I do not know about you, *Captain* A'lbaran, but I am willing to listen. And the sooner we get you offworld, the sooner I can offer proof that you are hale and hearty and your father is a mad king."

"If you can refrain from insulting my father," Xiri said, "I can send him a message. You or your *son* can review it. But I can convince him of my safety, and *perhaps* to come to the peace summit."

Queen Adrialla's deep eyes assessed Xiri for far too long. It took all her training not to fidget. "Very well. *If* you bathe. I understand it may be hard for you to accept a kindness from me, but you are not a prisoner here. I will not return you looking as one."

"It feels indulgent," Xiri admitted, "to waste water."

The queen stood, clearly out of patience for the E'roni royal. "If it's any consolation, it's mixed with salt water. But do clean up. Phan-tu will wait for you and take you to the ship when you are decent."

"I will?" he asked, then cleared his throat and turned it into a statement. "I will."

"We've all had to make sacrifices these last few years," Queen Adrialla said. When she didn't smile, she looked so very tired. It was a weariness Xiri, a girl less than half the queen's age, shouldn't have felt so acutely. And yet there it was.

The queen of Eiram took the supporting arm her son offered and made her way out of the suite, stopping at the door. "I can see in your eyes the toll of the war. You strike us. We strike harder. On and on . . . This may be our only opportunity to listen to one another without dissolving into chaos and take aim at a resolution. Let us not miss."

Chapter Nine

THE BRUSHLANDS, E'RONOH

Serrena took the EX communications droid apart piece by piece. It would have been lost to hyperspace if she hadn't moved quickly. With all attention on the drill ships ascending into E'ronoh space, Serrena had slipped by undetected, and intercepted the Republic's capsule with her *Vane*-class transport shuttle, a two-person shuttle she'd salvaged from scrap and armed with retractable magnetic clamps. She'd welded and assembled it with her bare hands.

She'd landed within the Brushlands, at an abandoned mining village that skirted the capital. There Serrena had found everything she needed to fulfill her mission. A quiet place to hide and serve her master well.

The front door hissed open, letting in the chill and dust of the windy night. Abda had returned, and the scent of fried scorpion filled the room. Serrena did not look up.

"I brought food. You've been at it for hours," Abda said, sitting on the threadbare rug.

She resented having Abda watching over her shoulder, pointing out every single detail as if Serrena hadn't thought of it first. But the elders had *insisted* on working in pairs, on making sure they were never vulnerable to the corruptions of the outside world. Serrena and Abda were, of course, both Kage, born to the dark shimmering world of Quarzite. Banished by their clans for refusing to fight. For Serrena, it wasn't the violence she turned from. It was the insignificance of it. Through the Path of the Open Hand, she had learned that every part of her lived in harmony, and her misfortunes? They were the fault of those who used the Force, like the Jedi. After years on Dalna, she had been called to a higher purpose, one she would fulfill with her last breath, because she was one of the Mother's Children, and Abda was not.

She snarled, "I'll eat when the work is done."

Abda sighed, taking a bite of her meal. "If you pluck the wrong wire, everything will be erased and we won't be able to learn why the Republic has come to this sector now. And if you can't dispatch it once we're done, they may get suspicious, and it'll lead back to us."

"I *know* what I'm doing." Serrena pushed back her hood. Her pale skin was covered in red burns from the unforgiving sun. She bared her teeth and seethed. "You forget *she* chose me for this honor."

"And you failed," Abda muttered, rolling her pink gem eyes. "Princess Xiri lives. The cease-fire still holds and your jamming beacon was destroyed."

Serrena slowly put down the Louar clamps. "Patience."

"You sound like a Jedi."

Serrena cursed, but focused on her work. She needed something useful to report back. Everything else was a distraction, even her partner.

A bead of sweat ran straight down her nose, and she caught it with her tongue. Her fingers were steady with purpose as she plucked a silver wire that would trigger a system reset. Then she turned on the EX droid, and a holo of two old Jedi, judging by their robes, flickered to life.

"That isn't Chancellor Mollo," Abda grumbled as they listened. She always was shortsighted.

"Even better," Serrena said. "We need to tell the Mother the Jedi have arrived."

Phan-tu Zenn had never been offworld before. Had the war never started, he would have been Eiram's ambassador to E'ronoh and the rest of the galaxy when he officially took his place as heir. Instead he'd remained rooted to his home, to the currents of oceans he knew better than the lines across his palms.

As they filed into the shuttle, all of Phan-tu's efforts went into keeping his earlier meal down. Eiram's delegation consisted of Queen Adrialla, her consort, Captain Xiri, a dozen of the queen's personal guards, and Phan-tu. He strapped into a seat toward the back of the shuttle, grateful for the low light to hide that he was sweating through his shimmersilk. He unfastened the top clasps of his tunic, but it did little to relieve the vise around his lungs.

He was vaguely aware that the captain was speaking, announcing their takeoff. He was too preoccupied by the sudden rattle. Were shuttles *supposed* to rattle? What happened when they got above the clouds? He'd seen ships split open in atmosphere, solid ships made of solid metal reduced to scraps. What was to stop their shuttle from doing the same? And then a darker thought wormed through his mind—what if the Monarch was as mad as they said? Mad enough to sacrifice his daughter in order to destroy the queen. All of them packed into little more than panels of steel hurtling through the sky. What if—

"Breathe." First came her whisper, then her hand on his.

Breathe, he commanded his body, and after several tries, he did just that. If he thought of flying into space as holding his breath long enough to dive for pearls in the Erasmus Sea, it might make things easier.

The princess removed her hand from his, then gave a bemused chuckle and shook her head. A red curl untucked from her braid and landed over her cheekbone.

"What?" he asked.

"You dived into the ocean, then clung to the hull of my starfighter as we plummeted several meters below water, but this makes you nervous?"

How could he explain that the ocean wouldn't hurt him? It was, of course, preposterous. People died from monsoons every year. Lost to boating accidents or krel shark in the deep, or swept off by riptides. He'd been pulled out to sea, and it had embraced him, returned him to the shore whole and safe.

"I know the ocean," he said, keeping his voice low. "I've never even flown across Eiram."

She nodded, but her brows furrowed. "We're through the worst of it."

Easy for her to say. Captain A'lbaran had been at the front lines of the war for half a decade. More than once, he'd heard General Lao curse her name during military briefings.

Phan-tu pressed himself back into his chair, feeling every dive, every turn, every list of the shuttle. Queen Adrialla glanced back at him once, then at Xiri. It wasn't quite worry that passed across her regal features, but sometimes, his mother was a mystery even to those closest to her. Perhaps she wondered if he was strong enough to lead Eiram when the time came. Perhaps she doubted, regretted even, that she had chosen him, a little boy from the silt. Perhaps his fear of flying was giving way to even greater fears, ones he could not put a voice to.

He knew, more than anyone, how quickly things could turn. One moment they were at war with E'ronoh, a war his grandmother had told him stories of. The next, he was blasting into the corridor between planets for a peace summit.

One moment he was in his house boarding up the windows as the storm raged, and the next he was pulled out to sea as a monsoon crashed through the slats and grabbed him like a fist.

One moment he was distributing relief, the next there was a red-headed princess holding a knife to his throat.

As they finally docked, Phan-tu knew that he had to be ready for anything. His mothers needed him to be strong, and that thought carried him as he put one foot in front of the other through the docking tube and aboard the *Paxion*.

A cohort of Jedi along with the chancellor himself greeted them before they were shepherded away by Republic aides. All except Xiri, who was being taken down a different corridor.

"The E'roni delegation will be on the port wing," the chancellor explained, reading the confusion on Phan-tu's face. Though it shouldn't matter to him where Captain A'lbaran stayed. They had done their part—his promise to keep her safe and bring her one step closer to home.

Xiri turned to the queen and consort and lowered her head slightly. "Thank you for keeping your word."

"It is my gesture toward a shared peace," the queen said. "Let us hope your father is swayed by your courage."

"He will be," Xiri said, her voice sharp as steel. Although Phan-tu had caught a slight hitch in it when she'd threatened to take her own life. He knew she'd go through with it, saw the resolve in her eyes. She'd been ready to make a sacrifice, despite her personal fear.

The Republic, the Jedi, E'ronoh and Eiram. Everyone was ready to contribute toward this effort.

That evening, Phan-tu lay awake for hours in a strange bed, far away from home, wondering what he'd give to see Eiram safe.

"Everything," he whispered to himself. "Everything."

LEVEL 2623, CORUSCANT

While Eiram and E'ronoh were deciding the fates of their worlds, Axel Greylark was arm wrestling a purple being named Cherro. She had been in holding for four days, ever since she'd been caught running an illegal Kowakian monkey-lizard fighting ring, and she smelled like it. The ring had finally been busted up by a Coruscant security patrol answering a noise complaint from a senator, whose presence at the gambling site was conveniently ignored, and who was in debt to Cherro.

The being hailed from a speck of a planet called Tunguray, which according to her was more oozing volcano than it was habitable land anymore. The last of her people had been shuttled offworld by a Republic Pathfinder team charting the hyperspace lanes near Sullust, and been given refuge on Coruscant.

Like most of her people, or what was left of them, Cherro had large yellow eyes and a vulpine face. Two leaflike antennae protruded from the dip between her brows, which she called her lie detectors and he called a load of bantha druk, as he'd been lying to her all night about his reason for being locked up.

Despite her obvious height disadvantage at barely a meter and a half tall, the Tunguray female was strong. Axel's biceps and forearm trembled, and he readjusted his grip around her stubby, furry knuckles.

"What are you doing when you get out of the hole?" she asked in accented Basic.

"I told you, you'd have to buy me dinner first, Cherro."

"Nerf-herder," she huffed. "I may have job for us."

"Another time, darling," he said, losing ground.

A drunk Toydarian who'd been hauled in at dawn for urinating on passing speeders on Level 1392 heckled them from the corner. "Why you have all those muscles for, eh? Pretty boy Greylark."

Axel grunted, ignoring the jab. But he was getting tired, and as sweat pooled between his shoulder blades and the cell's pungent odor wafted back to him, he finally let go.

Cherro pumped her fists into the air and chittered in her language.

"*Alli p'ami,* my friend," he said, rolling down the sleeves of his sweat-drenched shirt. She'd said that meant "good game" in Tunguray, but given that the language was nearly extinct, he could very well be saying anything. "Three out of five?"

Cherro slapped the air and plopped down on the bench, using the cape she'd won off him during the previous round as a pillow and his shimmersilk shirt as a blanket. He was down to his undershirt, pants, and socks.

"I'll take that as a no," he muttered. Forgetting the very tender bruise on the side of his face, he scratched there, then winced. The Toydarian laughed again. Axel leveled a smile at the being and said, "How about a friendly wager?"

"Greylark," came a voice behind the cell's glass door.

"Ah, Drave, have you reconsidered my request for a cell with a view?" Axel sniffed. "And air purifiers?"

The warden, a bright-green Twi'lek with a missing lekku, snarled, "You've made bail."

"I have?" Axel pushed himself to his feet. For a moment he wondered if the duchess he'd stood up had come for him. It wouldn't be the first time one of his paramours raced across the galaxy to get him out of a sticky situation. Axel knew he could evoke deep feelings in people—most of the time favorable. Though, as with Raik, it often went sour.

Instead of the duchess, he saw the very last person he'd expected to come to his rescue.

"Ah, Mother." He tucked the hem of his undershirt back into his trousers. Again, he grazed his face and winced. "What brings you down here?"

Kyong Greylark, better known as Chancellor Greylark, had never looked more out of place than standing in the jail's poorly lit gray corridor. She wore a deep-purple cloak that did little to hide her identity but added a flair of drama. The great chancellor of the Republic, co-leader of the galaxy's push outward, proponent of change, bringing millions of species together as one galaxy. And here she was pulling her cloak slightly over her nose.

She said nothing to her son, only nodded acknowledgment at the

companions in his cell before turning on her heel and strutting back
out, no doubt expecting him to follow.

"Ohhh, pretty boy's in trouble," the Toydarian cackled.

Axel flashed a smile, made a final rude gesture with his fingers,
then abandoned his cellmates. He rubbed at the back of his neck. He
had half a mind to ask his mother if they could stop by the saunas in
the wellness district, but even *he* knew he'd pushed it too far if the
chancellor had come to collect him herself instead of sending one of
her assistants or guards.

"Where's my droid?" he asked, stopping at the warden's desk.

The Twi'lek male was too busy groveling at his mother's daintily
clad feet to have heard him. He complimented her policies favorable to
his clan on Ryloth, the way she was a beacon of hope. Axel almost
wanted to return to his cell.

He looked up and down the halls, but there was no QN-1 to be
seen. Something inside him quickly gave way to panic. He'd been fine
the moment he'd woken up in the cell surrounded by beings that had
been attempting to pick his pockets for credits the warden might have
missed. He'd disregarded any worry knowing that he'd eventually make
bail because his mother would get too tired of "teaching him a lesson"
and her pride and sense of decorum would win over. But during all of
it he'd rested assured that QN-1 was safe and sound in holding waiting
for him when he got out.

It wasn't.

"I asked, *where* is my droid?" Axel ran agitated fingers through his
hair. He could barely stand the smell of himself, and neither could
those around him.

"Axel," the chancellor said. Because in that moment and in that
tone of voice she was the chancellor, not his mother.

He took a deep breath and shoved trembling hands into his pockets. Sure, yes, he could be reasonable. "Please, Drave, I just want—"

The doors behind the Twi'lek warden hissed open and out flew

QN-1, trailed by a security droid holding a tray with his things. The relief that flooded Axel was singular. He'd have to face a world of lectures and likely a massive donation from his trust fund to a good cause, not to mention public appearances, but as long as he had Quin, he would be all right.

"As I was saying, these are all the items found on the person when he was detained."

Axel rubbed his droid's dome, then put his vintage chrono and chain back in place, not missing the twitch on his mother's eyebrow. What had she expected? That he'd gamble with some of the only things he had left of his father?

The chancellor lowered her head in what Axel was certain was supposed to be humility. "Thank you, warden. And for your discretion."

"Everyone needs to blow some steam off here and there," the Twi'lek said, beaming at the chancellor.

"Some more than others." She flashed that winning smile, the same smile he'd inherited.

Axel supposed he got his charm from somewhere.

It was, to say the least, distressing.

"See you soon," Drave muttered to him, and it took everything in Axel's spirit to keep on walking.

As they exited the precinct, Quin chirped at his side, sharing what sounded like a horror story of a closet full of droid parts. The triangle on its chest panel pulsed a frantic red.

"I'm sorry they treated you like a criminal," Axel said, giving his droid a reassuring pat on the head. "And you're right. I don't think we are welcome back at Raik's anytime soon."

The chancellor whirled around, and the look she cut him with was definitely his mother, and not the leader of the galaxy. Kyong Greylark *harrumphed,* then climbed into the speeder limousine. Axel followed into the back seat with Quin hovering at his shoulder. They quickly ascended the levels of Coruscant. He'd been in the dark so long he couldn't even tell what day or time it was. Holos flashed across skyscrapers: The Mighty Helix Experience had released a new song. Can't-miss vacation packages to Baroo's artificially created beach resorts. Chancellor Mollo was bringing peace to the Outer Rim, interestingly without any mention of Kyong Greylark. But then Axel saw Chancellor Greylark's face appear across a gossip feed, alongside his own.

He leaned forward, but the speeder went by too quickly to read. At the next intersection, though, another screen replayed the moment of Axel fighting and being stunned by the security guards. This was bad. He knew this was bad.

He'd gotten in trouble before, had spent several years courting trouble, in fact. He'd had his mother's assistant bail him out of the hold on Canto Bight, and more times than he could count from nightclubs and less-than-legal races. Axel should have known that since she'd let him stew there for several days, this time had to be different. Before that, she'd left him on a jungle on Numidian Prime for two days because it had taken that long to assess the damage and transmit a "ransom."

After the fifteenth blinking screen, he'd had enough of looking at his own face, and his was his favorite face in the galaxy.

Quin nudged him and emitted a calming blue light beside him, whirring softly until they came to a stop.

"Thanks, buddy," he sighed, filing out of the speeder, suddenly feeling the wreckage of the last blurry nights.

His mother didn't wait, striding into the gleaming building they called home and remaining silent as she passed the gilded archways in the lobby, up the glass lift that had one of the best views of the behemoth city. Axel had benefited his entire life from this world. It had been the very thing that had spawned him, a line of politicians and military heroes, of explorers and daredevils with one goal in mind: to thrive, and in thriving make the galaxy better. So long as they were at the nexus of it, of course.

The lift dinged when they reached their family's penthouse suite, and his mother barely waited for the doors to slide open before walking ahead. The apartment was empty, freshly cleaned, with the scent of caf wafting from the kitchen, but he wasn't foolish enough to do anything but follow his mother into her office.

His mother moseyed past her glass desk and opted for a bench notched into the crook of the gurgling indoor waterfall, its base lined with thousands of pebbles and stones. She was attempting to collect at least one from every planet that made up the Republic. It was supposed to invoke a sense of calm. Axel did not think it was working as Kyong Greylark pushed back the hood of her cloak and sat on the wooden bench handcrafted by artisans on Kashyyyk. Her gaze flitted past Axel to the portrait of his father that took up the far wall. He'd often been told he looked like both of his parents, with his father's strong jaw and his mother's dark eyes, though he imagined that's where the resemblance stopped.

Axel imagined his father would have hated a life-size portrait, being inspected every day, in a home he'd never lived in.

His mother sighed deeply.

"Here we go," he whispered, and plopped into the spinning guest chair.

"Don't," she said, settling her hard gaze on him. "Don't. You are too old to still be getting into this kind of trouble."

Axel swiveled in the direction of his father's portrait. The man was in his admiral's uniform, and though he'd been the kind of person who smiled at everyone, who had a deep love for exploration, who went out of his way to make everyone in his vicinity feel at ease—he'd been immortalized in a rare moment of severity.

"You're right," Axel said, straightening up to face his mother. His body ached from his benders, and the nights he forced himself to stay awake because this time, every year, the nightmares returned. "You're right and I'm sorry. I really am."

"I know it's a difficult time for both of us," she said in that placating politician way of hers. "I miss him, too."

He swallowed the anger that rose to his throat. His mother would never understand what he'd been through, because she hadn't *been* there. She had the uncanny ability to put on a good face, to never let her emotions show, because she knew someone was always watching and she cared more about frowning in a candid image than showing any emotion. More than once she had said, "You need to move on." So he'd done just that, coping, compartmentalizing, figuring out how to move on in his own way.

Axel did not want to give her the satisfaction of being right, so he lied. "That's not what this is about."

Kyong's brow furrowed slightly, but she bent her head thoughtfully. "Is this all because I won't release your inheritance?"

Axel grinned. "I have to do something in the meantime, don't I?"

"You have degrees in agricultural economics and interplanetary politics from Reena University. You apprenticed in the Senate. You are a *Greylark.*" She seemed to hear her voice escalate and took a breath. "There are infinite possibilities for what you can do in the meantime, Axel. And yet you choose, you *choose* to humiliate this family and yourself."

Axel couldn't help but smile. "We both know I have no shame, Mother."

"Fools have no shame, either." Kyong picked up an agate, then more, and began building a small tower. "You are no fool, I know that much."

"What do you want, Mother?" Axel asked softly. "Normally you lock me in a room with your attendants and public relations secretary, but something's different."

"Why do you say that?"

"Because you're still here."

"Is that why you're upset?" Kyong asked, adding an onyx to her tower. "I'm not there enough for you?"

"I'm not a senator," Axel said. "Or some backwater tyrant you're trying to negotiate a treaty with. I'm your son, please just tell me what you want me to do."

Kyong puffed a small laugh, stacking a blue stone, an opal,

tourmalite, black moonstone. One by one extending the neat tower. She let him stew on purpose because she knew he was interested. Well, he wouldn't give her the satisfaction.

"I'm going to bathe," he said, and began to stand.

"There's a situation in the Outer Rim," she said, finally. Waiting for him to sit back down, she gave him her undivided attention. There was a time he would have done anything to have his mother look at him that way, like he mattered enough to confide in. "The Office of the Frontier has informed me that Chancellor Mollo redirected his last mission to aid the Jedi Order in the Eiram-E'ronoh system, and I need eyes and ears there."

Axel's lip curled with distaste. "I thought you trusted the Jedi. Implicitly. Don't you remember that?"

"I trust the Jedi *believe* themselves the defenders of this galaxy. I trust Chancellor Mollo *believes* in our shared mission to bring peace to the wilds of space. And I trust that my son can act as my representative while I must remain here on Coruscant."

"You want me to spy on them?"

"I want you to represent me." Kyong cast a glance at the door before she continued. "From the information I have received, Chancellor Mollo rushed our intervention in this system. We agreed to let them resolve it on their own. Knowing him, he heard the Jedi were on their way, and he saw the opportunity to try again to bring about peace negotiations."

Axel licked his canine. "Mollo loves a lost cause."

"It's more than that," she stressed. "We rule the Republic together. Eiram and E'ronoh are not the Republic. He thinks if he can bring them peace, he will change that, and then others will follow."

"Isn't peace part of your campaign promise? Double the chancellors, double the result." Realization dawned on him. "Unless, of course, he succeeds on his own."

"He should have *told* me first," she snapped. "That is how this is supposed to work. Together."

He only half believed her. "That and elections are never far away," he muttered—her refrain.

"Precisely." The chancellor regained her composure, the easy disposition that made her both a strong hand for justice and a soothing maternal figure. "I wanted to strategically bring these worlds into the Republic by showing them exactly how we will make them prosperous, and Mollo wants to rush in. He hates bureaucracy, but there is an art to leading this way."

"You are the indispensable one, Mother," he said.

She lifted her shoulder coyly, the lie believable but a lie nonetheless. "There is no Republic without the two of us."

"Regardless," Axel said, leaning forward. "You get regular reports. Mollo has his own delusions of grandeur, but he's not a traitor to the Republic."

His mother shook her head emphatically. "I don't doubt that. But the reports aren't enough. I need someone I trust who will tell me everything as it unfolds. Even the things I don't want to hear. This is the first time he's broken ranks. I simply want him to know that I've noticed. My hope is that your presence will make him reconsider some of his impulsive urges."

Axel glanced briefly at his father's portrait. "Aren't you afraid I'll make things worse?"

"That depends entirely on you." She offered him a rare, sad smile. "I know that you blame me for—"

Axel stilled. "We don't have to do this, Mother."

"No, we do." She raised her proud chin. "I know you blame me for your father's death. I know you wish it had been me instead of him, because between the two of us, he was a good man, the very best. He got to be your friend and I got to be your mother."

Axel couldn't bring himself to look at her. The memory always overwhelmed him, worse on the anniversary of it all. He'd been an idiot boy, not even twenty standard years. It had been the first anniversary of his father's death, and they'd had a private memorial with all their friends and family. He'd been raw grief and anger, and she'd been all smiles and pleasantries. When he'd started getting drunk, she'd shoved him into the kitchen, a thing to be hidden.

"If you can't comport yourself like your father's son, then stay here," she'd said.

"You act like he never existed!" he'd shouted. "When you're the one who sent us there. You're the reason he's gone. It should have been *you.*"

Though he'd apologized for speaking the cruel words, he could never take them back. Even if he had meant it at the time. She'd never forgive him for saying it, for how everyone had heard. And he'd never forgive her for suffocating him with his duty of being a Greylark.

Now she returned to stacking her rocks, letting their shared sorrow settle between them. With a final stone—purple from Quarzite—the tower fell into the waterfall. Kyong Greylark smiled at him, deepening the lines around her eyes. She could compose herself so easily. It had taken him time, but he'd learned that from her, too. Perhaps he was more like her than he wanted to admit, and the thought was troublesome.

"You want me to go to the Outer Rim and be your eyes and ears," he said. Mother or not, it was his turn to negotiate. "It'll take me ages to get there. I'd need the security clamps removed from my ship. A case of goldberry wine, a gift to the nations, naturally. I wouldn't object to a new wardrobe."

"Perhaps a new droid? There are state-of-the-art astromechs—"

He balked at the idea, and QN-1 trilled from where it stood sentry outside the office. "I haven't needed a new droid in thirteen years."

"As you wish." Kyong nodded. "We will include relief supplies for E'ronoh and Eiram as a show of good faith from the office of Chancellor Greylark. And when all is done, I will release your inheritance. All of it."

His mother was serious. As serious as he'd ever witnessed. His heart gave a hard thud of anticipation, like he was back at that gambling den. "What if the summit is a failure?"

Her dark eyes narrowed. "I am not asking you to be a negotiator. I am asking you to report back."

If she kept her word, and there was always a possibility of *if,* he'd be free of answering to the chancellor. He'd clear his very long ledger. Perhaps buy that yacht from the queen of Naboo. Fill the chaos in his heart with everything credits could buy. He—

He was already getting ahead of himself.

Axel cast a final glance at his father's portrait and stood. He could barely stand his own stench, but he squared his shoulders like the good Greylark soldier he'd been raised to be. He went to her side, kissed her on the top of her head, and said, "You've got yourself a deal, Mother."

"I'll have my assistant get you everything you need." She sniffed, then let her stoic features wrinkle with distaste. "Now go bathe, please."

Axel began to walk out of Chancellor Greylark's office, but he lingered at the threshold, almost hesitating. She needed to hear it again.

"You're wrong," he said, his back still turned. "I don't blame you for what happened to Father. I said things that can't be unspoken. Know that I am different, Mother. Perhaps not the son you imagined I'd be, but the son you have."

Axel had never seen his mother cry, not once in his life. Not in front of him, at least. But as he turned over his shoulder, he saw her eyes turn glassy with unshed tears. He let them both retain their dignity and walked on, lowering his voice for a final admission. "I do not blame you. Not anymore."

He blamed the Jedi.

PART TWO

THE FUSE

Chapter Ten

"Peace is a choice," Chancellor Mollo said.

Every morning, he rose to the same routine. Drinking tea of haneli flowers, taking a long, scalding shower, followed by lathering himself with moruga nut oil. The lack of humidity aboard the *Paxion,* and most worlds he'd traveled to, was terrible for his skin and nasal passages. He'd so looked forward to breathing in Eiram's briny air. That would have to wait.

As he polished his frontal tusks and selected a deep-turquoise shimmersilk suit that reminded him of home, he did his vocal exercises.

"*Peace* is a choice," he said, with a more severe intonation than before, then experimented with emphasis. "Peace *is* a choice . . . Peace is a *choice.*"

During the chancellor's morning routine, AR-K4, one of the Republic's top-of-the-line protocol droids assigned to ambassador ships, stepped forward from where she waited with his bowl of dry eels.

"I do say, Chancellor Mollo." Her voice had a high-pitched and pleasant quality. "You cut quite the figure."

"Is that a *but* I hear, Arkfour?" His tentacles wriggled with unshed nerves. He plucked the dry eels from her grasp and devoured them.

"But," AR-K4 continued, her copper-plated oval head tilting to the side, "perhaps your clothing denotes that you have chosen to side with Eiram, as their emblem and royal colors are turquoise and gold."

Mollo let out an aggravated sigh. He, of course, would have argued. The suit so matched his eyes. And yet, nothing must go wrong during today's summit. He'd maneuvered the vicious politicians in Coruscant with placid smiles and hidden fangs; he could traverse the tenuous ground in these outer planets.

"Perhaps you're right," he said, relenting. He could hardly eat or sleep the night before, constantly checking the status of E'ronoh's drill ships parked in orbit. The *Paxion* and the *Valiant* Longbeams were the only thing standing between them and Eiram. He would not, could not, admit that perhaps Chancellor Greylark had been somewhat correct in saying this system was not ready to see the light of the Republic. But Chancellor Greylark was not here. They had been elected and re-elected together. He admired her strength and knew that she would always put the galaxy first. But she had been born and raised among Coruscant's elite. She could never quite understand what it meant to him, a Quarren who'd lived through the tumult of war like the ones that plagued these worlds, to be the one to bring about peace.

Kyong didn't know the Outer Rim the way he did. She didn't know the complex histories, the vast worlds, the vivid cultures. She only saw the promise of it all. He would prove that he was capable of doing more for their shared cause, because in the end their shared cause trumped everything else. A united galaxy. In that, he was certain he could trust her. He only hoped she felt the same.

So he turned to his protocol droid and asked, "What would you suggest?"

AR-K4 set down the empty tray and shuffled over to the overstuffed closet of silks, linens, and brocaded capes, selecting a black suit with a deep-ocher cape. "Somber and stately, but with a dash of color."

"What would I do without you, Arkfour?" Mollo asked but did not wait for a reply as he spun back to his mirror to clean his gills. "Make certain our guests need nothing, and that everyone is on time. E'ronoh is still an unknown factor but they are smarter than to tangle with the might of the Republic."

"Presumably, sir," she said, but he'd already returned to practicing his delivery.

AR-K4 was having a very good day. Then again, every day she fulfilled her programming—to make sure everything aboard the *Paxion* was perfect—was a very good day.

She hadn't seen Chancellor Mollo so nervous since the first day of his new term. That morning, she'd found traces of ink on his sheets, which meant he'd likely had nightmares. No matter. Nightmares passed, and if anyone could get through it, it was the pride of Mon Cala.

AR-K4 knocked on the door to Eiram's suite. A human woman, approximately fifty standard years, with light-brown skin, dark eyes, and straight black hair answered.

"Yes?" she asked impatiently.

"Bright suns," AR-K4 said, trying out a greeting she'd learned on one of the last planets they'd visited. Her programming had not been updated for a while, nor did they yet have a complete data bank of Eiram's customs. "I am here on behalf of Chancellor Mollo. Are your accommodations—"

"The queen is getting ready," the woman said, tightening her robe. "If the chancellor is afraid that we've scuffed off in the middle of the night, let him know we are still here."

The door hissed shut before AR-K4 could acknowledge their statement. "How peculiar."

"Excuse me," said a low, pleasant voice just a door down. "Can you tell me where the kitchens are?"

AR-K4 turned to find a human male with a scattering of freckles,

Eirami delegation. She recorded that detail, as she'd never come across the likeness. "Your meal should be brought to you, sir."

"It's just Phan-tu. And it's all right. I'd like to walk, thank you."

What pretty manners for a pretty boy, she thought.

After pointing him in the right direction, she hurried onward, scolding the serving staff when she found that someone had moved her arrangement of pillows in the parlor room. They had royalty aboard. Didn't they understand everything had to be perfect?

AR-K4 reached the row of suites assigned to the Jedi but found them empty. She tracked the Jedi down in the training hall. Four of them, three humans and one Cerean male. Each of them sitting in a meditative trance.

Chancellor Mollo would not like his Jedi guests interrupted, and so she left the chancellor's esteemed guests to their Jedi business.

That only left Princess Xiri A'lbaran. When AR-K4 reached the E'roni captain's room, the door was still open. *How irregular,* she thought, and followed a soft voice into the suite. Sitting at an oblong table was a redheaded human female. Her hair was down, and she was dressed in her planet's scarlet military dress, the stitching noticeable along a rip in the arm. It was certainly not proper for the occasion, though her programming understood that a person of the captain's rank would not want to don anything but her world's regalia for this summit.

"I know we've not always agreed on our approach toward Eiram," she said. "But I am asking you, please, Jerrod. Help me to convince my father to come here. He has not responded to my comms but I know he thinks highly of you. As do I. For E'ronoh."

When the recording was finished, and a message blinked with confirmation, the protocol droid made herself known. "May I be of some assistance?"

The young woman blinked, then looked to her door. For the first time, AR-K4 noticed the heap of dresses scattered on the bed, boots and sandals strewn about. "I suppose I scared the last attendant away."

"I am Arkfour, galactic envoy to Chancellor Mollo," she said. "I cannot be scared away. How may I help you?"

"I've never had strangers help me dress," she admitted.

AR-K4 said, "I have been programmed with three hundred ways to prepare species for political assembly. May I?"

Hesitation, then the straight shoulders of a soldier. "Please."

AR-K4 got to work, twisting and braiding the thick copper waves into something most proper. "If I had the time I would—"

The pulsing sound of alarm sensors resounded through the room.

"What's happening?" Captain A'lbaran asked, launching herself to her feet and running out into the hall barefoot. That was most improper.

AR-K4 hurried behind her and found her farther down the starboard hall facing a viewport. She was joined by the young man with pretty manners—Phan-tu—and some of the serving staff running errands. Out in the corridor of space, the drill ships Chancellor Mollo had denounced were moving, breaking the formation they'd been in for approximately ten hours.

"Cannons to starboard, position locked," came an announcement from the bridge. "Awaiting orders."

"Where is Chancellor Mollo?" Captain A'lbaran asked her.

"You won't make it across the ship in time," AR-K4 explained. "They'll hold for the chancellor's orders."

"I must alert my mothers," the Eirami man said, but when he glanced at Captain A'lbaran, at the way she held her breath and kept her fists tight at her sides, he seemed to be pulled between staying and going.

He stayed.

AR-K4 should have been returning to Chancellor Mollo's side, but her programming warred with his last directive to make sure his guests were all right, and they visibly were not.

She computed the outcomes of each scenario ahead. "The likelihood of survival is a fourteen point seven, six, eight, one—"

Then, as the drill ships parted, a boxy orange shuttle hurtled through the space between and toward the starboard hangar, leaving the drill ships behind.

"Hold your fire!" shouted Chancellor Mollo through the ship's speakers.

"Deactivating cannons," the ship's captain repeated the directive.

The E'roni princess breathed slowly, then shut her eyes with relief. "That's my father's shuttle. I—I knew he would come."

"I think I lost several years off my life," Phan-tu said, prompting a strangled laugh from the princess.

The alarm sensor and blinking lights stilled as the threat was removed.

AR-K4 said, "Cumulative probability of death is one point—"

"Even now?" Phan-tu asked with a tone of surprise.

"Taking into account species behaviors, and adding the sector's mortality rate, including accidents, yes," AR-K4 explained, as her internal sensors recalibrated the day ahead. "Now we must hurry. This put us twenty-one minutes behind schedule."

"Thank you, Arkfour," Captain A'lbaran said, smiling for the first time that morning before running back to her suite. The Eirami man did the same.

"Don't thank me," she said, shuffling her way back toward Chancellor Mollo's quarters. "Thank the Maker."

The *Paxion* buzzed with news of the Monarch's sudden arrival as rooms were readied for his sizable entourage.

Gella Nattai joined the other Jedi, now all dressed in formal white-and-gold robes, in the wide, circular parlor room designated for the day's summit. The concave ceiling was dotted with lights to evoke the stars and the cushioned seats were lined with Ghorman velvet in an array of warm colors. The chancellor had selected the location instead of what he'd called "a boring meeting room."

Enya lowered her voice and asked, "Do all summits occur in parlors?"

Master Roy placed a gentle hand over her shoulder, and she stopped fidgeting with her tabard. "It leaves little room to wonder who is at the head of the table when there is no table."

"Right you are, my dear Jedi," Chancellor Mollo said as he entered. Even he had dressed somberly for the occasion, though his turquoise eyes sparkled as he lowered his head in respect to the Jedi. "An honor to work at your side."

The masters did not get the opportunity to return the compliment before Eiram's delegation approached the threshold.

Dressed in bright turquoise, deep green, and golden silks, they evoked the colors of their homeworld. Queen Adrialla stopped at the door to be admired and received. She kept her head high, her elegant braids dotted with dozens of gold rings, a slender diadem tucked behind her ears. To her left was her consort, covered by a sheer veil kept in place with a platinum band.

"My wife, Odelia," said the queen in a voice that exuded confidence and patience. "Our son and heir, Phan-tu Zenn."

Gella couldn't see the resemblance, but she knew quite well there were other types of families that weren't biological. He wore his brocaded honey-gold and blue suit like someone who hated formal wear. He offered the chancellor a handshake and bowed at the Jedi, though his sea-glass eyes kept wandering to the door. Even without reaching into the Force, Gella could feel how nervous he was.

"Weapons," a Republic aide said, raising a wide silver tray to Phan-tu.

"Uh, I can't," Eiram's prince replied. His hand went to a dagger holstered at his side, its hilt dotted in rubies. "It's not mine. I mean, I'm returning it to someone."

"Perhaps now is not the place, dear," the consort whispered to her son.

"I think it'll be all right," Chancellor Mollo said, waving the attendant back. The guards, however, did rest their electrospears against the wall, their discomfort at being separated from their weapons evident. The six royal guards waited behind their queen.

Queen Adrialla stopped in front of Master Roy. She craned her head back, and though she was dwarfed by the Cerean's height, she seemed quite comfortable with him.

"We are honored by your trust and willingness to listen," Master Roy said.

Her lips quirked. "Since my medical relief is now conditional, I suppose you could say I felt *encouraged* to be here."

"Come, my love," the queen consort said, threading her fingers through her wife's. "Let us hear what the wise old Jedi have to say on a matter so far from their home."

Master Roy blinked, startled, then tugged at his short black beard. Enya bit down on her laughter, and even Master Sun was doing everything possible to quell the slight tremble of his lips. Gella sharpened her focus on the open entryway.

Master Sun had said there were different strategies to who entered a room first. The Jedi and Republic were exempt as the hosts. Queen Adrialla's entrance was a show of composure, as if she was deigning to grace them with her presence while smoothly pointing out how her hand was forced. It also gave her the advantage of selecting her seat first. In the circular lounge, though there was no primary seat of power, she chose the cushioned seats at the heart of the room. While everyone would always have a view of the others, this was the focal point when a new guest entered. Yes, the hosts flanked the doors in greeting, but the first thing the E'roni's delegation saw would be the queen with her retinue at her back.

There was a ripple through the Force, like the aftershock of a groundquake as Gella sensed the final delegation near. Metal-studded boots stomped a staccato rhythm that announced their presence moments before they turned the corner.

The Monarch of E'ronoh paused before reaching the hosts. First he looked at Queen Adrialla. His thin mouth curled into what might have been a smile. With pronounced jowls and a full head of white hair, he was, Gella estimated, in his late seventies. From his holos, she hadn't expected a man so thin. His military uniform with the rank of commander hung on his crooked body. Wrinkled hands dotted with sunspots gripped a cane made of what looked like solid copper, the cane encrusted with rubies. Just like the dagger Phan-tu carried.

"Monarch A'lbaran," said Chancellor Mollo. "You honor us with your presence."

"I am sure," he said, a wheeze of a voice. "My daughter, Captain A'lbaran. But you know that of course."

"You are very welcome for her safe return," Queen Adrialla said.

Chancellor Mollo's face-tentacles danced, and Gella took half a step toward the E'roni. She was sure the other Jedi sensed the anger and resentment roiling from that delegation. Gella tried to separate them in her mind, to better understand their emotions in the event something went wrong. The tallest of the group stuck out. His posture was impeccable, even as he scanned the surroundings with one cloud-gray eye. The other eye was covered by a tight black patch. Raised white scars peeked from the edges and spoke to a very painful act that cost him the organ. Gella had seen replacement prosthetics for the loss of such body parts, but she wondered if in this sector of the galaxy it was less common.

"Captain Segaru," the Monarch continued.

Gella noticed Xiri glance up at the man with a faint smile, as if she hadn't heard his title before. He returned the look with a wink so quickly Gella would have missed it had she not been watching him.

"And Viceroy Ferrol," a redheaded third man introduced himself, nudging past Captain Segaru.

There, Gella realized. That was where the anger radiated from. She had to briefly quiet her mind to his emotion, because he'd left her feeling like she'd taken a plunge into an oil spill.

After the Jedi and chancellor were finished with their introductions, the Republic attendant stepped forward again.

"Weapons," he said.

Captain Segaru moved to place his blaster there, but Viceroy Ferrol stilled his hand. "The Jedi don't seem to have given up their magic swords."

"It's not magic," Enya said, keeping her arms at her back.

Master Sun and Master Roy locked eyes as if in silent conversation. Gella wondered if there would ever come a time when she knew one of her fellow Jedi so well, understood them so intrinsically, that they could make a pressing decision by a look and their connection through the Force.

The viceroy grimaced as he faced the chancellor. "Favoritism already?"

Chancellor Mollo did not step into the viceroy's verbal trap, though he did run his fingers through his tentacles. "I assure you, Eiram's delegation has already complied."

"I am not talking about Eiram, I talk of the Jedi." The viceroy split the last word into two long syllables.

"As I understand it," Captain A'lbaran said, "they are more than weapons."

"Right you are, Captain," Master Roy explained, his soothing voice easing the tension in the room. "For Jedi, lightsabers are extensions of us and our connection to the Force."

"And yet still a sword," the viceroy countered. He knew exactly what he was doing, and he smirked the entire time.

"*We* would feel safer if the Jedi kept their trinkets," Queen Adrialla said coolly.

Gella frowned at the word *trinket.* Masters Sun and Roy were often sent by the Order to negotiate in distant worlds, but this wasn't what she'd expected. This was letting all parties sink verbal teeth until they drew blood. If she remained with their team, would she learn how to navigate these waters?

"I did not come all this way to speak of *lightsabers.*" The Monarch leaned heavily on his cane and shuffled toward the left side of the circle.

Captain Segaru dropped his blaster on the tray. The attendant began to move to the next guard, but Segaru reached into his vest and withdrew two slender daggers, then a single-charge pistol from his boot, and a third blaster from around his massive thigh.

With an audible swallow, the attendant nodded at the man's dagger, sleek with a black hilt, and strapped snugly at his hip. Gella understood where Phan-tu Zenn had procured the one he carried.

"Our bane blades," Captain Segaru said, flashing a smile at Master Sun, who was the closest Jedi to him, "are extensions of ourselves."

Gella felt a ripple of displeasure through the Force. It was rare to *feel* Master Sun's reaction like that.

The others of E'ronoh's delegation followed until the attendant staggered away under the weight of the weapons.

Gella hooked her thumbs on her holster, opting to remain sentry near the door as Chancellor Mollo strode to the center of the parlor. He walked with a muted version of the swagger she'd seen at their first meeting, but he commanded attention nonetheless.

"Peace," he said, dragging out the word, "is a choice."

Someone cleared their throat. One of the pillows slipped off the velvet. The leaders of the warring worlds waited. The statement did not seem to have the effect the Quarren had wanted, because his tentacles resumed their excited wriggling.

"Aptly put, Chancellor," Master Char-Ryl-Roy said, getting up to join the chancellor's side. "This is the first step to a much brighter future. E'ronoh, a world rich in minerals and metals. Eiram, a magnificent mystery with depths that have yet to be discovered."

The leaders of each planet nodded, accepting the praise.

"As representatives of the Jedi Order and the Republic, we believe that together we can arrive at a lasting, peaceful resolution for generations to come."

"Thank you, Master Roy, for those placating words," Queen Adrialla said.

"For once we are in agreement, Adrialla," the Monarch said, clicking the heel of his cane on the floor. "You come here from your distant worlds and think you can tell us how to live. Who made you the keepers of the galaxy?"

Master Roy did not balk at the questions. He spoke with a calm grace, his long fingers moving to the cadence of his voice. It reminded Gella of the precise meditative movements of the Guardians of the Whills. "The Jedi Order goes where people need us the most. When Eiram called upon us, we were there. Had E'ronoh ever called upon us, we would have done the same. After the regrettable accident in the space corridor, we felt a duty to remain. We are here now, not to tell you *how* to live, but to give those beings on the ground, the beings on your planets, an opportunity. Not just to survive." The Cerean paused. Faced every being present. Let the silence hang with meaning as his gaze burned with intent. "An opportunity to plan for a real future. Here and now, you choose life and prosperity over annihilation. I truly believe that is why you are in this room today."

"I came because my daughter called upon me," Monarch A'lbaran said sharply. The hand squeezing his copper cane shook. "And because we have proof Bly's accident was no accident at all."

Queen Adrialla leaned forward, tenting her elegant fingers. "Be very careful of your accusations, Monarch."

"We make no accusations, Your Majesty," Captain Segaru said, holding his palms up to show he was reaching for a datacard, not a hidden weapon, and handed it to Master Roy.

Gella felt the discord crackle in the room as the Jedi inserted the datacard into a wall port. The holo flickered to life, magnified as the overhead lights dimmed. A simulation of the tragic devilfighter's trajectory. Bly Tevin sailing on a one-way arc into Eiram.

"That was a glitch," Xiri said, her amber eyes looking to Gella for support. "We were there."

"She's right." Gella's stomach squeezed at the memory. A boy she couldn't save, though she'd tried.

"We recovered parts of Bly's ship," Captain Segaru explained. A muscle on his jaw rippled with tension. "And it was programmed with a simulation that overrode any command until it overloaded the system. A manual restart triggered the—"

"Explosion," Gella offered after a beat of silence.

"We do not have this kind of technology," Phan-tu said.

The viceroy huffed. "Of course you do! Let us speak plainly. You have been building weapons against E'ronoh for half a decade."

Phan-tu Zenn shot to his feet, "That is a lie!"

"The only weapons we've had to endure are those monstrosities you have in orbit," Odelia, the queen consort, said.

The Monarch blustered, like a fish struggling to breathe out of water. "You cannot be reasoned with, Adrialla. You took one child away from me and now—"

"Niko drowned," Xiri whispered, her voice low yet somehow powerful enough to put a stop to everything. "It was tragic, and terrible, but we have seen the footage. My brother drowned on a diplomatic mission to Eiram, and nothing we have done in the last five years is going to bring him back."

Gella focused on the Force around her, around the Monarch's heartache, and found not anger, as she expected, but utter desolation. The absence of light and dark. A gray, barren thing that made her shiver. How had this man kept fighting for this long?

As the Monarch clapped a hand over his eyes, he seemed to crumple into himself. Xiri made to comfort him, but the old man shook her off.

"Princess Xiri is clearly still in shock from her ordeals." Viceroy Ferrol stood. He brushed a fleck of dust from his medals, then addressed the room. "Eiram's crimes are deeper than that."

Queen Adrialla narrowed her dark eyes on the slick viceroy speaking for the Monarch. "Please, enlighten us."

"Eiram took our colony, which we've had claim to for over a century, and handed it over to the Czerka Corporation. Let *us* speak no more about our prince's tragedy, but we know how his negotiations ended."

"You had a *lease* on a plot of land and stopped paying the tariffs," Queen Adrialla said, her soothing voice escalating. "Let *us* not forget who dropped the first torpedoes on civilians."

The viceroy continued, unbothered. "E'ronoh defended its colony and chased away the corporation polluting *your* oceans. E'ronoh defended itself against the queen's attack on our defenseless cities. E'ronoh was forced to adapt, to fight back against a world we once called an ally, and until those crimes are answered for, we can never have peace."

The Monarch stood and leaned heavily on the viceroy as they stalked out. Every one of E'ronoh's delegation followed, except Xiri. She remained seated, staring at the pixelated holo of Bly Tevin playing on a loop.

Gella crossed the floor and shut it off; the room emptied of everyone but the Jedi and Chancellor Mollo. The first thing Master Sun had told her about Eiram and E'ronoh was that there were some wounds that ran too deep. She had to believe that they could still do good, that remaining in this system was the right path. But what if the wound had festered too long? What if they were too late?

The Jedi Knight excused herself and went in search of answers.

Chapter Eleven

THE BRUSHLANDS, E'RONOH

Abda awoke to the soft beeping of a holoprojector. *Her* holoprojector. Ever since they'd been stationed on E'ronoh to survey the crisis, all communications had gone through Serrena. But Abda was not jealous. She knew that the Force provided. Her time would come to prove herself, to show everyone in the Path of the Open Hand that she was grateful for her second chance at life. That was all anyone wanted, wasn't it? A chance.

She slipped out from under her covers. Once the sun sank behind the orange and red canyons, E'ronoh's nights were unforgiving in their cold. Abda was used to cooler climates. Her homeworld of Quarzite was naturally cool, with its belly full of shimmering crystals and twisting tunnels. That was another life. Another version of herself, too weak to be the violent, ruthless warrior her family had expected her to be.

Abda had found people who accepted the broken parts of herself. They welcomed her. From the minute she'd left home—no. It wasn't home anymore. She had to shed the blinders in her mind. From the minute she'd left Quarzite, she'd become a different person with a new name and new purpose. She'd seen how wide the galaxy was. How cruel it was, too.

Her feet were a whisper against the stone as she shivered out of their abandoned shelter and into the night. She answered the call, and the pixelated holo came into view.

Abda's lips trembled from utter and complete joy. She dipped her head low. "Mother—it's you!"

Her lips were all that was visible under her long, hooded cloak, but Abda recognized her anyway. She only wished she were on Dalna to take in the Mother's beauty and listen as she whispered the truth of the universe. Now, she was smiling for Abda. "Hello, Abda."

"Do you want me to wake Serrena?" Abda glanced back, but the Mother *tutted* her tongue against straight teeth.

"Let's not wake her just yet. She has her instructions."

"I'm sorry we've failed you. I—"

"Never," she said, her image rattling. The private relay systems in their sector were unstable, and Abda cursed them for interrupting even a breath of her audience with the Mother. "*You* have not failed me."

Abda nodded, cheeks hurting from smiling. She didn't know it *could* hurt to smile. "I would never."

"I know you wouldn't. That is why I think it's time for you to go out on your own."

"Of course, *anything* for the Path of the Open Hand."

"Oh no, Abda. This is something for me." The Mother smiled as she rested her palm over her heart. "I want you to take your rightful place as one of my Children."

Abda's stomach clenched with nerves. She'd waited and waited to be noticed. To be one of the Mother's Children. She wasn't ready. Was she? Serrena always reminded her that she wasn't ready. But the only voice that mattered, the only voice of truth was the Mother's.

"I would do anything." Her voice trembled with need. "Anything."

"Good, Abda." The Mother glanced over her shoulder. "You must do exactly as I tell you. Can I trust you?"

"Yes," the young Kage cried. "With every part of my being."

ABOARD THE *PAXION*

The *Paxion*'s lighting dimmed, simulating the rotation of a standard day. The tech supervisor had told Gella Nattai it was both to conserve energy when they were far from refueling stations, and to keep the organic beings aboard on schedule.

In the training room, Gella Nattai did not notice the lights change, the rotation of techs, the changing of the chancellor's guard, the shouting that began in the E'ronoh suites and reverberated through the airshafts and into the cafeteria. The first day of the summit had been a disaster.

Gella was attempting the Aerialwalk once again. She sank into the hold of the Force, envisioned her body stretched out within a sphere, and walked with a clear mind. With every step, she tried but failed to keep images from squirming into the forefront. The viceroy's anger, like greasy maggots festering in rotten ground. The white-and-red light of Bly Tevin's exploding ship. The dark woods of Orvax and the screams of her crew. A distant sensation trying to break through, racing toward her, but obscured.

She sucked in a sharp breath and toppled onto her back. Less graceful than when Enya had interrupted her, but at least no one was around to witness.

That is, until he cleared his throat and made his presence known. Master Sun took a seat beside her.

"You're getting very good at that."

"At falling?" she asked.

He did not entertain her self-deprecation. Instead he said, "Have you been here since the end of the summit?"

Gella stretched her arm across her torso and pressed down on her elbow to loosen the muscle. She blinked at the low light. She'd missed supper, and now that she was out of her trance, her body felt it. Sitting in front of him, she said, "I was searching for answers."

"The situation is far worse than we'd anticipated," Master Sun admitted. "But the two young heirs give me hope."

"I'm having a difficult time seeing the path forward, master."

He nodded in understanding. "You aren't supposed to do that alone, nor is it your sole responsibility."

"That's easy for you to say."

His brow furrowed. "What do you mean?"

She sighed softly. "I watched you and Master Roy in that parlor. You didn't let anything get to you, no matter how much the viceroy tried to goad you. There was a moment when I wondered if it was best to *let* them fight. There have to be other worlds in the galaxy that *want* us there."

"I felt that way on my first mission to broker a treaty between clans on Ryloth," he said, his voice rough with exhaustion. "But that's a story for another night. Please continue."

Gella blinked, half expecting him to correct her. To give her a rousing speech about their duty as peacekeepers. But when she met his dark-brown eyes, she found patience instead. Would she ever have that kind of patience?

"Then I thought of Captain A'lbaran. How she begged her father to come. Of Phan-tu Zenn and the way he was so open when he stepped into the room. Perhaps you're right, and there is something there. I was hoping the Force would help me see, but—" She couldn't tell him. He was open and listening, but she couldn't tell this Jedi Master that her focus was muddled. "There is too much in flux."

Master Sun considered her words for a beat. "I admire you, Gella."

She didn't think she'd heard him correctly. "Can you repeat that?"

"When I was a Padawan, and then a Jedi Knight, I did everything I could to be the perfect Jedi." He eased onto the backs of his hands. Gella had hardly ever seen him slouch. "Then I started leaving the temples. I thought of my world as the Jedi Order and the rest of the galaxy as separate entities, which of course is a fallacy, as is the idea of a perfect Jedi. I quickly learned how connected I was to the galaxy through the Order."

Gella chuckled softly. "You admire me for being imperfect then?"

"You are as imperfect as me or Master Roy. Don't tell him I said that." He winked. Actually *winked.* "I do fear I jumped to conclusions when we found the jamming beacon on the moon. I shouldn't have tried to stop you."

"What do you mean?"

He glanced to the doors.

"What's wrong?" she asked.

"Master Roy and Enya have uncovered something." He leaned forward, casting his voice low. "But we aren't certain of what just yet."

"Where are they?"

"Aboard the *Valiant.*" He waited as a small sweeper droid entered, registered beings in the room, and backed up to keep cleaning the halls. When they were alone, and the silence felt magnified, Master Sun continued. "Enya retrieved pieces of the jamming beacon you destroyed."

"She did?"

Master Sun tamped down on his smirk. "It was a rudimentary design meant for temporary interference, and its parts come from all over, making it more difficult to identify a point of origin."

"Then what did you find?" she asked, a spike of nerves driving through her core.

"Some of the wiring was coated with orange dust. Clay from—"

"E'ronoh."

They sat with the realization. Gella's mind cast a dozen scenarios and answers to her own question. Perhaps someone from E'ronoh had placed the jamming beacon there to keep discord between the planets. She'd been out there and had witnessed firsthand how quickly things descended into mayhem. Not to mention, from what they'd seen of the desert planet's representatives, they could have done so at any time. Then again, perhaps the beacon came from Eiram framing E'ronoh, though there wouldn't be a guarantee of the device being uncovered.

"Someone is going to great lengths to make certain that these worlds fail to communicate," Gella mused. "But did not take into account our intervention."

Master Sun did not seem as bolstered as she felt. "Therein lies the problem. By the very nature of our discovery, if we enter the second day of the summit with even a *suggestion* that E'ronoh planted the device, we lose non-partisanship and risk the entire peace process."

"Viceroy Ferrol stressed favoritism between us and Eiram," Gella said. A shiver ran through her as she remembered the oil slick of his anger and hate. "What if he's behind it?"

"No one has been ruled out." Master Sun raised his brows as if he'd already considered it. "We, however, are torn. We would not want to appear as though we're hiding information. Yet the situation is too fraught to bring anything with even a whiff of accusation toward E'ronoh."

Gella's head felt heavy, the pressure around her shoulders exhausted. There was that sensation again, but what was it telling her? "And what if it's neither?"

"We need more than scrap coated in E'ronoh's dust before relaying this discovery to the summit." Master Sun stood and offered her a hand to help her up. "Master Roy and I would like our decision to be unanimous."

They were waiting on her, she realized. She'd gone off to try to find a path on her own, and it had led her back to the team she'd been assigned to. She saw the clearest path under the circumstances and did not question herself once. "We should wait. Gather more information."

Master Sun's lips unraveled into a wide smile. She didn't think she'd seen so many of his teeth before. "Then we wait, for now."

"Let's hope the Force is with us tomorrow," she said with a bite of frustration.

He gently chuckled, and when they stepped into the hall, his severe frown returned. She found she almost missed that furrow. Almost. "The Force is always with us, Gella. Always."

Restlessness spread through the *Paxion*. Braxen, the guard standing sentry at the Monarch's door, couldn't keep still. The viceroy's words sped through his clouded thoughts, and the heavy meal he'd scarfed down earlier made his guts seize. He hadn't been that full in months. Couldn't remember the taste of anything but the weak siltgrog brewed during drought season.

Braxen had been fighting since his youth, serving many years in E'ronoh's military before going to work in the quarries during a time of peace. But when the war reignited five years ago, Braxen reenlisted to pilot a drill ship. Those machines Braxen once used to gouge through layers of bedrock in the deserts had been retrofitted for war. E'ronoh didn't need gemstones and marble. E'ronoh needed to win a war by hitting harder and faster.

For some beings, the last half decade was a blink in the eye of time. But for him, it was an eternity. After he'd returned to the Rook from his last mission, he found he could no longer stand the quiet. He never could, but now it was worse than before. One moment, he was blasting his way through their enemy. The next, he'd been ordered to guard duty. He missed the drag from maneuvering through space, the rattle of flak against his shields, and the piercing spin of the drill ships. It was hard to think amid so much dim lighting and so many hollow metal halls.

He reminded himself that the Monarch needed him. That since their fleet had been recalled so quickly, many of his friends were on the ground waiting, futureless, rudderless. He'd wanted to stay in atmosphere, but the medics hadn't cleared him for active duty. Instead, he'd been pulled from the ranks by Viceroy Ferrol himself for one more mission.

And yet he knew that in his final mission, he wouldn't be remembered like Segaru or Rev Ferrol or Kinni or even Blitz. He had no voice, but deep inside, all he wanted to do was scream because even his own scream was better than this silence.

When Viceroy Ferrol had pulled him into a hidden corner of the *Paxion* to brief Braxen about the situation, he couldn't believe it.

"Captain A'lbaran has been altered by Queen Adrialla's secret weapons," the viceroy confessed. "That is the reason she spread those lies about Prince Niko. And if we go through with this peace, all of E'ronoh will be within the enemy's clutches."

It made sense that that would be the reason Princess Xiri had spoken to the Monarch in such a way during the summit. And if it could happen to the heir of E'ronoh, what chance did he have as an ordinary soldier?

"What do you need me to do?" Braxen asked, his voice distant.

Viceroy Ferrol clapped a sweaty hand on Braxen's shoulder. His breath smelled stale, and the sweetness of his sweat made Braxen sick. "I need you to be brave. I need you to do what no one else can to help me stop Eiram. You are the only one I trust. I fear the others are compromised."

"What about Captain Segaru?" Braxen asked, heat spreading through his muscles from an ache in his chest.

The viceroy's grip on his shoulder tightened. "Even the best of us can lose sight of what we're fighting for. You, *you* are a true child of E'ronoh."

And like the day he'd rained down fire on Eiram's western isles, he didn't hesitate, because he was a good soldier. "What do you need me to do?" he repeated.

After Viceroy Ferrol whispered the orders, Braxen left his post.

He walked and walked, and there was no one to stop him. No one to tell him that though he was following orders, he was dishonorable.

He, this aging-warrior, made it to the hangar. He stood on a precipice, but that was where everyone lived. Every day, every second, every waking moment someone was looming over an edge and there wasn't always someone to reel them back away from that dark. Viceroy Ferrol was giving him a chance to serve his planet one more time.

He stood in the air lock. Stared at the blue lines across his fingers. Swallowed a deep breath. When he punched it open, when the cold vacuum of space embraced him, he had one final scream left in him. "For E'ronoh!"

Phan-tu Zenn heard footsteps outside his door. He'd only just fallen asleep, the first sleep he'd managed since arriving on the ship. It did not take.

He pulled on a loose pair of pants and walked out of his suite. He saw someone hurry around a corner, too fast to be recognizable. Phan-tu followed, making his way through the empty halls. He felt the cool recycled air on his bare chest and realized he was sweating.

Approaching E'ronoh's wing, Phan-tu stopped. He caught a flash of thin red hair and gray clothes. Viceroy Ferrol. What had the Monarch's trusted adviser been doing in Eiram's wing? Phan-tu wanted to follow him. And then what? Skulking wasn't an offense and all their weapons had been locked up. Plus, if anyone caught him standing there alone, he'd also appear suspicious. Phan-tu rubbed his face and exhaled. His worry was getting the best of him.

He returned the way he came but wasn't ready for sleep.

Passing a lone sweeper droid, his restlessness took him through the empty corridors and to the aquarium. It was indulgent, but he'd longed to see Chancellor Mollo's collection of aquatic creatures from Mon Cala. He wondered if there were similarities between that world and his own. If perhaps despite the distance he'd recognize bits of Eiram in the sea beasts.

He was about to let himself in when he heard voices whispering at the still-open door. He recognized the first as Xiri. The second was the gruff, arrogant Captain Segaru.

Phan-tu knew better than to eavesdrop. He'd grown out of the habit since the time he'd been a little boy, new to the palace, and had taken to creeping along every ledge, banister, and column, until he'd seen things not suited for his young eyes. Now heat spread across his chest and he thought of Xiri and Segaru. He started to walk away, but curiosity dragged him back. He remained at the edge of the door, out of sight.

"I told you," Xiri said. "I couldn't sleep. I don't need an escort to walk around one of the most secure ships in the galaxy."

"Nothing is truly secure or safe," Captain Segaru countered. "We know that better than anyone. Or have you forgotten so easily after a single day of Republic comforts?"

"Do not forget yourself, *Captain,*" Xiri said sharply.

The man chuckled low. "There she is."

"Jerrod, please. It's been trying enough without having to worry about you hating me, too."

"You're the reason I'm here." The man's voice softened. "We had no word from you until you sent me that holo. We didn't believe the queen's message at first."

Xiri sighed hard, defeated. "It was my third holo."

"You know the comms—"

"It wasn't the comms and you know it. It was Viceroy Ferrol."

Phan-tu grimaced. He'd never had an outburst like the one in the summit, but he couldn't sit there and take the viceroy's vitriol, accusing his mother of such despicable things when E'ronoh was the one whose drill ships and torpedoes had decimated an entire hospital. Eiram was not guiltless in returning the violence; he knew that, too.

"I don't care for the man, either," Segaru admitted. "But he is loyal to E'ronoh's Monarch."

"The seat of the Monarch, not the person on it."

"Regardless. You cannot suspect your own simply because a few barnacles were kind to you."

Phan-tu's heart leapt to his throat. He wanted to barge into that room and punch the word out of the captain's mouth. And then what? Have Xiri join her captain? Have the Republic guards take him away? Wake his mothers? He wasn't this person. He did not want to hurt anyone. He choked on his anger, but he stayed put.

"Stop calling them that," Xiri pleaded. "I need your support. Without you and me there, Father only has Viceroy Ferrol. I don't know how to help him see through the past."

"Have you ever considered that, perhaps, the Monarch doesn't want to see through the past? He's lost so much. Your mother. Your brother. He almost lost you."

Xiri was quiet for so long, Phan-tu imagined they had slunk off so silently he'd missed them. Then she spoke.

"I have to believe the man I once knew is still there. He simply needs to remember that we're fighting for E'ronoh's future. Can I count on you, Captain?"

"You can always count on me," Segaru whispered. "Xiri. There's something I've been wanting to speak to you about."

"Can it wait until after the summit?" she asked, a slight tremor of alarm in her voice.

He made a disgruntled sound, then deflated. "Of course, Captain."

Phan-tu held his breath, grateful for the shadows as they stepped into the corridor and returned to E'ronoh's wing. *E'ronoh's* wing, he reminded himself. Xiri was his ally, nothing more.

When the way was clear, Phan-tu sat alone inside the expansive aquarium walls, surrounded by hundreds of sea creatures that he had no real names for but that felt familiar, nonetheless. Under the pale-blue light, he felt encased underwater, and finally slept.

Queen Adrialla envied her wife's ability to sleep anywhere. She kissed her beloved Odelia on the forehead, the consort hardly stirring as Adrialla slipped out of bed.

The suite aboard the *Paxion* had been equipped with the basics a visiting envoy might need—a comfortable bed, a small sitting parlor, a tray laden with food, and a pitcher of crisp, clean water. But by the time she'd met the cohort of Jedi and the chancellor, she hadn't been hungry. Now, as she slipped into a sheer sleeping robe, she padded quietly to the adjoining parlor. She didn't bother with the light, and had been fighting the sharp pain at her temples since they'd left Eiram. She forced herself to eat and drink because she would need her strength.

Phan-tu needed her to be strong. Odelia needed her to be strong. Eiram needed her to be strong.

The queen broke off a piece of bread, the spongy texture melting on her tongue. It was so sweet her taste buds ached as she washed it down with a sip of water.

What was she doing?

What was she doing *here*?

Her mother would never have accepted help from the Republic or anyone but a short list of her most trusted allies. Then again, the former queen hadn't lived to see each one of those allies abandon Eiram in its time of need. Adrialla had seen the very worst of what E'ronoh could do. She'd done unimaginable things herself.

It was not a future she wanted for Phan-tu.

That was why she was here. *That* was why she had to make things right. She only hoped it was not too late.

As she reached for her glass of water, she noticed someone standing in the corner of the parlor. There was a moment, when her body went rigid with fear and her heartbeat thundered, when Adrialla tried to make sense of her. A servant girl? One of her own guards? No, she'd never seen a being with such pale gray skin and startling eyes. Then the queen's attempt at reason plummeted into the dark—an assassin. Betrayed by the Republic. The Jedi. Lured to the corridor between worlds to die far away from home. She dropped her glass onto the rug and the cool liquid pooled at her feet.

"I'm not here to hurt you." The girl's pink-crystal eyes seemed to glow in the shadows of the parlor. Her lips pulled back into a sneer. Queen Adrialla knew quite well that there were dozens of ways to hurt someone without drawing blood.

Unarmed, the queen raised her palms to show it. "Who are you?"

Adrialla thanked the sea that her wife was such a heavy sleeper. Thinking of Odelia, the queen's mind pushed away her rush of fear. She had to keep the stranger focused on her and call for help.

But when Adrialla glanced at the door, the intruder was faster and blocked her path.

"I'm here to talk, Your Highness," the girl said.

"Then talk." The queen breathed hard but managed to remain steady on her feet. "There are better ways to request an audience with me."

"Oh, but you haven't been listening." The girl's eyes were wider. "You were warned of what would happen if you broke your bargain."

Adrialla placed her palm on her stomach. All at once, she knew who this girl was and who sent her. She trembled as she said, "I already told the Mother. That was all of it. E'ronoh destroyed the facility."

The intruder stepped closer. "She *knows* you're lying."

Adrialla moved back and hit the edge of the couch. She stilled, desperately needing the room to remain quiet. It was her first mistake. "I can't."

"You don't want anyone to come help you," the intruder observed. "Because you don't want anyone to know what you did. What would your *peace summit* say? What will your son do when he finds out what you're keeping from him?"

"Leave my son out of this."

"We tried to help you," the girl continued; her whisper had a zealous calm that made Adrialla's skin crawl. "Who filled your barrels with grain when Shuraden cut off your trade? Who sent healers to help take care of the injured after E'ronoh raids? Who filled your ships with fuel when the Republic rerouted the hyperlanes?"

And because the girl waited and waited for the answer, Adrialla finally said, "The Path of the Open Hand."

"No." The Kage shook her head slowly. "The Mother."

In her most desperate moments, Adrialla had made a bargain that haunted her still. At first, the leader of those who called themselves the Path wanted nothing, not even gratitude. The Mother generously offered medical supplies, rations, fuel. The queen never asked where they came from, and she never told anyone, save for General Lao, of her dealings. Adrialla told herself it wasn't because she was doing something wrong, but because she wanted to protect her wife and son. She told herself every action was just if it meant the survival of Eiram. At some point, gratitude was not enough. The Mother wanted payment, and credits would not do.

"I delivered. The rest of the shipment was destroyed." Adrialla's heart thundered with the admission because it was a lie, and the girl knew it. Somehow, she knew it.

"It's your poison." The girl bared her teeth. "Make more."

"And if I don't?" Adrialla asked. "If I confess?"

Those pink-crystal eyes blinked. Her lips set in calm reflection. "You saw what happened to the E'roni starfighter and Captain A'lbaran's ship. Perhaps, we will set our sights on a different heir."

Queen Adrialla couldn't think of anything but the threat to her son as she launched herself away from the couch and at the intruder. But the girl was quick, and she leapt back.

The red blaster shot illuminated the dark. Adrialla gasped, then searched her own body for a wound. But she wasn't hurt. The intruder swallowed her cry and clutched her shoulder. At once, they looked back to the threshold leading into the bedroom. Odelia stood there with a slender blaster, trained on the intruder.

"No!" Adrialla shouted.

In the confusion, the girl recovered her strength. She raced across the parlor and struggled to climb back out through the vent in the ceiling.

The guard at the queen's door was punching the door, ready to sound an alarm. She couldn't jeopardize the peace summit.

"What are you doing?"

"I'll explain," she begged her consort. "I promise."

Taking the blaster from Odelia's shaking fingers, Queen Adrialla composed herself, and opened the door. Her guard blinked in surprise, her electrostaff crackling and ready to defend.

"My queen, I heard a blast."

Adrialla held up the weapon and smiled. "I was cleaning my blaster. I couldn't sleep."

And because she was a good soldier, the guard took her queen at her word with only a quick glance around the room. "I'll be right here if you need anything."

When the door slid closed, Adrialla pressed her body against it. The cool metal was a relief against her sweat-drenched sleeping gown. But the night wasn't over. Odelia brushed her fingers along the queen's jawline.

"Oh, my love," Odelia said. "What have you done?"

Chapter Twelve

ABOARD THE *PAXION*

Gella had studied countless accounts of neighboring planets, symbiotic worlds falling into chaos and war. She'd never quite understood how beings so dependent on each other for life and prosperity could lose sight of that and give in to hate and destruction. But now she understood. This. This is how peace is lost.

On the second day of the peace summit, Gella resumed her place against the wall, closest to the door. Chancellor Mollo paced and Master Char-Ryl-Roy was a beacon of serenity. Eiram's delegation arrived first, and E'ronoh's last. Gella heard whispers among that camp of a deserter in the dead of night, but it was quickly quieted as they were called to order.

When asked to present their proposals for a resolution, Eiram's queen consort handed a datacard over to be played. The recording displayed the day E'ronoh dropped proton torpedoes on the oceanic planet's southern rain forest, unaware that the previously uninhabited land had a new outpost. There were no survivors.

The day after that, Viceroy Ferrol read from his datapad—a list of every fallen E'roni soldier starting with Prince Niko A'lbaran.

On the third night, after what felt like reliving the first day of the summit, Gella went to the *Paxion*'s training room to burn off pent-up energy. Only . . . someone was already there. Phan-tu Zenn and Princess Xiri were fighting.

Gella leaned against the entryway and watched the pair spar with wooden batons. Phan-tu had excellent reflexes, though Xiri was faster. His sweat-drenched shirt clung to his lean swimmer's muscles, and though he blocked her every move, he remained open to her every strike. Xiri was small, but understood the weight of her muscular curves in motion. She locked her leg between his and got him onto his back, resting the baton across his throat without what looked like any real pressure.

"See?" Xiri panted. "You're pulling your punches."

"I agree," Gella said.

Xiri nearly leapt off the Eirami heir, standing less than gracefully. She used her sleeve to wipe the sweat off her forehead and offered a smile. "Master Jedi."

"Jedi Knight, actually," Gella corrected, though she found herself amused.

"What's the difference?" Phan-tu asked, trying to catch his breath as he crossed the room and poured water from a carafe into two glasses. "I don't mean to be rude. I've only ever seen the Jedi from afar, and, well, now."

He offered a water to Xiri, who accepted. She looked at the glass for a long time before she drank. Guilt rolled off her in waves.

"Experience." Gella rattled off the list on her fingers. "Readiness. Preparation. Devotion to the next step in the Jedi Order."

"Huh," Phan-tu said thoughtfully. "So it's eventually your next step."

Eventually, Gella thought as she picked up the discarded batons, a little shorter than her lightsabers. "I have a long road ahead of me before I can prove myself a master."

"Is that what you train all your life to be?" Xiri pried curiously.

"I've trained all my life to understand the call of the Force," Gella explained. "Through that understanding, I can serve the galaxy, whether as a lone Wayseeker or by taking on an apprentice. Similarly, you train for skill and for your planet."

Assessing the Jedi, Xiri set her bottle down and grabbed a staff off the wall. "I've always wondered if the stories of the great skill of the Jedi are exaggerated."

"It depends on who is telling the stories, I suppose." Gella rested the baton across her shoulders and stretched. "I'm not a Padawan. I won't be taunted into a duel. It's not a fair fight."

"Then, I challenge you." Xiri walked to the center of the mat. "Use your skill and not your magic."

"It isn't *magic*."

"Perhaps I should remain as witness," Phan-tu said, though worry notched his brow.

Gella's curiosity at the challenge won out. She bowed to the princess and sank into a fighting stance. Xiri swung first, arcing the staff wide. Gella diverted, leaping to the side. She felt herself call on the Force to stabilize her jump, but pushed down on the instinct. Landing in a crouch, she swept her leg under Xiri, who leapt back.

"If it isn't magic, then what is it?" the princess asked.

"The Force is everything. The seas of Eiram. The canyons of E'ronoh. It is the current within me and you, and everything in between. The energy that makes life flow." Gella went on the offensive, and pushed Xiri forward, slapping her batons against the staff in a steady rhythm that carried them across the entire floor, until the princess stumbled off the mat and fell on her backside. "And the one thing I am always certain of is that the Force is with me."

She held out a hand to help the princess stand, and Xiri took it amiably.

"I've never heard it explained that way before," Xiri said, her amber gaze turning to Phan-tu. "Even the Jedi didn't pull her punches."

"I did no such thing," Phan-tu assured them. "On Eiram, we don't have hand-to-hand combat."

"That's right," Gella agreed. "But as I understand it, E'ronoh has mandatory military training."

Xiri snatched a towel from a rack, her smile gone and defenses up. "It's how we survive. From our very first rite to our service, to the very end."

"If this summit is a success," Phan-tu said, "perhaps you'll learn to survive in a different way."

"It's not that simple," Xiri said, dabbing the sweat on her brow. "Though admittedly, this is now the longest we've gone without killing each other in quite some time. Perhaps the Jedi being here is not so bad."

Gella scoffed. "It's always nice to be appreciated."

"I've heard stories of Jedi all my life," Xiri said.

"Everyone has stories."

"We don't," Phan-tu said. "But we do have the old gods. The way you talk about the Force, it reminds me of how the elders speak of the first god."

Gella wanted to explain to him that the Force wasn't *a single* being but thought better of it. Not everyone wanted a lesson on the workings of the Jedi's beliefs. Though she was always ready if anyone asked. "And what do they say on E'ronoh?"

"Some people believe you're miracle workers. The way you levitate and read minds and use your light swords. Others—"

"We don't really levitate," Gella said, just shy of defensive. "And why does everyone think we read minds? It's not— You know what? It's too late for this. We have a long day tomorrow."

"A long day is one way to describe it." Xiri drifted away, tossing her towel into a bin. Gella could see the princess's hope wavering like a flame fighting not to get snuffed out.

She felt the urge to say something comforting, the way Master Sun might. "I've been through your history records, and there *was* a time when Eiram and E'ronoh were friends."

Phan-tu's face brightened with a smile. "Perhaps that's how we were created. First we were one, then three: Eiram, E'ronoh, and Eirie, our moon."

"Please. Do not say that in front of my father," cautioned Xiri. "Only Eiram calls it that."

Phan-tu nodded. "Of course, but you have to admit it is better than the Timekeeper Moon."

"I meant," Gella emphasized, "the centuries of peace."

"As you said, that was centuries ago. There is likely not a soul alive who remembers that age."

Gella wouldn't let the captain despair. "That's what records are for."

"I know what you're trying to do, Jedi Knight," Xiri said. "I haven't lost hope. My father was sensible once. He wanted the peace we are here to discuss. But the older he gets the angrier he becomes. He's resentful of what we have lost. We can't feed our people. The drought is the worst it's ever been. Everyone is looking to him to make things right, but in the end, it'll be me. I'll be the one who has to fix it because it'll be my war, when he's gone."

Xiri pinched the bridge of her nose. Her eyes were glassy, but she did not cry. It wasn't the E'ronoh way, it seemed, though Gella's skin practically prickled with the raw emotion coming off both young royals.

"Jedi Nattai is right. Our worlds have known centuries of peace in the past," Phan-tu said firmly. "We will get there again, Xiri."

"There was a deeper connection between your worlds," Gella said, pulling what she remembered from the archives. "You get along better than your parents. Maybe that's a start."

Xiri smiled, and it made her look younger, unburdened. "Maybe that *is* a start. Let us hope, at the end of this, we can all go home."

Home, Gella thought. But she couldn't conjure a single place to attribute that word to.

On the morning of the fourth day of the summit, Gella returned to her post at the parlor entrance. She noticed the way Chancellor Mollo dragged his feet into the parlor room. His face-tentacles were limp as he somberly called the meeting to order. Eiram screened another holo, this time of E'ronoh's drill ships tearing right through the bulbous hulls of a dozen starfighters and a hospital. Gella watched the viceroy, the only one among his party, look the other way until the recording came to a stop.

E'ronoh did not return for the next session later that day, and Eiram's queen would not be made to wait on anyone.

This is how peace withers.

But after spending days observing the delegations, Gella Nattai saw an opportunity. She arrived at supper with her cohort. Master Roy's suite was extraordinarily neat, his bed as if he hadn't slept in it at all. By the soft shadows under his blue eyes, Gella suspected he hadn't.

"I thought Chancellor Mollo was joining us?" Enya Keen asked, pushing food from one side of her plate to the next. The cook's special was braised fish and legumes.

Gella pushed her empty plate aside. "He's sulking."

"He's regrouping," Master Roy said thoughtfully.

Master Sun propped his elbows on the table and tented his fingers. "I fear our brazen chancellor may have thought this would be an easy win. But not all is lost. Remember Ryloth? We eked out a victory, or I should say, you did."

Char-Ryl-Roy took a small bite of food, mostly because he hated being wasteful. "Let's call it a team effort."

"You didn't at the time." Master Sun smirked as he chewed.

"I am not keeping score, friend," the Cerean chuckled. "That was different. The clans of Ryloth have been embroiled in civil wars for generations."

"Like here," Gella said, then added, "Only, on one planet. What happened on Ryloth?"

"We were searching for a holy heirloom, a gem the size of my hand, that had been stolen," Master Sun explained. "Found it on the first day. A third clan wanted to start a war."

"Only Creighton dropped it off the side of a cliff," Master Roy said. "That's what took us so long—digging through every nook and cranny."

Enya snorted into her goblet, and Gella tried to picture the Jedi Masters at her age. Capable of making mistakes, even with the world at hand. She'd always thought that serving the Order, serving the galaxy, meant she had to achieve an impossible kind of perfection. It showed how much she had yet to learn.

"Do Eiram and E'ronoh have any holy relics?" Enya asked.

"None that might resolve a crisis," Gella said, setting down a holoprojector beside her empty plate. "But I believe they do have their own weaknesses."

Master Sun pressed the center button and a blue projection was emitted. Recent imagery from E'ronoh's and Eiram's streets. A riot in one capital, and trails of refugees filling the canals. A troop of soldiers running across the desert, and the ensuing explosion that shattered the feed.

"How did you get this?" Master Roy asked, more curious than anything else.

Gella glanced at Enya. "Someone in the communications room owed us a favor. They sent out an Ee-Ex droid to take these recordings. We need to get them back into that parlor room and make them remember *who* they're fighting for."

"And then?" Enya asked. "We've let them talk for *days*."

"Yes, my Padawan," Master Roy said. "They needed to. We, almost more than any beings in the galaxy, know that we cannot hold emotions back or else they fester. If the Force is a balance, then so is peace."

Master Sun was deep in thought for a long while before he pushed the holoprojector back toward Gella. "Feed it through the rooms. All of them."

This is how peace endures.

While the recording ran on a loop, Gella opened herself up to the Force. Aboard the *Paxion,* emotions rose and fell like the peaks of a great mountain range. Amid them all, one called her attention because of its proximity.

The library, to be exact. She pressed the door open.

Captain A'lbaran sat in the tall, upholstered chair in the center of the room. On one wall was a screen that scrolled to vistas from distant worlds. The only ones Gella could name were the mega city of Coruscant and the great palace of Naboo. While there was a small shelf of ancient flimsiplast books, the rest of the walls were lined by a prism of holobooks.

The E'roni princess, however, wasn't reading. A red holobook was on the floor, as if she'd dropped it. The projection of the recordings Gella had acquired took up her entire line of sight.

"Did you do this?" Xiri asked, her voice hard.

Gella felt the rolling waves of the captain's distress. "I did."

"Thank you."

They weren't the words Gella expected to hear, certainly not from her. She slowly stepped into the library and took the seat beside Xiri. Gella knew there was nothing she could offer the other woman but comfort. She hadn't known her for very long, but they shared a small connection she couldn't quite explain. Perhaps it was akin to the friendship Masters Sun and Roy had after their journeys together. Sitting with her, the Jedi was plunged back into the memory of the dogfight. Opening herself up to their shared memory, Gella remembered the fear of that day, the senseless loss of all of it.

Gella ran her fingers through her hair and sighed. "I don't suppose the others will thank me."

Captain A'lbaran shut off the holo and picked up her book. "I've cowered to my father's viceroy for too long. It is a relief to know I'm not alone in this anymore. I simply hope Eiram sees it that way, too."

"Time will tell," Gella said. "But the Force is with us."

Xiri leaned on the arm of the chair and narrowed her eyes. "I'm curious, Jedi. Is this what you do all the time? Go here and there saving worlds with your light swords?"

"Lightsabers. And they are for defense first. We go where we are called," Gella said, remembering Master Sun's words. "I'm still learning my way."

"Don't you miss your home?"

Gella blinked at the question. "The concept of home is not the same for me as it is for you."

"I suppose your temple is your home."

"Yes, though sometimes we're assigned to different temples on different systems, and sometimes, like now, we live aboard a ship."

"Strange," Captain A'lbaran said wistfully, "you fight to save so many homes for so many beings, yet you have none of your own."

"It's not as simple for Jedi." Gella turned to the flickering landscapes on the far wall. If she thought about the enormity of the galaxy for too long, how she would never see all of it, she'd get too lost in her own thoughts. "I've never actually thought of it that way. The galaxy is my home, then."

"*Hm,*" Xiri mused. "That sounds like a lot of upkeep."

"Upkeep does not do such a thing justice, I think." A warm sensation spread from Gella's chest. Certainty. Every Jedi, whether in the temples, on Pathfinder teams, or serving as Wayseekers, had a shared goal—peace and justice in the galaxy. "It is my calling."

"I feel that way about E'ronoh. That's why I came here, actually." She waved a hand to the books around them. "I was trying to find some history on us, but the Monarchs of my line have never liked it when outsiders come into our sector. We had a Pathfinder team try to make contact and they blinked right back into hyperspace. That's what my brother told me, at least."

Gella sensed the young woman's sadness at the mention of her brother. But it wasn't the same as her father's. It was love, distant, but understanding.

"What about your own libraries?" Gella asked.

"Destroyed during the first year of the war."

"Phan-tu said the last time your worlds were in harmony was centuries ago."

"Yes, he was right. I found a note on that here. It's but a page." She scoffed. "Entire dynasties, and we are but a few lines of memory."

"What does it say?" Gella sensed Xiri's kinetic energy before the princess spoke.

"That our royal families were united by marriage."

"Well, Queen Adrialla already has a wife," Gella noted.

Gella had the distinct impression she'd said something wrong as Xiri stood abruptly and reshelved the holobook.

"I should go," the captain said.

She did not wait for a response before sweeping out of the library.

On the fifth day, Xiri A'lbaran entered the parlor room last. Her father, or one of his attendants, had brought her clothes to change into. Instead of her military uniform, she chose a scarlet dress and heels. She wanted to evoke E'ronoh. She hadn't come of age with her mother, but upon watching the queen of Eiram every day, she understood the importance of making sure all eyes were on her.

She strode inside, leveling her shoulders like the captain, the princess, she was. Red satin clung to the narrow dip of her waist then spilled onto the floor. In the tradition of most E'roni dresses there were loops for a metal holster, though hers were empty as Phan-tu Zenn still had her bane blade.

With only a glance, the Cerean Jedi and the chancellor ceded the floor.

"Daughter," the Monarch began, his bushy white brows drawing together in confusion. The viceroy started to stand, but Captain Segura clapped a beefy fist on his shoulder and forced the man back into his seat.

"Enough." The word cut through every person in the room. The protocol droid in the corner, AR-K4, even raised her arms, offended by the outburst.

"I—"

"Enough," Xiri repeated, this time to Queen Adrialla.

Xiri felt her chest rise and fall, her heart swell with the righteous anger she'd swallowed over the last days. Most surprising was the strength in her words. "I am finished with your blame. I take it everyone on this ship saw the recordings someone distributed of our cities descending into riots. My first thought was to wonder who would do such a thing." She paused to glance toward the Jedi cohort. "My second was to thank them."

"Xiri," her father said, but she leveled her gaze with his. She had her father's clear whiskey eyes, her father's love of E'ronoh. She used to think if she had more of him, it would be enough to move him past their sorrows. She was beginning to realize she had to decide when it was enough. The Monarch quieted.

"Our soldiers enlist for an extra ration that is dwindling by the day. They are standing right here. Those that are gone, you list their names"—she turned to Viceroy Ferrol and bared her teeth—"when you have *no* right . . . We have no right if we do nothing differently. We talk of past transgressions. We talk of what came before without even a mention of what comes after because I fear that for you there is no after. There is no future."

She glanced at the domed ceiling, a deep longing for her own desert sky. For E'ronoh. Always for E'ronoh. She pressed on. "E'ronoh and Eiram's future isn't yours. It's ours. Monarch A'lbaran, Queen Adrialla, I am ready to move forward while we still have a future to look toward. But I cannot do it alone."

There was stunned silence, but Xiri held her chin high even as the viceroy's rotten eyes burned a hole in the side of her face, and even as Captain Segaru slowly rose to his feet. She wouldn't look at him.

"I sense you have a proposition, Captain A'lbaran," Master Roy said.

"There is no stronger alliance than the one shared between E'ronoh and Eiram during the Greatest Age," Xiri explained. She would give E'ronoh every piece of herself because she was the daughter of the canyons, the heir of the thylefire scorpion, the next Monarch of a world that had so much potential running through its rocky veins. Xiri A'lbaran would do what needed to be done. "Then let's return to that time."

"I don't understand," Queen Adrialla said slowly. "You speak of something that happened two hundred years ago."

Xiri gestured to Gella. "It was this Jedi who made me realize that the only way to heal what has been done is to forge a new future. What I propose is a marriage alliance between E'ronoh and Eiram."

Xiri felt the room shift. "You can't," came from Captain Segaru. A soft gasp from the veiled queen consort. "I do love weddings," came from AR-K4. Phan-tu Zenn turned to his mother. The Jedi had their nonverbal conversations. Her own father was so at a loss for words, he called the room to order by beating his walking staff on the floor.

Master Roy was staring at Gella Nattai but speaking to the room when he said, "It is a neat resolution considering the history of your worlds."

Chancellor Mollo's tentacles resumed their jovial dance for the first time in days. "I would have suggested it myself if I'd thought it an option."

"It isn't," said Queen Adrialla, gesturing to her consort. "I have chosen my mate. And the Monarch looks old enough to be my father."

Xiri glanced up at the chrome ceiling. May the old gods grant her patience. They were so gone, so obtuse they couldn't even imagine a solution outside themselves.

"The Monarch is five years your senior, Your Benevolent Majesty. But I speak of myself and"—she extended a hand toward Phan-tu Zenn—"your heir."

The queen placed a hand over her son's forearm. Xiri had noticed that at their palace. Small gestures and touches of affection. She imagined trying to talk to her own father with a mere look, a slight brush of the wrist, or even something as common as a smile. He hadn't even hugged her when he'd docked on the *Paxion* and found her alive and well.

"Absolutely not," said the Monarch. "I will not have my only daughter, the product of E'ronoh's *longest* royal line, sullied by—"

"I would choose your next words very carefully," Master Roy warned.

The Monarch blustered. "Your Jedi sorcery doesn't work on me."

The Cerean methodically touched his beard. "It is not sorcery to remind you that this is a peace summit, Your Grace."

The Monarch pointed at Gella. "This is your doing. You come out here into our space and tell us how to rule our worlds. Now you will have us tied to the very people who killed my son."

He clutched his chest. Xiri reached for him. She had never, not in a million years, heard her father speak this way. Worst of all were the tears spilling from his eyes.

E'roni did not cry. The Monarch did not cry.

It was the thing he'd drilled into her head since she fell and split open her knee on a sharp rock. *Get up, my heart. You are thylefire-made and the scorpion does not cry.* She'd been four. But she'd done as she'd been told. As she always had.

"Why are you doing this to me?" her father asked, then shook to a stand. Despite the cane, the Monarch found the strength to burst out of the parlor and through the corridors, and the rest of the delegation with him.

Xiri turned to Phan-tu and said, "I will await your response."

She kicked off her shoes and ran to her father's chambers, heart thundering in her ears. The guards stood at attention when they caught sight of her, but it was Captain Segaru who blocked her path. His broad chest was like a granite wall under his uniform.

"Get out of my way," she demanded. "That is an order from your captain."

He raised his brows in defiance. "We have the same rank."

"Then from your princess."

With that, he could not argue, though she saw he wanted to try. The moment she stepped into the suite, Viceroy Ferrol stepped into her path.

"This is tantamount to treason!" he shouted.

Xiri grabbed the slick man by the collar and pulled him close. She could not be weak now. *Get up, my heart*—she thought of her own father's words from so long ago. She hadn't fallen, but she had opened a new wound. *You are thylefire-made.*

The viceroy hadn't seen a battle in decades, and he was slow. Too slow to stop her from wrapping her free hand around the hilt of his bane blade. "Say it again."

"Guards!"

"Call me a traitor one more time," she said with a deadly calm she did not feel inside. "Or challenge me."

"Unhand my daughter, Viceroy," the Monarch said from his chair.

Though she was the one who held the counselor in her grasp, he threw his arms into the air with a dramatic scoff and stalked out of the room muttering, "You will regret this."

She brushed off his words and knelt before her father. His fist clutched around his heart. As much as she talked of moving forward, she didn't know how to move forward with *him.* Her hands itched to hug him, to tell him that she would do everything right. They were not like Phan-tu Zenn and the queen of Eiram. They were E'ronoh.

"Get up, my heart," Xiri whispered at his temple. "You are thylefire-made, and the scorpion does not cry."

He blinked, a clarity there she hadn't seen in years.

"We will be in the parlor."

Chapter Thirteen

ABOARD THE *PAXION*

Jerrod Segaru watched the princess slip from the room and walk right past him. As if she hadn't known him her entire life. As if he hadn't trained her in combat, taught her how to fly, how to take aim by shooting armored rats in the Ramshead Gorge. As if he wouldn't have helped her put an end to this war himself.

"Xiri, stop," he shouted, but she marched through the stale metal corridors.

She whirled on him. "It is done, Jerrod."

He swallowed a foreign ache in his throat. He blamed his unquenchable thirst. He blamed the Republic ship. The meddling Jedi. "What did they do to you?"

"This is the only way forward. A shared peace with shared consequences."

He threw his hands up. "I don't believe you. You spent one day on Eiram and you're ready to throw away everything we've worked for to tie yourself with the enemy?"

"The queen loves Phan-tu Zenn, she'd never—"

"Phan-tu." He spat the name. "If you wanted to bed the barnacle you could have done it without betraying your people."

They'd traded punches before, sparring in the barracks. When she was seventeen, just before she'd gone off to university, she'd gotten into a fight with a merchant's son. He'd insulted Xiri's brother and called her the Monarch's "spare." She'd punched him. A week later, Jerrod had spent hours teaching her how to do it again without spraining her wrist.

Now she had the same fury in her eyes, and he almost wanted her to do it. To hit him. If only to keep her there with him so she would not go into that parlor. But she pressed her fists to her stomach and put more distance between them.

"You think me too soft." Xiri tugged on her dress. He knew she hated dresses. He knew she preferred to roll on a pair of pants and sleep under the stars. That man would never know her enough, as well as he could. "But I am willing to give everything I have, all of me, to secure the best future for our people. I need you by my side."

She began to turn around, but he grabbed her hand, hard at first, then let her go as she pulled away. "Xiri. Xiri, you and I could secure the future of E'ronoh. I would declare myself to your father. I could give you that security. I could make Eiram pay for everything they have taken from us."

This time, when she touched him, she placed a hand on his cheek. He saw her resolve. He'd seen it every time they went into orbit. Every time she visited the families of the fallen herself. Before that even, when they'd climb the steepest canyons without harnesses and breathe in the dust, the glory of E'ronoh.

"That is exactly it," Xiri told him. "You want to get that by fighting, just like my father and the queen. I see another way."

She slid her palm to the place over his heart, his strong pulse frantic, and then she left.

Jerrod swung at the wall. Pain flared through his knuckles, the split, callused skin there. He reached for his blaster, but he'd surrendered his weapon at the meeting like a good little soldier. But not his bane blade.

He unsheathed the small dagger, the blade as long as his open palm. The first inhabitants of E'ronoh survived the desert with these very weapons during their coming-of-age rites. Gutting open small black thylefire scorpions through their bellies. Sharpening staffs, tools. Threatening an opponent. To throw the blade on the ground was to issue a challenge of life and death. Eventually, the blades became shorter, ornamental. No longer pure metal but decorated with gems. His was pure steel, and a marble hilt of E'ronoh's veins.

Jerrod Segaru marched through the corridors, having memorized the network of halls the very night they'd set foot aboard the *Paxion*. He would right this injustice with his last breath.

He punched open the door to Phan-tu Zenn's room. Breathing hard, he scanned the empty space. An unmade bed. A half-empty bowl of starfruit. Clothes heaped on the gray settee. Somehow, despite being kilometers in orbit and away from the wretched planet, the room stank of the sea.

Jerrod heard footsteps behind him. E'ronoh's newest captain spun around in surprise. It took him a moment to register who was at the door. He lowered the bane blade.

"I know you," he said. "What are you doing here?"

When bright-red plasma fired, they were the last words Jerrod Segaru would ever say.

"Marry." No matter how many times Phan-tu Zenn had said the word since the E'ronoh royals had fled the room, he still wondered if he'd dreamed it. Namely because for one night, just one, he had.

"Truth be told," Odelia, the queen consort, said, adjusting the thin band keeping her sheer veil in place, "like the chancellor, I wanted to suggest such a thing myself, but I thought it impossible. That the princess Xiri is making the offer—well—it gives me hope that there is someone in that family line with reason. You were right about her, my love."

"Mother, say something, please." Phan-tu brushed his palm over the queen's. She'd been distant, not only after Xiri's declaration but before that. He knew she'd tell him when she was ready. She always did.

Queen Adrialla rested her chin on the top of her hand in that elegant way of hers and peered at the Jedi cohort. "I suppose this was your idea of peaceful resolution."

The Jedi, Gella Nattai, stepped forward. Her loose black waves reminded him of a spill of ink. The stern set of her brows softened as she tried to explain herself. "We were simply talking about the last enduring peace. I did not think the princess would act so swiftly."

"Is this how you control your Jedi, Master Roy?" his mother asked.

The Cerean loomed to his full height. "We trust Gella had all the best intentions. We all want the same thing."

"Do we?" the queen asked, but pitched her voice so low, Phan-tu wondered if the others heard it.

"I think it's romantic," the youngest of them said, gesturing toward Phan-tu. "I sense you are excited."

He stood, tapping his torso. Was she *in* him with her Jedi magics? He was embarrassed to admit he didn't quite understand the limits of their abilities.

"When I was a girl," the queen said, "my mother chose a husband for me. One of the barons from Pantora who wanted to dig our oceans for fuel. It would have been a good alliance."

Odelia rested her hand on top of her wife's. "Too bad for the baron you'd met me first."

Queen Adrialla smiled, her brown eyes softening as she turned to face Phan-tu. "I don't want to do the same to you. I want you to experience love. Partnership. We are not like E'ronoh, cold and calculating with hearts made of stone and clay."

Phan-tu bristled at the words. Even though it was a common enough refrain about their enemies, he did not like speaking them out loud with their delegation gone from the room. Especially if he was to *marry*. First and foremost, he had to train his mind to not think of them as the enemy. Though if he searched his heart, he never truly did.

Gods, could he even do this? For his queen. For his family, the ones who had chosen him and the ones the sea had taken. For the people that would one day look to him as a leader.

He remembered being under the water and seeing Xiri's face, the fear there even as she was seconds from drowning. Would she always have a fraction of that fear when she looked at him? When they'd come ashore, she would have fallen on her blade rather than be taken prisoner. The same blade she'd nicked him with, right under his chin. He touched his finger there, to the spot that hadn't even left a scar. His pulse was frantic at the memory, and now she wanted to unite them, their worlds, their families, their planets.

"She *is* very beautiful," the queen said.

"Mother," Phan-tu whispered. "You mustn't worry about what you wished for me. You have given me everything, things I'd never dreamed of having. With this war over, we could rebuild. We could—"

"Are you saying you'll do it?" The question came from Chancellor Mollo. The Quarren had been watching so tensely from the other side of the circle, Phan-tu kept thinking of him as a statue or a powered-down droid. Now his tentacles wiggled, and he honked a nervous laugh. "Marry, that is."

His entire body numbed at the word. Was it anticipation? Or was it dread? He didn't have time to determine which, because all he saw was the flash of red as Xiri reentered the room. Phan-tu could hold his breath for approximately eleven minutes, but in that moment, a second was all it took for him to feel the burn of his lungs. Tendrils of red curls had come undone from her plaited crown, and her toes were bare, yet she strode in like someone who had always known she would be queen. He should probably offer to give her his shoes. Would that be improper?

He shook off the assault of questions in his mind as the Monarch followed her in. This time, he was alone. There was no Captain Segaru, no Viceroy Ferrol, and no guards. His cane clacked hard with every decisive step as he returned to his seat.

Xiri smiled like someone who was so close to victory. He would help her meet it.

"Have you thought about my proposition?" she asked, seating herself beside her father.

"Dear," Queen Adrialla said, a bite of humor in her reprimand. "If we are to be family, I am going to need to know that you care about my son as more than a mutual understanding of peace."

Xiri shifted uncomfortably for a moment, her large amber eyes flicking toward him. He tried, and failed, to suppress his grin. "There is much I must learn about your ways, as you will learn about ours. But from what I know of Phan-tu Zenn, I know he is kind and brave. He will make an admirable partner. If he agrees."

Everyone turned to him. The Jedi, who likely were already in his mind and knew what he'd say, and the Monarch, and every member of the Republic delegation.

"I agree with Captain A'lbaran's proposal," he said, switching on his most proper, most courtly behavior. "So long as E'ronoh recalls their ships from orbit immediately."

The Monarch scrutinized Phan-tu, the jowls of his cheeks trembling as he nodded. "Very well."

Xiri released a sigh, her nerves finally showing as the tension in the room gave way to celebration. She smoothed out the front of her dress and wasted no time. "I've studied the holos Jedi Nattai procured, and I noticed activity and unrest across the planet. We'd have to visit those sites as soon as possible."

"Have the acting general issue a statement of retreat," Queen Adrialla said, then turned it over to the Monarch.

"My viceroy is—indisposed—but we will issue it immediately," the Monarch added tersely.

"What about the wedding?" Consort Odelia asked, tapping the tops of her fingers together.

Xiri's face was calm, as if she were discussing how much sugar she wanted in her tea.

"I anticipate we will need ceremonies on both E'ronoh and Eiram. Phan-tu?"

"Naturally," Queen Adrialla said before he could.

"If I may," Master Sun cut in. The severe human man stood with his hands clasped in front. "This may be an opportunity to show the galaxy what you have done."

"Excellent, Master Jedi," Chancellor Mollo said. "Think of the invitations. 'The Forever War has come to an end.' Leaders from all over the galaxy will flock here and see that this system is safe for trade routes once again. You will be a symbol of hope for the entire galaxy— enemies united at last."

Phan-tu let the chancellor's words sink in, and saw another opportunity. "As much as we would love to host hundreds of people, we cannot. Unless we have the help of the Jedi Order, and the Republic to rebuild in time for the ceremonies, that is."

A corner of Xiri's lips hooked into a smirk. "The Republic would also have to lift the sanctions on E'ronoh."

Chancellor Mollo looked chagrined at that, but he'd backed himself into a corner and he knew it.

Phan-tu realized then that he needed to do things properly. He had to present Xiri with a fresh catch of pearls. He had to share a meal with her family. Would they live on Eiram or E'ronoh? Would they have *children*?

"How soon can we arrange this?" Consort Odelia asked.

"First," Xiri said, "we must tell our people."

Phan-tu nodded in agreement. He thought of the cities and small outposts devastated over the years. His heart ached for an entirely new reason. "We should go personally."

Xiri looked at him curiously, like he'd surprised her. "Agreed. We will bring the news and help distribute relief as a sign of unity and peace."

"That is not an option," the Monarch said, jabbing his cane on the floor. "We cannot forget this all started because my daughter's life was threatened. I fear the news will upset many who will always oppose such a union."

The queen sighed. She rarely agreed with the Monarch, but she chose that moment to do so. "Upon both worlds."

"We will provide security escorts," Master Roy said, glancing back at Gella. "We remained here to help establish a peaceful resolution, and we will see it through."

"A campaign," Chancellor Mollo suggested, waving his hand in an arc, as if he were writing the words across the simulated sky.

"Then it's settled," Xiri said.

Phan-tu had never been engaged before. He had never really considered it, even though he knew, eventually, it would be expected. It wasn't a matter of *if,* but when, and as he stood and made his way toward Xiri, captain, princess, his betrothed, now seemed as good a time as any. She rose and met him halfway. He unsheathed her bane blade and presented it back to her. She wrapped long fingers etched with thin scars around the hilt and pressed it to her heart, then offered her free hand.

"For Eiram," she said.

He felt the barest tremble at her touch. Fear? Hope?

And he said, "For E'ronoh."

There was no celebration, not yet. As Phan-tu Zenn stepped into his suite, he still couldn't believe the last hours. He shed his clothes at the door and stepped into the bathroom. He was to marry. He was to marry the princess of E'ronoh.

He took that thought with him as he showered away the cold, nervous sweat on his skin. When he was finished, the tension in his body gave way to exhaustion.

Before he stepped into bed, he caught the smell of something he hadn't before. A hint of smoke, and a cloying sweetness.

"Hello?" he called into the empty room.

When nothing and no one answered, he scoffed at himself. He was wound up. Who wouldn't be?

Then Phan-tu pulled back the heavy covers on his bed and found the body of Captain Jerrod Segaru, eye and mouth open even in death.

Chapter Fourteen

ABOARD THE *EVENTIDE*

Axel Greylark was on his way.

He'd made a few pit stops. His mother had said to leave for E'ronoh immediately, hauling a full cargo hold of durasteel crates stuffed to the brim with food rations and whatever else the benevolent Republic saw fit to send to the backwater planets. And he had left immediately. However, Chancellor Greylark had said nothing about the route he should take.

Axel had plunged the *Eventide* into the first sequence of jumps through hyperspace. Once, it was his father's ship, equipped with four turbothrusters and gleaming chromium plating. The only upgrades Axel had allowed himself to make were a first-class hyperdrive and a cannon turret—which was useless as he no longer had need to hire a crew. That had been a different life, one he'd left behind. Mostly. It was just him and QN-1, who disapproved of every deviation along the charted route to the Outer Rim.

There had been a cantina on Bardotta, a quick getaway from an old business partner on Lorta, and a race. In the last case he'd been an ac-cidental participant, but he'd held his own, testing the limits of the

Eventide as he cleaved through the blackness of space like a chrome sickle.

When he'd finally reached a sector with better connection to the holonet, his mother had sent a reminder that he needed to fulfill his promise. The only problem was that he couldn't bring himself to care. He didn't care about the war on Eiram and E'ronoh. The only certainties in the cosmos were war and chaos, and only one of those things appealed to him. And he didn't care that his mother and Chancellor Mollo had likely poked and prodded at that sector with their mission to "unite the galaxy." The galaxy wanted to be left alone. Or perhaps he was projecting.

And so he hadn't finished the race, not that he would have won. He simply wanted to fly faster, deeper into the stars until something, or someone, stopped him.

He redirected course to Eiram, landing there through a shortcut of backroad lanes he'd learned from some less-than-polite company he kept. When his navicomputer announced their approach, Quin trilled a warning.

"We're not late," Axel said adamantly.

For the first time since he'd left Coruscant, Axel had that sinking sensation at the center of his chest again. Quin nudged him with its dome, emitting a calming blue glow from its chest panel. The therapy droid he'd had since his father's death was more attuned to his emotion than even he was.

Axel shook his head. "I'm perfectly all right. Assessing the landscape is all."

The copper and turquoise planets loomed ahead. He noted the curious silver moon between them, the river of junk, and two Longbeams stationed at the heart of it all. He hailed the *Paxion* but no one answered. No matter, he had automatic clearance codes.

The hangar bay shield dropped, and he sailed onto the crowded launch pad. Perhaps he was late. He secured the clasp of his gray cape and lowered the boarding ramp. QN-1's white thrusters leveled out at his shoulders, keeping up with his long strides.

"That's odd," Axel said. "Where is everyone?"

QN-1 suggested they were sleeping. But the lights were still bright, and besides, that wouldn't account for the traffic controller not being there. Not that he'd expected a welcome party, but he'd expected some familiar faces from the crew. Unless everything had already gone south and they'd killed each other.

"No matter." It wasn't his first time aboard the Quarren's retrofitted ship. He even had a favorite room, one decorated like a city in the sky. He made his way there, needing a quiet moment before he announced himself to the peace summit. His mother would get her update when he was well and ready. But as he made his way into the *Paxion,* hazard lighting blinked overhead.

"Let's wait in our suite," Axel told Quin.

Republic staff and droids turned a corner in a hurry, while the following corridors were full of very aggressive, confused soldiers dressed in red and gray. A few people glared at him as if *he* were the anomaly, and not the obviously failed peace summit.

"Record this, Quin," Axel whispered.

When he found his suite, it was locked. Of course it was. He rubbed the back of his neck and moved on to the next one. Also locked. He pushed forward and found a suite wide open.

"Mollo," he said, surprised to see not just the chancellor standing there, but several others. The Quarren seemed too preoccupied to give him a proper greeting and didn't even question Axel's arrival though he'd sent no word that he was coming. The chancellor waved him in. Axel'd clearly interrupted something, but as no one was talking, he kept moving. A needle of ire pricked him when he saw two robed Jedi. He locked eyes with one of them, a dark-eyed woman with a burnished complexion, and saw her instant disapproval in the subtle purse of her full lips.

He nearly tripped. Nearly. He was quick on his feet and launched himself onto the plush settee beside a human man with dark curls. QN-1 beeped a confused sequence and conferred with a frantic protocol droid.

Axel sat forward, plucked a starfruit from the bowl on the table, took a bite of the crisp, sour fruit, and asked, "What did I miss?"

Gella couldn't keep standing still. A man was dead. One of E'ronoh's captains found in the bed of Eiram's heir. When they'd rushed into the suite at the first signs of alarm, they'd found no one but a very pale Phan-tu Zenn. No signs of a struggle, and no murder weapon. Gella Nattai and Enya Keen had been tasked with keeping the royal delegations and the chancellor safe. The only additions to the room were a stranger and his droid, who sauntered in like—like they were out for an evening at a saloon.

Gella sensed nothing from him. But because the first word out of his mouth was "Mollo," and the Quarren waved him in, she stood down.

"Why aren't they back yet?" Phan-tu Zenn asked, knees bouncing with nerves.

Master Sun had been questioning the attendant who'd locked up the weapons, while Master Roy helped with the search. Gella felt a surge of anxiety, which she tamped down with a deep breath.

"What if the killer is still here?" Queen Adrialla whispered from her seat. Her consort squeezed the regent's shoulders.

Captain A'lbaran, who radiated guilt but had an alibi, said, "It was Viceroy Ferrol. It had to be."

The Monarch shook his head. "I won't believe it."

"He *was* skulking about the other night," Phan-tu said tightly. "But he's been cleared."

Master Roy had interrogated the viceroy, who'd been found near an air lock. Viceroy Ferrol was certain he'd find evidence aboard the *Valiant* that the Jedi were favoring Eiram. When his search came up empty, he'd foolishly stolen a spare robe. Gella could not make sense of the small, petty gesture, but Master Roy had been certain he'd gotten the truth from the viceroy. Now, he was in the ship's brig until they decided what to do with him.

"Pardon me but did someone say killer?" the stranger with the ridiculous cape asked, more awed than alarmed. The narrow corners of his eyes crinkled with amusement. "Another one of your themed parties, friend?"

"No! A man is dead, Axel! Dead. On *my* ship," the Quarren boomed, and the chastened man, Axel, finally seemed to understand what he'd wandered into.

"Chancellor," Gella said, easing toward his side. "We will find whoever did this."

"And if you don't?" the Monarch asked, unable to stop the tremble of his hands.

"Every part of the ship is being scoured," Enya said, though Gella sensed her Jedi companion also felt the rising agitation in the room.

"We're just sitting here. What if they come back?" Mollo asked, pressing his fingers against the sides of his head. "It'd be like shooting krakanas in a barrel."

His copper-plated droid turned around. "Krakanas are too large to fit in a standard barrel."

"Oh, you know what I meant, Arkfour!"

"Master Roy thought it safer if we all remained in one location," Enya reminded them.

Xiri frowned at the man the chancellor had addressed as Axel. "Then how did *he* get aboard?"

The corner of Axel's lip curled. "I assure you I am extremely authorized."

"I presume your mother sent you," Chancellor Mollo said curtly. "We will talk later."

"Chancellor Greylark sends her best," Axel said to the room, making himself comfortable with a lazy spread of his arms across the back of the settee.

Gella reached out into the Force again. Most beings carried their emotions on the surface, but Axel was shuttered off in a way that was surprising. She didn't have time to linger on him, though, as the chancellor's guards reentered the room.

"What news?" the Quarren asked.

The guard at the forefront gave a solemn shake of her head. "We believe the killer traveled through the vents. One of the escape pods was jettisoned. We're scanning the area."

Queen Adrialla gripped her wife's hand for comfort.

"They could be anywhere by now," Phan-tu said.

"Stay with them," Gella told the head guard, and sprinted into the hall.

Enya snatched the edge of her cloak. "Where are you going?"

"I have a feeling—" Gella stopped. She had to think. To focus. She'd sensed a disturbance the night before. All the Jedi had. Like them, she'd blamed the mounting emotions on the ship, its proximity to the warring planets surrounding them with beings crying out for help. She couldn't ignore her instinct again, though. And she wouldn't make the mistake of running off alone. "Come with me."

Enya seemed to weigh the orders of her master against the certainty in Gella's eyes. She gave a single nod, and they sprinted all the way to the hangar bay.

"There has to be one of these ready to fly," Gella said, gaze falling on sleek curved ship like no other in the hangar.

"I don't think I've ever seen you smile like that before," Enya noted.

Gella was already boarding the still-open ramp and climbed into the two-person cockpit. She'd never paid attention to the scent of a ship before, but this vessel reminded her of a dense forest and something she couldn't quite name.

"Can I?" Enya asked, straining a smile as if not to hurt Gella's feelings.

"Arrogance would not be becoming for a Jedi," she said, buckling into the copilot's seat.

"Neither is stealing." Enya readied the ship for launch and read from the display screen. "The *Eventide*."

She engaged the engine and eased the controls forward. They both gasped at the speed of the ship, zooming forward in a downward arc.

"It's not stealing. We're bringing it back," Gella reminded the young Padawan. They'd have to face that Axel Greylark, but they would bring it back. "Head toward the moon."

Enya pulled up. On their Jedi starfighters, the move would have felt choppy, but the *Eventide* glided, smooth as molten metal.

"Why was Captain Segaru in Phan-tu's room in the first place?" Enya asked.

Gella gripped the hilts of her lightsabers, something she did for comfort, to ground herself. "We can only speculate. Whoever stole that blaster from the hold might not have been expecting the E'roni captain."

"I can't sense anything," Enya admitted as they approached the silver sphere. "What are we looking for? An escape pod could be anywhere by now."

"I'll know it when I see it." Gella watched the debris bounce off the *Eventide*'s deflector shield. That same lonely, desolate feeling she'd had the first time on the moon returned. "But we found the jamming beacon, perhaps there's something else there."

"This thing has sensors," Enya said brightly. She scanned the moon as they flew around its circumference. There were so many nooks and crannies in there. It would be the perfect hiding place.

Enya pressed more buttons on the panels. The lights of the cockpit flashed with a rainbow of colors, and the intro keys of a classic harp-rok played. With the next button a hidden panel opened, but there was nothing in there.

"Whoops," Enya said, and put everything back into place.

Gella was beginning to think she'd miscalculated in rushing out there when something hard thumped against their viewport. She started, trying to make sense of the debris plastered to the transparisteel. Gray, ice, and then a red uniform. Realization crept in as Enya gasped, and Gella unbuckled her harness. She raced to the air lock to bring the remains of the dead E'roni soldier in from the cold.

The Monarch's shuttle led the return to E'ronoh. Trailed by the *Paxion*, the *Valiant*, and Eiram's own royal vessel, it was a sight every being stepped into the dusty streets and canyons to behold.

What they couldn't see were the bodies in the morgue. A chancellor holding on to the threads of hope. The Jedi searching for the shadows of disruption. A man scratching the surface of the chaos in his heart, and a Jedi Knight seeking out her path. Two heirs walking toward each other, toward their future, by clasping the tender seeds of peace, vowing that nothing and no one would stand in their way, because this—this is how peace holds on.

PART THREE
THE SPARK

Chapter Fifteen

THE ROOK, E'RONOH

Long ago, a Monarch of E'ronoh gutted the side of a mountain and built herself a fortress, called the Rook. From such great heights, she would watch her capital city grow in orderly, spiral streets leading out into the vast crooked canyons.

Jedi Knight Gella Nattai treaded the same dusty road for Captain Jerrod Segaru's funeral procession. The Segaru clan forged the way, four of his kin bearing the weight of a metal coffin several kilometers out of the Rook and into the cemetery, where they heaved it into the aboveground rows of dead. The towering structures reminded Gella of a hive of Qieg on Lan Barell.

"They do not bury their dead," Enya mused at her side. "I've never seen that."

"Nor I," Gella admitted. "Would a captain not be placed somewhere else?"

Phan-tu Zenn, who'd been very still and very somber beside them, shook his head. "Even the Monarchs of the past are in these towers. No matter the rank, they are equal in death."

They kept a respectful distance from the hordes of mourners dressed in deep red, along with Eiram and the Republic's delegations. She didn't want to feel like a spectator, but they hadn't known the captain long. The circumstances of his death were clouded by shadows even the Jedi could not yet illuminate. The only certainty was that he was one with the Force, as was Braxen, the guard she and Enya had uncovered floating near the silver moon. He, however, did not get a war hero's funeral.

As Captain Segaru's coffin was interred and sealed, a plaque on the outside blinked to life. Gella could not make out the symbols from afar but deduced it would be similar to surrounding plaques. Dates of birth and death, a loving mother, an honorable father. Some even had images. Some of the older ones were in the ancient E'roni language. For a moment, Gella wondered what hers would read. What would her fellow Jedi say about her? It was a passing thought, though. When her time came to return to the cosmic energy of the Force, she'd be cremated and her kyber crystal added to the Kyber Arch.

One by one mourners, beginning with the Monarch and the princess, stepped up to the Segura clan to pay respects. Gella stretched into the Force, casting wide. Sorrow, anger, worry. Particularly from Captain A'lbaran. Cries echoed on the jagged mountainsides, carried on the wind like the fine copper dust that permeated everything. Emotion swelled and broke over her like the harsh sun. News of the peace treaty and marriage alliance had been overshadowed by the funeral and immediate distribution of food and water rations. But as the crowd shifted, and someone sidled up beside her, Gella did not think that would last for long.

"Do you think it's rather morbid?" he asked.

Gella turned to find Axel Greylark. Somewhere in his admittedly beautiful ship, he'd dug up a crimson suit tailored to his broad shoulders, with black silk piping down the leg seams and a cape embroidered with silver thread. His small droid hovered close. Gella had only ever seen that model as a child, a prototype therapy droid that emitted a calming light from the triangular panel on its chest. But all she'd seen this one do was serve the chancellor's son drinks.

"I understand death is generally morbid for many beings," she said, keeping her arms at her back and her gaze focused on the weeping family as they lowered their heads in respect to Masters Sun and Roy, next in the receiving line.

An open silver flask appeared in her line of sight. "Drink?"

She glanced up at him, recalling his outburst when they'd returned to the *Paxion.* "Are you going to yell at me again?"

"You stole my ship." He lowered his flask and blinked slowly, thick black lashes casting long shadows over high cheekbones. When he smirked, mouth full of whatever was in that flask, it accentuated laugh lines, which made sense: From what she'd seen of him, he did not understand how to take anything seriously. It appeared that this included a funeral.

"The situation called for it," she said. "And we brought it back."

She turned to Enya for assistance, but the Padawan was strolling across a tower of the dead, passing the plaques one by one, and the other Jedi were deep in conversation with the chancellor and queen.

"Would you feel the same if I borrowed your lightsabers?"

Reflexively, she tightened her grip around their hilts. "Very well. I accept your reasoning."

"Is that how the Jedi apologize?" He scoffed but did not let her interject. "No matter. It is forgiven. What do you think happens if your friends and family aren't the ones to write your eternal byline?"

"What are you talking about?"

"I mean"—he gestured with his flask toward the plaques—"what if your worst enemy writes HEREIN LIES THE MAN WHO STOLE MY WIFE AND ALL MY CREDITS."

"Do you imagine that's what *yours* will say?" She looked him up and down. She could certainly imagine it.

That smile again. "See something you like?"

Gella sighed, exasperated. "I noticed that you came prepared to mourn."

"I'm always prepared, darling," he said. "Red happens to be my favorite color. I couldn't decide what to wear to the great wide frontier, so I packed the lot. One never knows when one will need to—let's say barter."

"How resourceful. But I didn't think I'd need to barter with my Jedi robes, or that I'd get much for them."

Axel scrutinized her robes, the bracers clasped to her forearms. "I know several collectors who'd pay for Jedi trinkets."

She frowned at that and turned slightly away from him.

"Well, I'm off then," he said, striding past Gella nonchalantly. "Save me a seat at dinner."

She certainly would not, but glanced around. "You're leaving? Now?"

He held out his hands, walking backward into the crowd, droid at his side. "Perhaps this market has better entertainment."

The words were so glib, so callous, she blinked after him for a long time, a slash of crimson disappearing into a sea of red. Death was a part of life, inevitable for all beings. As a Jedi, she accepted that, knew it as a pillar of her understanding of the galaxy. But she *cared* and he did not.

As Master Sun approached, he searched Gella's face. "That is a very frustrating young man."

"Have you met him before?" Gella asked.

"I've seen the tabloids with his exploits," he said, scanning the crowd.

"You see tabloids?"

"The headlines," he corrected her sheepishly, "to stay up to date on the galaxy. A thoughtful choice of envoy for Chancellor Greylark, though."

Gella tipped her head to the side in question. "What do you mean?"

"Had she sent one of her secretaries, it might suggest she did not trust Chancellor Mollo. Instead, she sent relief, and her son. I feel she is asserting her place."

"Do you sense deception from the other chancellor?" she asked.

He could not answer as music rose, loud reedy pipes that mingled with the wailing, and the final blessing from a robed priest. Amid the noise came a distorted crackle from the distance. Confusion gave way to shouting and shoving.

Master Sun unholstered the cross-guard hilt of his lightsaber. As he ignited the blue blade, Gella felt the threat through the Force. An object sailing low through the air, aimed at Eiram's delegation. The large rock was disintegrated with a slash of the blue blade. A group of E'roni launched a second volley, which Master Roy deflected with the Force. The jagged rocks hung in the air before clattering to the ground.

Gella drew upon the Force and jumped back to Phan-tu and his mothers' side, Captain A'lbaran joining them. There were too many bodies shoving their way back out to the dust road. Xiri shouted orders to her guards, who shoved their way through the crowd toward the center of the aggression.

The Monarch brushed off any attempts at being protected or restrained. He stepped forward and fearlessly faced his people. So different from the man she'd seen aboard the *Paxion*. Though Gella knew that strength could manifest in different ways when one needed it.

"What is the meaning of this?" Monarch A'lbaran thundered, his voice reaching the peaks of the surrounding canyon.

The mourners bowed, nearly every single one of them creating a wave that fanned out to the edges of the open-air cemetery.

All except a group of four. Leading the insurgents was a stocky Pantoran in soot-covered coveralls shouting through a loudhailer. "Traitors to E'ronoh! The Monarch allows the enemy's soldiers on our soil! He gifts our princess to the Eiram! Enacts a curfew on our lives! The Children of the E'ronoh won't stand for it!"

A single person in the small crowd shouted their agreement before they were tackled to the ground. More tried to run but were apprehended by others in the crowd until the guards could reach them.

"We need to get back to the palace," Gella told Captain A'lbaran.

Pain flashed across the princess's features for a moment before she steeled herself. She raised her comlink and called for a speeder shuttle.

"It's only four people," Enya said, trying for comfort. "They'll see this is the best thing for everyone."

But all it took was one drop to create a ripple.

"Is this what you call protection?" Queen Adrialla asked.

Though her question was pointed toward the Monarch, Gella couldn't help but feel her tone suggested all parties involved.

After being shuttled back to the Rook's palace, they'd filed into a cavernous dining hall. Eiram's queen and her consort sat on the left, along with the Jedi, though Phan-tu doubled back and took a seat beside Xiri A'lbaran.

Marble sconces dotted the stone walls, and silent attendants hurried to set the table with goblets of a weak, bitter ale, which Gella understood had become popular, if necessary, during droughts. Gella felt the heightened nerves from a redheaded young woman as she spilled some of the drink and quickly apologized before wiping down the surface and scurrying out of the room.

The Monarch, who'd gazed off into the distance in silence, did not respond to the queen's question.

"No one was hurt," Phan-tu said, though he averted his eyes from his mother's gaze.

"First it's rocks," the queen pressed on. "Then it'll be thermal detonators. Then what? Perhaps—"

"Perhaps we need to move faster," Captain A'lbaran said tensely.

"*Perhaps,*" the queen bit back, "we should not have spent so much time celebrating a man who was going to try to hurt my son."

Captain A'lbaran rested her hands on the table, as if she was gathering patience. "I will not argue with you, Queen Adrialla. We do not know why Captain Segaru was there, or *if* that is the place where he was killed. You forget, both of our lives have been threatened in so many days. Right now, we must provide relief and quell any more fighting across *both* our worlds."

"Captain A'lbaran brings up an important point," Master Roy said, his deep, assertive voice turning everyone's attention toward him, even the Monarch's. "We have reason to believe, now more than ever, that someone is working to make certain that your great worlds remain in a state of disruption."

Master Sun set a holoprojector on the table. The projection showed a rotating image of the jamming beacon Gella had destroyed. "We uncovered this on your Timekeeper moon."

"Was this when you found that unfortunate soldier?" the queen prodded. "On Eirie, you mean. That is our name for the moon."

"No," Master Sun said, clearly understanding that even the shared moon between worlds was not without its claims. "Shortly after the collision that began all of this."

The Monarch made a sound of disgust. "And you did not think it pertinent to inform us? You Jedi like your secret ways, don't you?"

"I do not know what you mean by that, Monarch A'lbaran," Master Roy said, leveling that stare that made even younglings stand at attention. "At the time, we thought it best to gather as much information as possible before being a source of disruption ourselves."

"And what did you find?" Xiri asked eagerly.

"A rudimentary thing, assembled from junk and salvage." The Cerean master paused before continuing. "Traces of dust from E'ronoh in the wiring."

The queen started to get up, but her consort placed a gentle hand on her regent's. Her sheer gold veil rustled as she shook her head.

"This changes nothing." Phan-tu sighed his frustration.

The queen looked beseechingly to the room. Gella had never seen the woman struggle for words before. "Twice now people have died in places intended for Xiri and Phan-tu. Can't you see someone is trying to hurt you?"

"How is that different from what we've been doing for the last five years?" Captain A'lbaran asked darkly. "Phan-tu is right. This changes nothing."

"It may be an opportunity," Gella whispered to Master Sun, but her voice carried in the stone halls.

"Say more," Queen Adrialla instructed her with a curl of her long nails.

She gestured to Phan-tu and Xiri. "Once the heirs are on the move, if the aim is to hurt them, then the assassin would follow and be ferreted out."

"You want us to be bait?" Captain A'lbaran smiled slowly.

"Well." Gella tried to think of a different way to phrase it. "Yes."

"I like it," said the princess.

Phan-tu turned his pale-green gaze to her, watching his betrothed curiously. Like he was trying to understand a sunrise. "You do?"

"I have been a trained warrior of E'ronoh since I was a child," the princess said, pride in the set of her shoulders.

The Monarch was not in a hurry to agree as he said, "And what of your son, Adrialla. Do you train your soldiers in anything other than swimming?"

"We—" Phan-tu began, but his mother cut him off.

"We do not shove knives into the hands of our children and call it 'coming of age,'" Queen Adrialla said crisply. "We teach them to honor our seas and serve their communities."

"I can fight," Phan-tu said, but it almost sounded like a question.

As if to move the conversation along before another fight broke out, Captain A'lbaran then leveled a hand toward the Jedi cohort. "And we will be accompanied. If the Jedi were serious about their commitment to our shared peace."

"Of course," Master Sun agreed.

Chancellor Mollo ran his fingers through his face-tentacles. "The

Republic would also be of assistance. We would be spread thin between drafting the treaty and distributing rations on both sides of the corridor."

"What about the one with the floppy hair?" the queen of Eiram asked.

Phan-tu rolled his eyes. "I beg your pardon, but what sort of training goes into being the galaxy's most eligible bachelor?"

"Ah, you've read up on me," Axel answered.

He sauntered into the room with his droid and made himself at home at the empty seat beside Chancellor Mollo. He wiped something that looked like sugar from his bottom lip. "The answer's easy, my friend. A lot of training. Right, Mollo?"

Gella felt an eagerness radiate from the chancellor. She thought of what Master Sun was saying about the hint of friction between the leaders of the galaxy when it came to Eiram and E'ronoh. "Mister Greylark *was* at the top of his class at university and excelled in hand-to-hand combat. Besides, he has a great deal of diplomatic knowledge."

"I worry," the Monarch rasped, "that having strangers with you will stir the same sentiments we heard from that dissident. You should have E'roni guards."

"My son will not be surrounded by armed soldiers who might decide they are, what did that man call himself? Children of E'ronoh. In that case we will send a small retinue of Eiram's best."

"No," Phan-tu and Xiri said at the same time.

The queen balked and the Monarch grimaced.

"What we mean is that we cannot be flanked by guards," Captain A'lbaran stressed. "We are there to defuse any lingering violence and distribute aid. Showing up with a battalion tells our people that we fear *them.*"

"Gella and Axel can travel with them, undercover," Master Roy stated calmly, as if it were obvious.

Master Sun nodded and added, "Attendants and chaperones for the couple."

Gella felt a hint of disappointment come from Enya, and she understood. As a Padawan she, too, had longed to be sent on journeys out of the temples.

It was true, Jedi on undercover operations had to dress the part, but the thought of wearing anything but her robes made Gella feel vulnerable. As the servants set down plates of roasted tip-yip and root vegetables, she studied the E'roni style of dress—so structured compared with the freedom of her robes. She'd have to adapt, and quickly.

Axel arched his brows. "Glorified nannies?"

"I would feel safer knowing my son and future daughter-in-law will be with such a great warrior," the queen said.

"Thank you," Gella and Axel said at the same time.

Gella sensed he'd done that on purpose to get under her skin. Jedi were guardians of peace, *not* glorified nannies. Still, she wouldn't let him ruin the spark of excitement this mission was for her. Her dreams of training across the galaxy felt so very far away. But as Master Sun tried to make her see, she could learn here and now. Prove to herself that she could lead. The Force was calling her down this path, and she would follow it.

"You can count on me," Gella assured the queen.

"Us," Axel added, raising his flask in her direction, then to the others.

"Good," Xiri said, finally taking a bite of her food. "We leave at dawn."

Chapter Sixteen

THE ROOK, E'RONOH

Abda walked through the Rook's market with her last handful of pezz. On Dalna, they didn't need patina-covered coins or Republic credits. They grew food right from the ground. She'd learned to love the smell of worms fertilizing the soil, the way there was always dirt under her fingernails to prove she was an asset to the others. Because the Force provided. More than that, it had saved her once, and she owed it all to the Path of the Open Hand. To the Mother.

As E'ronoh's dust slapped her cheeks raw with the passing morning windstorm, she missed the place she'd learned to call home. And she missed standing in Mother's grace.

Abda took a curving market street and ducked into a narrow alley, avoiding a small group of Path members who shouted against the winds, "Look no further for the root of your suffering! It is the Jedi! The Jedi misuse the Force, and the Force must be free!"

Once, Abda had been among them, taking their teachings wherever the elders sent her. Now she almost felt sorry for them, because they may be part of the Path, but they were not chosen by the Mother, as she had been. They were not special.

Abda pressed on, turning into an even narrower alley.

Clothes dried on crisscrossed lines up above. She had to turn sideways to walk all the way to the other side. Once she did, the winds had stopped. Vendors quickly reopened their stalls. One advertised fried thylefire scorpions. Another shouted, "Fifteen pezz a kilo, get yer tip-yip." A double-headed Troig set up an instrument with what looked like a hundred strings and began to play using all four hands. Scores of children kicked a ball, then cried as it was flattened under an ikopi's hoof.

A hooded figure knelt in front of a screaming boy and handed him a pezz. The child snatched it with grubby fingers and bolted.

Then the hooded figure made straight for Abda. In the angular shadows of the alley, he revealed himself, a green Mirialan skin with a smattering of black markings. Binnot Ullo had a twisted smile and a keen eye for opportunity.

"She sent *you*?" Binnot asked smugly.

Abda's lips pursed in distaste. "That's right, she sent me. Mother trusts me."

"Really?"

"Yes. We—we are her Children."

Binnot's eyes and smile widened a fraction with surprise. "Well, then you should know the Mother isn't pleased." He reached into his pocket and withdrew a small pouch. She recognized the shimmering gold lichen that grew on the canyons. The locals liked to call it asterpuff. He took a pinch and inhaled it. When he offered her some, she declined. "Suit yourself. Have to make this rock tolerable until we can clean up your mess."

"Not my mess," Abda said, seething at being lumped in with Serrena. But blame would not get her anywhere.

"Mother won't see it that way." He sniffed, wiping his hand across his nose. He held up one long finger at a time and said, "Serrena killed the wrong target. The Jedi convinced two children to get married and come out looking like heroes. Queen Adrialla thinks she can get away without keeping her end of the bargain, and now Serrena is injured." He flashed that twisted smile. "No wonder you need our help."

Abda shook with powerless rage. Anger rose to the back of her throat. It wasn't her fault. It was Serrena's. She'd failed, but it was Abda's turn to prove herself. "I'll fix it."

His eyes dilated, and his smile broadened. The tip of his nose still shimmered gold. He reached into the pocket of his cloak again. This time, he withdrew a slender metal tube with a narrow glass pane. Inside was a turquoise liquid coagulated with silver bubbles.

"This is all of it," he said. When she reached for the tube, he gripped her hand hard. Her bones pressed together, and she panted, struggling when she thought they might break. "Do not miss."

Binnot let go, then rucked up his hood and blended into the busy market streets. She slid down to the alley floor and cradled her hand against her chest. Her eyes burned against the dry heat. She thought of the cool, blue skies of Dalna. The Mother's caring face. Being embraced as one of her Children. That's what Abda was. Not someone who let her family down. The Mother was counting on her.

Abda rose to her feet and made her way into the market. She used the last of their pezz to refill her canteens. Then she began the journey back to the Brushlands. Along the way, the royal desert barge sailed right past her into the canyon. She stopped to pull her hood low when she noticed two dead scorpions at her feet. Small blessings. She'd learned to like the taste of them.

Smiling, she shoved them into her pockets and whispered, "The Force will provide."

ABOARD THE *AMARYLISS*, E'RONOH

Phan-tu Zenn couldn't take his eyes off the canyon road. Though the rivers of E'ronoh had long since run dry, he could see the mark they'd left behind in the smooth, undulating patterns of the rock faces. Gold lichen shimmered under the scorching sun, and though he stood at the forward lookout of the Monarch's luxury desert barge, the angled sails did little to provide shade.

Where there would normally be a full staff of servants and protocol droids, the crew aboard the *Amaryliss* consisted of Xiri, Gella Nattai, Axel Greylark, his small droid, and himself. The belly of the ship was loaded with relief aid, and though he knew his mothers feared for his safety during the journey, there was no doubt in his mind that he was exactly where he needed to be.

As the Rook became little more than a speck on the horizon, the silence among the four of them stretched. Phan-tu realized the last time he and Xiri had been alone, truly alone, was under the Erasmus Sea.

Axel Greylark had made himself at home in his cabin belowdeck, while the Jedi Knight inspected the top deck of the barge, as if she were expecting to find their would-be assassin clinging to the rear of the sail barge. Though considering everything they'd been through, Phan-tu didn't think anything could surprise him as much as Xiri A'lbaran's marriage proposal. She'd, understandably, been quiet since Captain Segaru's murder, and he wished he knew what to say.

As if he'd called her with his thoughts, E'ronoh's princess appeared at his side. Her dark-red hair was plaited in an intricate loop, the tail draped over her left shoulder. His Eirami clothes were so bright in contrast to her gray tunic. Her black leggings had corrugated pads at the knees, like they were meant for climbing the crags of a canyon instead of embarking on a diplomatic mission.

"Here," Xiri said, handing him a sort of helmet.

"What are these?"

"Sun visors." She placed the bulky eyepiece on his face. "The workers in the marble quarries use them to protect their eyes."

Through the sun visors there was a dark film over the landscape, swallowing the most intense oranges and reds. Prisms of light bounced off the metal rail of the deck, and the shimmering lichen dotting the canyon.

"Thank you."

Thank you? He couldn't think of more to say to her than a simple *thank you.* Perhaps that was enough, but it didn't feel that way. Not when the woman beside him was supposed to be his fiancée. His future queen. Down in his cabin was a glass box filled with pearls his mother had given him. He'd had every intention of giving them to her the night before, but he'd been afraid she'd think the gesture childish, and it didn't feel right since he hadn't caught the pearls himself.

"Phan-tu, what is it?" Xiri rested a hand on his back, guiding him half a dozen paces to the cushioned seats. "You look like you're about to say goodbye to your morning meal."

The sun visors made everything worse, so he removed them and set them on the nook table between the seats. Blinked at the sun-drenched deck and focused on her face.

"It's suddenly—"

"Overwhelming." She smiled hesitantly. "Last night I couldn't sleep. I was thinking that you were going to wake up and take it back, and we'd be right back where we started."

The honesty in her words gutted him. "Wild krel sharks would have to devour me alive before I renege on my word to you." It felt too intimate to say that, so he added. "To our worlds."

She pressed her lips together into a flat smile. "Good."

"What's a krel shark?" The question came from Axel Greylark.

The man the holomags liked to call the Coruscant Prince sauntered onto the barge's deck and fell onto the long-cushioned seat. Honestly, did he have to throw himself onto every surface? It was hard enough having Axel wear the attendant clothes of Eiram—trousers and a long cerulean tunic trimmed in gold, though he'd taken it upon himself to undo the clasps down to the apex of his stomach. Phan-tu would have much preferred to have a second Jedi with them.

The princess waved at the Jedi, who remained close to the control column at the rear of the deck. "Join us."

"Someone should stand watch," Gella shouted over the wind.

Phan-tu had hardly recognized the Jedi that morning without her robes. Her hair was tied at her nape in two elegant buns. She wore a stark-gray E'ronoh handmaiden uniform, with silver and red embroidery over the shoulder to show her rank as working for the princess. Where her bane blade holder would have been, had she grown up on the desert world, hung twin lightsaber hilts.

"We've checked every part of the barge," Axel said pithily. "And we're moving at sixty klicks per hour. Whoever wants these two dead is going to have to *fly* aboard."

"Leave her be," Xiri warned.

Phan-tu couldn't understand why Axel, who seemed to flirt with everything that moved, including droids, was so brusque with the Jedi Knight.

Gella moved closer but remained near the railing on the starboard side. Phan-tu suspected it was because the only available seat was beside Axel.

"No one answered my question," Axel continued. "What is a krel shark?"

"A shark from Eiram," Phan-tu said, exasperated.

"Clearly." The Coruscant Prince smiled. It was a smile intended to wear someone down, pleasant, inviting, kind, even. "Any reason it's called that?"

Axel must have been getting under Phan-tu's skin because if it had been anyone else asking, he would have launched into the story of his favorite creation myth. There was a year he'd made his birth mother tell it to him every single night. In all the tumult he had yet to stop to wonder what she'd say if she could see him now.

Thinking of her, of the animated way she told stories, he channeled her spirit. "Long ago, when our planets and the moon Eirie exploded into being, Krel was born at the heart of Eiram. His birth unleashed the oceans and storms. When he swam across the Erasmus, waves carved mountains into flat coast lines. Krel tended to Eiram, nurturing his world until it began taking on a life of its own, plant life and creatures sprouting from land and sea. As the ages passed, he transformed into his shark form—though he retained his beard—which is why they have tusks under their lower mandibles."

Xiri smiled, tucking back a renegade curl. "I've never heard that one before."

"That's the short version," Phan-tu added.

"See, I don't think we even have myths like that on Coruscant." Axel leaned back on the entire couch, tucking his arms under his head. "There are ruins in the lowest levels, but it's uninhabitable. Then again, I've never really looked. What about E'ronoh?"

"People talk about the old gods, but their names were all lost," Xiri said, turning wistfully toward the view ahead. "We do have the thylefire scorpion, the symbol of my house and E'ronoh's strength."

Axel propped himself up on one elbow. "The things people fry and turn into candies in the market?"

"A creature that can survive this desert and give sustenance," Xiri explained. "Nothing like the blue ones of Eiram. Those are venomous."

"Eiram has bearded sharks and poisonous scorpions?" Axel mused. "Perhaps our journey should have started there."

"We'll get there," Phan-tu said, wanting to remind the man that he wasn't on some cruise. "One village at a time."

"What about you, Gella?" Xiri asked.

The Jedi Knight considered the question. "It isn't quite the same. Many beings have myths about the Force—where it came from and how to interpret or even wield it. The Jedi have stories that have fallen into legend of a dark age. But I suppose my master, Arezi Mar, told me a cautionary tale that her master told her, who had been told by her own master, and so on. It was about a Jedi who wished to see the entirety of the galaxy in his lifetime. He sought out an oracle and was told that all he had to do was walk along the seam of the galaxy until he reached the end."

"But that's impossible," Phan-tu said.

"Precisely." Gella smiled wryly. "The Jedi Knight spent years, a life span, walking and walking."

"Did he find it?" Xiri asked. "The end of it, I mean?"

"No. Along the way, he felt the call of voices crying out to him. Worlds that needed him. And so, he left the path of stars, and returned to fulfill his duty to guard the galaxy."

"I would have kept going," Axel mused, his ever-present grin falling for just a moment. As if he realized it himself, he cleared his throat and reached into the bowl of fruit on the nook's table. "Also, that is a terribly depressing story to tell children."

Gella flicked her eyes skyward. "It's a fable, Axel."

"What about from the world you were born on?" Phan-tu asked.

"I wouldn't know, actually," she said, leaning her elbows against the deck's railing. "My parents, whoever they might have been, dropped me off at the Jedi temple on Devaron. I was too young to remember anything, but they knew enough about Force-users to know where to take me."

Phan-tu felt incredibly sad. He knew very well that family could be chosen, but wouldn't she always wonder where she came from? Perhaps Jedi simply did not have those questions.

"I can't miss something that was never meant for me," Gella said without a trace of doubt or melancholy.

Even Axel decided not to antagonize Gella after that. Instead he sat upright and helped himself to more of the fruits on the table. He held up a purple one with crooked white stripes. Phan-tu had never seen its equal. It must have come from the Jedi or Republic relief crates. Axel tossed it off the side of the ship.

Gella extended her hand and the thing sailed back, midair. Phan-tu could barely react to the Jedi's power, as he whirled on Axel.

"There's a food shortage! Are you mad?"

"Are you *trying* to kill me?" Axel asked, indignant. "I'm allergic to jogan fruit."

"Then don't eat it," Xiri snapped, taking it back from Gella and sinking her teeth into it.

Axel leaned forward to argue, but Phan-tu caught a glimpse of a communications tower up ahead, ending their argument as he walked across the barge to get a better look as they arrived at their first outpost.

BARAKAT OUTPOST

Xiri A'lbaran basked in the arid air of her world. She hadn't stopped moving in so long that she was afraid of what would happen if she did. Axel Greylark, as insipid and arrogant as he was, was a welcome distraction from the overwhelming realization that Jerrod Segaru was dead, and she might never know the circumstances of his death. She would eventually mourn the man who had once been a friend and mentor, even when they fought. But as the *Amaryliss* came to a stop, she had to steer forward.

Barakat Outpost was small, with mostly the families of the quarry workers populating the apartments built into the canyon walls. A layer of white dust settled everywhere as the great machines drilled into the ground and carved out hunks of marble. There had been a time when E'ronoh supplied marble to surrounding systems, but when the war began again, their off-planet contracts had become few and far between. Now this marble was being used to plug the holes in E'ronoh herself, to fix the destruction left behind.

As the barge came to a stop, a group of villagers gathered for their arrival. Because the war had demanded all her time, Xiri hadn't visited the quarries, or anywhere beyond the Rook, in years, but there were fewer people and far fewer children among the worker families than she remembered.

"Oh, good," Axel said, shielding his eyes with the flat of his hand. "A welcome party. Though they don't look happy to see us."

"We sent word to the outposts and villages along the route to come and collect rations and supplies," Xiri explained. "But the aid has been a long time coming."

Gella frowned. "I don't like this. We should stop here and Axel and I will take the shipments in the raft."

Xiri gave a decisive shake of her head. "We cannot cower. I must face them."

"Can't you wave from the deck?" Axel offered.

"Xiri is right," Phan-tu said.

Understanding their resolve, Gella nodded and lowered the ramp. Together, the four of them loaded the raft with the allotted crates for Barakat.

Before they even reached the crowd, a muscular blue-skinned Pantoran man stepped forward. "You are not welcome here."

"Do you know whom you are addressing?" Xiri asked.

The crowd of about twenty murmured. One of the children said her name in an innocent little squeak. There had been a time when the Monarch made sure the people saw him, loved him, even if they feared him. She did not want that, but she had to assert herself and her intention. Phan-tu Zenn stood beside her, though he remained quiet, even as curious eyes darted in his direction.

"The Great Princess of E'ronoh," said the Pantoran. "My family came here a generation ago on the promise of the great E'ronoh. But what has the Monarch given us?"

Gella took a step forward. The Jedi's lightsabers were obstructed from view by the long silk cape clasped at her throat, and Xiri brushed the woman's arm as she reached for them. Gella's frown deepened, but she stayed her hand for the moment.

"You're right," Xiri addressed the Pantoran who seemed the leader of the quarry. "But my betrothed, Phan-tu Zenn, and I are here now. We are here to help. We—"

"You are here to die." The Pantoran unlocked a bulky piece from his belt. Xiri's heart gave a hard pang as the bane blade landed at her feet. The challenge was clear.

Gella bent down to retrieve it, but Xiri shouted, "No!"

Xiri snatched up the dagger by the hilt. It reminded her of Jerrod's blade, simple E'roni steel, so different from her ruby-encrusted one.

"Xiri," Phan-tu whispered. The worry in his voice grounded her, but it was a reminder that there was no other way. She had asked Viceroy Ferrol to challenge her aboard the *Paxion,* and she would have gone through with it. This was the E'roni way, and though many things could change, this was not one of them.

"I accept your challenge," Xiri said.

"My aquatic prince," Axel said to Phan-tu. "What is she talking about?"

Phan-tu's face twisted with a look she hadn't yet seen from him. Anger. Frustration. As Xiri peeled off her tunic to better move in her undershirt, she let her betrothed explain, curious about how an Eiram would describe it. "I've only heard tales about it. An archaic E'roni rite. A challenge for honor, for life, for the throne."

"So if this fellow wins, *he* gets to be the heir of E'ronoh?"

"It won't come to that," Xiri said.

"I cannot let you do this." Gella's dark eyes pleaded with Xiri. "Let me fight in your stead. There is too much at stake."

Axel's eyes darted to the Pantoran, and then back to Xiri. She could see his skepticism there. "I can't believe I'm saying this but I agree with the Jedi."

Xiri unsheathed her bane blade, the rubies catching the sun. She imagined Niko was with her as she secured it at her hip. She faced her crew. "I know she's right. There's too much at stake. It is precisely why I have to do this. There is nothing more cowardly on E'ronoh than turning your back on a rite. It is our most ancient challenge. If I let another duel in my stead, what would that say to my people?"

"As you wish it, Captain A'lbaran." It was the first time Phan-tu had

sounded so formal when he addressed her. She needed him to understand more than anyone why this was important.

She took his hand firmly. "Trust *me*. Please."

His sea-glass eyes searched hers, and she saw the moment he relented, opening up to trust her.

Xiri marched ahead and followed the people of the Barakat Outpost
toward a clearing in the quarry where a natural battleground formed
from slats of marble. The people of the outpost sat along the stone edge
and covered their heads with swathes of cloth to protect from the sun's
rays. Her challenger accepted cautious praise from his friends and
sauntered to the center where he waited for her.

Xiri leaned on a massive boulder and stretched. Gella, once again,
stood in front of her. "You know I can't let you die, right?"

"I thought a Jedi would have a few more encouraging words," she
said, hoping her bravado masked her nerves.

"He favors his left leg when he walks," Gella said. "He's big, but
you're fast."

"See?" She smiled.

Gella squeezed Xiri's shoulder. "May the Force be with you."

"I don't need the Force," she said inhaling the scent of stone. "I am
the heir of the thylefire scorpion and that is the only strength I need."

Gella joined Phan-tu on the sidelines. Axel was nowhere to be
found.

As Xiri strode across the clearing to face the Pantoran, she said, "I
have the right to know the name of my challenger."

"Bruzo." Up close she could see the thin white scars on his face from
some sort of accident. He sized her up, too, and he sneered.

Xiri had dealt with people like that her whole life. Those who looked
at her and saw someone small and weak. But she'd walked the deserts
of her world, had nearly been buried by the sands, but made it out
alive. She'd led her people into battle. Bruzo could challenge her, but
she knew that she would win, because she had come too far to lose
now.

They circled each other. One of the villagers, a brown-skinned man with nervous eyes, approached to referee. "Third blood."

Xiri and Bruzo nodded. Anything could be used—bane blades, fists. She'd once seen two dueling vendors use carpentry tools.

"There was a time when the warriors of E'ronoh were legendary," Bruzo said, goading her. "It is another thing your family has dishonored."

She knew she shouldn't have taken the bait. He wanted her erratic, easy to distract. But she did it anyway. She landed a hard jab to the Pantoran's nose. Blood gushed from it and ran into his teeth, turning his sneer red.

"First!" the referee shouted. "Princess Xiri."

She lunged forward with her dagger, poised to slash across his arm, but he grabbed her arm and tossed her several meters across the clearing. Pain burst from her shoulder and a scream ripped from her throat. For a moment she couldn't see past the blinding light of the sun and the fine powder that stung her eyes.

With her palms on the ground, she felt the vibration of his heavy boots running toward her. Panting, Xiri got up to her knee, blinking hard and fast. There was a blue blur and she lashed out with her bane blade. Bruzo grunted as he swerved away from its edge, but doubled sideways. She tried to turn but felt steel bite into the top of her shoulder.

"First, Bruzo," said the referee.

The crowd gasped and murmured. She turned to find Gella and Phan-tu huddled in silence, while Axel had returned, and raised his flask while shouting less-than-sportsmanlike encouragement.

"There's no shame in giving up," Bruzo taunted her.

She laughed. He said he'd been on E'ronoh for a generation, likely on the wave of refugees that had come from Pantora and other systems before she was even born, back when E'ronoh was prosperous and a beacon of promise. But if he'd truly been here that long he knew that there was no greater shame, no greater dishonor.

Xiri climbed to her feet. This time, she searched only for Phan-tu among the others. He hadn't moved, but his hands were fisted on his thighs and his eyes never left her. A thought wormed its way into her mind. *What if I do lose? What then?*

She heard Gella first, shouting, "Xiri! Behind!"

Xiri snapped back to focus and drove her elbow back. She struck muscle but it did nothing. Bruzo was like a blue marble wall. Hands shoved her forward and she fell. She ate dust and spat it out. Rolling sideways, she avoided the crunch of his boot in the place her throat would have been. She scrambled on her belly until she could climb to her feet, turning swiftly and balancing herself as Bruzo approached again. Xiri had fought in the rites tournaments as a young girl freshly out of the academy. She'd defeated challengers as big as Bruzo. But now she had poisonous fear getting the best of her because there was more than honor at stake. There was her whole world.

So Captain A'lbaran, Princess Xiri of E'ronoh, fought harder. She dashed forward, crouched, then tumbled between Bruzo's legs as he swept his arms forward, trying to grab her. Punching the backs of his knees, causing Bruzo to stumble, Xiri dragged her blade across his shoulder. He roared as the referee called, "Second, to the princess."

Now Bruzo fought with blind rage, lashing out with his fists. She ducked again, but this time he anticipated her movement and grabbed hold of her, squeezing her until it felt like he'd shatter her bones. She dropped her dagger, gasping for air. Desperate to break free, she brought down her face against his, felt the crunch of bone, then something warm spilling into her gasping mouth.

"Second, Bruzo," the referee stuttered.

"Thanks for that," her opponent chuckled as he released her from his grasp and prepared for their final encounter.

From somewhere Axel Greylark was booing. Xiri supposed someone should be enjoying themselves at the expense of her and her future.

But that wasn't right, was it? It wasn't only her future or E'ronoh's.

It was Phan-tu's and Eiram's future, too. The reality of that crushed her and fortified her all at once.

She picked up her dagger, glad to see the Pantoran was also struggling to breathe.

"You are not worthy of us," Bruzo told her.

"Perhaps not today," she said, her voice carrying in the natural amphitheater of the quarry. "But I will do everything I can to make sure that when the time comes, I am worthy of you. All of you."

There was silence, and a hateful grunt from her opponent. She ran forward but she couldn't use any of the tricks she already had. Instead of going low, she launched herself on him, climbing him like the marble slab he was. Her legs wrapped around his waist and she whacked him across the throat with the side of her palm, stunning him just long enough for her to drag her blade across his cheekbone. He choked and staggered back, gripping her to fall with him. She leaned into the fall and landed on her feet.

"Third, to the princess!" the referee shouted.

Bruzo pressed the back of his hand to his face to examine the cut. He stayed down.

There was half-hearted applause, and she caught her breath as she faced her people.

Breathing hard, she welcomed the surge of emotion, and pressed a fist to her chest. "My name is Xiri A'lbaran and I will fight for you every day, every way I can."

There was a scream, and she didn't understand why until she saw Phan-tu Zenn racing toward, then past her. She spun just in time to watch Phan-tu intercept a charging Bruzo with a lunging punch. In one swift movement, Bruzo was down and unconscious with Phan-tu standing over the body.

Phan-tu turned to her and took her hand, threading his fingers through hers. "Together," he said to the crowd. "We will fight for you every day, every way we can, together."

He never took his eyes off Xiri.

Chapter Seventeen

Axel Greylark counted his well-earned pezz.

"I can't believe you bet on whether or not Princess Xiri would win," Gella said.

"Your incredulity is killing my buzz," he said without sparing her another glance. "And at least I bet she'd win."

It had been several hours since they'd left the outpost. After Xiri's victory—and Phan-tu's impressive punch—the citizens of Barakat had embraced both of their new heirs. With the first of the aid now distributed, they were back on the barge, moving at a glacial pace across the desert. To Axel, the entire endeavor would have been faster if they'd let *him* pay for the fuel required to take his ship. But he was beginning to understand how proud and stubborn the Outer Rim was.

"*And* that Bruzo would win," Phan-tu added sharply. His knuckles glistened from the healing ointments. Eiram's heir was full of surprises Axel would have to watch out for.

Meanwhile Xiri hissed as Gella finally finished treating her wounds. The Jedi had been meticulous despite Xiri's frequent protests that she was fine.

Axel shook his head. Not a single visionary in the lot of them. "Hedging my bets. Here are your cuts." He set their shares in four neat piles. "On second thought, Jedi probably don't need money to buy anything. I'll take your cut, Gella."

Gella had truly learned how to turn the other cheek when it came to Axel. It made getting under her skin that much more of a challenge. She crossed her arms and set her wide brown eyes on the desert road ahead. "We require the same things as everyone. Food, shelter, fuel."

"But you're not going to go out and buy yourself something nice. Something just for you. Art to hang in your room. A cask of Alderaanian wine . . ."

"Stop picking on her," Princess Xiri warned. "Or I'll take *your* cut as a fine for talking too much."

He laughed brightly, and Quin chirped a warning.

"I *know* she means it," Axel whispered to his droid. Then he raised his voice so his new reluctant friends could hear him over the wind. "Though if you two *really* want to take this show on the road I know a few places where we'd do very well."

Phan-tu narrowed his eyes. "How exactly does political royalty and a minor celebrity end up knowing places like that?"

"Minor? Please." Axel scoffed. "I make it my business to know. Plus, it is my goal to burn a hole through the galaxy and never look back."

He felt Gella's stare on the side of his face as he said that. Generally, it seemed she avoided looking at him because she couldn't control her displeasure at everything he did. "That feels chaotic."

"Then it's a good thing," Axel said, gracing her with his best smile, "that I thrive in chaos."

After their initial collision with the locals, Axel had expected every outpost and village they visited would include a similar financial opportunity. Unfortunately for his funds, the next two days were filled with routine drops. Jallen Outpost received the princess and her betrothed with open arms. The people of Heliol, a curious village settled in the underground caverns of the region, had welcomed them with fried thylefire scorpions and something called iazacal brew. The liquor was so strong it burned his eyes the moment he brought the glass to his lips. It did, however, give him pleasant dreams. He'd almost forgotten what it was like to sleep through the night. To dream at all, instead of reliving the memories he tried to drown out and thoughts he tried to keep at bay during his waking hours.

When he wasn't helping the others unload supplies from the barge or letting the E'roni sun gild his skin, Axel detailed daily accounts on Quin's recorder in his tiny room belowdeck.

One morning, he'd been going over the events of the previous night for his mother's report while he dressed for the day.

"Who are you talking to?" Gella asked, hesitating at the open doorway. Her spill of dark hair was coming undone from the loose braid over her shoulder.

"There are many people waiting to hear from me." Axel grinned and tapped Quin's recorder closed. His little droid pulsed violet and spun toward the Jedi Knight, and she pressed a hand to its round dome.

"I'm quite sure. More likely, you're reporting to Chancellor Greylark on everything going on here?" Gella's eyes fell on the red crescent scar that curved over his heart. The only reason he still had a mark was that he'd refused medical attention when it happened.

For a moment, he'd forgotten the state he was in. He quickly grabbed his tunic from the narrow bed and finished pulling it on. He hadn't wanted her to see him that way yet. He blinked. He hadn't wanted her to see him that way *ever*. People acted strange when they saw the scar, either asking too many questions or muttering pitying remarks. *Poor Axel Greylark. How sad, how tragic, his poor mother.*

He stood from his bed, the room so small, he was closer to Gella than he intended. He leaned against the wall, facing her. "I'm sure you're used to living in close quarters and seeing much more than this."

She shrugged, crossing her arms over her chest. "You're deflecting."

"You call yourself an attendant to royalty?" he asked, frustrated at how her hair was coming undone.

"It's a little more complicated than a Padawan braid," she said, tugging at the clasp.

He pointed. "May I?"

Gella scrutinized him, before relenting. He wondered if it cost her to let someone help her with something so trivial.

By the maker, the lengths he would go to in order to, what did she say? Deflect. He unraveled the plait, and ran his fingers through the soft black strands, sectioning off three parts. When he was a little boy, when things had been different with his mother, he'd helped her brush her impossibly long hair at bedtime. It was one of the only times he remembered they spent together, and he got to be part of her ritual.

Finished, Axel tightened the metal clasp so it would stay, and took a step back. "There."

Her face softened with gratitude, then that frown of hers returned. This time, it wasn't directed at him, as she turned toward the ladder and the hatch leading to the deck. He'd seen her face focus that way aboard the *Paxion*, right before she'd taken his ship, as if she could hear sounds, feel things the rest of them simply couldn't. Because she was a Jedi, and he could not forget that.

"What's wrong?" he asked.

It was Xiri who answered with a shout, "Both of you, get up here now!"

Axel followed behind Gella as they climbed up the rungs.

"Stop the barge," Xiri ordered, peering through binocs from the lookout point.

As he emerged on deck, Axel was closest to the control podium. The

Amaryliss lurched to a halt. The four of them crowded at the mast. He searched the rocky desert that spilled into the horizon until his eyes adjusted on two glinting objects separated by several meters. *People,* he realized. But they weren't moving. One was standing, one on their knees.

"Those are two Eirami soldiers," Phan-tu said gravely.

As one of the soldiers fell, it triggered a blast that boomed through the Badlands.

Chapter Eighteen

Gella began to climb the deck's railing. She calculated her jump through the Force, her landing so she could get to the remaining fallen soldier faster. But then she stopped. She looked back at her charges. Fear for the soldier and fear for them was making her leap without thinking.

Wait. She felt the word run through her, as if her past self were speaking.

This mission had to be different from her others, which meant she couldn't keep doing the very same thing that had landed her on E'ronoh in the first place. Her instinct to help was right, but she couldn't leap into a minefield.

"There's a mine scanner in the cargo hold," Xiri said, her voice distant. She glanced at Axel. "Before you say anything, yes, my father is always prepared."

The Coruscant Prince had enough self-preservation to remain quiet. Gella followed Phan-tu to release the boarding ramp. They waited at the edge. Out here, the rocky ground was dotted by spindly thorn trees and stone archways. Unrelenting sun drained all moisture from the land.

Xiri returned, holding up the wide scanner. She seemed to be hold-ing her breath while the sensors crackled as she raised it across the desert. It trilled a single beep when Xiri trained it directly at the kneel-ing soldier.

"Okay. Here's what we do. I'll hold back the trigger. You two get him to safety." Gella knew asking the heirs to stay behind would result in an argument they did not have time for. She also recognized it would help for the Eirami soldier to see Phan-tu.

"The way is clear, but tread carefully," Xiri warned.

Gella stepped off the ramp first. The ground was solid rock so dry it split open in patches, like something from beneath was trying to hatch. Though the way to the soldier was clear, she used the Force to guide her, placing one foot directly in front of the other. Gella had never disabled an explosive device, especially not one that was activated. But she could buy them time. For a moment she wasn't in the desert but in a forest of Orvax. Damp earth instead of desert. Shadow instead of sun. She'd forged ahead then, and made mistakes. The difference was that here the path was clear.

When they reached the Eirami soldier, he was in a crouch. Palms and knees on the ground, a tremor racking his frame from the exertion of holding that position. His hands were red and blistered from the sun, and the blue-green metal plating of his uniform had been badly warped across the shoulders. He lifted his head, mouth ringed with white film as a wheezing sound scraped from his throat.

Gella felt his pain through the Force. So much pain, not just his body but his spirit. What terror had he endured before this?

"Water," Phan-tu said.

To her surprise, it was Axel who'd brought a canteen. She hadn't looked back, and assumed he would stay behind. Quickly, he poured water into the cap and carefully brought it to the man's cracked lips. The soldier wept as the clean, cold liquid fell into his mouth.

"Go!" he rasped. "Don't."

"I can help you," Gella pressed.

"You can't." The soldier looked down. A small red dot blinked from the sliver of land mine peeking out from under his knee.

The soldier trembled violently. "Can't hold on much longer."

Gella steadied him through the Force, careful he didn't slacken too much and tip over. She turned to Phan-tu. "Be ready to carry him away."

She felt their eagerness and the fear that kept them sharp. As she moved her attention to the land mine, the soldier focused on them. Recognition filled his green Eirami eyes when he noticed Phan-tu. Confusion quicky gave way to panic as he threatended to scramble away from the prince. "Where am I? Is it really you?"

"You're safe," Phan-tu said. "You're safe. I've got you."

"It's too late," the man whimpered.

"Now, now!" Gella shouted, her control slipping as she tried to keep the land mine pressed down and the frightened man calm. Phan-tu lifted the man and began to pull him away from the land mine as fast as he could. Cold sweat pooled between Gella's shoulders as she reined in her focus, the charge from the land mine whining as it engaged.

At the same time she pushed the mine as far away as she could through the Force, someone was dragging her back across the ground as it blew.

Gella bit down on the scream in her throat as she regained control and deflected the shrapnel of rocks.

Her pulse hammered, and she allowed herself a moment to shut her eyes against the sun, against the ringing in her ears. Dust still settled to the ground, but as everyone stood and brushed themselves off, she thanked the Force for guiding her.

Phan-tu wasted no time in hurrying back to the soldier's side. "Let's get you on the barge."

"Too late," the injured man repeated. "Save the others."

He kept a hand against the center of his chest where there was a wound she hadn't noticed before. They might have bought him a few more moments, but now that his head was resting against Phan-tu's chest, now that Axel stood in just the right place to give a dying man shade from the sun, she felt him slipping.

"My prince," the man said, in his delirium. "I made it back."

"What's your name, soldier?" Phan-tu asked, the end of his words hitched with emotion.

"Salas, sir." His eyes were unfocused, every blink slower and slower. "The others—"

"We will find them, Salas," Phan-tu promised.

"D'you know the sailor's lament?" The soldier slurred his words. A trickle of blood ran down the corner of his mouth.

"I—I'm sorry," Phan-tu looked up at them for help, still trying to keep pressure on the wound. "I don't."

It was Xiri who answered. "I do."

And as the man slipped into the Force, the princess of E'ronoh sang.

The ground was solid rock, and so they could not dig a grave. Instead, the Jedi Knight, the heirs, and the Coruscant Prince covered his body, and the remains of the second soldier, from the sun and scavengers with large stones. Phan-tu carried the remains of Salas's breastplate to take to his family. But first, they had to investigate the fallen soldier's claims.

Aboard the *Amaryliss* Gella cleaned the scrapes on her palms and a fine slash on Axel's cheekbone. Painless compared with what Salas had gone through, but it forced Gella back into a feeling of failure she thought she'd moved past. She was beginning to realize that perhaps it was a feeling that never went away, something she would always have to work to overcome.

Night fell quickly in the desert as they gathered on the deck. They ate cold meat and bread in silence, all except Phan-tu who leaned against the lookout point just as he had the morning they set out on their journey.

Gella attempted to regain her focus, then thought perhaps the best way to do it was to replay those moments in a mental loop. To relive it, to see every moment as it unfolded. And then to let it go.

Beside her, Axel kept touching his cut and wincing. He'd been the one pulling her back from the blast, she realized.

"Thank you," she told him.

He acknowledged her with a curt nod, took a sip from his flask, then passed it to Xiri, who passed it to Gella. When she turned the cool metal in her fingertips, she wondered how he was so adept at burying his emotions. Perhaps some people were contradictions. Perhaps understanding someone completely meant accepting those contradictions. And why should it bother her when after this, she might never see Axel Greylark again?

When Phan-tu returned to sit beside Xiri, she commenced her debriefing. She pulled up a holo of the topography. More dry lands, more canyons.

"In the recordings Gella attained while we were aboard the *Paxion*," Xiri said, "this area was a dead spot. There was never any ground fighting here."

"Whoever left the land mines behind did not get the directive," Axel chimed in.

"Those were supposed to have been recalled early in the war." Xiri wore her guilt for all to see. "Before things got worse again."

"What about prisoners?" Gella asked.

She glanced at Phan-tu as she said, "All prisoners were ordered to be released—"

Axel took a nip from his flask. "My point still stands."

"What do we know about the nearest village?" Gella asked.

Xiri expanded the region on the holo. "A'ranni is in the heart of the Badlands and on our relief route. Mostly iazacal farms. But since the drought, the war, and more drought, production all but stopped."

"If there are more of Eiram's soldiers there," Phan-tu said, "how do we get them out?"

Axel lifted a finger in question. "Not that I am calling our collective skill into question, but if we're venturing into a place so charmingly called the Badlands, shouldn't we ask for backup?"

"We should know what we're up against first," Gella countered. "The very reason we're here is because Captain A'lbaran did not want soldiers marching across E'ronoh."

"If we leave now we'll get there in a few hours," Xiri said, "then proceed under the cover of night. A'ranni is small."

She dragged her finger across the projection of the map. "But over this ridge, there's a network of stone arches and caves. It's where I would make a stand if I were leading the charge. There's a lot of cover, a lot of places to hide."

"Not to mention likely more fun little toys to blow us up," Axel muttered. "Might I suggest you pull rank and order them to stand down and free any prisoners?"

"After Barakat, I want to prepare for anything." Xiri frowned, like she was readying herself to meet any more challengers who came her way. "Once we've gathered intel, we'll know how to proceed."

"I'll take the first shift," Phan-tu volunteered.

The weight of the day settled on Gella, and she joined Princess Xiri as she excused herself to go belowdeck.

"The Force will be on our side," Gella assured her.

As she took the first step on the ladder, she caught the Coruscant Prince grimacing toward the horizon and saying, "I'd much rather have luck on my side."

Phan-tu Zenn crept over the crags of the ridge that bordered the farming village of A'ranni. Their way was illuminated by Eirie's silver moonglow and the pinpricks of stars. Even at a distance, he could see that the groves of iazacal trees were dry and lifeless.

Axel Greylark was at his side, his chrome blaster pistol drawn as they crawled the rest of the way on their bellies. Phan-tu could just make out the silhouettes of Xiri and Gella, as well as Axel's little droid.

"I still think you should have left Quin," Phan-tu whispered.

"And I still think we should have called for backup," Axel hissed back. "Besides, do you know how many times Quin has saved my life?"

"He should get a medal," Phan-tu murmured.

"I'm starting to get the sense you don't care for me very much." The Coruscant Prince scoffed. "Are you still mad about the music?"

Phan-tu was not this man. He did not act so rudely to others. He had patience for everyone, even some of the cruelest courtiers he'd met back home. Perhaps Axel reminded him of those people, and that was why his wry smiles and ability to walk through the world as if he were the only person in it bothered him. That, and Axel had spent the entire night blasting terrible music. After the horror that was the previous day—mere *hours* ago—Phan-tu was weary. Axel was an easy distraction for his anger, a feeling he loathed.

He loosed a frustrated sigh. "It doesn't matter what I think of you."

"Shh," came the admonition from Gella. "I see figures. Looks like two soldiers, both pinned down."

The Jedi passed the binocs to Xiri, and on down the line. When they got to Phan-tu he peered through the lenses, light adjusting for the dark. Far down beneath the ridge was a hole in the ground—the jagged mouth of a cave. Stalagmites jutted out and boulders clustered around the lip. Phan-tu's adrenaline spiked when he noticed the Eirami military transport shuttle. It appeared to have crash-landed. Its wing was charred and bent, the cargo hatch still open, and part of the hull crushed beneath the stone lip.

He kept scanning for life as far as the cave entrance would allow. Though the movement there was obscured by a barricade of durasteel crates and the overhang of the stone crags, he recognized the red uniforms. The only way in was the same way those ships had gotten themselves stuck—from above.

The four of them turned around, lying on their backs.

Xiri raised her wrist comlink and whispered, "All units, come in."

They waited. Phan-tu felt like he'd swallowed a hive of bees as the dead air of the comm was the only answer they received. Xiri repeated herself and added, "This is Thylefire One."

"Looks like we're doing this the hard way," Axel said, voice low.

"Blast it," Xiri hissed.

"What about the droid?" Gella asked.

"What *about* the droid?" Axel repeated defensively. The little QN unit was small enough that its thruster didn't emit a loud noise, and smart enough that its response to Axel and Gella was a simple, low beep.

Axel grunted a sigh, but said, "I suppose you could try to talk to the ship using a different frequency. That is *if* either ship has any fuel left and is powered on."

"Let me try," Xiri said, urgently.

As the small unit flew into her hands, Phan-tu crept back over the ridge to keep a lookout. Both camps were quiet. Perhaps, he wondered, they'd gone to search for Salas. But no, they would have crossed paths. Unless, of course, these caves gave way to tunnels. Phan-tu's education about E'ronoh had focused on the wars that marred their shared histories. His own grandmother had told him about the first time she'd seen the red slash of E'roni starfighters fly over her island in the southern isles. The destruction had been the reason she'd sailed alone, at ten years old, to the Rayes Canal at the capital. Others had left on refugee barges for Tawl and Bespin. But the surrounding planets had stopped trying to get involved by the time the war became something Phan-tu would have to endure.

Never again, he swore.

A nearby scuttle drew him out of his thoughts. He let his eyes adjust to the dark as the noise, familiar in so many ways, crept closer.

"Don't move," Phan-tu warned Axel, keeping his voice calm.

But Axel had already seen the small thylefire scorpion that had landed on his chest. He bit down on his lip to avoid shouting a curse, but Phan-tu clapped his palm over the Coruscant Prince's mouth.

"It isn't venomous, don't scream," he whispered. "Unless you want unwanted visitors."

Phan-tu pinched the critter on its torso, picked it up, and set it on a craggy mound, where it scuttered off. "See?"

Axel combed his long fingers through his hair and whooshed his relief. Phan-tu could see the white of his teeth as he smiled through the night, glancing at QN-1 as if to make sure Xiri hadn't somehow destroyed his property.

"Indulge me," Axel said, turning his head toward Phan-tu. "How did a street urchin become the heir apparent to the queen of Eiram?"

"This." Phan-tu shook his head, heat rising to his face. It took every part of him not to shout. "This is why I do not care for you very much."

Axel didn't seem fazed. He only shrugged. "I find those I meet want to either kill me, bed me, or save me from my worst impulses. Sometimes a bit of all three."

"Do you hear yourself?" Phan-tu asked. "My world has been moments away from ending, every day for years, and you've done nothing but joke."

"Worrying just makes you get old fast." Axel was losing steam.

"Let me guess. You want to be young forever?" Phan-tu knew how precious a thing like old age was.

Axel hummed his thought. "Not exactly. I want to burn quickly, in a blaze of glory. Like a supernova."

It was decidedly not what Phan-tu thought the arrogant man he'd come to know would say. They were quiet for a long time, listening to Gella and Xiri try to make contact on the comm. Why had he pushed so hard against Axel's question? He wasn't ashamed of where he came from. He was quite proud, actually. The people of the Rayes were survivors.

"You remind me of every glugheaded ass who made my life miserable my first years at court."

Axel held back a snort. "I grew up with the type. Politicians' kids are worse. I should know. But if I'd been there, I would have just been bigger and meaner for you."

Dammit. He managed to smile.

"When I was a boy," Phan-tu said, giving in to Axel's earlier question, "we had one of the worst monsoons in Eiram's history. The weather shields hadn't been repaired in the Rayes Canal part of the city. My mother managed to get my sister and me on the last skiff out of town but there wasn't room for her. I was scared and I wanted my mother. So I ran off. My sister, Talla, followed me."

It was then he realized Xiri and Gella were listening, too.

Every time he closed his eyes, it was the nearest memory he could summon. "When the wave came, it felt like a fist had grabbed hold of me and yanked me out to sea. I was in that ocean for what felt like an eternity. It was me and the krel sharks, thousands of sea creatures displaced by the storm. But they didn't harm me. Eventually, the sea spat me back out and I was rescued by the royal guard. Queen Adrialla and her consort were on the ground helping in the medic tents and they tended to me. I don't recall exactly how it happened, but they took me in. At first, I was Consort Odelia's attendant, then they adopted me, and that's the whole sordid tale." He nudged away another scorpion crawling across his ankle, disturbing the pebbles on the ground. "Satisfied, Mister Greylark?"

"Extremely," the Coruscant Prince murmured. "May your luck never run out."

What Phan-tu didn't say was that part of him was still under that wave, swimming in circles trying to find his mother and sister. He never did. Xiri had lost her brother to the same ocean, but she never talked of him. He hoped, as they grew closer, that would change.

"I think I've managed to get something through," Xiri said.

He sat forward with every intention of going to her side. He stood up, but the next step he took, he sank right through as the crags crumbled under his weight. He opened his mouth to cry for help, but sucked in gravel as the ground broke and pulled him underneath.

Chapter Nineteen

A'RANNI OUTSKIRTS, E'RONOH

Gella snapped toward the cry of Axel Greylark's curse. It echoed against the cliffside for the longest second of her recent memory.

"What just happened?" Xiri asked. Gella could feel the captain's denial, then the sinking realization that her betrothed had vanished. "Where's Phan-tu?"

The three of them stood over the place where Phan-tu Zenn had been kneeling.

"I don't know! I just blinked and he fell through." Axel scrambled back and ordered, "Quin. *Glow*."

The QN-1 droid illuminated the hole in the ground that hadn't been there before, then flew down into the darkness. Pebbles rained down as the cliff eroded. Xiri crouched, but Gella yanked her back in the event the chasm spread. Quin's light faded from view, and couldn't let them see far enough. Gella didn't think her lightsabers would either.

Xiri sifted a fistful of the pebbles through her fingers. She turned to the silhouette of the cliff's ridge. On the other side were the pinned down camps of Eiram and E'ronoh. "I wonder . . . if they tried to blast their way out and have weakened the caves below."

Axel fisted his hands through his hair. "I regret calling him lucky."

Gella opened herself to the Force to try to sense Phan-tu's presence. She sensed *life*, but the proximity of the warring camps added to a feeling of confusion. The pit of her stomach churned with fear. It spread and threatened to cloud her actions as she remembered what happened on Orvax. It had started the same way. "It's happening again."

"*What's* happening again?" Axel asked.

The strong tenor of his voice cut through her memories, and reminded her that Phan-tu and Xiri needed her. "I should go down there."

"Wait," Xiri whispered. A faint light sped up from the tunnel.

QN-1 flitted back up to the surface, the small droid trilling an excited sequence.

"Quin thinks it heard him," Axel said, slowly translating the trills and warbling sounds. "But there are too many tunnels."

"*Thinks?*" Xiri asked.

"Why don't *you* go down there, Princess," Axel said, defending his droid.

Gella cautioned, "Axel, you're not helping."

"Please," Xiri whispered, but Gella did not think she was addressing either of them.

High-beam lights flared from down in the cave. Shouts rose to the top of their ridge as blasterfire lit up the dark.

"We have to trust that Phan-tu is safe," Gella said. "Right now, we have to free these soldiers."

Axel leaned over the ridge and craned his neck. "That's going to be a bit difficult if they end up shooting at us."

Gella joined him and studied the maze of stalagmites, the rows that lined the cave. Boulders were piled up below, and as pebbles skittered beneath her boot, she saw that with every attempt to blast their way out, they'd buried themselves deeper into the rocky cave. But she saw her way through, and perhaps, they'd be able to get everyone out safely.

"I'll draw their fire," she said, drawing her path between the narrow rock spires with the tip of her finger, "while you and Axel climb down. Once I have their attention, you can order them to stand down. If changing Quin's frequency didn't work, they may not even know the war is over."

"And in the event they do not stand down?" Axel asked.

She thought of Axel and Phan-tu's conversation, which she'd been quietly listening to as they tried to make the comms work. Taking a deep breath, she turned her back on the steep drop of the basin, balancing on the edge of the ridge with her boots.

"Wear them down," she said, and took the leap.

Phan-tu Zenn never used to fear the dark, until it devoured him. Falling through the network of tunnels beneath the mountain ridge, he lashed out. Clinging to nothingness. It was a recurring dream, that feeling that everything he had was a dream and one day, he'd tip back into reality and the plunge would be nothing like the comfort of his ocean. That safety was an illusion, an unfulfilled promise he made to the people of his planet. And now, the people of E'ronoh.

When he landed, he didn't move for fear of having broken something. Slowly, he wiggled his fingers and toes, pushed himself up, only to have the ground move. Shift. He could see nothing, not even his hand flexing in front of his face. He dug into his pockets, but carried nothing that would provide light. He reached down to touch the ground, and his fingers came away dusted with powdery sand. He inhaled the cool, mineral scent of stone, felt the indentations of tiny particles embedded into it. Remnants of when E'ronoh's canyons might have been split by rivers, covered in oceans. A time so long ago, only the fragments of shells petrified in stone remained as evidence.

Perhaps there had been a time when his world and Xiri's were not too different.

The thought of her, of Gella, and even Axel snapped him back to life. He needed to get back to them, but he did not know a way out. He heard a distant shouting from the surface. He tried to find grooves and notches along the stone but the tunnels were too smooth, and he only slid back down. His knuckles and palms raw from trying to climb, he remained on his knees.

He'd never for a moment thought tying himself to Princess Xiri would have landed him here; nor had he thought it would be easy. Simple. A hurt that could be smoothed away like the grooves in stone around him. That took time. It took erosion, wearing away. He laughed, alone and in the dark. Wasn't that what Axel had said to him moments before? But if the heir of his world's longtime enemy could sing a sea chanty of Eiram to a dying soldier, then wasn't that something they could build on?

Phan-tu closed his eyes and settled into the dark. Was it different from being under the seas of E'ronoh? They both had cold, quiet, solitude, and creatures scuttling in the corners. Instead of a current of water, he felt air.

Wind.

A thin breeze, like the ribbon in Xiri's hair. He followed it, climbing into a tunnel and crawling his way out. Eiram's soldiers needed him there. With every nudge forward, the current got stronger. Light seeped at the distance. The noise, too.

He'd crawled right into the center of a nest of thylefire scorpions.

Gella Nattai loved the sensation of falling. True, she did not care for flight. Flying was a seesaw of movement, and depending on the pilot, she was left excusing herself to the restroom. But falling? That was different. As she leapt into the night sky, she unholstered her twin lightsabers, trusting the Force would carry her safely. Why couldn't she always trust herself as implicitly as she did in moments like this? Wasn't every decision she made similar? With no guarantee but the guarantee that it was as the Force willed it.

As she landed in a crouch at the center of the cave, she felt the soft shock through her legs. Then when she was steady, she ignited her lightsabers. The vibrant hum within the core of her moonstone hilts ran up her arms. She inhaled the cool scent of stone mingled with decay.

The contingent of E'ronoh's red-clad soldiers noticed her first. An older woman sporting a head bandage did a double take and then re-directed her fire to Gella. The Jedi Knight raised her left blade and deflected the blast.

"Where the hell did the Jedi come from?" the soldier shouted to the man behind her.

"The Jedi are with Eiram," a rough scrape of a voice said from the inner, shadowed corners of the cave. "Shoot her down!"

Gella glanced up to the rocky ridge for signs of Xiri and Axel Grey-lark, but the high beams being used by both shuttles washed out the corners of the basin. They would make it, she knew it.

"Jedi, run!" The sharp cry came from the wreckage of the blue Ei-rami shuttle.

In that moment of distraction, Gella nearly missed the second shooter from the E'roni side. She had just enough time to lean back, the centimeter of proximity grazing heat at the tip of her nose. She righted herself with a nudge of the Force, and used the severed stalag-mites as stepping-stones to draw even more attention. Red blasterfire sailed toward her. Gella spun, each bolt ricocheting off her violet plasma blades and illuminating the E'roni camp. She heard someone scream, a blaster clatter against stone.

Gella balanced on the spur of a stalagmite and used the reprieve from blasterfire to let her voice carry. "Stand down!"

"Go make trouble on some other rock, Jedi," the rough voice said. The threat was made clear as a large, bearded man stepped out from the shadows. He leveled a heavy blaster at her. He didn't wear military clothes, instead had on stained coveralls. "You have no authority here."

Gella looked up to see Xiri and Axel slide the rest of the way down the stone and land on the shelf of the cave above. Axel drew his blaster while Xiri stepped forward into the light. She gestured at the Jedi.

"She doesn't," the princess said, "but *I* do."

"Captain!" the woman with the bandage gasped. She saluted and stood at attention. "Acting Lieutenant Marlo, here. Have you brought backup?"

Gella had been right. They didn't know the war was over. That meant they'd been down there for days.

Slowly, half a dozen battered soldiers emerged from behind the barricade. "Who issued your last orders?"

"Lieutenant Segaru, ma'am," Marlo said, "two weeks ago. We got intel that an enemy ship was attacking A'ranni. A few of their soldiers died on impact, and we took care of some others. We've been pinned down ever since."

"Lost all comms," a younger soldier said, turning to the bearded man in the coveralls "Some of the villagers like Hix came to help blast us out but it didn't work."

Hix, a bearded farmer, made a deep grumble. "We've run out of food, water. All we had left were ammo and a bit of courage to fend off the attack until you *remembered* us."

Gella felt the thrum of discontent. It was like the cemetery all over again, except these E'roni had blasters *and* rocks.

"That is a lie!" an Eirami soldier in a dirty uniform shouted. She stepped out of the cover provided by the stranded shuttle with arms up. "We did not come to attack. Our ship was shot down and we crashed. We've lost all communications with Eiram."

Someone fired at the woman, and she ducked. Gella, who'd been attuned to the crackle of feelings, blocked it with her lightsaber. It lanced against the top of the cave and caused a small avalanche of pebbles.

Gella sensed Xiri's worry and her nearly impossible stance unraveled quickly. This E'roni unit had been forgotten on their own soil. They were starving and holding out hope that someone would come for them, but no one had. Now Xiri had to reveal that not only had peace been brokered, but their perceived enemy, the beings whose lives they'd taken, had died in vain.

"By decree of Monarch A'lbaran of E'ronoh and Queen Adrialla of Eiram," Xiri said, her strong voice filling the cave. "A ceasefire is in effect, and a permanent treaty of peace is being drawn up as we speak."

"I don't believe it," came a whisper from the dark.

"Impostor!" Marlo cried, pointing a finger at Xiri. Then the acting lieutenant turned to her soldiers, any sort of formality she'd shown her captain and princess was gone. "Why does she travel with an Eirami guard? This is another deceitful trick. We cannot trust her."

E'ronoh's soldiers trained their guns at their princess. Axel shoved the shocked Captain A'lbaran and the pair broke into a run as far as the shelf of the cave as the soldiers opened fire.

Gella used the Force to leap, spinning and deflecting fire as she worked her way across the maze of stone. She wouldn't be able to keep that up for much longer. She jumped to the ground and took cover behind one of the stalagmites. From there, she had a clear view of E'ronoh's barricades. Axel and Xiri joined her side, flinching as red fire carved away at their shelter.

"Well, that went as expected," Axel said airily, dusting the front of his tunic. "How are we to prove you're *you*? Unless . . . *are* you an impostor?"

Xiri glared at him. "Now is not the time to test me, Greylark. And it isn't their fault. We abandoned them. I did this. And Phan-tu may be—"

"We *will* find him, Captain A'lbaran," Gella said. The Jedi had faith, but the princess, Gella understood, needed tangible proof. "First, we must subdue your army. I'll give you a clear shot to stun."

The princess of E'ronoh raised her blaster. Axel pressed his back against a rock formation. Their eyes met, and he nodded. They were ready.

Gella seized the crates and yanked them through the Force, bursting through rows of crumbling stone. The fine particles billowed in the air, obscuring the soldiers' view of them.

Axel moved with a swiftness she had not expected. He felled the nearest soldier with a shock of blue, then took cover. Every time she'd tried to gauge his emotions before, she'd felt nothing—as if he were cocooned in *beskar*. But now she felt a trill of excitement, a burst of his adrenaline. He looked at her, and in the warped shadows, he smiled like he knew every secret in the galaxy.

Behind her Xiri cried out. She staggered forward into plain sight, grasping the blaster burn on her shoulder. Axel yanked the princess back in time before another hit could land.

"It's just a flesh wound," Xiri said, switching her blaster to her good hand.

Still, cold fear threatened like a vise at Gella's throat at the thought that her charge was hurt. But she would not allow it to take hold. She drew deep from the well within her and stepped into the line of fire. This time, she advanced fast, engaging her lightsabers and moving with them in an arc. Violet light slashed and crackled against red blaster fire. She made herself the bigger threat, and that gave Xiri and Axel the opportunity to flank. Blue energy pulsed and pulsed until one by one, all the soldiers fell.

The dust settled, coating everything within reach in E'ronoh's crimson dust.

Xiri fell to her knees beside her people, and Gella knew this was not a victory.

"Check on the others," Xiri said solemnly, getting up to wade deeper into the ship that had been repurposed as an encampment. "I'll find restraints."

Gella still crackled with energy, though it was beginning to fade. She hadn't needed to call on the Force with such fervor before. Her body ran so hot, the cold desert air felt like a gift.

"That was impressive," Axel commented, keeping pace at her side.

"Thank you."

"I clearly mean me."

She grumbled but found a strange comfort in his levity. They marched ahead in the network of stalagmites. On the other side of the cave, where the Eirami ship had crash-landed, three soldiers emerged. The woman and two men. Gaunt eyes peered at them from hollow, bruised faces. Like Salas, they were in bad shape, though their injuries didn't appear fatal.

"Is it true?" the woman who'd spoken earlier asked. She favored her left leg and had her arm tucked into the crook of the other. "About the treaty?"

Gella suddenly felt very cold from the inside. She slowly moved her hand to one of her lightsaber hilts.

"It's true," Gella said, trying for Master Roy's serene voice. "Princess Xiri is to marry Prince Phan-tu Zenn. We will get you medical attention and then get you home."

The woman breathed hard, pale-green eyes scanning the area behind Gella and Axel. Her bottom lip trembled. "Where is he then? Where is Phan-tu Zenn?"

"He's with Salas," Axel said, gesturing toward the exit with his hands. "He was badly injured, but we found him." At first, Gella didn't understand why Axel was lying. But the truth was, they didn't know Phan-tu's fate. She didn't agree with the way he was trying to gather their trust, but she understood.

"Our queen would *never*." The woman pulled her arm free. Not injured but hiding her blaster.

Axel drew his chrome pistol and pointed at the men. They raised their hands in surrender. "Don't."

Gella couldn't move fast enough. Weighed down by their fear, their doubt, she hesitated for one moment too long. That cold sensation returned as the woman took aim at Gella, and the other two reached for their weapons.

Axel Greylark fired.

Chapter Twenty

A'RANNI OUTSKIRTS, E'RONOH

Over the span of the war, Xiri A'lbaran had endured many things. The first was her brother's death. Niko was their father's joy. When he was alive, she'd understood her place on E'ronoh. She was a warrior in her own right. Thylefire-made. She'd completed her coming-of-age trek through the canyons and survived. She'd gone to university, away from their system, to learn, to find an eligible match to bring home—perhaps someone of industry or titled. She'd be expected to train her children to be warriors, too, because the only certainty in E'ronoh was that war would one day come.

As she watched over the burning ruins of the basin, she wondered if war only came because her family willed it. Would her brother have made the same decision she had? Would her father have found another reason to take up arms?

But that night was not the time for guilt.

It was a night for courage.

With the help of Gella and Axel, they'd lined up the dead bodies of the soldiers from both E'ronoh and Eiram and built a pyre. Only flame could burn the things these stranded soldiers endured. Pinned down in a cave, without food or water, cut off from home, fighting a war they didn't even know might be over. Xiri had seen terrible things over the last five years, but she had never seen *this*.

Axel watched the fire roar. Xiri would not have believed he had it in him, but he'd saved Gella's life. She watched him wander away in silence, and Gella take a step to follow. But Xiri was certain he wanted to be alone, and she gripped her Jedi friend's wrist.

"He'll wander back."

Gella turned her attention to the barge and lowered the ramp. The dissenters who had fired upon them and refused to stand down dragged their feet up the boarding ramp into the cargo hold of the *Amaryliss*. When they reached the next village and got back on schedule, they'd have the prisoners sent to the Rook for disciplinary hearings.

"My father would have killed them on the spot." Xiri wasn't sure why she'd said that out loud.

She met the Jedi's curious gaze. "And that is why you are the one who put a stop to the Forever War, and not Monarch A'lbaran."

She felt like one big bruise, inside and out. The weight of the years past that should not have belonged to her pressed down on Xiri.

"The Forever War. I never thought it rang true, but now I know it does."

"You and Phan-tu are forging something stronger," Gella said.

Xiri watched as dawn approached. She let herself voice her fear. "What if Phan-tu is lost?"

This time, the Jedi did not give her any assurances.

At the sound of tumbling rocks, Xiri and Gella reached for their weapons. QN-1 flew out of the cave. Its triangular light panel pulsed red.

She pressed her hands on her stomach. Hunger fought with her unease. "Any sign of him?"

Axel was not around to translate the little droid's trills, but she caught the moment when Gella tilted her ear to something Xiri wasn't connected to in the same way.

"Do you hear that?" Gella asked.

Xiri listened to the hoot of a night bird, the warming metal under fire, boots scraping against a ramp. "Nothing that wasn't there before."

Shhh, Gella whispered softly. The Jedi closed her eyes and turned her ear away from their battleground, and toward the rest of the Badlands. Crimson slashed across the base of the blue night and illuminated a moving beast.

"By the old gods," Hix, the bearded farmer, rasped. The giant man had been fearless enough to fire at *her* but now he staggered back and fell off the ramp, taking the remaining soldiers with him.

At first, Xiri thought it might be one of the E'roni stags, with their long necks and massive black horns. But as it crept closer, she saw it was a scourge of scorpions. Hundreds of them walking across Phan-tu's arms, shoulders, his torso. The biggest one nested in the soft brown top of his curls. He was smiling as he approached.

She felt the urge to run to him and make certain that he was all right. But something stopped her. *Should* she show affection? She didn't know what was appropriate for an arrangement such as theirs.

"Thank the old gods you're safe," she said, and hoped her voice was not too tired to show her sincerity.

"Krel's beard!" Greylark exclaimed, returning to complete their cohort. "How'd you get over there?"

Phan-tu lowered his arms to the ground, creating a human land bridge for the scorpions. "It was the strangest thing. I fell into the tunnels beneath the ground, and I came upon a nest clogging the entrance. At first, I was terrified, but then I kept going and they clung along for the ride."

As the scorpions scurried across the ground, some of the older prisoners whispered, "Thylefire-made." She rejoiced at the words. Now more than ever, she needed the approval of her people, even if they had tried to kill her.

"What does that mean?" Gella asked.

Phan-tu's smile fell as he rose to his feet and took in the scene. She'd have to tell him everything as soon as they were on the move again. For now, she wanted to remember that moment. Eiram's son flanked by a desert dawn.

"We mean *of* the scorpion," she said. "*Of* E'ronoh."

Axel Greylark wanted to get out of the Badlands as soon as possible. He told himself that was why he helped rearrange the cargo to make a temporary brig and not because he'd hated the look on Gella's face when he'd shot and killed the Eirami soldiers about to attack them. He didn't need to be judged by a Jedi, and he didn't need his actions questioned, especially when he had saved her life.

As they finished loading up the *Amaryliss,* Axel told Phan-tu everything he'd missed while he was making friends with scorpions. Horrified at their discovery, the young Eirami prince said, "That's unthinkable."

He just shrugged and excused himself to his tiny room. He regretted ever agreeing to get himself involved in Eiram and E'ronoh's mess, no matter the prize waiting for him at the very end. He forced himself to forget the day, Gella sailing across that cave in a magnificent arc. Forget the heat of his blaster, the shock on the faces of the Eirami soldiers as they fell. He wondered if his mind would ever get too crowded to hold memories he'd rather forget. His mother was an expert at it. She walked through the halls of their Coruscant tower, the halls of the Senate as if nothing and no one had ever hurt her. Perhaps. *Perhaps* he was more like her than he'd ever imagined.

As Axel regained his composure, he undressed and wedged himself into the narrow shower tucked in the corner. When he was done with this place, and he hoped that day came sooner than later, he was certain he'd never get its dust out of his orifices. He lathered himself in soap and had only begun to rinse through his hair when the water shut off.

"Ration complete," a warbling voice chirped.

"*Ration,*" he spat. "This day couldn't possibly get worse."

Quin flew to his eye level and offered up Axel's flask. For once, he was not in the mood. "Can you beg one of the others for some water?"

His droid flew out of the room, only to return moments later. Axel stuck his suds-covered torso out of the shower stall to find his droid wasn't alone. Gella chased after Quin, trying to pry a canteen out of its grip. When she realized she was in Axel's room, her eyes flared with fury.

"I can explain," he said, but didn't move any further. As a general rule he never exposed himself to anyone who didn't ask. He retreated into the stall and rested the back of his head against the wall. "I didn't know there's a water ration. We brought them all that water!"

She sighed, somehow righteous and exasperated at the same time. "You do know what a drought is, don't you?"

He was too tired to laugh, and managed to rub suds into his eyes. "You'd be surprised. I've met plenty of leaders who live in luxury while their people suffer. Please, Gella. I'll give you whatever you want—within reason." Then he added just for good measure, "Please. I did save your life."

A better man wouldn't have reminded her of it. But he was who he was.

The ration sensor was practically gloating at Axel when he heard the knock on the other side. He cracked the shower stall door open. She handed him the canteen and he made quick work of using the tepid liquid to rinse his eyes. When he was finished, she was still there, leaning at his threshold, with her back turned to give him privacy.

He chuckled darkly, then yanked on his robe and sat on the edge of his bed. He cast a long glance at Quin, who let out an innocent warble. Gella glanced over her shoulder and took back her canteen.

"Thank you," he said.

He watched her face. The tension around her eyes when she inspected something. Currently, it was the vintage chrono on the thin shelf, and his family ring. He was very good at reading people, and he'd noticed that Gella looked at everything like she was trying to make sense of it. She'd done it at the funeral procession, and at the dinner after, and at every village and outpost they'd visited. He wondered if she knew she was doing it.

He pressed his fingers against the ghost of an ache in his chest. "Is there anything else I can help you with, Jedi?"

"I want to know why you're so antagonistic toward *Jedi*," she said, the last word soaked in the same derision he normally used.

He knew the longer he spent on this mission with her, the more it might come up. Everything that had to do with the events of his father's passing threatened to rise to the surface. But he couldn't do it, not in this state.

"I will. I promise," he said. "But not tonight. I have a million useless facts stored up for moments such as these."

Her brow furrowed in confusion. She likely thought he was being literal.

"Why don't you tell me what you meant when you said, *It's happening again.*"

She broke their eye contact. "Not tonight."

Why was he even entertaining her? He was exhausted. He was beginning to regret ever agreeing to return to the Outer Rim. Frustrated, he raked his fingers through his damp hair and changed the subject. "Do you believe in this mission, Gella? That the heirs will make it?"

"Those are odd questions." She rubbed the side of her neck. She'd fought like hell tonight. He could admit that. "It matters that Xiri and Phan-tu believe in it."

Axel shook his head. "I could never do it. Marry under such pressure."

"Well, you are all very different," she said. "They are selfless."

"And I am selfish," he stated with a grin on his lips.

She glanced down at her canteen as if that was proof.

He chuckled low. It was a good reminder of how matter-of-fact Jedi were with their words.

"Good night, Jedi Nattai," he said wearily. He had no energy for more.

"Good night, Axel Greylark."

The moment she was gone, Axel stretched out on the bed and stared at the dark.

THE ROOK, E'RONOH

The honorable Viceroy Ferrol burst into the meeting office, trailed by his son, Rev. Several guards rushed in, blubbering apologies to the Monarch and his guests.

"What is the *meaning* of this?" Eiram's queen asked.

The viceroy would not acknowledge any presence but that of his own ruler. No matter what he'd done, it was not enough to choose strangers over a lifetime of fealty to E'ronoh.

The self-righteous Jedi remained the tall statues they were. Though the one who questioned him slowly moved a hand to his weapon, resting it there as if it were the viceroy who was a threat when the only threats to the Monarch and their planet were the strangers in that room.

"Ferrol," the Monarch began.

The viceroy lowered his head in apology. "Your Grace, you cannot keep me in the shadows. I am still the viceroy."

Queen Adrialla took two steps around the holotable, her long nails tapping against the surface. Good, let her be nervous. He knew she was hiding something, and in the end, he would uncover the truth and set their planet free from the ridiculous bargain orchestrated by the Jedi and the Republic.

"Monarch A'lbaran," the viceroy said, standing firmly in place. "I've served you my entire life. My son has dedicated *his* life to the only thing he's ever wanted—to fight for our future."

"I am aware of that." Monarch A'lbaran at least had the decency to look him in the eye.

"Then *why* am I being treated like a criminal?"

"You confessed to spying on and stealing from the Jedi during a peace summit," the Monarch said.

He'd had to confess. It was a testament to how lost his friend had become in his old age. He never imagined he'd see the day where the queen of Eiram, a Republic chancellor, and Jedi commanded more respect than the Ferrol name.

"Monarch A'lbaran," the towering Cerean Jedi began with that pedantic flourish all Jedi seemed to possess. "Do not keep your viceroy at bay because of us. We understand it was a trying situation."

Ferrol would have scoffed in his giant face if he could get away with it. Likely, a Jedi deception to keep an eye on him.

"Do not patronize *me*," Viceroy Ferrol blustered.

"I will summon you when I require your counsel." Monarch A'lbaran turned toward the flickering holoprojection of the surface of both their planets and every drop shipment of relief being distributed.

And a third image just out of his view—the route Captain A'lbaran and her *betrothed* were on.

"That is all I ask, my monarch." He bowed low to show his penance for his supposed blunder, then turned on his heel and marched out.

When the viceroy and his son were safely out of the palace and in the busy market, he finally allowed himself a moment to breathe. To remember what was at stake. Everything he did was for E'ronoh, and that was what mattered. They wandered past the like of beggars and street musicians.

A couple of beings dressed in tattered gray and blue clothes tried to make eye contact with any poor sap who wanted to listen to their proselytizing about *Jedi*. He had enough to worry about.

They stopped in front of a fruit vendor. The cacophony of the market was enough cover for their conversation.

"Did you get a good look at it?" he asked his son.

Rev Ferrol nodded, reaching into a bin of starfruit and plucking one. They turned to go, and the vendor stammered after them, asking for payment. The viceroy tapped the sigil and medals that decorated his chest and kept walking. The audacity of the man.

Under a stone archway, a brazen girl with a buzzed haircut shook a can of paint and scrawled graffiti on the stone wall. The viceroy bared his teeth in a smile as he read the words—RISE, TRUE CHILDREN OF E'RONOH.

"Yes, Father," Rev said. "We know exactly where the princess will be. She will never see us coming."

Chapter Twenty-one

ABOARD THE *AMARYLISS*, E'RONOH

As the *Amaryliss* sped between the high desert ridges of E'ronoh's northern villages, the news of Captain A'lbaran's betrothal and the end of the Forever War was received with cautious hope. Word was even beginning to spread of Xiri's victory in a rite of challenge, which brought further admiration. For his part, Phan-tu Zenn was welcomed, with his sweet, charming smile and eagerness to heave crates of medical supplies, roll barrels of grain, or simply hold a screaming toddler while its parents unburdened themselves to their princess.

Days slipped into nights, and their small crew's routine became a great comfort to Gella, who loved routine. In some ways, rising at daybreak and meditating had stayed the same. Sometimes Xiri and Phan-tu joined her. It fascinated her the mundane details they wanted to know about temple life—yes, she had her own room, yes, she was given a small allowance, yes, she had more than one set of robes.

One morning, when they were a few hours away from the mining village of U'ronoh, Gella climbed up to the deck. She'd slept restlessly, and blamed Axel Greylark playing music at all hours of the night.

Because he'd made every possible effort to avoid even looking at her since the night at the caves, she thought he was doing it on purpose.

"Morning," Gella said, then noticed that the sails were pulled back. "Are those *clouds*?"

Xiri smiled from behind her cup of bitter E'roni tea made of the severed heads of desert nettles. She tilted her face toward the gray overcast sky. "Let us hope so. It will be a novelty only having to worry about something like rain."

Gella joined the princess and poured herself some tea. She sensed Xiri's dread, rising like the tides of Eiram. "What is it?"

"The comms tower at the mines hasn't responded since last night," Xiri said, that pinch between her brows deepening.

Gella understood immediately. "You're afraid it'll be like the Badlands."

"It's more than that. I'm afraid the citizens of E'ronoh won't accept me as Monarch when the time comes. Not because of Phan-tu, but because I'm not doing enough. It must sound silly to a Jedi Knight." Xiri drummed her fingers against her teacup. "You're not afraid of anything."

The sincerity of the words made Gella smile. "We have this Jedi Master. He teaches us as younglings. Yoda's his name. One of my earliest recollections was being afraid of the training spheres."

"What are those?"

Gella held up a round fruit roughly the right shape. "Imagine if this shot lasers."

"At *children*?"

Laughing, Gella explained, "They tickle, as do our training lightsabers. But I didn't know that. I was always quiet, wandering around the temple halls and trying to find hidden passages or secret tombs. But when it came to practice, I was the first one there. I thought I'd be a natural, but that first day, when I saw that sphere covered in what looked like mechanical eyes, I ran out of the room."

"Poor little Gella," Xiri said sympathetically. "Did they yell at you?"

Gella blinked at the suggestion. "Not at all. Master Yoda found me. He just sat with me in the garden and we watched this one frog try to leap over a stone wall into a waterfall. It kept missing. Miscalculating. Falling. Getting back up. Then he said, *Like that frog, you must be.*"

"Did you get it eventually?"

"The next day I got hit right here." Gella tapped her nose. "Eventually, though. So, yes, much of what Jedi do is confront fear, feel it, conquer it. Accept that it is a part of me like anything else."

"What happens if you can't?" Xiri asked. When a beam of light broke through the clouds, Gella could feel her disappointment. "Conquer it, I mean?"

The refrain came so willingly, she could hear it in the voice of Master Arezi Mar. *Fear is the path to the dark side.*

But as Phan-tu Zenn and Axel Greylark climbed onto the deck, she never got to finish.

"Axel was eavesdropping," Phan-tu said, sitting beside Xiri. Every morning, Gella noticed, they sat a fraction closer together, as their comfort in each other seemed to grow. He smiled widely, then helped himself to breakfast.

Axel sat beside Gella, scowling at Phan-tu. The pair had developed a strange sort of friendship. Sometimes they'd be sharing in a joke one moment and the next they'd be shouting. If Axel used the deck sail rung to do pull-ups, Phan-tu would try to do twice as many. When Axel won, likely *cheated,* at cards, Phan-tu would want to play until he won at least one game. At least when they competed to see who could unload more crates, they delivered their rations faster.

"Good news," Phan-tu said, "U'ronoh's mining tower let us know they were awaiting our arrival in the launch bay."

Up ahead, white sandstone homes dotted the side of a sprawling mountain covered in prickly, dry brush. A communications tower and hangar bay sat at the top, and the mine entrances were on the other side of the mountain.

"I don't think I've ever been to a mine," Axel said, biting into a star-fruit. "What exactly do you dig up?"

"Gems mostly," Xiri said. "The last time I was here was to recruit. This entire street was filled with the families of the workers."

Gella craned her head back to look at the tower, and the glint of a shuttle landing up there. "Are we expecting anyone?"

"U'ronoh has its own security detail," Xiri explained, though she reached for the security of her bane blade.

"I can imagine it's a tempting target for marauders," Axel said, a spark of excitement in his eyes. "It's far enough away from a major city, there's only one unit to dispose of, and you've got civilians to use as leverage."

Xiri frowned at him. "It is disconcerting how quickly you formed that plan."

"I've had a lot of lives, Princess."

"Something tells me if not for your pedigree you'd be in prison," Phan-tu said.

"No one wants me there," Axel assured them. "I'd just run the place in no time."

They shared a laugh, though Gella was certain the Coruscant prince wasn't joking.

Axel cast his eyes on the core of his fruit, the table, Xiri, Phan-tu, before finally landing on Gella. She would not look away first. She hadn't forgotten that he still owed her an answer about his father. She didn't even blink, offering him a smile as she picked up the jogan fruit.

He made a disgruntled sound as he lost their staring contest, and she took a bite of the fruit, ripe and sweet.

As they rode over the top of the mountain village, the first thing Gella noticed was that there was not a single being there to welcome them. Every other location, no matter a town or a hamlet, had eager crowds waiting to collect their rations.

Gella cast a wide net into the Force, but Xiri and Phan-tu's anxiety overshadowed anything else she might sense unless she concentrated.

Though she could not feel his emotion, she could see Axel realizing the same thing she had.

"Where is everyone?" he asked.

Xiri went to the control podium and coasted the barge to a stop. Gray still clung to the sky, and the wind whistled sharply so high up. The comms tower looked vacant, as did the town's tavern and row of white stone houses. She'd *seen* a ship land, though the hangar bays were closed.

"Stay belowdeck," Gella said sharply. "Axel, turn the barge around. We need to leave."

He must have seen how serious she was because he didn't even argue, only took the controls from Xiri.

"Wait a minute," the princess said, turning to Phan-tu for help. "We don't know what's happening. If something is wrong, we need to help."

"I agree, but we're too exposed," Gella said as something hit the *Amaryliss.* The unmistakable sound of a blaster shot pinging on metal.

The barge lurched to a stop. Axel punched the control panel and cursed. Xiri and Phan-tu hit the deck, and Gella scanned the area until she spotted the soldier making a run back to the hangar bay. She grabbed him through the Force and he staggered, remaining in place. Boots tried to drag against the dusty ground, and he fought hard against her will.

Another shot was fired, this time hitting the deck railing right in front of her. Gella released her hold on the soldier. It was only as he ran for the cover of the hangar across the platform that she realized he hadn't been wearing E'ronoh's red-and-gray uniform.

Gella whirled to Phan-tu. "He's from Eiram."

The young prince shook his head in denial. "What?"

"We have a bigger problem. The engine is fried," Axel said, then began to adjust the sails. They could get back down the mountain coasting on the winds.

Gella had the dawning sensation that they'd entered into a trap. She trained her eyes on the hangar bay. Whatever was behind those doors wasn't going to be friendly. The ship she'd seen was another one of Eiram's. "If they wanted a kill shot, there'd be a shooter up top."

Xiri nodded, getting to her feet. "Or the tower."

"Someone is going to a lot of trouble to get our attention," Phan-tu said, the four of them gathered at the portside of the barge facing the bay doors.

"I would suggest we not give it to them," Axel said, resigned. "But I know you won't listen."

The metal doors of the hangar rattled open and a squad of Eirami soldiers in white-and-turquoise uniforms and patina-covered helmets stormed out. Gella counted eight, each carrying a blaster, except the soldier leading the charge. He raised the crackling end of an electro-staff and shouted, "We've come for the traitor Phan-tu Zenn and Xiri A'lbaran."

"They're a bit busy at the moment!" Axel shouted back.

"We've got a little wedding gift from Eiram."

Gella sensed the overwhelming anger in Phan-tu, then fear as he turned to Xiri. They followed the circle the leader drew around the town center. The missing miners appeared at every threshold, every doorway. Standing on the rooftops. Around their chests were strapped blinking devices. Detonators.

Veins popped at the side of Phan-tu's throat. "Let them go!"

"We'll disarm them as soon as we're en route to the Timekeeper moon—as long as you come unarmed. This is your only warning."

Phan-tu turned and made for the hatch leading belowdeck. His resolution was stronger than durasteel. Xiri's, too, as she grabbed his wrist.

"I won't stop you," the princess explained as he tried to pull away. "Together."

Even QN-1 flitted to Phan-tu and bumped his dome against the Eirami prince's chest.

"Whoa, wait a moment," Axel said, gesturing between himself and Gella. "We're not letting them go off with those lunatics, are we?"

Gella was desperately torn. They were entrusted with protecting the heirs, yes, but in her heart, Gella would make the same trade without hesitation. It was the only way to buy them time.

Phan-tu clapped Axel's shoulder and flashed a pained smile. "You'll just have to come save us."

Xiri removed her blaster and her bane blade, then she and Phan-tu began their march across the flat mountaintop and into the hangar. Gella calculated the speed they'd have to sail the barge, *if* they caught the right wind. Or if she could jump far enough to get to the bay first, but she'd never jumped that far. Then she saw the small white blur flying right at Phan-tu's back.

"Phan-tu trusts me to save him," Axel said, more in wonder to himself than to her.

She wondered who had ever made him feel otherwise.

"Have faith, Axel."

He scoffed. "In what, the Force?"

Yes, she thought. But also in QN-1. She motioned with her gaze and watched his smile unfurl as he saw what she did. "In your droid."

When Quin flew undetected into the bay behind Phan-tu, the usual mischief returned to Axel's face.

He pressed one of the side buttons on his wrist comlink. Hushed voices came through, but it was hard to hear against the groaning sound of metal as the hangar roof began to open.

"We're not going to make it," Axel said.

A serene calm fortified Gella as she stepped onto the railing of the barge and extended her hand to him. "Do you trust me?"

He said nothing, and she felt nothing break the shields around his heart and mind. Except he climbed up beside her, squeezed his fingers around hers. She drew strength from the Force, and together they jumped.

Gella steadied their landing as they managed to cover half the distance. They sprinted the rest of the way to the hangar bay.

Axel trained his blaster at the hangar lock, and took the shot. The panel blew in a shower of sparks and the door cranked open.

Then it stopped.

The space was too small to let them squeeze through.

Gella powered up her lightsabers, drove them through the metal, and pushed outward against the resistance of the material until the last threads holding the door together clanged to the floor. It was Quin who came through the small gate, trilling excited little warbles.

"Slow down!" Axel shouted at his droid. He turned to Gella and said, "Xiri and Phan-tu were taken aboard, but Quin managed to steal the detonator."

Relief washed over Gella as the little droid revealed the trigger stored in its panel. There was no time to lose. She squeezed Axel's arm. "You get everyone free. I'm getting on that transport."

Gella crawled through the opening she'd made in the hangar door, narrowly missing the blaster shot that landed a meter from her head. An Eirami military transport was taking off, the loading ramp slowly drawing closed as the thrusters engaged. A blue-clad soldier clung to a rung and fired at her.

Igniting her lightsaber, she deflected the blasts. Red plasma shots hit the soldier across the chest. Gella looked up to find Axel beside her, pistol drawn. The soldier rolled off the ramp and onto the hangar floor. Gella stirred with lament, but she knew that he would not be the first casualty of the day.

Holstering her lightsabers, she then stacked her palms, one on top of the other. "I'll boost you up."

Predictably, Axel made a face, but he did not argue. Gella buoyed his weight through the Force, then jumped behind him. She clung to the edge of the ramp and hefted herself aboard as the vessel listed, trying to shake her off. She saw the red flare of a blaster, followed by a guttural gasp.

When the transport made a turn, she rolled across the floor, colliding hard against Axel—and the second dead soldier. As they evened out and ascended, the dead body lay across them both.

"This planet is nothing but nightmares," Axel said darkly, then they hefted the unfortunate dead Eirami off them. Axel picked up his blaster and covered the entryway. If the entire squad had gotten aboard, there would still be six left.

Gella removed the soldier's helmet. She felt a pang of dread. She'd seen the woman before. Auburn hair, amber eyes, just like Xiri's, stared into nothingness. None of the distinct green freckles many Eirami had. Because this girl was not Eirami. She was a servant in the Monarch's household. She'd been there that day, so nervous she'd spilled Gella's drink. What had the leader of the captors called the moon? *The Timekeeper moon.* That's what it was called here.

The Jedi stared at the helmet in her hands as realization dawned on her. The turquoise flecks of patina along the arched metal spaces for the eyes. There was a groove along the brow, charred at the edges as if from a fatal blast to the head.

"What is it?"

"These soldiers are not from Eiram," Gella said.

"This is an Eiram military transport and that is an Eiram uniform, so then who in the *bowels* of Coruscant is it?"

When he was done shouting, Axel blinked at the ceiling. She followed his gaze to the graffiti scrawled across it. It read CHILDREN OF E'RONOH.

Chapter Twenty-two

U'RONOH VILLAGE, E'RONOH

Xiri A'lbaran was falling. Not in body, but in her mind. She dreamed of her brother's face. Marlo shouting at her. *Impostor. Traitor.* She dreamed of Phan-tu Zenn covered in scorpions, his smile like the sickle of a moon. *Thylefire-made,* even the dissenters had called him.

Get up. Her father's voice roused her. Then it transformed.

"Get up." Still familiar, but not her father. The owner of that voice kicked her.

Head spinning, she blinked Rev Ferrol's face into view. All at once, she remembered where she was. In the commotion, she thought she'd seen QN-1—and then, well, it all became fuzzy after that. But she was alive, in the stolen Eirami transport. She'd recognized Rev's voice from the years he'd flown in her squadron.

She searched the hold, currently used for weapons, and for them. Phan-tu was beside her. Something frantic and urgent slammed into her when she realized he was still. Too still. She tried to go to his side to check his pulse, but her wrists were clamped with binders.

"Relax, Princess," Rev said. "He's alive."

Xiri had never longed to challenge someone to a rite so badly before. "Why are you doing this?"

Rev's brown hair was matted at the temples. The olive undertone of his skin was crosshatched with scars she hadn't seen before the cease-fire.

"For E'ronoh, Captain A'lbaran," he said mockingly. "After that dog-fight from a cease-fire *you* orchestrated, I woke up in the medbay with orders to go home. That's it. Go home. You are done."

"What would you have us do, Rev?" Xiri seethed. "Fight forever? Until we are dust and they are drowned?"

"*Yes.*" The venom in his voice terrified her. The others who were part of these Children of E'ronoh weren't fighters. She could see that from the way they handled their blasters. But Rev was, and he relished it. "No matter. Only the true Children of E'ronoh understand."

"Is that what you do? Strap bombs on our own people and kidnap the Monarch's daughter?" She laughed at him, focusing his attention on her. She could hear fighting in the other rooms and hoped and prayed to the old gods that it was Axel and Gella, and that they were winning. "You're a fool."

"A fool you've underestimated." Rev crouched on the floor before her. There was a disturbing sort of calm about the way he blinked, the way his lips split his face into a smile. He leaned close to her ear, and confessed, "I killed Jerrod Segaru."

She breathed hard, biting down on her lower lip to stop it from trembling. Her eyes burned with anger. She remembered seeing Sega-ru's body on Phan-tu's bed. How he hadn't fought back because he'd known the man who shot him. They'd blamed Braxen because it felt like the only problem they could solve and the family needed closure.

"You framed the guard." Xiri kicked hard, but he was ready for her and moved aside.

He eased back. "Me. Well, I had help. My father has such a way with words."

"Viceroy Ferrol." She remembered the man's words to her the day she proposed to Phan-tu. *You'll pay for this.* "Why?"

"Jerrod was a good soldier. The best, honestly. But he'd always be loyal to you, and you are compromised, Xiri. I'm taking you home. Some of us are willing to give our lives for the cause you forsook."

Xiri laughed again, unable to control the fear that raked down her throat. She laughed because she'd reached her breaking point. Rev was every one of her fears come to life. Unquenchable anger. An endless cycle of war. How did she fight that?

"Everyone is willing." She lifted her chin at the parachute he was wearing. She hadn't noticed until that moment. "Just not you."

Rev slapped her hard, losing himself to his own fear. "I am the bigger picture."

"You're a fool," she repeated, licking the blood that spilled from a crack on her bottom lip. "What will you do when people investigate? When the transport is recovered? Maybe I will be dead, but whoever is with us will be *children* playing dress-up."

"It won't matter. Those in U'ronoh will tell the story of the day Eiram threatened their lives and kidnapped their princess."

The sounds of fighting were getting closer. Rev looked over his shoulder, and she saw the desperation of someone in such a hurry to win that they became careless, and careless people made mistakes.

"You'd rather go through all of this than challenge me?"

Rev's grin vanished. "I've already won."

"Land this shuttle," she taunted. "Fight me to the death like the first families of E'ronoh. Isn't that how our stories go? The line of A'lbaran unseated the lesser Ferrols."

The thing was, she saw the spark of temptation there. Only for a moment, and then his false sense of victory returned.

But over Rev's shoulder she could see a familiar figure stand in the doorway. She never thought she'd ever be so thankful to see Axel Greylark's face. She truly hoped she understood the ridiculous hand gestures he made, and threw herself on the ground.

When Axel took the shot, Rev moved to the side, and the blast hit the spot right over her head. She could smell the burn against metal, the sweat on her skin. Rev whirled on Axel and slammed his stolen helmet upward. Greylark bellowed in pain. Xiri rammed her boot upward, kicking at the back of Rev's knees just as Gella rushed into the room, lightsabers drawn. The violet light hummed as she crossed the blades under Rev's chin.

"Don't worry, Princess," he said. He'd been in her squadron. Thylefire Thirteen. They'd grown up together, and she'd seen his twisted anger and told herself it would pass. "You always taught me not to go into a fight without a way out."

He raised his fist and pressed the top button of a trigger. The door of the cargo bay blasted open, and the ship shuddered. A torrent of wind filled the cargo hold, dragging everything not bolted down straight out of the hole. Prepared for it, he'd gripped a metal rung on the ceiling and dived out feet first without looking back.

Xiri watched Gella use her Jedi magic to barricade the door with weapons crates, the suction of the wind keeping them in place even as they began to plummet.

"Who's flying the transport?" Xiri shouted.

"Autopilot," Axel said, the lower half of his face covered in blood.

While Gella freed them of their binders, Axel grabbed the parachutes. Xiri shook Phan-tu, pressing her hand on the sides of his face.

Get up, she thought. *Get up, get up.*

His eyes blinked awake slowly, then all at once, taking in their situation. "Did you get the detonator?"

"Yes," Axel assured him. "Now we just have to get off this transport. I'm changing coordinates so it crashes in the middle of nowhere instead of the capital."

"You're both pilots. Can you land it?" Gella asked Xiri and Axel.

Greylark opened a control panel and assessed the damage to the ship. "He blew a hole through it, and I'm good but not that good."

"I'm glad you've learned some humility," Phan-tu said.

"I'm glad my inappropriate sense of humor is rubbing off on you," Axel shot back, "but we have another slight problem."

"We're going to have to jump," Xiri shouted over the rattle of the vessel. She opened the latch to the compartment stowing the parachutes. She looped her arms inside one and secured it, then tossed another to Phan-tu. When she grabbed a third one, she froze.

"What is it?" Phan-tu asked, buckling the harness around his torso.

"That's the only one left."

She held the last parachute in her hand.

Axel opened other compartments, but they were empty. For the first time since she'd met the Coruscant Prince, he seemed nervous. All it took was the fear of death.

"I can hold you, or he can hold you," Xiri shouted, gesturing between herself and Axel.

Gella closed her eyes. Her dark lashes fluttered in that way of hers when she meditated at dawn. She turned to Axel and said, "Put it on."

He looked down at the vest Xiri shoved against his chest and blinked. "What?"

The shuttle tilted downward, and they slid onto what were the walls.

"There are too many variables," Gella said. "This is the only way at least three of us make it back. Let me do what I was assigned to do." She raised her fingers and *moved* crates out of the way to give them an escape.

Gella turned to Axel again and shouted, "Put the vest on now!"

Axel moved mechanically. Xiri had seen that look on the faces of soldiers before. Had experienced it herself. It was like walking in a dream, your body not truly yours.

"Go!" Gella squeezed Xiri's hand like a metal claw and shoved Phan-tu out the door. "Make for U'ronoh!"

Then that great invisible Force that Gella always talked about, Xiri *felt* it, like a pressure against her chest, Gella's promise and faith.

And then it was gone as Xiri fell in earnest through her E'ronoh skies.

Gella pressed her body to the wall, right beside the gaping hole in the hold. "Axel, *jump*. I can't hold back these crates much longer."

"Why?"

"You don't even *like* Jedi," she said, a terrified, trilling laugh escaped her. She didn't think she'd ever made that sound before. It felt good, like a release.

"I need to tell you—"

They were losing altitude. He looked around desperately, but he knew it was too late. Gella grabbed him by the collar and shoved him out of the breach in the hull. She believed the Force would carry her friends safely to the ground.

Now it was her turn. She'd fallen from great heights in the past, had leapt off the edge of a cliff in a trust-fall—and the person she'd been testing had been herself. But this was a new sensation, and instead of fear, she found excitement. Gella Nattai had never considered herself a daredevil before, but in this moment, the word felt right. Her place in the Force felt right, with nothing between them but trust. No expectations.

She watched the rocky ground come closer and closer. She couldn't leap too soon or too late. The Force did not *speak* to her, but she felt its nudge. *Now.*

Gella Nattai took the leap.

When Phan-tu Zenn landed, he found himself situated about halfway up the mountain. Everything hurt. He supposed that was a good sign. It meant he was alive. He patted his entire body down, then unbuckled the parachute and tested the strength of his legs.

He wanted to thank his lucky stars, but he knew his gratitude belonged to Gella Nattai. He knew the Jedi well enough to know that she would have said, *Thank the Force instead.*

As he scanned the cloudy sky for Xiri and Axel, he begged the Force, prayed to it the way his mother Odelia still prayed to the god

Krel. Though he supposed Gella had said that wasn't what it was like at all.

He squinted against the sun and noticed that new green and brown freckles had sprouted across the tawny brown skin of his arms. He hadn't noticed before how E'ronoh's sun had brought out his most distinct trait from Eiram. He felt the urge, the need to tell Xiri.

Then he heard the crunch of rocks behind him. It was one of the E'roni desert creatures with long necks and great black antlers. It hopped up the side of the mountain. *Make for U'ronoh,* Gella had said.

The comms tower was silhouetted at the top of the mountain. He cast one last glance behind, then marched forward. He had to trust that Xiri would find her way there. Luck, the Force, Krel. Perhaps it was all the same thing, in some ways.

Phan-tu trekked up the mountain toward Xiri, and toward his future.

The town called it a miracle.

Xiri A'lbaran remembered sailing through the sky. She did not remember landing, or even getting up. The next thing she remembered was being surrounded by every being in U'ronoh. The town had survived. Now the town was embracing her. Reunited families hugged one another, while a hairy rodent-faced Tintinna raced across the village searching for her missing husband. The buildings and the tower remained intact. The *Amaryliss* was still parked exactly where they'd left it. And beyond it, Phan-tu Zenn made his way on shaky legs. It seemed she always noticed his smile first.

She ran to join him the rest of the way, propelling herself into his solid embrace. Xiri couldn't remember the last time anyone had held her this way, like she was safe, but she couldn't let herself scratch at the meaning of that touch. Not yet.

A third figure appeared on the curved road that led to the top of the mountain.

"Gella!" Xiri shouted.

The Jedi Knight appeared unharmed, though covered in grime.

Phan-tu pulled her into their shared embrace and wild relief. When she pulled back, Gella's palm was pressed firmly against her chest, not in injury, but in some sort of silent Jedi prayer or thanks.

Xiri watched her friend's eye take in the town, searching each face.

"He isn't here yet," Xiri said. "And I haven't seen Quin."

"Probably managed to find a sabacc tournament happening exactly where he crashed," Phan-tu said, but his chuckle was hollow. Xiri felt a tendril of shame at how she underestimated Greylark, but that was tempered by everything that needed her attention. As battered as they were, there was no time to rest.

"We have to return to the Rook," Xiri said, "and tell the Monarch of this new threat. I want to question Viceroy Ferrol myself before he plays to my father's loyalty and weasels his way out."

"We won't go anywhere until we repair the barge," Phan-tu said.

As they assessed their damages, a Mon Calamari woman approached. Dark-purple spots dotted the sides of her head, likely from living on the sun-drenched planet. Around her neck was a sort of climate regulator that puffed a tiny cloud of mist.

"Captain A'lbaran, thank the stars you're safe." Xiri took the Mon Cala's claw-tipped hands in hers. "I am Iana Percei, marshal of U'ronoh."

Xiri introduced Phan-tu and Gella, and quickly explained their situation.

"What is the galaxy coming to?" the Mon Cala lamented. "While we await the fate of those still missing, we must tend to your wounds, and your barge."

Phan-tu used his hand to shield his eyes as the sun reached its zenith. "Didn't you say there was a patrol ship stationed here?"

"Recalled to the war effort some time ago," Iana said. Another puff emitted from her climate regulator. "We patrol the tower ourselves, though U'ronoh has been less tempting to brigands since the mines have not yielded in some time. You've seen the reports."

Xiri had not. She'd been busy with recruitment, with resorting to buying water from smugglers because merchants wouldn't come to a war zone. She'd been trying to find a way out of this. Now that she had, they would have to turn their attention to the parts of E'ronoh that had been left behind.

"In the meantime," the Mon Calamari said, "we will hold a Remembrance for those lost. Come. We have a med droid scanning for injuries."

Xiri was about to refuse. They still had to unload cargo, fix the barge. But she also needed to be at her best. This fight was not over.

"What's a Remembrance?" Phan-tu asked at her side. They walked at a slow pace behind the Mon Cala, who was fascinated with the presence of the Jedi and pulled Gella into a conversation.

"It's a celebration for the dead," Xiri explained, looking into the weary faces that bowed in respect as they passed by. "Sometimes it's only among family, but in rural areas the whole town comes together. They tell stories of the dead, sing their favorite songs, cook their favorite meals. Harder to keep up during wartime."

"We have something like that. Only it's one day a year, and the whole of Eiram celebrates."

She would like to see it someday soon. Though given their journey so far, she worried about what was waiting for them on Eiram.

When Gella stopped walking abruptly, Xiri reached for her weapon before remembering it was on the barge. She'd seen that look on the Jedi before, the warning that meant something was approaching.

From the road snaking to and from the mines emerged Axel Greylark. He walked slowly. At first, she thought he carried his parachute with him. But as he drew closer, she finally saw what he carried, and a scream slashed through the noise of the crowd. The Tintinna woman who'd been searching for her husband pushed her way toward the dead body bundled in Axel's arms.

As the red sun yielded to the night, the mourners of U'ronoh gathered in Siggi's tavern. Xiri and Phan-tu sat with the families telling stories of the small Tintinna and the tower guard. Both killed by the Children of E'ronoh. Gella hadn't seen Axel since he'd been scanned by the med droid and couldn't shake the feeling that he shouldn't be alone. Still, every time she thought of going to search for him, she remembered how he'd *wanted* to be alone after the night at the caves.

Gella tucked herself into a corner booth and nursed a drink called a stinger. She'd watched the bartender make it by pouring amber iazacal liquor and adding a drop of some red syrup extracted from thylefire scorpion blood. The drink was strong enough to make her eyes burn when she merely brought the glass to her lips, and then it burned again going down her esophagus.

"An acquired taste." Iana Percei, the Mon Calamari marshal of the town, joined Gella in the dimly lit booth.

Gella offered the marshal a warm smile. Earlier, they'd eaten bowls of puffed rice, gravy, and little purple beans Gella had no name for. She'd eaten ravenously, despite the spices making her nose run.

Marshal Percei coughed, then pressed the button of her climate regulator. "Pardon me. This desert air doesn't always agree with me."

"Perhaps Eiram's climate might suit you better," Gella suggested.

"Oh, I tried," the Mon Cala said ruefully. "But the fighting had broken out, and there was a blockade. E'ronoh needed workers in the quarries and mines since they'd drafted everyone else. Beings came from all over the galaxy. Many left again when the drought set in."

"Why did you stay?" Gella asked curiously.

"You might not understand. You Jedi are not rooted to anything. You're warriors always going here and there. I've now had the pleasure of meeting two Jedi in my life. But it is not so easy to pick up and *go*." Another puff of humid air made her voice phlegmier. Gella waited patiently for the Mon Cala to continue. "When I left Mon Cala because of our own civil war, I thought the farther I went, the better I could escape it. But here, there, I cannot escape it. All I can do is root myself like coral trees and live through it because the only other choice is not living."

Gella considered the marshal's words. "Home is not so simple for a Jedi, but we are not an army of warriors. We're guardians. We fight when we are called to, when we must defend the lives of others."

"Fighting for peace is like coming to the desert for rain," said a human woman sliding into the seat beside the marshal. "You will wait forever."

She had startled eyes and hair pulled back into a tight braid. Gella sensed the apprehension as the woman looked the Jedi up and down. Farther into the tavern, the singing had turned to dancing.

"Don't mind Kala," Marshal Percei said apologetically. "Her pessimism is not contagious, I promise."

Kala sucked her teeth and glowered at Gella. "It is not pessimism to know something is true, and my truth is that nothing changes down here in the dust. But up there?" She pointed a scrawny finger to the ceiling. "Up there you Jedi change things."

Gella realized the woman was talking about her, but she did not understand. "What do you mean?"

"Kala, stop it," the Mon Cala chastened her. "Go sleep it off before you insult our guests with the ramblings of strangers."

Kala shot to her feet, but Gella sensed no real threat, and so did not move. The woman's pinched face gave way to a deep, unshakable bitterness that no words from the Jedi could soothe. She did not want it.

"What strangers?" Gella asked.

The marshal gave a weary sigh, then flagged the bartender for another drink. "Travelers from a system—Dalna, I believe—called themselves the Path of the Open Hand. They offered a *better* way of life away from all of this, and . . . away from the influence the Jedi have with the Force."

Gella had never heard of such a group before, even on the sacred moon Jedha where sects of Force-wielders and worshippers coexisted. She'd have to ask Masters Roy and Sun if they'd ever heard of the outlandish claim.

"What else did they say?" she pressed.

The marshal knocked back her drink, a drop of amber liquid running down one of her chin barbels. "Only that the Force does not belong to the Jedi."

"We have never made such a claim. We find balance *in* the Force."

"I would not worry, young Jedi. Many of the younger ones in the town left with them, but I think their families would have done anything to have them escape the draft." She looked back to the heirs, being pulled into the dancing. "I do look forward to a new age for E'ronoh."

With that, the Mon Cala left Gella to join the dancing. Gella did not dance, and Kala had left a lingering cloud of worry. Gella took her barely touched drink and stepped out of the tavern. The night was surprisingly balmy, the stars covered by clouds.

The mining town was dark, except for the light coming from the rear of the *Amaryliss*. There, Axel Greylark lay on a creeperlift, half tucked under the belly of the barge. QN-1 hovered nearby, its chest panel working double time as a torch. Its dome turned at Gella's approach and trilled a greeting and dropped the hydroclamper onto Axel's stomach.

He let out a curse, then pushed out from under the vessel. He removed his goggles, a frown twisting his features. "Don't look at me like that, Gella Nattai."

She hadn't thought she was looking at him in a particular way. When she focused on the Force, she didn't find his usual walls. He was kinetic, all chaotic energy without release. He *wanted* to pick a fight.

"Why aren't you at the Remembrance?" she asked, sitting on the ground beside him.

"I told the mechanic I'd take over." Axel leaned forward on his knees. He plucked the drink from her hand and drank it. A familiar irritation returned. Though she supposed she *hadn't* wanted it. She just hadn't wanted to be wasteful.

"God, what is that?" he asked, pounding his chest. "It's terrible."

"That man's family wanted to thank you for bringing his body back. They think he might have been trying to run for help."

QN-1 nudged Axel's shoulder, its triangular chest plate pulsing faster, flickering colors before opening to hand him his flask. Axel took it, held it, but placed it back into his droid's compartment.

"Yeah, well," he muttered, "a lot of good it did him."

"I don't understand you." Gella shook her head. "The day I met you, you walked into a dead man's room without a care in the galaxy. You act and talk like you don't care. Why is it different now?"

He sighed deeply. "Some mysteries aren't to be unraveled, Jedi."

At that she couldn't help but laugh. "Most of my Order might disagree. Our lives are dedicated to the Force. Unraveling our understanding of it. Finding balance in it. What bigger mystery is there than the cosmic thing that binds us all together?"

Axel turned his dark gaze on her. The corner of his lips quirked. "Are you saying you want to unravel me?"

Gella didn't know how the conversation was getting away from her. But Axel Greylark was good at deflecting, and she wouldn't let herself be flustered. "I want to understand why you are the way you are."

"Do you do that to the others?"

They both glanced at the tavern, the musical sounds of strings and horns spilling out from the open doorway.

"Xiri and Phan-tu are clear to me. They have made a vow to their worlds, and to each other. They are driven by a legacy of war they never asked for."

"And you? Are you driven by your rank?" He needled her again. "Grand Master Jedi in the making."

"I'm driven," she said softly, "by a feeling I can't always explain, but one I trust wholly and truly. I'm driven by curiosity." Is that why she searched for him? Because she was curious about what made Axel Greylark do and say the things he did?

"You're like that story. That Jedi walking along the seam of the galaxy." Axel rested his forearms on his knees.

"And you? You can do anything. You can go *anywhere.* I almost envy that. The possibilities—"

"Why didn't you fight me for that parachute?" he asked, interrupting her with that stare again. "Were you that certain of your odds of surviving the jump?"

Gella closed her eyes for a moment and remembered stepping out into the sky. "The only certainty I had was that I had to protect you." Then she added, "All of you."

"That is maddening," he said, rubbing the exhaustion from his eyes.

"Why? Because you don't want to be friends with a *Jedi*?"

Gella felt his earlier riot of emotion flare as he glanced up at the sky. "No, I don't."

"Tell me."

Axel hesitated, but then relented. "When I was eighteen, I accompanied my father to the Cadavine sector on a diplomatic mission to Melida/Daan. My mother was on her campaign for the Senate. My father was a senator on Coruscant, and he was working with the Jedi to negotiate the release of the Daan's leader held captive by the Melida.

"It wasn't until the extraction that we realized it was a trap to show all of Daan's allies what could happen. We were trying to get back to the ship, and there was an explosion. We got separated. I was badly injured."

"Your scar," she said.

He nodded. "My father was trapped under the rubble, and I was trying to get him out. I could hear him, but the Melida were coming and we had to go. I wouldn't budge."

QN-1 flew to its master and nudged Axel on his chest. Axel rubbed the droid's dome as it emitted a calming blue glow. Gella understood what happened then.

"In order to save me, save all of us, and get back to the ship, the Jedi Knight had to drag me with her abilities." Axel cleared his throat, and Gella sensed that armor of his going back up. How much effort did he spend doing that every single day? "Then once again when I tried to turn the ship around. After that, I passed out from exhaustion. When I woke up, she told me it was the will of the Force. And then she just walked away and discussed a cargo manifest like nothing had happened. Like they hadn't made me leave my father behind to die."

Was that why he'd asked, *Why didn't you fight me for the parachute?* Had he thought she would have left him behind? Gella wanted to comfort him, but the words she would have said were the ones he hated. It was the will of the Force, the way it was the will of the Force that they would find each other sitting there together. Instead she placed her hand on top of his. He stared at it like he couldn't make sense of the gesture. Like he was expecting her to be defensive, not this.

"I have perspective now," he said. "You know, I saw that Jedi Knight again. She didn't even remember me. Why would she? What is one grieving boy in a galaxy full of them?"

"Everything," Gella found herself saying.

She felt it then, as he pulled his hand away from hers, the wound in his heart. That was the thing he was protecting.

"There you are!" Phan-tu shouted from the tavern. He glanced between Axel and Gella, like he couldn't make sense of them.

"I was just coming to give you dancing lessons," Axel said, his voice huskier than usual.

Something wet landed on her cheek. Gella looked up at the overcast night, saw the tendrils of lightning, felt the roar of thunder that shook the mountain. She inhaled the scent of petrichor.

The music slowed and the singing and laughter died down, as everyone in the tavern spilled onto the street and turned their faces up.

Rain had returned to E'ronoh.

Chapter Twenty-three

THE ROOK, E'RONOH

Enya Keen's first solo interrogation hadn't gone quite as she'd expected. When he'd been accused of murder aboard the *Paxion*, Viceroy Ferrol had confessed almost willingly to stealing from the Jedi. Now that he was under house arrest in the palace of the Rook, and accused of treason in light of his son's actions, his resolve was made of solid phrik. He denied all of it.

The first thing Enya had done was sit across from the ruddy-faced man. The room smelled of sticky sweat. Sunlight oversaturated the luxury suite that overlooked the prison tower and market.

With a flourish of her hands, she'd reached into the Force and shuttered the tall windows, then she'd waited and watched him sweat as the heat rose in the room. She'd seen Master Char-Ryl-Roy use the same technique when interrogating a baron from Dimok who'd managed to get his hands on two Force-sensitive orphaned children in an attempt to cultivate powerful army generals to fight his war with Ri:poblus. Master Roy had gotten him to confess in the first hour and uncovered where the children were being kept. The kids had been too old to be trained as Jedi but were taken to Jedha and adopted by other orders.

Enya hadn't had the same results.

Now she ran through the halls of the palace to give her report to the assembled summit. Bursting into the meeting hall, her boots almost slid on the marble floors. She took the empty seat between the Jedi Masters.

Princess Xiri, who'd arrived in the middle of the night with the others, sat forward. "Well?"

"If Viceroy Ferrol knows where his son is hiding, he won't reveal it," Enya assured them.

"Unacceptable!" Monarch A'lbaran clacked his cane on the floor. Chancellor Mollo's face-tentacles wriggled anxiously. Phan-tu Zenn started, while Axel Greylark, sitting to his left, studied the beds of his nails. "Can't you send a fully grown Jedi?"

"I assure you, Enya Keen is one of our brightest," Master Roy said, his usually calm voice clipped.

Enya frowned, anger and hurt flaring. What was she supposed to do, torture it out of the man like the Monarch wanted? Master Roy had already told him this was not the Jedi way.

"He told me other secrets," Enya said, trying to rein in her smugness. She knew she had their interest when they simply waited for her to continue. "He had been giving clearance codes to pirates in exchange for credits," she said, then grimaced as she remembered, "and also that he likes his toes—"

"Perhaps," Queen Adrialla interjected, "we should reconsider the Monarch's earlier offer."

Monarch A'lbaran huffed. "A saltsnake using the scorpion for its sting. The irony."

"Don't forget your war helped create soldiers like Rev Ferrol," the queen said haughtily. "*Children* of E'ronoh. This treaty isn't safe until he is brought to justice."

"We still don't know how many there are," Gella said. "Or if they had any involvement in the initial sabotage that started all of this."

"I agree," Master Creighton Sun said. He dragged a finger along the stubble on his jaw. He normally shaved every morning, but nearly two weeks of drawing up the treaty had taken a toll on everyone. "I sense something moving in the shadow."

"We should move up the wedding and relocate it solely to Eiram," Queen Adrialla suggested. Enya sensed the woman's crackle of nerves, but she was very good at keeping her emotions at bay.

"And cancel the public ceremony," the Monarch added.

Phan-tu shook his head, his voice more assertive than Enya remembered. "That's what they want, isn't it?"

"The whole reason to have ridiculous ceremonies," Xiri said, "is so that our worlds and the galaxy can celebrate *with* us. Anything else feels like hiding."

"It is true," Axel said. He flexed his fist, like he had a twinge at the center of his palm. He glanced at Gella. "Phan-tu and Xiri have them believing their union brought down the rains."

"We obviously cannot control the rain. Right?" Phan-tu also looked to Gella, who shook her head with amusement.

Xiri bit her bottom lip to keep from smiling. Why did the people of this planet try so hard not to smile? Enya couldn't wrap her head around it. Even the oldest, best, most serious Jedi she knew, like Master Yoda, *smiled* on occasion.

"Clearly," the Monarch said drily. "But I am pleased approval among the population has increased. Even still, the Ferrols have influence. Turning members of my household against us."

Enya had been disappointed to discover one of the servants who'd been so nice to her had then left and attacked her own princess with Rev Ferrol.

"That is why I agree with Queen Adrialla that we should move up and relocate the union ceremony," Xiri said, then held up a finger as the royals tried to speak over her. "We still need the Monarch's blessing for it to take place here."

Phan-tu turned to her, a resigned smile on his face. "Will you ever stop trying to make yourself bait?"

The princess let out a laugh before bringing her fingers to her lips. Even the Monarch was surprised to hear her perfectly normal outburst.

Enya sensed Xiri's defiant hope. Phan-tu Zenn's love for his world. When she moved on to Axel, she felt a burst of anxiety spike the moment he glanced at Gella, who in turn stared directly at Enya.

"E'ronoh has its traditions," Xiri said. "This is the first union we've had since my parents married *fifty* years ago."

"Fifty-two," the Monarch corrected softly.

"Fifty-two years," Xiri repeated. "The sooner Rev strikes, the better."

"If I may," Master Sun said, and stood. "We've examined the grid of the palace, and I believe there are two places Princess Xiri will be the most exposed. We can play that to our advantage."

"Then it's settled." Xiri stood, and Phan-tu rose and stood beside her.

"We will update the invitations," the Monarch said to Chancellor Mollo.

With the summit dismissed, Enya followed the Jedi cohort to Master Roy's chambers to debrief with Gella.

As they looped through the courtyard gardens and gem-encrusted fountains, Enya bumped into someone. The woman had the pale-gray skin and rose-gem eyes of a Kage. The Padawan was going to apologize, but the young woman narrowed her eyes angrily.

"Watch where you're going, *Jedi.*" The words dripped with contempt.

Enya knew it was a trying time for everyone, so she smiled anyway, then hurried up the palace stairs.

Abda hated weddings. Her brother's wedding had been the biggest their family ever threw. That had truly been the day she'd decided to leave Quarzite. Knowing that she'd be expected to do the same, to follow the same life as her parents. To know that no matter what she did, she would never be as good a fighter, as good an anything. Not the way her brother was. The galaxy always seemed to be harder on daughters.

But things had changed when Abda had taken the turbolift into the spaceport in orbit and hopped on the first transport scheduled to depart. She'd landed on a busy way station on Bardotta.

She'd wandered the way station alone and desperate, until she'd met Binnot. He bought her hot food, introduced her to the ways of the Path, and then the Mother. Her life changed.

She could not face the disappointment on the Mother's most beautiful face. There were dozens, hundreds of others lined up and waiting to take her place. Just as she'd done when Serrena returned wounded from her failed attempt to convince Eiram's queen to fullfill her bargain. Abda had meant to treat the wound, but she'd had a revelation. The Force provided. Unbeknownst to Serrena, Abda had used a single drop of the poison Binnot had given her. It was over quickly.

Serrena had failed the Mother for the last time. Now Abda had something she hadn't had before. The Mother's love.

As the Monarch's blessing got under way, Abda slipped through the crowds in her servant's uniform. The gray material was too soft on her skin. *Indulgent.* The princess talked of the beings of E'ronoh needing to witness her dedication to them, but all Abda saw was indulgence.

In the central courtyard, under the clear cerulean sky, Princess Xiri sat on a dais wearing a sheer gold dress with a ruby crown perched on her royal head. Icy resentment filled Abda's heart. None of this would be happening if the Monarch's daughter had just boarded the sabotaged starfighter. Instead, she received adoration for her part in ending the so-called Forever War.

E'ronoh's citizens lined up to give the princess a blessing, hundreds of excited revelers stretching out of the palace, into the circular streets of the city and out onto the canyon road. Every guard in the palace watched the line for danger. Jedi perched on the roof of the palace, and another remained sentry beside the princess keenly watching as each being stepped onto the dais, and let the future Monarch place a cube of food into their mouth. It was a consecration, they said.

For a moment, Abda wondered if the princess's gifts were a thinly veiled bribe. She fed them a morsel, and her people returned it with a blessing. But the Path of the Open Hand had taught Abda that gifts should not carry a burden. This *consecration* of the future Monarch felt little more than a ritual to give their lives meaning when they didn't understand that there was something greater, something *worthy* of devotion. Real loyalty didn't require gifts. It required courage.

As she adjusted a tray laden with drinks for the onlookers, she walked the perimeter of the courtyard until every glass had been snatched up. She returned to the palace kitchens where the Monarch's chef shouted orders and other servants ran in and out. As the hours slipped past, Abda prepared. She allowed herself to check once, just once, that the cylinder Binnot had given her was in her apron pocket.

Her heart raced like a subtram and when she turned around, someone bumped into her and she sent the tray of drinks flying. With uncanny reflexes, he managed to save one before the rest shattered.

Every guard turned to them, and she shrank into herself. All the courage she'd summoned was replaced with fear.

"Apologies, darling," said the man dressed in a long black cape. His cheeks were flushed with drink. His hooded eyes settled on Phan-tu Zenn.

"Axel!" the Eirami heir hissed.

"I apologized," the tipsy man whined.

Pale-green eyes settled on Abda. She lowered her head and apologized. "It's all right everyone, false alarm."

Mouth dry, Abda returned to the kitchen for another three trays of drinks.

When the ceremony was over, the princess gave the very last bites of food to the Monarch, and then to her betrothed.

The desert night shielded her as she waited for the halls to empty, the celebration to move into the streets, and for the princess to return to her bedroom.

She shoved her tray into the kitchens and returned to the servants' quarters. There, she crept into the laundry lift and opened the latch. She pressed a hand on either side of the wall and climbed up, up, up.

Her arms burned and trembled, but the closer she got to the princess's rooms, the more a thrilling warmth spread through her. Abda was certain that every one of her actions was in service of something greater. Queen Adrialla had reneged on her word to the Mother and needed to be reminded of that cost. When the queen came to her senses, and when the Mother was satisfied, Abda could rest and journey at her side, as they traveled far away on the *Gaze Electric*.

When she reached the right level, she listened for voices, but the princess was alone. Abda opened the hatch and landed like a whisper. She stepped past the ceremonial clothes and into the dark bedroom.

Abda reached into the inner pocket of her apron for the glowing cylinder.

But there was nothing there. Impossible. She'd had it the whole night. She'd checked just before—

The shadow on the bed moved, sheets rustling. Abda scrambled back as a yellow lightsaber illuminated the dark.

Chapter Twenty-four

THE ROOK, E'RONOH

"Hello, Chaos," the Mother said into the hololink.

She made herself comfortable in the command chair of the *Gaze Electric*. Running her fingers along the smooth armrests, she shut her eyes and smiled. This would do.

"Mother," he said.

The live comms cut out, but he'd said enough. She knew that tone of voice and had been far too used to it lately. Something had gone wrong. "Where are you?"

"The market." The image cut in and out. "Perhaps this is lost. The wedding is still happening. The Jedi are set to arrive in droves. The Republic, too."

"It seems my invitation was lost in hyperspace," she purred, gripping the armrests and leaning forward. With him, she let the hood of her cloak fall and her hair spill around her shoulders.

"Abda was captured. I can break her out. Get her back to Binnot."

"No." The Mother rested her delicate chin on the top of her wrist. "A pity. I had high hopes for her. It falls on you now."

He stared at her intently. It was his dark stare that had drawn him to her so long ago. Angry, defiant, but lost, too. "I don't think you understand. The heirs are irritatingly committed to this union. The civil unrest is bringing Eiram and E'ronoh closer together."

"E'ronoh and Eiram are *nothing*," she said. "Queen Adrialla, on the other hand. I owe her a kindness. She will understand what comes of betraying her word to me. She chose to align herself with the Jedi. They are teeming all over this sector and interrupting our plans."

He chuckled, that defiant smirk returning like lightning. "Our plans, is it?"

"I know what's going on," she said.

He scowled, and glanced away. "You do?"

"You're angry with me."

He shook his head. "No."

The Mother smiled into the holo. "I kept you waiting for too long, but I have never forgotten you. No one is ever going to let you feed your chaos heart."

What were promises in the grand scheme of the galaxy but tying someone's hopes around her little finger?

"Maybe I want to get things my own way," he said.

"And how has that worked for you before?" When he didn't answer, she relaxed back into her seat. "Get rid of Abda. She's become a loose end. Let these planets choose their peace, for as long as it will last them. While the Jedi are preoccupied, find that poison, and come home."

"What are you going to use it for?" he asked.

He'd never truly questioned her before, but she did not let her smile falter. "I'm going to use it for us. For the safety of the Path." But she knew he was not *exactly* like her Children. He did not need the comfort or assurance that the Force would be freed. Perhaps that was why she added, "And so that I can finalize the *Gaze Electric* without being vulnerable to those who seek to hurt me. Hurt us. Can I count on you?"

He wavered, then cleared his throat. "Yes."

"As for the Jedi Knight you've told me so much about, I'm sure you can manage something."

He was silent for a beat, then said, "I'll figure it out."

"You aren't having doubts, are you?"

"I said I'll figure it out, Mother."

"Of course. I know I can always count on you, Chaos," she said. "My Axel Greylark."

That night, Gella found Master Sun in the gardens of the palace, silvered in moonlight. Incandescent sparkflies drifted in the cool breeze. At the ledge of the reflecting pool, the Jedi meditated.

Sensing her presence, he opened his eyes. "Sleep eludes us all this night."

With admirable control, Master Sun lowered himself back to the garden floor. He reached for his robe and pulled it over his nightwear.

Gella had woken to restless memories of the last several weeks, from the moment they'd entered Eiram-E'ronoh space, to the long tour into the desert and back again. None of it revealed an answer to the true identity of the young Kage woman in the prison, or why she'd been found in Xiri's room, weaponless.

"My thoughts are unsettled, master," Gella admitted.

The older Jedi turned to the reflective pool. Marble tiles and gemstones from E'ronoh's quarries and mines created concentric patterns. A breeze disturbed the surface of the water.

"I fear we are yet operating in the shadows," he said gravely, "obscured by every choice being made in the light."

"The more I try to unravel, the less I seem to make sense of," she said. "Xiri thinks that the Children of E'ronoh, the sabotage, all of it was orchestrated by the Ferrols. Rev had access to the military hangar bay. It accounts for the beacon containing E'ronoh dust. He confessed to worse. So why send a weaponless assassin to Xiri's room?"

Master Sun looked up. She could feel him sensing for threats, but he seemed to find none. "Perhaps now that she's been in holding for a few hours, the Kage is ready to talk."

"I don't doubt your skill, Master Sun," Gella told him. "But she is protecting someone."

Still, they made their way up the spiral stone steps of the tower. Up there, the wind whistled.

"I was going to mention in the morning," Master Sun told her. "The Council is sending several Jedi to help with the security detail on Eiram. Your short time with the heirs has been impressive, and by all accounts, after the wedding, you can return to Coruscant and continue your training."

"Really?" The news should have thrilled her, but a dull ache nestled between her ribs.

"Unless you feel you are called here."

The choice was hers. But as they approached the top of the prison tower, both Jedi were on alert. The only problem was that instead of sensing danger, they sensed nothing at all.

The Force would provide.

Abda repeated the refrain again and again. She sat at the center of the cell and stared out the rectangle cut into the ceiling. A sliver of the moon, a slash of night, just visible. She traced and retraced her steps. She'd been so careful. *So* very careful.

Binnot would come for her. He'd get her out. She would hate the smug look on his face when he'd remind her of her failure. The Mother would not be pleased. At least she hadn't said a single word to the Jedi. Her mind and her heart were impenetrable because they belonged to someone else. A greater being, and a greater purpose.

As the wind howled through the lone gap in the wall, Abda shut her eyes. She heard a soft hiss, like a sigh. It was in the dark with her. Abda tried to duck, to kick, but an arm hooked around her throat.

"*Shh shh shh,* you tried your best," he whispered, low and familiar. "But the Mother needs better than your best."

Abda's body tried to remember old training with her brother and parents. She threw her arm back, but she couldn't breathe. Couldn't beg for another chance as she heard the release of the injection. The thin needle pricked the side of her throat and sent the poison coursing through her bloodstream with every beat of her failing heart.

He let her go, but her airway swelled shut. Blisters bubbled along her collarbone, and even as her vision darkened, she crawled on her belly to the door. Her mind was an onslaught of images, one after the other—her parents. Did they even remember they'd had a daughter once? The steep plains of Dalna. Chasing scorpions in the desert. What had it all been worth?

When the heat in her veins subsided, the image behind her eyelids surprised her. It had been years, but the violet caves of Quarzite finally beckoned her home.

Phan-tu Zenn needed to see the body. He walked to the morgue, even though his entire body screamed at him to run. If the reports were true, then he needed to see for himself. Guards watched him pass, their amber eyes trailing after him like they saw something they needed to crush under steel-toed boots.

The young Eirami prince only smiled. He had what mattered, in the end. Xiri's trust. Now if only he could hold on to it. He couldn't afford to be reckless. Not when they were so close to a major event in their shared planets' histories.

When he arrived at the marbled room in the lower levels of the Rook's palace, he was startled to see there were people there. Master Char-Ryl-Roy, Gella Nattai, Axel Greylark, and Xiri were already present.

The way Xiri's eyes brightened when she saw him twisted something in him. She'd looked at him with fear, suspicion, a dash of murder. Later hope. Perhaps one day, when things were settled, when they got to know each other the way his mothers knew each other, the way someone can know another by touch and scent and sound—she might look at him with love.

"We just sent the little Padawan to fetch you," Axel said.

The Jedi Master, whose bald oval cranium barely cleared the low ceiling, glanced at Axel with disapproval. Greylark was an acquired taste, like that stinger drink from the U'ronoh mines. But he couldn't imagine having survived the journey without him or Gella. It was strange how for several weeks it had just been the four of them for long stretches of time. Once back in the capital, he'd barely seen any of them, even Xiri.

"I stopped by the market," Phan-tu said. "But I heard the autopsy is complete. What have you found?"

As he made his way deeper into the sterile cold room, though, he could see for himself. Her body had been covered for privacy, but the deadly gray pallor of the Kage's body was marked with an undeniable truth. Blisters peppered her skin like a pox, and at the side of her neck was a clear puncture mark. From its center stretched thin tendrils of raised pearlescent scars.

Master Roy shook his head grimly. "In all my years I've never encountered something like this. Though I have seen cases of Dexstri Skin Pox that leave behind lumps on the skin."

"Isn't that contractable by meat?" Gella asked.

Phan-tu pressed his own hand to his stomach. The chances that he was going to be sick were rising.

"Yes. And this poor girl's stomach contents were nothing but bile and undigested scorpion shells."

Xiri reached down to pull the cover over the Kage's face. They'd all had enough. "Did anyone know her name?"

"None of the servants or the majordomo," Gella said.

"They wouldn't be able to tell you the names of the living, and poison isn't the E'ronoh way, which, as much as I hate to admit it, rules out the Ferrols." Xiri turned curious amber eyes to the Jedi Master. "And there was no weapon found?"

Gella shook her head. "Master Sun is still investigating the cell, but there was nothing when we arrived. Only this." The Jedi Knight picked up a small metal tray. On top of it was a round disk made of some sort of black alloy.

"Aren't the Kage warriors?" Xiri asked. "Perhaps she's a bounty hunter."

"That is not a bounty puck," Axel said matter-of-factly. "That's an invitation."

"To what?" Gella asked. When she turned the disk between her fingers, there were no markings on it.

Axel shrugged, hesitating, likely because of Master Roy's presence. "A sort of game, really."

Phan-tu snapped his fingers to recall his conversation with Axel. "Is it that championship you lost a bunch of credits at?"

The Coruscant Prince looked like he was going to jump over the dead girl on the table and throttle him. "Do you even know how to keep a secret?"

He did, actually. That's why he needed to get the Jedi away, for a moment.

"I would need a skilled fighter," Axel said, his somber stare falling on Gella, then Master Sun. "Can you spare your best Jedi Knight?"

Master Roy tugged at his beard. "We are needed on Eiram to receive the arriving Jedi, but that depends on her. Gella, have you decided to stay?"

It was news that she might have decided to *go,* especially by the flash of hurt on Axel's and Xiri's faces.

"I can accompany Mister Greylark, yes," Gella said.

"But I should warn you." Axel tented his fingers. "It is a very bad idea."

Chapter Twenty-five

Nestled in the copilot's chair of the *Eventide,* Gella Nattai stared at the sea of stars ahead. It was her second time aboard Axel Greylark's ship, though he was decidedly more used to its controls.

"You seem troubled, Jedi," Axel said. Was it progress that he did not say *Jedi* with his usual derision?

Gella didn't like that he could see it in her. That he was perhaps paying too close attention. It bothered her for reasons she could not meditate on. Not until the treaty was signed and until Phan-tu and Xiri were wed, and their threats eliminated. That was why, when Master Roy had asked if she was going to stay, she'd agreed to investigate their lead with Axel.

"Someone was murdered while we slept," she said.

"Do you lament the death of an assassin?" he asked flatly.

"Death is inevitable. I lament the circumstance."

She watched his unflinching, strong profile as he steered the ship. She realized they hadn't been together since the night it rained on U'ronoh, and since his confessions, he'd smiled her way less often.

Perhaps he regretted sharing his wounds. Or perhaps, she hadn't given him the reaction he'd wanted.

"Do you know what I've learned, Jedi Nattai?"

She thought this would be amusing. "Please, do share."

"I have learned that you have three serious faces," Axel said, holding up one finger at a time.

She crossed her arms over her chest. "Go on."

"The first is *Oh, no, Axel, how could you possibly talk without thinking?* Then there's your Jedi fighting face. And finally, the one you've had this entire ride to the Hesperys."

"And what's that?"

"The burden-of-the-galaxy face."

Gella grinned despite herself. "It isn't a burden, Axel."

"Then what is it?"

She waited for his derision. She waited for the cocky smile, the spark in his eyes, but there was only Axel Greylark, or a version of him, trying to understand her. If they weren't sailing straight for a carnival stationed on a dead asteroid, if they had more time, then perhaps she'd like to talk to him all day.

"It is a choice," she said.

"Is it?" he asked. "I swear I'm not—being myself—but if it's all you've ever known, then wouldn't you *have* to feel that way?"

"I've spent my entire life trying to understand my power and my place in the galaxy." She brushed her fingers along the hilts of her lightsabers. "Youngling, Padawan, Jedi Knight. Master. Every ascension brings us closer to understanding the Force and fulfilling our vow. I was so eager to be the ideal Jedi, get to the next step." She met the intensity in his eyes with her own. "Being here is making me realize I'm still listening to the Force."

He blinked first, pushing the controls of the ship forward. "Right. The Force. And what is it saying?"

"The galaxy is not my burden, Axel. I choose it."

"That's the difference between us, I suppose," he said softly.

Could he not see that his burden was the bruise in his heart? Gella turned to dig at his response. But he focused on the viewport, on the bit of pale-gray asteroid growing in size as they approached.

"How did you first find this place?" she asked.

She sensed it then, a pressure against his emotional wall. His hesitation, but something wanting to emerge like a sapling working its way through cracks in the side of a mountain. "The year after my father died, I said terrible things to my mother. She, in turn, sent me on a grand tour of the galaxy to gain *perspective.*"

Gella had only ever heard of the galactic pleasure trips embarked on by wealthy royals and children of politicians. Drunken galas on exotic beaches and debauchery in sacred ruins. It felt like the opposite of what she'd wanted to do when she'd first joined the Pathfinder team to Orvax.

"Instead of joining the other senators' kids, I took Quin and my father's ship and went off on my own." He brushed his fingers across the console. "Made it as far as I could and wound up on a little planet called Skye, not far from here, actually. Do you know, it is amazing how quickly you can lose a fortune without actually trying?"

"No," she said, as Jedi didn't *have* fortunes.

"Chancellor Greylark wanted to teach me a lesson and cut me off. But I found work."

Curious, she asked, "Doing what?"

"Hmm," he mused. "Freelance shipping redistributor."

Gella laughed. "That's a lot of words when you can just say smuggler."

"Call it what you like," he said. "I'd get by, make a fortune, lose it the next day. Get bloodied up in a cantina pit brawl, then go back to Coruscant. Be a 'Greylark' in society. Then when it got to be too much I'd do it all over again."

"What do you mean by too much?" she asked.

"I think you're only allowed to be broken for so long before even the people you love start to wish you'd get over it. At least, that's what it was like being the chancellor's son. Anyway, I have a contact who might be able to identify our mystery Kage."

As they approached the Hesperys station nestled on the surface of a dead asteroid drifting in the Dalnan sector, all Gella could make out was a riot of multicolored lights beneath an environment shield. Axel gave the code phrase on their black invitation disk to the traffic control tower, and the shield opened to let them through. They docked the *Eventide* on a crowded launch pad.

"This is not what I imagined when you called this place a carnival," Gella said, keeping a tight grip on the loops of her holsters.

A group of Sullustans loaded cages of puffer pigs onto an Orlean starcab. A Hutt, not fully grown judging by their size, snaked between disorderly rows of shuttles, racing pods, and salvage ships. A single, wide street shot straight down the center of the station and was lined by dank buildings.

"The Hesperys is everything you want it to be," Axel said, leading the way with a vulpine smile, QN-1 flashing an array of lights at his shoulder.

Axel was different here than on E'ronoh. Electric, like he fed off the cacophony, the feast of sparks igniting the air. The fireworks seemed to come from a tent that advertised droid-versus-gundark wrestling. A large orange Twi'lek collected entry fees at a blurrg rodeo, the stench of the muddy grounds mingling with that of the ronto roaster across the street.

"I've never seen anything like it," she marveled.

Axel gave a surprised laugh at her side. "I assumed you would hate it."

There were some highly illicit things—a woman selling spice from the back of her neon-blue speeder. A Wookiee with a shock of green running down the center of his head had an open case of what looked like unsanctioned blaster cannons.

Gella stopped in front of a boxy building with a red pulsing light. She was trying to peer inside the window when a muscular humanoid male with blue skin stepped outside. He leaned against the threshold and smiled at her.

"Not tonight, darling," Axel said, yanking Gella away by the sleeve of her robe and hurrying three doors down. "Here we are. The Rusty Rancor."

The building was painted black, newer than most on the station. A pink holographic rancor blinked over the door.

Axel did a double take at Gella and brushed a lock of her hair back, then adjusted the buckle of his azure-blue cape. He leaned in and whispered at her ear, "Ney Madiine doesn't like strangers, so please just let me do the talking."

She wanted to argue, but this wasn't her world. She inhaled the recycled, musty air and decided she would have to follow his lead.

Inside, they were swallowed by the dark. The only source of light was a raised fighting ring. The crowd pressed in tight, shouting for blood and violence. The fighters, two fish-faced Patrolians, clawed at each other across a stage made of reinforced glass. Within the fighting ring's circumference, rectangular metal slats were suspended in scattered rows. The fighters used them like stepping-stones or ladders to climb up higher. When one Patrolian reached the top, the slat under his feet malfunctioned, and he flailed as he fell to the glass stage two stories below. A hatch opened and the loser fell under, while the winner leapt across the ring in victory.

"Come on!" Axel shouted over the frenzy.

He waltzed right past the Trandoshan bouncer. The lizard-faced being snarled at them before doing a double take at Axel and pointing a claw to a door on the other side of the room. The soles of Gella's boots stuck to the surface with every step. She sniffed at the metallic scent of blood and spilled grog.

Axel glanced back once, as if to see if she was still there, before ascending two flights of stairs and heading down a narrow hall. Her senses twitched, but how could she pinpoint the danger in a fighting hall full of beings chanting, "Tear 'im to shreds! Bite his head off!"

"Axel," she said as a warning.

He shot her an overconfident wink.

When they reached the end of the hall, a security guard punched open the door to an office. An entire wall was made of glass, to better see the pit below. An older Theelin woman looked up from her table lined with datapads, holoprojectors, bounty pucks, and what looked like stacks of currency from several worlds. Ney Madiine, the Jedi Knight presumed, had pink skin and green hair pulled so tight, it seemed to smooth out the fine wrinkles of her face. She had a scar that went down from her lip to her clavicle, and fingers dotted with jeweled rings.

"Axel Greylark," she crooned, "as I live and breathe."

He walked around her desk and into her outstretched arms. Gella stayed put in front of the woman's desk, and glanced away as Ney kissed Axel's cheek for far too long.

"Ney, my darling," he said, peeling himself out of her grip.

"This is a surprise." Ney finally turned to Gella, her gem eyes raking down Gella's robe, lightsabers, and boots. "And what did you bring?"

"Jedi Knight Gella Nattai, meet Ney Madiine."

Gella tipped her head as the woman's tooka-cat grin widened. The Jedi tried to reach into the Force to feel the woman's intentions but sensed only excitement, and it was all targeted at Axel.

Axel held up the invitation they'd found on the dead Kage and placed it on Ney's table. "I need a favor."

"You know the rules." Ney studied her rings. "My champion against yours."

"*Axel,*" Gella gritted through her teeth. What champion? She looked down at the floor and stepped aside in case there was a trapdoor.

He simply waved away any of her concern, pressing a palm against her lower back and steering her away from Ney's earshot, and against the glass wall overlooking the pit. "It's just a little thing I forgot to mention. Winning a round's the only way she grants favors."

"*Forgot* to mention?" She grabbed him by the buckle of his cape and pulled him closer, propelled by a burst of anger.

His eyes flickered to the snarl of her lips, and he said, "Just know I have every bit of faith in you."

Warm, musty air filled the office as the glass wall at their side opened and a metal slat appeared, like a plank on a sail barge.

Gella didn't get another word in as Axel shoved her onto the plank. She stretched out her arms and pulled at the Force to regain equilibrium. What had she expected from Axel Greylark? She could see him through the office wall as he returned to negotiate with Ney. *Fine.* She'd do her part if he did his.

As the metal slats reset themselves two stories in the air over the fighting ring, the spectators down below went wild. She heard the telltale crackle of a lightsaber being ignited.

Across the ring was another Jedi, raising a double-bladed lightsaber straight at her heart.

Chapter Twenty-six

HESPERYS STATION

The Pa'lowick descended from the ceiling on a spinning mirrored ball affixed to a metal rod. She cleared her throat and spoke into a slender microphone. It was the only time since Gella Nattai had stepped into the Rusty Rancor that the crowd down below was quiet. She took that opportunity to prepare herself for the match, clearing her thoughts of her anger at Axel Greylark.

"Fiends and friends!" the Pa'lowick shouted in a nasal soprano. "Welcome back to the Rusty Rancor! I'm Goldy Bex, the master of ceremonies of your most favorite place aboard the Hesperys Station, for a one-of-a-kind *rrrrumble.* Your champions have been chosen!"

Goldy spun on the mirrored ball, the contraption easing her through the levels of the glowing light slats. She winked a beady little eye at Gella. "Please give it up for a Jedi Knight all the way from the mystical land of Jedha—Jellie Nattal!"

Jellie Nattal? Mystical land? Gella had never felt more insulted at being treated like a spectacle. Her opponent laughed along with the crowd. She sized him up. He was twice as big as she, muscles nearly straining from Jedi robes made of green velvet that matched the double blades of his lightsaber. A band of neon, geometric tattoo mods decorated the polished brown skin of his throat.

Goldy Bex twirled, egging on the spectators. "And it wouldn't be your *lucky* night without the reigning champion. With ninety-nine wins, he is the Wrath of the Jedi, and king of my heart—Dario Melek!"

Dario blew a kiss at the Pa'lowick for good measure. The crowd gave a deafening roar.

Gella knew something was wrong. Was he *undercover* here? She couldn't think of any Jedi in the Order who would use their abilities in the Force like this. Perhaps that's why Axel hadn't told her the entirety of his plan. She wouldn't have agreed. Would she?

And yet here she was, unholstering her lightstabers to defend herself.

"Remember! First opponent to knock the other onto the ring floor wins! Will it be Dario's one hundredth victory?" Screams of adoration. "Or will Jellie make her stand?" Light clapping.

Gella fumed as she ignited her twin blades. The crowd multiplied until they were nothing but arms, horns, heads, and flashes of ravenous mouths shouting for the fight to begin. Gella had seen holos of piiraya fish acting the same way when they sensed a drop of blood in the water. Her heartbeat hammered in her ears, the staccato rhythm disparate from the electronic music thundering all around.

A buzzer rang, and Gella felt it reverberate through her as she sank into her fighting stance, though the metal at her feet did not give her much room to sink deep.

She wanted to look back, to see if Axel was at the glass office wall. She didn't.

Dario lunged first, skipping across the air like he'd memorized every place the light slats would move. Gella stood her ground, lightsabers forward. If it had been her, she would have used the Force to guide her into a jump.

When he was centimeters from her, she parried his blow. Dario's green blades crackled against her violet ones, and she saw the way his arms trembled. He looked at the moonstone hilts, and his brows drew together in worry. Something was wrong. The feeling nudged hard against Gella's senses as she bore her blades against his and pushed.

Dario staggered back, but because he seemed to know which of the fighting ring's metal slats could malfunction, he knew where to fall. Catching himself on a ledge, he simply *waited* another second for the opportunity to regain his footing.

Gella landed in front of him in a single jump.

"Impressive," he growled in a booming voice. "But I am the only true Jedi on this station."

He twirled the shaft in one hand with expert movements. It must have taken great practice to guide their motion, especially when the man was *no* Jedi.

"You are no Jedi I know," she said, anger building. "Where did you steal that lightsaber?"

"Where did you steal *yours*?" Dario glanced around, still holding his blades up, and lowered his voice, changing his tenor entirely. "Wait, is this part of your bit?"

Gella realized all at once. Not only was he not a Jedi, but he had no connection to the Force. He was a grifter, using a sacred weapon that had once belonged to another.

She couldn't fight a man with such a disadvantage, but he resumed his character. This *Wrath of the Jedi.* This showman making a mockery of everything she believed in.

"I *am* a Jedi." Gella holstered one of her blades. Then she reached out into the Force and seized the lightstaff right out of his hands. He gasped, then looked her up and down.

"Maybe you're the real deal." Dario looked up in the direction of Ney Madiine's office. His face twisted into something scared, then mean, like whatever was up there was scarier than Gella ever would be to him. "But you're not taking this win from me."

He screamed as he hurled himself at Gella. She felt him a little too late to move out of the way of his momentum. She grabbed onto his slippery robes, and they fell together, slamming into the glass floor with a painful thud. Pushing herself up, she wasn't sure if the liquid on the floor was her blood or other secretions. But that wasn't her biggest worry.

The Trandoshan bouncer and a few others shoved their way through the dispersing crowd.

"Too late," Dario said as he sat up. "Ney does not like her shows interrupted."

She held the stolen lightstaff in her fist, and felt the hum of its crystal within. She'd get it back. She was sure of that. First, she threw it back. "Defend yourself. We're leaving this place."

But as a magnetic force ripped her blades from her hands, and the hatch of the floor snapped open, Gella knew she wasn't going anywhere.

Moments before Gella Nattai fell into the underground level of the Rusty Rancor, Axel Greylark was talking his way into getting what he wanted.

"My, my, Axel Greylark." Ney rested her sharp chin on her folded hands. "I'm jealous. I've never seen you smitten before."

"Don't be *ridiculous.*" He ran a palm down his torso. He did his best not to turn left and peek at the fighting ring. Gella could handle herself. She'd survived a shuttle falling out of the sky, she'd survive this without him. "The Jedi is a means to an end, nothing more."

"I'll never understand why you run back to the Path." Ney raised her brows. When he didn't answer, she said, "My sweet, whatever you're doing, it is not going to turn out how you think it will. You're better off coming to work for me again. You barely lasted a year back on Coruscant before winding up right back here in this chair."

"Ney. My magnanimous Theelin rose. Level with me. Can you dig something up on Viceroy Ferrol?"

She arched a brow. "What kind of something?"

He leaned forward. "The kind you don't come back from. You know you owe me."

"You're no fun anymore," she said, clicking her tongue. "It's straight to business. And you're right. I never took care of you for bribing that Chandrilan senator for me. Even if you broke his daughter's heart."

Axel felt a twinge of guilt, but then buried it. The senator had been lobbying for an Outer Rim police force that would destroy places like the Hesperys. And even if he hadn't been, why did he need a reason? Everyone in the galaxy was a means to an end, and the end was his chaos.

Ney grinned at her mischief. "And now I will do you a favor."

Axel frowned. "What do you mean?"

"This popped up earlier today on my feeds." She flicked to a holo of his face. A bounty had been placed on him by *Raik.* "That's not a very flattering angle."

"All my angles are flattering." Axel ground the back of his teeth. It was definitely time for him to go. "Is the favor that you're going to let me out of here without collecting it yourself?"

"You're more useful to me alive," she said. "But I will give you a head start."

Ney slid a datacard across the table and he pocketed it before she changed her mind and made him crawl for it. Wouldn't be the first time. As he swallowed the dryness in his throat, he finally turned to the fighting ring.

Gella and Ney's "Jedi" champion had fallen off the Theelin's aerial playground. As her lightsabers were snatched by the magnetic clamp on the stage, the floor latched open and she plummeted into the cellars.

"You should see your face, Axel," Ney teased him. "Thank you for bringing her. She will make a fine champion. Once we break her."

Axel flashed a smile. That's where Ney was wrong. He knew the Jedi Knight well enough now to know that a place like the Rusty

Rancor wouldn't break her. In his haughtiest voice, he said, "I'm bored now, I must be getting back."

"Don't forget your head start," Ney reminded him as he made his way out of her office.

Opposite Axel, one of the Theelin's security detail was hurrying to his boss. In his hands were three lightsaber hilts to be stored in between fights. Axel drew his blaster and shot the human man in his chest. Because of his surprise, he rocked back and cracked his head as he fell.

Axel holstered his blaster pistol and bent down to gather the lightsabers. The lightstaff, he tucked into the hook of his holster. Gella's twin hilts, he held for a moment. He'd seen her fight half a dozen soldiers with them. Glide across stalagmites like she was walking on air. He squeezed his fists to stop them from shaking, and slid the twin hilts into his cape pockets, hurrying out of the corridor before someone noticed the body.

Retracing their steps from when they first arrived, Axel took advantage of the dispersing crowds, furious that the last match was stalled. The little Pa'lowick sang into the microphone during the slight intermission, but there was too much confusion.

On his way out, QN-1 stopped him, trilling obscenities.

"Where did you learn how to say that?" Axel asked, affronted. "And we have to go. There's a bounty on my neck, and the minute I'm gone, my mother will throw you into the Coruscant recycler."

Quin's triangular panel pulsed red, as it did when the droid was angry or afraid.

Axel kept walking. He knew he should just *keep* walking. But with every step out of the Rusty Rancor, he found it became harder to breathe. He got down on one knee, pressing his palm to the place over his heart. He rubbed the place there. He had a small scar from the day his father had been buried in the rubble of Melida/Daan. It didn't hurt. Not anymore. Not physically. But he touched it because it was a reminder, years later, that his father had been real. He wasn't a memorial statue in a Coruscant park, and he wasn't a tactless painting in his mother's office.

Quin tried to stop him again, bumping his dome hard against Axel. This time, the little droid's light pulsed violet like Gella's lightsabers. Gella, whom he was supposed to leave behind. Gella, who was supposed to mean nothing. Gella, who looked at him with a kind of patience he had never felt or been given.

Axel stopped walking. Bodies pushed against him in the throngs of revelers. He looked back. He had his story. *Gella fought and lost.*

It was the way of the Force.

It was the way of the Force.

As soon as the thought burst into his mind, he whirled around and let out an exasperated scream. He knew the Rusty Rancor's levels and doors. He pushed through the angry crowds waiting for the next match. There was an elevator on the other side of the fighting ring, but he'd never get there in time.

Squished right against a three-eyed Gran, Axel grabbed the being's holstered blaster pistol and shot it into the air, before dropping it. Screams ripped through the room, the crowd churning like a wave. He coasted through the mob, then repeated the act, this time lifting a blaster from a panicked Aqualish. With the security detail running to the areas where the shots rang from, Axel and Quin slipped through the back door leading to the sublevel. Bright-white cells lined the row housing Ney's prized fighters. Some were willing permanent houseguests, and some, like Dario, who had a gambling ledger to pay off, were chipping away at what they owed the Theelin.

Axel walked past Gella's cell. Through the reinforced glass smudged with her fingerprints, he watched surprise bloom across her face. It was quickly followed by anger as he withdrew one of her lightsabers from his pocket.

He'd call it payback for the time she took the *Eventide* for a joyride.

It was a good thing he always knew what button to press. As the purple light of Gella's lightsaber elongated, Quin flew out of the way before it could get cleaved in half.

"Sorry!"

Gella punched at the glass. Axel only stared at the sword in his hand. He'd never actually held a Jedi's weapon before, not that he'd ever had the opportunity. It was disturbingly intimate. The coolness of the hilt in his palm, the very weight of it. The whole thing felt like an illusion, like he shouldn't need to grasp it with both of his hands to bear it. That's exactly what he did as he drove the violet blade into the glass and cut a way out.

In the other cells, the champions banged against the glass. "Get us out of here!" But he concentrated, struggled to cut a door because he kept flicking his gaze to her. To the way she bounced back and forth on her heels as if she was getting ready to burst through the doorway.

When he was done, Gella ducked out of the cell. She swallowed, the bottom pout of her lip trembling. He knew when someone was getting ready to yell.

Instead, Gella Nattai whispered, "Thank you, Axel. You could have left without me."

He was going to. He *should* have. He was supposed to. "Quin wouldn't let me live it down. Let's go."

"Wait!" Gella grabbed a fistful of his tunic, then turned off the lightsaber and holstered it. "The others."

"We have to go, Gella," he repeated. There was a bounty on his head. There was no time for this. Was there? Perhaps once, when he'd been a boy, when his father had been alive, when he'd been primed to lead. Perhaps then his first thought would have been to rescue them all, instead of just one person.

As she found the override lever that opened all the doors, Axel's thoughts spiraled. But Gella wasn't like him. She wasn't like anyone he'd ever come across in the cosmos. She chose the galaxy and he chose himself. She chose the path of a peacekeeper and he chose a different way. She was justice and he was chaos. The thought made him want to run.

A dozen champions spilled out of the cells. Some remained behind. He watched Gella exchange a look with "the Wrath of the Jedi." Then, together, Axel and Gella shot out of the belly of the Rusty Rancor and raced back to the *Eventide*.

Axel breathed hard as he punched in the flight sequence. Gella strapped into the seat beside him. He couldn't look at her. Not after what he'd almost done.

"Well?" she asked. "What did you find?"

He pulled himself together, piece by piece. He reached into his pocket for the datacard Ney provided. "Everything the Monarch needs to get rid of Ferrol."

Chapter Twenty-seven

ERASMUS CAPITAL CITY, EIRAM

The docking bay in Erasmus Capital City was situated on the south end of the coast. The city's transparent shield dome opened above that sector to let in ship after ship arriving for the wedding of Phan-tu Zenn and Xiri A'lbaran. Senators and royal households had started arriving the night before, and they hadn't stopped. As Chancellor Mollo had predicted, the galaxy was curious about the fate of E'ronoh and Eiram's promise.

From there, all the way to Coruscant, tabloids created their own narratives, spinning the couple into legend. A peaceful union became a marriage of convenience became star-crossed lovers became fate—as evident by superstitions being bolstered around each world by the presence of the brave and true Jedi, and representatives of the Republic.

Phan-tu Zenn was not aware of the way the galaxy perceived him. As he waited in Docking Bay 26 for the *Eventide,* he only worried the forces trying to break their worlds were stronger than the ones trying to keep them together.

The guard Vigo, standing nearby, noticed his nervousness and cleared his throat.

"When you pulled the princess out of the sea, did you imagine you'd marry her?"

Phan-tu only shook his head, distracted by the *Eventide* landing in the docking bay. Then he answered earnestly. "No, I didn't. Why do you ask?"

"Soon, half of you will belong to E'ronoh. How do we know you will love your people as much as you always have?"

Phan-tu turned to him, shocked at such a brash and direct question, but Vigo had already retreated out of speaking distance, staring evenly at the Prince of Eiram. Phan-tu shook it off as the sickle-shaped Republic vessel landed. He nervously waited for the ramp to lower and for Axel Greylark and Gella Nattai. Trailed by QN-1, the pair stomped out of the ship and onto the tarmac.

"You look terrible," Phan-tu told his friends.

Gella's onyx hair was loose over her shoulders, and her beige and brown robes stained with—was that blood? Phan-tu always knew she might throttle Greylark one day, as they'd all taken turns feeling during their desert voyage. Axel, on the other hand, looked freshly showered and had changed clothes on the return trip from his asteroid playground.

Axel loosened the collar of his tunic, and hugged Phan-tu. "I expect a personal welcome every time I come to Eiram."

Phan-tu shook his head, and Gella waited patiently. Was that a third lightsaber she was holding?

"What did you find?" he asked.

"Proof against the viceroy," Axel explained.

He would find peace in seeing the viceroy pay for what he'd done. In the meantime, he needed Axel's help.

"I need a favor," Phan-tu said to Axel. He hoped that his new friend could sense that it was urgent. Then again, the Jedi likely could as well. He decided to add, "Wedding things."

"I'll take the datacard to the summit," Gella said.

For a moment, her worried gaze lingered on Axel, then Phan-tu.

When the pair of them waved at her, she shook off whatever was bothering her and hurried to the palace.

When she was out of earshot, Phan-tu asked, "What did you do?"

In his defense, Axel did not deny it. He scratched the side of his head and winced as he said, "I shoved her into a fighting ring and got her trapped. But I did rescue her."

"Well, yeah, that should do it."

The ramp of the ship closed behind them. Axel led Phan-tu inside. It smelled like desert rose incense from E'ronoh, and the earthy-scented oils Greylark slathered on himself. He admired the classic details in the ship, the soft brown leather in the lounge and cockpit seats.

Phan-tu strapped in, much to Axel's confusion.

"I'm sorry, are we going somewhere?" the Coruscant Prince asked.

"I need you to take me two hundred klicks north of here to Arium Island."

Axel sat back in his pilot's seat, turning things back on that he'd just turned off. "For wedding things?"

"Yes," Phan-tu said.

"Krel's beard," Axel muttered. "Do you need me to draw you a diagram for your wedding night?"

"Why do I bother with you, honestly?"

Axel shrugged and laughed at his own humor. "Because you want a favor no questions asked, and you know you've come to the right person."

Phan-tu shut his eyes as the *Eventide* peeled back into the sky. Even though he'd been to E'ronoh and back, the takeoff still made him dizzy.

As Axel navigated to Arium Island, Phan-tu drummed his fingers on the console to the rhythm of the song blaring through the cockpit from his custom transmitter. When his fear of flying vanished, Axel lowered the music, almost as if he knew.

"We got word your mother is on her way," Phan-tu said.

Axel acknowledged it with a faint nod.

Phan-tu didn't know much about one of the chancellors of the Republic, but he understood the pressure Axel felt. His own mother *was* a queen, after all. Sensing that his friend didn't want to brush upon the subject, he updated Greylark on the nearly finalized treaty, and the distribution he'd done with Xiri on the day Axel and Gella were gone.

Axel tucked a hand under his head and propped up his feet on the console. "If you want honeymoon destinations, I'm happy to suggest."

"Perhaps. If—" He wanted to say, *If there's still a wedding after today.*

"You're a terrible liar, Phan-tu Zenn," Axel said, lowering the thrusters as they approached the small island. "So just tell me why we're here."

"I know what poison killed the Kage assassin," Phan-tu said after a moment of silence.

Axel eased the control down. "I take it that's why we're at this island?"

"There's a research facility here," Phan-tu said. "I thought it'd been shut down when the war first broke out. But when I saw the body, it looked so familiar. The thylefire scorpions on E'ronoh may not be poisonous, but the ones on Eiram are. The death looked like an extreme reaction to something that should be survivable."

Axel's wrist comlink beeped. He looked at it and frowned, ignoring it. "My mother."

"Blame the salt groves," Phan-tu said. "They grow a lichen that seems to disrupt some comms."

"Is it like the happy lichen on E'ronoh?" Axel's eyes glittered with something dark, something Phan-tu had come to realize was self-destructive.

"Are you sure you're all right?" he asked the Coruscant Prince. There had been a noticeable change in his reluctant friend since he returned from the asteroid. Though, if he really thought about it, he could trace Axel's erratic mood swings to his arguments with Gella that night in U'ronoh. "Are you perhaps lamenting something you can't have?"

"Darling, the only thing I can't have is jogan fruit." Axel flashed his famous smile as he busied himself with their landing.

They stationed the *Eventide* in the bay behind the research facility perched on the tallest hill of the dark-green island surrounded by rough waves. Overhead, storm clouds rolled with the promise of rain.

"Before we go inside," Greylark said, pointing to the viewport that faced the stark gray compound, "I need you to ask yourself two things. What are you going to do if your hunch is right? And are you going to tell Xiri?"

Phan-tu had asked himself those questions since he saw the dead body. "The Jedi Masters said there are too many things obscuring us from the truth. I don't want to add to that. I don't want to start this with Xiri with a lie. Even if that means confronting my mother."

"We could make a run for it," Axel said. "I have enough fuel to get us a one-way trip to Coruscant."

He laughed. Axel Greylark had been right. The man had worn him down like sea glass. "If we have a weapon, I want to destroy it. That's why I didn't want the Jedi around. We would have been lying to them all, and it could give credence to Viceroy Ferrol's mad ravings."

"Though if it turns out that your mother has been secretly manufacturing a poisonous weapon, they wouldn't be mad ravings anymore."

Phan-tu got up. What was the galaxy coming to when Axel Greylark started sounding reasonable?

As they stepped off the *Eventide*'s loading ramp, Phan-tu found himself asking, "Do you ever want to get married?"

Axel looked taken aback. "By the stars, no. Though I have been engaged three times."

"Three times!" Phan-tu led the way into the facility. He pressed his palm against the lock scanner, and the door hissed open. The moment they strode in, rain began to fall.

Axel shrugged like it wasn't a big deal. His little droid warbled something Phan-tu could not understand. "Another time, perhaps."

Someone waited for them in the wide hall of the research center.

The woman had long blue braids twisted in two knots at the top of her head. Her pale-green eyes bounced from Axel to Phan-tu and back, then at her datapad.

"My lord, we were not aware of your visit," she said, bowing to Phan-tu. "You may tell the queen all samples are about to be destroyed as she ordered. That is, of course, except for the ones archived in the palace. The problem is we've had to divert power to the weather shield because of the storm and have had to delay the process."

"Lord Phan-tu would like to oversee the destruction for himself," Axel said. Though he was no longer dressed as his "attendant," he seemed to have no trouble slipping back into the role.

Phan-tu had only ever accompanied his mother to the facility once before, when they were working on developing more advanced water purifiers, but then the war started and, to his understanding, everything had been shut down. Even as they took the lift to the labs in the sublevels, the building felt hollow.

"What have you been doing, Mother?" Phan-tu whispered, opening the door to the lab. His breath came away in tiny, cold clouds.

Everything, it seemed, had already been cleared out. Phan-tu went to the holotable but all information had been scrubbed. He had the sudden urge to break something, but there wasn't much for him to shatter. He had to think clearly. Axel had asked him what he was prepared to do. He'd simply have to face the queen of Eiram.

"Anything?" Phan-tu asked.

Axel tapped open a small refrigerator, his face bathed in the blue light. QN-1 pulsed red, then mimicked the glow of the room.

Phan-tu came up behind him and found the tray of metal tubes full of marbled white-and-turquoise liquid. At least a dozen of them. His mother had lied to him. Kept him in the dark. Now she was hurrying to erase anything that she might have done.

"Well?" Axel asked. "What are you going to do?"

The poison had to be destroyed and he had to be the one to do it because he would not hesitate. He'd have to deal with the "archived" samples later.

Phan-tu went to the corner of the room where he opened the incinerator chute. He could not leave matters to chance. Grabbing the tray away from Axel, he launched it into the fire. He stepped out of the way as the metal doors shut and there came the roar of flame, warped metal and liquid hissing.

His relief was short-lived when he stepped back and noticed an empty cage, the door still open. The rattle of a stinger filled the sterile room.

Axel turned slowly. "What is that?"

"Don't. Move." Phan-tu tried to pinpoint the scorpion's location, but it scurried too quickly, under the table.

Axel drew his blaster and shot, but it only made the thing screech and hide again. Phan-tu shielded his eyes against the next round of shots, until one landed true. Axel bent to pick up the dead, charred scorpion by a twitching pincer, nearly as long as Xiri's bane blade. Its carapace was a sun-bleached blue and three times as big as any he had ever seen.

"You never said these were *enormous*. This is the size of my head! You mean to tell me *these* are just crawling around your planet filled with poison?"

"The shields do keep them out. Besides, I've been—"

Phan-tu heard the scuttle of the critter against metal. He turned around and came face-to-face with a second scorpion that had been nesting on a shelf. Its sharp, ridged pincer rattled and hissed as it got ready to sting. Axel fired and missed.

Phan-tu raised his arm to shield his face from the pincer, but Axel stepped right in from of him, taking the full brunt of the sting as the barb drove through the hollow beneath his clavicle. Axel's blaster clattered to the ground first. Clutching his chest, he scratched at his throat, wheezing for breath.

"Warning," an automated voice spoke. "Initiating storm lockdown."

"No, no, no!" Phan-tu shouted, trying to shoulder Axel's weight as the lab doors shut.

Axel Greylark was on his way. When he'd left Coruscant with a ship full of gifts on behalf of his mother, Chancellor Greylark, Axel had every intention of making the exhausting trip to the Outer Rim without any unscheduled stops. Instead, he'd stopped along the way. That's when he'd bumped into an old friend.

Binnot found him at a saloon on Lorta. They hadn't seen each other in some time, but some bonds were deep enough to survive long absence.

"You're getting predictable," the Mirialan said. "You always stop here on your way to Dalna."

Axel smiled into his drink. He had to shout over the caterwauling of the screeching band. "Maybe I want to be found!"

His friend smiled. "She has a job for you."

"Maybe she's the one getting predictable," Axel said, staring into his glass. "Dare I say, careless, even?"

"Don't." Binnot glared at him for a long time before continuing. "She misses you. All members of the Path are dear to her—"

Axel interrupted, "I'm *not* a member of the Path."

"Of course. But the Mother *never* forgets her Children," Binnot said, taking Axel's drink and knocking it back. "She wants you to come home."

But Dalna wasn't his home. When he'd been at his lowest, it might have been, but no more. Axel Greylark was not a member of the Path of the Open Hand. Even the thought that he'd ever uttered the words "the Force will be free" made him grimace. The only freedom he cared about was his own. How could he ever achieve that if his entire life was bound to who he was. His very name. *Greylark*.

Once, the Mother had taught him to not simply channel his chaos but to embrace it as a good little soldier. She'd seen his potential since the moment Ney Madiine sent him to the Path to deliver ship parts for the skeletal frame of what would be the *Gaze Electric.*

Back then, on Dalna, it seemed he'd found the one corner of the galaxy that did not worship the Jedi Knights. That's why he'd first lingered. But the Mother was why he'd stayed. She reminded him that his pain, that bruise in his heart, was the only reminder that he had survived while his father had died. He needed to press down on it, to remember. When he began to forget, to return to the Axel Greylark that Chancellor Kyong wanted him to be. When he closed his eyes, and he couldn't conjure his father's face from memory. When he couldn't breathe, when he began to settle like dust. He pressed down on that bruise, and he learned to need the pain it brought.

When the Mother realized he would be better suited positioned in Coruscant, at the heart of the Senate, she sent him away. When she needed him—the whispers people divulged to him, the threats he could wield with a smile, or even the skill of his blaster—he returned because if she was his moon, then he was the tide.

At least, that's how it had been.

Then, on Lorta, on his way to join the *Paxion,* he told Binnot, "Already have a job."

"Do you want a job? Or do you want purpose?"

Axel shrugged, but grinned. "Let's hear it."

Binnot glanced around the room, but in this nook of space, no one cared about the dealings of strangers. "She needs someone to keep track of some Jedi."

Axel was beginning to think he might never outrun his past. Who was he without it? "Why would the Mother care what a bunch of Jedi are doing on Eiram?"

Axel Greylark hadn't been prepared for what he'd truly find.

PART FOUR
THE COLLISION

Chapter Twenty-eight

ERASMUS CITY CENTER, EIRAM

For the last several years, the queen of Eiram had spent her nights in the old study where every royal before her had strategized before a fight. Portraits of her family covered one wall, while a paper map of Eiram, so old it was disintegrating, was framed on another.

After her son had returned with a very sick Axel Greylark, Queen Adrialla hadn't been able to sleep. She paced her study, robe kissing her bare feet and long curls spilling over her shoulders. The queen turned away from the remains of the map and toward the intricate holo-rendering of Eiram. She had a list of every delegation attending the wedding and considered what alliances could be struck.

When the doors to her study opened, she turned to find her son. Normally, he brought her a gift—a flower from the garden, pearls from his trips into the canals of the city, or simply an embrace.

Now, as he stalked into the room, she realized she hadn't been prepared for this confrontation.

"Mother," he said, a tone her sweet, caring Phan-tu Zenn had never taken with her, or anyone for that matter. There was something in his hands she could not make out in the low light. Not until he tossed it on the holotable. The cylinder rolled until she snatched it up. An empty metal vial.

"You were at the research facility," she said coolly. She'd known it the moment the Greylark boy had been taken to the medic.

Phan-tu struggled, not for words, but for the courage to ask her the things he was afraid to hear. "What did you do?"

"I was protecting us."

"You lied to the summit!"

"I was protecting *us*." She stepped around the table, took his face in her hands. "E'ronoh had its new ships. Don't you think the Republic has weapons we don't know about?"

"And who do *we* have deals with?" He stepped out of her grasp.

"No one," she said, knowing it was the truth now. "Not anymore."

"Mother—"

"You're hurt I did not tell you." Queen Adrialla moved toward the large arched window. "I could not tell you. What if you'd been taken from me? It was best to keep you in the shadows. That way you would never have to compromise yourself."

Phan-tu scoffed, hurt lacing his words. "You did more than keep me in the shadows. You *lied* to me. I defended you when E'ronoh accused us of this very act."

"My darling boy," she said. "What would be the point in telling you? When our attempt to test it on E'ronoh failed—"

Phan-tu turned to her slowly. "*When?*"

Queen Adrialla inhaled deeply. "The crashed ship and soldiers you found in the Badlands. They had an aerosolized version, but it didn't work. We were going to try again, but when we implemented the cease-fire, I shut it down."

"You've known this whole time. Haven't you?" Phan-tu began to walk away, shaking with anger. Then he doubled back. "Who?"

Queen Adrialla pressed her lips together. "She calls herself the Mother. She came to me to offer relief when our friends had turned their backs on us. She was offering it in exchange for nothing, at first. Then, she asked for an experiment. She'd heard about the creatures of our world and convinced me that we needed to arm ourselves against E'ronoh because we would never match them with their ships."

He leveled an accusatory finger at her. "You told me we were above using our enemies' tactics, you told me—"

"I was *wrong*," she thundered. "And I was afraid. For you. For Odelia. For years, I did not see an end to war, and I thought *this* could fix it. But, she wasn't satisfied with a simple injection. She wanted it to become airborne."

"I suppose it's good to know you have a line, Mother," her son said bitterly. Then he stilled, looked at her almost without recognition. "Did you kill that girl?"

"No," Queen Adrialla said firmly. "No, I swear it."

He had no choice but to believe her. And yet, he still couldn't understand. "Why, Mother?"

"When I backed out of our agreement, she threatened me. I thought she'd go after you. I *never* thought Xiri would be harmed. But we will destroy the facility if it means you will forgive me."

"You should have told me!" he shouted. "I would have reminded you that we were supposed to be better. I—I have to tell Xiri. We cannot begin this on a lie."

Queen Adrialla gave him a sad smile. "She's a smart girl. And she is already here. Come in, Captain A'lbaran."

"Xiri," Phan-tu said, whirling around.

The princess of E'ronoh entered the queen's study. By the solemn set of her lips, Phan-tu knew she'd been there a long time.

"You followed me," he said.

"You're not a very good liar. I suspected you were keeping something from me when you left with Axel."

Xiri moved to the paper map. She squeezed her fingers, like she wanted to touch it but was afraid it would only crumble further. "Don't destroy the research facility."

"We already stopped production and have moved the last stockpiles to the palace archives for safekeeping," Queen Adrialla said.

"That isn't what I'm worried about."

"Xiri . . ." Phan-tu began.

Queen Adrialla chuckled. The princess of E'ronoh *was* her father's daughter. She might not have chosen her, but she would make a good balance for Phan-tu. "What are you suggesting?"

"Do you hear yourself?" Phan-tu asked.

"No, Phan-tu, listen to me," Xiri said. "Even now, delegations are flying across the galaxy for our wedding. To prove that we are stronger together. But what happens when other enemies appear? Rev Ferrol is still in hiding, trying to start a civil war. His father will be executed for his crimes. What happens when—if—the Republic one day decides they don't want to be our ally? What happens when we can't get help?"

"The Republic and the Jedi Order *are* our allies," Phan-tu said.

"But will they be in ten years? Thirty?" the queen asked.

"Axel and Gella have risked their lives for us, and I am truly grateful." Xiri walked slowly to Queen Adrialla's side. "But this is about us. For what comes after. The last poison is a fail-safe for all our people against threats from the galaxy. But the factory? You're right. I'm not talking about manufacturing weapons. I'm talking about technology that won't put us at the mercy of other systems. Our water, our mines, our quarries."

"Our worlds as one." Phan-tu stared at Xiri and took her hand. "I know empirically that you're right. After everything we went through on E'ronoh and everything we've witnessed here, I know the cruelty beings are capable of. I—I need you to remind me of those things. I never want Eiram and E'ronoh to suffer. But we can't let it change who we are."

Xiri nodded slowly. "We can remind each other."

Looking into the faces of her son and his future bride, Queen Adrialla saw the future of not just their worlds, but their system. She would do everything in her power to protect it.

Chapter Twenty-nine

ERASMUS CITY CENTER, EIRAM

Axel Greylark had always wanted to burn bright, hard, fast like a supernova.

But trapped in his mind, he could not stop the fire in his veins. The scorpion sting coursed through him the moment the pincer jabbed under his throat. He remembered staggering. The abrasion like sand under the top layer of his skin. He remembered Phan-tu screaming, a desperate ride back to the Eirami palace. He remembered the swell of the dark, the memories of people he'd hurt, by sheer stupidity or by careful action.

On usual nights, Axel did his best not to sleep, or at the very least not to sleep deeply, because that is when the memories flood back. He relives the worst day of his life, and if he could wake up, he would take himself to the nearest parlor or game or lose himself in someone until it starts to fade for a time. But the poison kept him anchored to his own thoughts, and he wondered if the one person he was trying to run from was not a memory, but himself.

There was a moment of reprieve. The heat in his veins iced over and his heart beat so fast it might stop.

There was another moment of solace. A tendril of hope worming its way into his heart. Hope looked like Phan-tu Zenn and Xiri A'lbaran and Gella Nattai.

But as the venom returned, he heard voices. Uncertain if they were in his head or in his room, he listens—*Axel, Axel, please.*

You giant fool.

Don't do this, Greylark.

I need you, Chaos.

When Axel Greylark's fever broke, he still thought he was dreaming. Through blurry eyes, he saw a young woman in brown robes at his side. He reached for her hand.

"Gella?" He brushed a finger against hers, too weak to hold on. "Gella, I'm—"

"It's Enya," the girl whispered. "You've been asleep for five days."

"*Five* days?" Axel blinked, regretting the piercing light being shined into his eyes by an older-series med droid.

"Patient stable," it said, then jabbed something into his arm and he felt the cold rush of medicine as he breathed through the pain.

Axel sat up despite the protests of the Padawan. Eirami servants had left behind a jar of water. He reached for it but dropped the cup. Enya took pity on him and poured him another.

"Thank you," he said, barely recognizing the scrape of his voice. He had lost so much time.

"I'll tell everyone you're awake," the Padawan said.

"Don't." Axel's *voice* hurt. He tried to sit up. "Not yet."

Enya watched him for a moment. "You should rest. The wedding rehearsal is tonight, and Chancellor Greylark is here."

Axel's adrenaline spiked. His mother had come. And he'd been out for five days. Quin flew over to his bedside and nested in the crook of his arm, like he was a child again. "Please just let me rest."

Perhaps he looked and sounded as awful as he felt because the Padawan looked at him with sympathy he did not deserve. As he asked, she left him alone, and when she vanished into the hall, he grabbed his comlink from the bedside. He pressed the button and waited for a response.

He took the comlink to the bath, where he let the pressure of the lukewarm water beat against his shoulders. During their voyage, Phantu would say that it was the salt in the water that made him feel alive when he swam, that the people of Eiram said it had healing properties. Axel was many things, but he was not superstitious. Yet with every moment letting the saltwater mixture cleanse him, he came more and more awake.

When he toweled off and inspected his wound in the mirror, he was surprised he still looked the same. There were shadows under his eyes and his skin was a bit pale. The dreams from the poison made him feel like he was being ripped from within, so he was relieved he still looked like himself even if he still did not quite feel it.

The moment his comlink beeped, he grabbed it from the side of the sink.

"By the Force," Binnot's voice came through. "You're alive!"

Axel did not have it in him to laugh, even if he missed his friend. He cleared his throat, rubbed at the scar over his pectoral. "I have the parcel."

"Good. Send your droid." There came the hollow sound of a comlink remaining on, but Binnot took a deep breath before he said, "You were supposed to get rid of the Jedi. The Mother is not pleased with you."

Somehow, Axel found it in him to smile, laugh even. "Then, my friend, she joins a very long list."

When he turned off his comlink, he dressed in a dark-blue suit of Ghorman silk that had been left for him. He slid on his family ring, his vintage chrono, his suede slippers. He loved beautiful things, but they were more than that. They were a cloak most people could not see through.

"Quin?" Axel called out into the empty room. His droid answered immediately, apparently worried given the faint purple glow of its front panel. Axel tapped the center, and it opened. Instead of his usual flask and his blaster pistol, there were three slender vials of Erami poison he'd smuggled while Phan-tu wasn't looking. He'd been too preoccupied with the realization that it was the queen who had the vicious poison made.

Axel trembled at the memory of the burn of the poison. *This* was what the Mother wanted?

Quin trilled, waiting for orders. Axel rubbed his palms across his face. He was tired, more than in body. He was tired of following orders. After everything he had done over the years, he knew he was not good. If he stripped down his family name, the inheritance waiting for him, the trinkets, the lies, what did he have left?

He rubbed at the ache on his chest. It was *lighter* than before. He thought of Gella Nattai. He'd told her some things weren't meant to be unraveled. Well, what if that was what he wanted?

Quin trilled again. Its triangular panels pulsing violet—like distant nebulas, like a Jedi's lightsabers.

"No," Axel said. "You're not going to Binnot. I'm keeping it."

Quin warbled in alarm.

Axel chuckled, but it hurt. "Not for long. I'm going to destroy it."

Rev Ferrol waited for the light. With the shipyard north of the Rook empty, Rev sat in one of the three drill ships he'd stolen, and patched himself in to the *Paxion*'s channels, to keep tabs on the situation and wait for his next best moment to strike.

He came from a long line of people who had given their lives for E'ronoh, whether in war or in the marble quarries, the mines that made his distant world rich with possibility. When he'd attacked the mining town of U'ronoh, he needed every citizen there to wake up. To see that the Monarch couldn't protect their own.

His father had been loyal, and where had it gotten him? Branded a traitor, conspired against, framed for a murder he hadn't committed. All Viceroy Ferrol was guilty of was being a true son of E'ronoh. Axel

Greylark had somehow falsified evidence, but he'd get what was coming to him. Rev had broken his father out of jail and stashed him in the abandoned Brushlands to recover. That was what Xiri's little peace summit had done to such a great man. They'd broken him.

Rev had been a good soldier. Until the moment his captain, his princess, had chosen to marry the scum across the space corridor instead of fight. He'd fight for the ones whom the Monarch left behind because once they stopped fighting, others would come. They already had.

The Republic had their hungry expectations to swallow their sector whole. And the Jedi? *Puh.* Who gave so much in exchange for nothing?

Everything he'd done, and everything he would do, had been to secure the future of an E'ronoh free from the Republic and free from Eiram. He'd taken a loss at U'ronoh, but he'd find others. Courage took time.

He sniffed gold asterpuff, wound a scarf around his face to protect against the sun, and imagined what it would be like to destroy his enemy. To end the line of A'lbaran.

When first light came, it would be time to go.

The night before the wedding, the ballroom glittered with glowing anemones and iridescent coral. At the behest of the chancellors of the Republic, delegations had come from Naboo, Mon Cala, Cerea, Lasan, Toydaria, and more, all dripping with their cultural finery.

Gella tried to count all the worlds represented but there were too many to keep track of. Among them, dozens of Jedi in formal robes had arrived a day ahead of the wedding. Some laughed, some stood somber sentry, some indulged in the feast. But all in attendance shared the goal of protecting the peace for the wedding.

Chancellor Mollo tapped his goblet with the tip of one of his nails. Every being at the rehearsal slowly turned to the plinking sound. Gella searched the faces in the crowd for Axel. Enya had said he hadn't wanted to be disturbed, and she knew he needed rest. Gella knew that was best, but she imagined he'd enjoy such a luxurious party more than she did, and besides, his mother was in attendance.

"Friends," Chancellor Mollo began, "we are overjoyed to share in this moment. Eiram and E'ronoh, united. I have traveled all over the galaxy, to many of the worlds represented here." He let that moment settle on the crowd. "I have survived a war myself. I know the dedication that goes into forging a lasting peace. We see that in Phan-tu Zenn and Xiri A'lbaran. We see it in our allies, the intrepid Jedi who helped foil attempts to disrupt peace. And we see it in everyone present, because peace is a choice, and you have all chosen it."

There was an excited round of applause. Behind her, she felt a familiar presence. "I do say, he's been working on that speech for quite a while."

Gella turned to the sound of Axel's voice. Her relief was overwhelming. Not only that, but Axel's *emotion* also overwhelmed her. Perhaps he was too sick to push it all down and pretend it did not exist. He did not seem his usual self, but Gella understood how long it took to heal.

Behind them, Phan-tu wrapped Axel in a crushing hug.

"Everything hurts," the Coruscant Prince eked out.

"Oh, right," the groom said, letting go with a final clap on the back.

Axel's smile was weary but genuine. She was learning to tell the difference.

Xiri, who did not hug, rested her hand on his shoulder. "Are you sure you should be up?"

"I heard a little dancing is good for the convalescing." He winked at the princess, but then held out his hand to Gella.

"Oh. I don't dance."

"Please." She'd heard him say the word when he wanted something, but she'd never heard it like this. Soft, final.

Gella took his hand and joined other dancing pairs at the center of it all. The music was all strings and instruments made of giant conchs that sounded melancholic. They made a strange pair, she thought. Perhaps that was why so many heads turned in their direction.

His hand was firm against the middle of her back, the other threaded with hers as they began to glide around the room with other dancing couples who were far more graceful.

"Where will you go after this?" he asked. "Back to your training, finally?"

"I may remain here, actually," Gella said brightly. "I believe in Xiri and Phan-tu. There is a lot of work to be done, and I'd like to help them. We make an admirable team. All of us."

Axel smirked but had no pithy remark. "Gella."

"Axel."

"Do you think . . . that if you weren't a Jedi and I wasn't, well, whoever I am, that perhaps you and I could be real friends?"

Gella stepped back as the music crested and couples spun. She thought on his words, on the sincerity that dug at feelings she couldn't name. "If I were not a Jedi, then I would not be who I am. I have dedicated my life to my vow. I—I can't separate that person."

"Oh, my Jedi Knight, I know." He brushed an errant strand of hair away. "You know, the Eirami have another superstition. That they live many lives. Perhaps in the next life."

She wanted to say that this was the only life she'd get before becoming one with the Force. Axel took her hand, and placed a soft kiss on the top of it. They remained there for a moment, his thumb on the pulse of her wrist. She let go first, but before they could part, Chancellor Greylark was there.

Draped in opulent golds, the woman was austere, elegant in her beauty. Gella could see Axel in her eyes, but her face was set in an almost unbreakable stoicism that could rival even Master Sun.

"Chancellor Greylark," Gella said.

"Mother," Axel murmured.

"You must be the Jedi Knight who helped keep the heirs safe." She brushed Axel's shoulder, and they both noticed him tense from his injury. "Gella Nattai," she said. "I came to pay my respects. It is technically against protocol for Chancellor Mollo and myself to be at the same functions without more security. Tomorrow I will view the wedding from aboard the *Paxion* since my own ship is docked near the moon."

"Mollo must be thrilled," Axel said, his smile faltering.

Chancellor Greylark's smile was tight. "I do hope my son did not embarrass himself too much on your relief campaign."

"But then how would you garner sympathy from the galaxy if you didn't have me to embarrass you?" Axel snatched a drink from a passing tray, but only held it. His fingers shook.

The chancellor's face paled, her lips parted in surprise.

Gella frowned, sensing Axel's anger, weariness.

"Excuse me, Jedi Nattai, Mother," Axel said curtly, then vanished into the crowded ballroom.

What no one could see, as Axel Greylark waded into the dense ballroom, was a slender beacon in the palm of his hand. He jammed it into a thick, potted plant of coral. Its winking light blended into the bioluminescence of the gnarly organism, and broadcast his location to a wide enough radius.

In hindsight, Raik had done him a favor by putting a bounty on his head. Axel had needed to regroup, *remember.* Press down on that bruise, as the Mother had told him so many years ago.

He hadn't wanted to leave the party just yet. He'd liked dancing with Gella; even if they could never be close, he was drawn to her. Then again, he liked it when things hurt. But his own mother had put a sour taste on the night, and he wasn't back to his full strength.

As he stepped back into his chamber, he scanned the room for Quin. He unclasped his cape and suit jacket. He'd sweated through his clothes and needed another bath.

"Quin?" he called out. Surely Binnot and the Path would be hounding Axel for the vials. But Axel was suddenly forming plans of his own. "Quin, I need a drink, please."

He heard the warbled sound first. A sound his droid had never made before. It was like he'd been speaking and then powered down in the middle of a sentence. Axel froze at the foot of his bed, where Quin had been ripped apart. His dome was askew, strung to his small lower half by fraying wires. The light panel on his chest flashed a burst of violet light, and then turned off.

Lost in his anger, Axel didn't hear the man creep up behind him.

Viceroy Ferrol grabbed Axel around his throat and held a blaster to his temple. Weak, muscles trembling, Axel hopped up on the bed frame and shoved back with all his strength. Ironic, that Axel had killed the Kage in a similar way, but he should live by hurtling himself at the floor. The blast grazed his ear, and he smelled burnt hair and heard ringing.

"I know it was you," the Viceroy seethed, taking advantage of Axel's weakened state and climbing on top. He extended his blaster, holding it with both hands.

Axel *laughed* and stared down the barrel. This man had never killed anyone in his life judging by the way he trembled. "What can you prove?"

"You framed me. I don't know how but you framed me!" His amber eyes were bright as he said, "I saw you enter that tower."

"We both know you're guilty of far worse than what I scrounged up," Axel said. Then he grabbed the bane blade from the viceroy's side and drove it into the fleshy skin beneath the man's ribs.

Axel could barely shove the viceroy off him. His heart beat wildly at his throat. Then he picked up the blaster and took a shot.

Someone would come because of all the noise. He could already hear confused commotion come from the open window. He considered staying. He was an excellent liar, but he'd have to twist himself into knots to explain *why* the viceroy had targeted Axel. There were too many variables.

He staggered to his feet and started to gather the pieces of Quin, but he couldn't carry his droid and disappear quietly through the palace.

"I'm sorry," he whispered. "I'm sorry, Quin. Please." *Please forgive me.*

He choked on the last two words as he opened the panel, withdrew the cylindrical vials of poison, and hurried away as fast and far as he could.

Chapter Thirty

ERASMUS CITY CENTER, EIRAM

Gella was leaning against the balcony overlooking the dark sea when she felt a disturbance in the Force. There was a weight pressing in against her heart, there and then gone. Up above, the palace was quiet, save for the party.

She hurried back inside and scanned the crowd—cackling Toydarians, waltzing Twi'leks, even two tipsy Gungans. Phan-tu and Master Sun were deep in conversation with Chancellor Mollo. All appeared in order.

"What is it?" Xiri asked, sidling up beside her. "I know your Jedi face by now."

Gella found a strain of the anxiety as a servant girl ran along the periphery of the room then tugged the sleeve of a guard and hurried him along.

Xiri and Gella shared a look that said everything. Gathering up the hem of her dress, Xiri ran alongside the Jedi Knight through the sandstone halls of Erasmus palace. Even before they turned the corner that led to the guest rooms, they heard a scream.

Axel, Gella thought. His room was down there. Every step felt like wading into an unknown current. She'd known something was wrong, but attributed it to his illness.

The Eirami palace guards parted as Xiri entered Axel's room first and found Viceroy Ferrol sprawled on the floor with a pistol in his hand and a dagger in his belly.

"Gather the leaders from the summit. And the Jedi Masters. *Discreetly,*" Xiri ordered the guard, who at first seemed reluctant, likely not used to being given orders by the princess from their neighboring planet. But when he looked at the lifeless body, he did as he was told.

Gella Nattai gathered QN-1 and brought the little therapy droid into her chamber. One of the Jedi Knights who had arrived that week, Aida Forte, had brought with her a repair kit. Aida was a Kadas'sa'Nikto with green scaled skin and horns that formed an arc on either side of her face.

"If you'd rather join the search party, I can fix the droid," Aida said, her sunny voice welcome in the shadow of Gella's thoughts.

The rest of the Jedi had dispersed through the palace, led by Master Char-Ryl-Roy, while Master Sun went to deliver the news to Chancellor Greylark. But Gella felt she needed to remain behind instead of rush forward. Axel didn't go anywhere without his droid. There had been an obvious struggle, which Axel had won. But why was Viceroy Ferrol on Eiram? No one could say it was because of the evidence against Ferrol—the summit had kept its origin secret.

"I should be here," Gella said, but she thanked her fellow Jedi Knight and got to work.

The QN-1 was so small she needed the tiniest screws and drivers. Piecing together the droid was its own form of meditation. She had to clear her mind and focus, on a wire, memory bank, the energy cell that powered Quin's light panel.

They knew Axel had run because his ship was no longer in Docking Bay 26. She remembered Master Sun saying that someone operated in the light. She felt the slow realization creep up, and then her mind denying it. What if—she had been wrong? What if they had all been wrong?

When Quin was assembled, Gella accessed its memory bank, scrolling through all the recordings. She did not sleep. She listened to every single one. The first were reports to Chancellor Greylark of their journey. Mundane things. Sometimes, he spoke, or complained, about Gella. Once he made a reminder to send a wedding gift to Phan-tu and Xiri. After that, it wasn't a voice recording, but a holorecording.

Gella closed her eyes, summoning strength from the Force. She rubbed her fingers across the top of her hand and watched him speak to someone who had no name or face. Given his injuries, the holo was from the day they'd been attacked by Rev Ferrol and the Children of E'ronoh.

He sat, face bloody, on the side of the mountain.

"And the Jedi didn't survive the crash?" the susurrous voice asked.

"There weren't enough parachutes, but I won't know for sure until I get back to the village," Axel said, his voice dark. "This Jedi is different. Impressive, I mean."

"Chaos, you're not sad, are you?"

Axel's face twisted back into his carefree mask. "Of course not. I did just fall out of a burning ship. Actually, I think I was pushed."

There was a sound. Rocks clattering.

Axel scrambled to his feet and drew his blaster. "What did you hear?"

The wailing voice of a Tintinna tried to speak but Axel pulled the trigger.

Gella watched holo after holo, then watched them again presenting them to both royal families, her fellow Jedi, and both chancellors. By the time the sun rose the next morning, the day of the wedding, Gella thought she could quote him from memory.

Of one thing she was certain. Axel Greylark was still in the capital, toting three vials of deadly poison, and she was going to find him.

Enya Keen raced across the roofs of Erasmus Capital City with Gella and Aida Forte to reach the docking bay. The streets were like congested arteries, too crowded to run through.

In the southern parts of the city, the buildings were closer together, which made every jump, every leap feel that much faster. When they reached the bay, they perched high up under a canvas overhang and clothesline.

"That's a lot of wedding guests," Enya said.

Every bay was taken, so ships clustered anywhere else they could. Some of the smaller ones had the same idea as the Jedi, and landed on any available roof. Though as they watched beings disembark and stomp through the canal streets and toward the palace, Enya couldn't help but think that these guests did not appear to be dressed for a wedding.

"Are we sure this Greylark is even still on planet?" Aida asked.

"He's here," Gella said firmly.

Enya sensed her friend's eerie calm, like it took all her focus to concentrate. Axel's final holorecording had said, "Change of plans." That was it. No "Hello, fellow criminal, let me reveal my detailed intentions so the Jedi can thwart me."

"I don't understand," Aida said. "Why not postpone the wedding until the threat is eliminated?"

Enya clapped the Nikto Jedi Knight on her back. She was new to the world and hadn't had to sit through all the shouting between the older royals. "Something in the air feels like now or never."

"And you really think he'll strike at the wedding?" Aida asked as she scanned the crowds. "From what Master Sun told me, he's had plenty of easier opportunities to attack both heirs."

"He's here," Gella repeated just as firmly. "Keep looking."

"It's strange to me that so many guests would arrive underdressed," Aida said, squinting as the sun shifted out of a pocket of clouds.

"Perhaps they're not guests," Gella said.

Enya watched a group of lizard-faced Trandoshans weave through the crowd, hips armed with blasters. A small, furry Lurmen with a prosthetic metal eye and a bandolier across his skinny chest limped his way through the crowd.

A short, furry purple being with two green antennae stopped right in the middle of traffic. She was consulting a holoprojection from her gauntlet, a spear clutched in one hand and several daggers sheathed on her belt. It was the cape that looked familiar to Enya. Its hem cut in jagged lines to fit the being's height.

"Doesn't that cape remind you of someone?" Enya asked Gella.

Gella jumped first, landing in front of the traveler in a crouch, and Enya and Aida followed right behind.

"Hello, there. I'm Enya," she said. "Where'd you get your cape?"

The vulpine-faced being made a little growling sound, then looked the Jedi up and down. Perhaps she recognized a threat. Perhaps it was something else, but she said, "I'm Cherro. Won it from a nerf-herder on Coruscant."

She raised her arm and the holoprojection was clear. Axel Greylark smiled at them from what looked like a detention photo. Every single comm device around them seemed to be pinging, as if from a tracker.

"He's broadcasting his signal like he wants to be found," Cherro chuckled, and ambled away to join the foot traffic on the way to the palace.

"These aren't wedding guests," Enya said, dread pooling in her stomach. "They're bounty hunters."

"Warn the Jedi!" Gella Nattai shouted. "And tell the queen to order the dome closed to prevent more ships from getting in!"

Aida began to run, but braked to a stop when she noticed two neon-blue Joben S-14 speeder bikes. She hopped on the saddle of one, and Enya held on tight behind her. Gella mounted the second one and heard a surprised "Hey! Come back here!" as she bolted.

She had a distinct memory of Axel's reaction when she and Enya had commandeered his ship. As she bounced against the shock of the repulsorlift, she blasted into the humid street that lined the coast. She felt him through the Force, a tether she had not understood was forming but couldn't sever. Not yet.

Gella.

It was as if he were in the clouds, the mist, changing shapes the way he changed clothes and smiles. But she couldn't see the *Eventide* in the sky, and it wasn't small enough to be on one of the shanty roofs.

Gella.

Louder, angrier. She tugged at their tether and followed the reverberation of her name. She wondered—was he even aware that he was calling her? Broadcasting himself like he'd done to those bounty hunters?

Gella snaked the speeder along the coast, hugged by crashing waves. Where E'ronoh was all jagged stones and canyons splitting the ground like wounds, Eiram's edges had been weathered away by relentless seas.

She gave up her body to instinct in a way she never had before. She trusted in the Force. She trusted that it'd brought them together for reasons that might not be clear from the moment he sauntered into the *Paxion.* Cold air rushed around her, and every muscle in her body tightened. In that breath, she turned the speeder onto a narrow rocky path that led to the tower emitting the energy dome.

She hadn't fully powered down the bike before she dismounted. The door was blasted shut. When she unholstered her twin lightsabers, Gella remembered Axel cutting a hole in a reinforced glass wall. He'd been ordered to leave her behind, so why hadn't he? She'd been locked in that cell with nowhere to go. Instead, he'd returned. She'd seen how he vacillated between selves. So why, when it would have been as neat as a cauterized wound, had he turned around? Gella needed to know. Holding on to that thought, she cut her way into the tower.

Gella punched the lift open and stepped inside. She ascended a few levels before it shook and came to a stop. She used her lightsabers to cut a hole in the ceiling, then climbed up the empty shaft.

Gella. He didn't say her name. But he was thinking it, so fervently that she could sense its impression in her mind.

When she reached the top, the lift doors were open. She hopped onto the ledge and found Axel, still dressed in the clothes from the night before, standing in front of the tower's control panels. Blue light pulsed from a slender blue vial affixed to an explosive.

"I had every bit of faith you'd find me," he said, turning the detonator between his fingers. "My Jedi Knight."

Chapter Thirty-one

ERASMUS CITY CENTER, EIRAM

Xiri A'lbaran, daughter of canyons and deserts, thylefire-made, would be married by the sea. The protective dome kept the lapping waves away, but thick storm clouds clung around the city. From her balcony in the Erasmus palace, she watched her guests fill the sandstone courtyard where she and Phan-tu would become symbols.

Xiri had never wanted to be a symbol, but as she'd gotten to know the Jedi, and as she'd watched the people of Eiram and E'ronoh turn to superstition to accept their union, she was beginning to understand the power of it all. She'd barely considered traveling the galaxy and now the galaxy had come to her.

Chancellor Greylark, in a sweeping gown and headdress, sat alone in the front pew. Xiri decided she had great admiration for the woman. At dawn she'd been told that her son was loose in the capital with three poisonous weapons, and close to sunset she sat with her head high after giving an order to capture and stun on sight. Soon, perhaps sooner than expected, there would be fallout. And if she ever saw Axel Greylark again, she'd make him pay for breaking their hearts. But for now, everyone at the peace summit agreed the wedding had to proceed. Xiri most of all was eager for it to start.

There was some commotion at the front gates, but she trusted in the ability of E'ronoh and Eiram's guards, as well as the noble Jedi.

"You look like an E'ronoh sunset," the Monarch said. Dressed in staid black and gray, he waited for her at the door.

As she took his arm, and they descended the spiral stairs that led to the courtyard, she *felt* like an E'ronoh sunset. The gown had been her mother's, reds and pinks dipped in gold. Queen Adrialla and Consort Odelia had gifted her a matching veil heavy with pearls. Phan-tu had caught them all himself. Her gift to herself was a weapon, very cleverly concealed.

"For E'ronoh," her father whispered, leaving her to walk the rest of the way on her own. "You are my greatest joy, Xiri."

"I will make you proud," she said.

He kissed her knuckles. "You already have."

Barefoot, Xiri stepped onto a sandbar that stretched the entire length of the courtyard where Chancellor Mollo waited to officiate. On the other side, Phan-tu Zenn waited. Eirami married in all white, but at his hip, he sported a new bane blade with a handle made of pale-green gems.

This was the easy part, she thought. Everything else—the rest of their lives—would be the real test.

As the music began, Xiri and Phan-tu began their walk across the sand to each other.

Before she could meet him halfway, the first blaster shots fired.

Master Creighton Sun believed he'd taken every precaution.

All entrances to the courtyard were funneled to a single gate. The last guests he welcomed were a pair of Ithorians wearing colorful heavy tunics. With all seats filled, he gave a cursory glance to the E'roni guards stationed on the palace turrets. Jedi were placed all around the palace, some blending in with the guests, and some, like himself, in formal Jedi attire.

The Erasmus Sea crashed in looming waves against the dome. The storm season had chosen quite a day to arrive early, though Creighton knew of all the things within their control, the weather was the least of it.

"Creighton . . ." Master Roy said into his comm.

"What do you see?" Creighton knew the Cerean Jedi was up on a balcony ledge and heard the worry in his voice.

But as Xiri, Phan-tu, and Chancellor Mollo took their places at the edge of the courtyard, Creighton sensed the disturbance through the Force. The six Eirami guards posted at the gate moved like a ripple, engaging their electrostaffs as tardy guests drew nearer. Creighton positioned himself between them and the uninvited guests. A broad Trandoshan and his pack edged to the front of the crowd. Each one sported double-crossed bandoliers.

Creighton motioned for E'ronoh's guards to join them on the courtyard level, then held up his comlink. "How much longer is the ceremony?"

"It hasn't started yet," said a voice he recognized as Jedi Knight Laan. The man was somewhere among the guests.

"Speeder approaching," announced another.

"Hold!" Char-Ryl-Roy ordered. "It's my Padawan."

Creighton heard the revolving hum of a speeder bike before he saw it cut a path through the crowd. Enya Keen and Aida Forte zoomed up the rocky palace path, narrowly missing the entrance as they broke to a stop beneath the sandstone arch.

"Master, we have a new problem," Enya said breathlessly, pointing in the direction they'd sped in from.

"Yes, we've seen them." All of Creighton's worry and fear transformed into energy. He felt the deadly calm that came before a storm, and he even allowed himself a wry smirk as it began to rain against the city's protective dome.

"Maybe the royals are just friends with a lot of mercenaries?" one of the younger Jedi mused through the comm.

Enya shook her head. "Axel's got a bounty on his head and something is broadcasting his location. They all think he's *here*."

"Gella's still looking for him," Aida added.

"Someone find this beacon and shut it off," Creighton ordered. He trusted Gella would find Axel Greylark. In the meantime, there was a truce to protect. "The rest of us will stall as much as we can."

The music rose above the churn of waves as Xiri and Phan-tu took their first steps toward each other. The horde of bounty hunters and guns for hire crowded the gate, shoving one another in agitation. Behind the Jedi, Eiram's guards formed a living barricade, propping up electrostaffs like links in a chain.

"I don't believe you have an invitation," Master Sun said, attempting to reason with the crowd, at the very least until the ceremony was finished.

"*Actually,* I do," the lead mercenary sneered. Behind him, dozens more raised the same holoprojection: *Axel Greylark invites you to catch him if you can.* "If the only thing standing between me and three hundred thousand credits is you, then I like my chances, *wizard.*"

"Honestly," Enya said, sinking into a fighting stance. "Why do people say wizard like it's a bad thing?"

Creighton quickly glanced at the ceremony underway, Phan-tu and Xiri standing before Chancellor Mollo, and then at the Trandoshan snarling at him.

"I can assure you, Axel Greylark isn't here," Master Sun said, his voice a deep rumble.

A blue-skinned Pantoran woman with a shock of gray hair slammed her staff on the rocky ground. She held up the signal broadcasting from the palace. "That's not what *this* says."

The restless crowd shoved from all sides, and Creighton knew there was no stalling.

"I've always wanted to fight a Jedi," the Trandoshan said, raising his blaster.

Creighton gripped his lightsaber and ignited the blue plasma blade in defense. He shielded his face from the blast. One by one, he felt the familiar hum of a dozen lightsabers flare to life, a prism of colors deflecting a volley of blaster fire. Most of the mercenaries shot wildly, for the sake of destruction and to get inside. But the better shots landed blows. A Jedi gripped her shoulder and fell back. A guard in patina-flecked armor cupped his knee.

Creighton doubled his effort and pushed against the frenzied crowd. He snatched blasters through the Force, but some mercenaries had blasters strapped to every hip, tentacle, or hunched shoulder. As he slashed the Pantoran's staff in two, another mercenary slipped through their defenses. Farther down the road, the next wave of intruders seeking to claim their prize approached.

"What's the status on the beacon?" Master Sun shouted into the comlink. The crowd had begun to shoot blindly at them. "I need a barricade around the guests. The last thing we need are easy targets running around."

"Everyone's a little *busy* at the moment, master." Enya Keen raised her yellow lightsaber and deflected a red blaster bolt. She nearly missed another, when Master Roy leapt in front of her, blocking the fire with his green blade.

"All Jedi to me!" Master Roy bellowed.

One by one Jedi stood side by side, a blur of blades while the wedding music escalated in tempo. While the guests ran for the safety of the palace, Phan-tu Zenn and Xiri A'lbaran reached for each other's hands.

"This wasn't what I had in mind when I thought we were bringing worlds together," Creighton admitted, cleaving a blaster rifle in half. He almost felt pity for the Twi'lek as he used the Force to fling her into a saltwater bush.

"Perhaps it's better?" Master Roy said, though he framed it as a question.

"Time will tell."

Creighton ducked as a massive Lasat twirled a bo-rifle with electric blue energy. He missed but slammed it into Jedi Laan's chest. The Falleen Jedi shook violently for a moment that stretched painfully before Master Sun's eyes.

Creighton swung his cross-hilt lightsaber upward, severing the Lasat's hands. The wound cauterized instantly, and the hands rolled into the mass of bounty hunters.

Creighton gathered the felled Jedi in his arms, already knowing it was too late. He took a steady breath and closed the young man's eyes. "Rest well, my friend."

Beside him, an Eirami guard dropped to his right. Another to his left. He heard the crack of a cranium, blood rushing to fill the cracks in the sandstone. Creighton watched the light leave the woman's green eyes, one with the Force.

Master Sun centered himself. He stood, raising his lightsaber and opened his connection to the Force. It was the place where he found strength, where he knew he belonged. He added that strength to his fellow Jedi. They were a linked chain, the might of the Jedi a wall united as one upon which the bounty hunters beat their fists and fired arrows and bolts. And the Jedi would hold together.

An angry Lurmen with multiple prosthetics climbed up a coral tree and cried, "Hand over Axel Greylark!"

"He isn't here!" Aida Forte roared over the tumult.

"Focus," Master Sun reminded them as small but furious mercenaries threatened to slip through their flanks.

The Lurmen jumped high, using the strength of his mechanical arm to pull himself up a sandstone column leading to a balcony. There was the sound of blasterfire, screams from on high.

Something metal landed at Creighton's boots and rattled to a stop. A gas canister. He seized it and tried to throw it skyward. Too late—it exploded into billowing yellow gas. He screamed as his eyes burned and choked as he inhaled the sulfurous clouds. He felt the Jedi lose their connection in the Force one by one, as pain lanced through him.

Momentary relief came when someone poured a liquid onto his face.

He spat out the acrid remedy that ran from his eyes to his mouth. When he blinked, his eyesight was partially blurred, but he got back up. A cheer went up among the remaining guests, and the orchestra burst into a raucous, joyful song that signaled the end of the wedding ceremony. He spat on the ground once more. Squeezed the hilt of his lightsaber, then smiled at the Trandoshan who'd fallen back.

"What's so funny?" the bounty hunter hissed. "What's that sound?"

Char-Ryl-Roy returned to his side, as they had been for years. Now they were joined by their fellow Jedi and the delegations they had stayed to protect. As bells rang, Creighton knew the wedding was done. It was over.

But his fight was just beginning.

While the bounty hunters and mercenaries charged through the gate, Xiri remained rooted to the ground.

"I don't care if there's a monsoon coming for us," Xiri told Chancellor Mollo, "you do not stop the ceremony."

"Perhaps a shorter, more poetic version," the Quarren said, nervous face-tentacles dancing in the sea air.

On their sandy perch, the princess squeezed Phan-tu's hands. Many of their guests had run for cover, but some delegations, including the Twi'lek and Mon Cala security details, remained to fight. E'roni civilians and veterans protected the ceremony by upturning pews and making barricades. On the other side of the shield, the Erasmus Sea swelled, crashing in waves that would swallow the palace if there were no dome.

"Repeat after me," Mollo said, his voice admirably even and strong. "My blood is the ocean, my bones are the salt."

Phan-tu's gaze never wavered, a coy smile tugging his lips when he said, "My blood is the ocean. My bones are the salt."

"But I give you my heart."

He flinched as something heavy crashed. Shattered. Xiri inhaled as the shouting came closer. Still, they didn't move.

"But I give you my heart," Phan-tu said.

"Until Eiram's last breath."

"Until Eiram's last breath."

Chancellor Mollo's expression betrayed his anxiety. But to his credit, he continued. "Now you, Princess."

Xiri held on to her husband's hands, an anchor in the storm, and said, "My blood is the ocean, my bones are the salt. But I give you my heart until Eiram's last breath."

"With the sea as your witness, and my authority in the galaxy, your union is bound." Chancellor Mollo turned and called out to one of his security officers. The officer tossed a small blaster to the chancellor, who caught it and commenced firing at the wedding crashers, using the overturned bench of the front row as cover.

Xiri and Phan-tu had a single moment together. He gripped her waist and pulled her close.

"Can I?" he whispered.

"Hold that thought." Xiri rucked up her wedding dress. She unholstered a tiny red blaster, leveled it at an encroaching bounty hunter, and fired.

"I am madly in love with you," Phan-tu said.

"Good." Xiri pushed herself up on her toes and kissed him like their world was coming to an end.

As the *Paxion* appeared over the city, its hull blazing fire, their end felt like a certainty.

Chapter Thirty-two

ERASMUS CITY CENTER, EIRAM

Gella Nattai and Axel Greylark stood on an edge at the heart of the tower powering the dome. She took a step closer to him, and he held up a narrow trigger, resting his thumb there. Detonators blinked from the control panels that emitted the dome that shielded the city, and wedged between them a poison vial he'd stolen.

"Why, Axel?" Gella finally asked. She thought she'd had him figured out every time they kept meeting—aboard the *Paxion,* at the funeral, at the summit, traveling the deserts of E'ronoh together.

Axel Greylark was ephemeral, molten and slippery.

"You have to be specific, darling," he said.

There was so much to choose from, but she started with, "Why are you trying to destroy the dome?"

"I'm not trying to do anything," he said, devoid of humor. "I will bring down the shield."

He was cruel to mock the words she'd grown up hearing.

"Gella, do you know why these shields are up during Eiram's fragments of peace?" He turned the trigger between his long fingers.

"Because of their storms." She scratched at the inside of her palm where her bracers dug into her skin. "Phan-tu told us the stories."

"It is the city's best protection. Even now, in what Eiram probably considers mild weather, the waves rise high and fast. If E'ronoh hadn't been trying to destroy it, Eiram's own waters would slowly erode the coast. It's the only thing keeping even the palace from washing away."

Gella had been blind to the truth in front of her. Now she could see. "There are other ways to destroy the poison. Axel, I know everything."

Axel turned to face the darkening clouds. The shadows under his eyes were more pronounced. "Then you know I was supposed to deliver the vials to—someone—but I've had a change of heart."

She took a tentative step forward. "You want to destroy it? I'll help you. I'll do it right now. Think of the Rayes. Phan-tu's home."

Axel shrugged, but his usual bravado wasn't in it. "I'm sure Eiram's used to a little destruction. What do I care?"

"Why did you risk your life for Phan-tu and Xiri if you didn't care?" Gella took another step.

"Because I am very good at wearing people down," he said. "Their love is a dream. Give it a few years. Maybe a generation or two and they'll be right back where they started. The only certainties in the galaxy are war and chaos, Gella."

"That's what she called you. That woman from your holos."

He stopped smiling then, and pressed down on the spot over his heart. "You want to know the truth?"

"Do you know how to speak it?"

Axel's lips tugged into a smile. "I killed Viceroy Ferrol."

"I know."

"I've spent part of my life trying to be the perfect Greylark, and another being the best of the worst. When the viceroy attacked me, there was a moment when I knew it was over. And then I came to my senses and saw my opportunity to simply stop. Stop being a Greylark. Start new somewhere."

That was one of the first things he'd said about himself. He wanted to burn fast and bright. A supernova. That's what he was to her, a distant star, fading and fading.

"But you won't lie for me, will you, Gella?" He held her stare, and she thought of every time they were on the *Amaryliss* and played the same game. This time she lost. "You won't lie for me because you are good, truly."

Gella took another step toward him. "So are you."

"You can't fix me, Gella."

"I don't want to fix you."

He laughed. "You want to fix the whole galaxy, but not me."

"I don't want to *fix* you," she stressed.

"Then what do you want from me, Gella?" Wind swept through his hair, the open collar of his tunic. Bruises blossomed across his throat where he must have struggled against the viceroy.

She sought strength from the Force. "Why didn't you leave me behind when your master ordered you otherwise?"

Axel glowered. She felt him grasp for a lie, then redirect. "I don't have a master. I'm not an apprentice. I don't need anyone to teach me."

"Then who are they?"

He shrugged. "They are free—from the Jedi. They are simple."

He truly didn't know anything about life as a Jedi if he didn't think life was *simple*. "Free from Jedi but not from murder? They are simple—says the man who lives in a glass tower at the center of the galaxy."

Axel's vulpine smile reappeared. "Are you angry, Gella?"

"Of course I am!" She gestured at the sky. "You have all the potential in the galaxy."

"You wouldn't say that if you knew the things I've done," he said darkly.

"I put Quin back together," she told him and watched his face soften. "We watched your holos. All of us. Your mother. Xiri. Phan-tu. I know *exactly* what you're capable of, and I'm not afraid. I can help you."

He crossed his arms over his chest. "Help me be better? Tell me, what will you do to Queen Adrialla for creating a poison she intended to use on E'ronoh?"

"We don't punish people, Axel. You know enough to know that."

"There was a moment," he said, blinking rapidly, "when I was unconscious that I relived everything I was afraid of. Everything. The pain was excruciating. I never want to feel that way again. I wouldn't wish that even on beings I hate, and there are many. No one should have weapons like this."

Gella felt his nudge of doubt. "We will destroy the poison, I promise. Tell me where it is."

"And then what?" He scoffed. "It is over for me. I can't go back to being 'Axel Greylark' anymore. Go home, little Jedi. Wherever that may be."

Why, out of every cruel thing he'd said, did that last part hurt the most? Gella took a deep, calming breath and reached into the Force. She seized the trigger control from his fist and put it into hers. Gella would keep her promise and destroy the poison so that no one could claim the terrible weapon. She pressed down on her comlink to call for the Jedi, but then Axel spoke.

"Did you know," Axel began, with such deep calm she knew instantly she'd made a mistake. He peered at his watch. "That there are three shield towers in this saltwater wonder, and if one goes down, so do the others?"

Bells rang around the city. The wedding. It must have finished. Gella ran to the edge of the tower balcony. Even if she pushed herself to the limit, even if she could vanish and reappear somewhere else, she wouldn't have made it to the other two locations.

"Axel," Gella said, as the electrostatic shield towers in the north and east sectors detonated.

Eiram stood still.

One moment the dome was operational, the following moment there was an explosion, then another, and the elecrotstatic dome came down. The white bands around the city crackled, and as the dust settled, the first waves lapped along the coasts and canals.

Confusion filled the streets as celebration gave way to fear and panic. Even the bounty hunters who had come in droves began to cut their losses, fleeing back toward their ships while they still had a chance.

The *Paxion,* which had appeared in the sky moments before, began to change course. Chancellor Mollo couldn't understand what he was seeing. Then he dragged his palms along his face and bellowed for the crew aboard. Everyone in the courtyard gathered and watched the sky fall.

"Come in, *Paxion,*" Vigo shouted into a comlink. The guard waited a breath for an answer, then said again, "Come in, *Paxion.*"

Silence. Then a low, vicious voice. "The Children of E'ronoh will rise."

"Rev Ferrol," the Monarch said with distaste.

As the Longbeam sank between the clouds, a cadre of drill ships tore through the hull. Screams filled the city, rising and cresting like the ocean that swept in.

Xiri A'lbaran, still in her wedding dress, set her shoulders in defiance and said to Vigo, "I need a starfighter."

Phan-tu's fear-stricken face said it all. "You can't. Look at what he did to the *Paxion.*"

She clapped her palms on his shoulders and squeezed. "Those are E'ronoh's ships. This is a mutiny and I have to stop it."

"I'll come with you."

"You have to be here. And I have to be up there. We have to make sure our people are safe. Together."

"Together," Phan-tu repeated.

As Phan-tu Zenn took a contingent of guards to help evacuate the city, a small squadron of guards from E'ronoh and Eiram marched up to Captain A'lbaran led by Kinni and others Xiri recognized as some of her Thylefire Squadron.

"Reporting for duty," said Kinni.

Xiri hooked an arm over the older woman's shoulder and led the way to the palace's hangar bay. With no time to spare, Xiri boarded one of Eiram's starfighters. The metal had a blue tint, the canopy bulbous as the familiar pressurized hiss sealed the cockpit. The last time she'd been in a starfighter she'd fallen from the sky and nearly drowned. It was the day Phan-tu had appeared in her life and saved her. Had she ever truly thanked him for what he'd done? More than pull her out of the ocean, he'd breathed hope into a fight she'd begun to think couldn't be won. She wouldn't let anyone tear apart what they had built.

"All right," Xiri said, marveling that this might be the first time soldiers from their two planets had fought side by side in her lifetime. "Thylefire Squadron, on me."

They called off their numbers. Thirteen altogether. E'ronoh and Eiram. United. As they blasted into the air, Xiri A'lbaran, the heir of E'ronoh and future queen consort of Eiram, had known she'd have to defend their peace, but she hadn't expected it to be so soon.

They would simply have to make this one count.

Debris fell from the sky as Phan-tu Zenn raced on an agopie to the Rayes Canal. Above, the *Paxion* split in two, listing toward the Erasmus Sea, the nose of the ship headed for a sliver of the coast. Bulbous Eirami starfighters shot at the contrails of flaming wreckage, breaking up the biggest pieces, while navigating around the escape pods jettisoned into the sky.

The tide was high, and waves flooded the thresholds of the sandstone shanties. Some people carried what they could bear, a child in one hand, and a small bundle in the other, and made their way toward shelter.

On the ground, Phan-tu had a different problem. Many of the inhabitants of the Rayes wouldn't budge. Elders, too frail to move on their own. Some were indifferent to the shower of debris, saying, "The monsoons are worse."

Phan-tu rode out to the small bridge connecting the canal to the other networks of waterways. He tugged his agopie to a stop.

"You know me," he shouted. "I was born on the farthest house on this canal. I know you're afraid. So am I. My *wife*, your princess, is fighting for you. But we can't protect you if you remain here."

"What about our belongings?" a wrinkled old woman shouted from one of the houses on the upper level. As a piece of shrapnel fell into the water, they all flinched.

"When I was a little boy, my mother wouldn't go, either. You remember her. You knew her. I ask you now, put your trust in me and I will do everything I can to keep you safe."

Phan-tu turned his steed and waited. He had never been a fighter or a pilot, but he was strong in other ways. He could lead his people when they needed him the most. Slowly, families emerged from their homes, their packs and duffels filled with the belongings they could shoulder. The old woman stayed. Some people were so rooted, nothing and no one could get them out. It was their choice, and he respected it.

For now, he did what he could. He gave up his steed so that a pregnant woman and her two children could ride. He shouldered the weight of an elder, and led them all to safety.

As they made their way back to the palace, the entire ground trembled.

Chapter Thirty-three

ERASMUS CITY CENTER, EIRAM

Farther out in the water, the *Paxion* was listing. Xiri called for a water evac, and prayed to the Force that there were survivors.

Xiri hailed Rev Ferrol as her squadron sighted and approached the three drill ships that loomed over the capital city.

"Rev Ferrol. You are not authorized to take decommissioned ships offworld."

"I do not recognize orders from the future queen of Eiram," he said, dripping with anger.

"Retreat, or we will open fire. This is your one and final warning." Xiri kept her controls steady, despite the fear coursing through her. She welcomed the fear. It gave her something to fight against.

The three drill ships didn't budge.

"Fire."

Every Eirami starfighter was half the size of a single drill ship, and every single one of her squadron gave everything they had, lighting up the massive drifting clouds and blue skies with red laserfire. But it wasn't enough. Not yet. She thought of how a constant drop of water could wear a hole through solid stone. There was something there, she just had to find it.

"My turn." Ferrol's voice crackled through the comm as all three drill ships returned fire, accelerating forward and picking up speed. One of them activated their drill nose, gutting one of Xiri's pilots. She swore and flew evasively, firing from all sides, then diverted energy to her forward thrusters.

They couldn't keep firing at impenetrable ships. Her father had bought those drill ships with funds reserved for the drought, and all she wanted was to see them buried. Below, the *Paxion* slipped into the sea. Xiri's mind raced as she flew. Then she thought of Gella telling her *He's big, but you're fast.* Underestimated.

The thought sparked.

"Thylefire Two," Xiri said, "Kinni, come in!"

"Yes, Captain?"

"Do you remember that move you taught me and Segaru?"

The veteran pilot chuckled. "The Kestrel's Dive or the Oricanoa Sweep?"

"The Dive," Xiri said. "Those ships are solid but they're clunky. Damage versus speed."

"Loud and clear, Captain." Kinni whooped as they gave chase and flew far across the ocean until the coast of the city felt distant. But before they could go down, they had to climb higher and higher.

"Is this what you had to do, Rev?" Xiri asked. She needed to make sure that he chased her and kept the momentum on her tail. "Too scared to challenge me for the throne?"

"When I'm done with you and your father, I will sit on that throne." His reply was a deep snarl. He gained on her. One of her fighters blinked off her screen. Her pulse roared in her ears.

The way to someone like Rev Ferrol was through his zealous pride. "I suppose 'courage' takes longer when the leader is you."

He growled low. "*I* would never surrender."

"You already did, remember? Do your Children of E'ronoh know that you declined a rite?"

Rev seethed. "And what honor is there in fighting a *traitor*?"

"Did you tell your soldiers it was you who murdered Jerrod Segaru?"

When Xiri heard a small gasp through the open channel, she pressed her advantage, climbing the stormy Eirami sky higher and higher. "It's not too late for your pilots. Listen to me. You can come home."

Xiri pushed her starfighter higher and higher, then drifted into a wide arc. Her squadron followed like the tail of a comet at her back. Not one fighter broke formation. But one of Rev's did. The drill ship changed course suddenly, but the hulking ship was moving too fast to maneuver and it rammed into one of the other drill ships.

Rev roared in anger. "You will never know peace, Princess. I swear it on my father!"

"When I'm through," Xiri promised, "no one in E'ronoh will even remember the Ferrol name."

"You wanted a fight to the death, Princess?" Rev asked. "*This* is your rite."

She smiled wide, and knew she had him. She keyed the comm over to her squadron. "Thylefire Squadron, break off. Head for the *Paxion* and help rescue survivors. I'll deal with Rev." The other Eirami starfighters turned away in unison, leaving Xiri alone, with Rev on her tail.

Together they plummeted toward the ocean, faster and faster, the devastating spin of the drill closing in on Xiri's starfighter.

Her sensors blinked that they were losing altitude and coming up on water, *fast*. Drill ships were vicious but heavy, clunky. But she was in an Eirami ship, and they were built to travel underwater.

Rev's ship wavered erratically behind her, trying to pull up as Rev finally realized the cost of his blind rage, but it was too late. They were on a single trajectory. Xiri pushed her controls to the limit and dove beneath the waves first. She remembered that morning at the caves when Phan-tu had told the story of being swept out into the ocean, how safe he'd felt. She could finally understand why. The first time she'd gone under, she'd been alone, trapped. Phan-tu had swum to save her. This time, she was not alone. She had Phan-tu, her pilots, Eiram and E'ronoh, and the promise of a future united.

Rev screamed as the drill ship crashed into the sea, tearing into the bedrock, splitting the underwater trench. Xiri knew what it felt like, to stand on that precipice and live. Now she turned back to the surface, and did not look back as the drill ship was swallowed into the deepest dark.

Before Xiri led her enemy beneath the sea, Gella Nattai watched space junk and bits of debris from the *Paxion* fall. It split and careened toward the water, but not before a couple of drill ships broke off parts of the canopy. Gella had the sinking memory of Chancellor Greylark saying she would be on the *Paxion* that day. She couldn't remember if she'd kept her word or not.

"Mother," Axel whispered, panting slowly.

"What did you think would happen, Axel?"

Gella was so focused on him, she didn't notice something hit the tower until it was too late.

Metal crunched and warped, driving straight through. The ceiling above was falling in on them. It was only her control of the Force that kept the two of them from being crushed by a slab of metal. She held on by a thread—the stubborn will to keep them alive.

"Gella, I'm—"

"Shut up and *help* me." Her arms trembled from the concentrated effort. Face-to-face, there was nowhere for them to go.

Axel, perhaps for the first time in his life, listened without making another quip. He stood, putting everything he had into supporting the metal slab above. It was too much. Her elbows were bending at the joints.

"Where are the vials, Axel?"

He shut his eyes and took a long moment before he said, "The ones I stole are in the first two towers."

"And the others?"

"Ask the queen," he shot back. "I knew I couldn't reach the archives beneath the palace. I needed to create enough chaos to draw attention to what I did. I fed a holo I recorded into an open channel. Everyone knows what I've done." He struggled against the weight of the falling ceiling. His eyes were unfocusing.

"Snap out of it," Gella barked. Her arms trembled as she tried to maintain her grasp through the Force. "You can't fake your own death if you die."

He grunted and dropped to one knee.

"I'm still weak, Gella. Can't you, I don't know, siphon my strength to make yourself stronger?"

The sound she made was between a cry and a laugh. "After all this time, you truly don't understand the Force, do you?"

"I never wanted to. Not before you."

Axel's side of the roof tilted, the ground groaning like a terrible metal giant. Beads of sweat ran down the arc of his nose from the effort. He shook his head, slipping. She grunted with the effort it took to suspend the ceiling overhead.

"If we don't live through this . . ." he began.

"We *will* live through this," she corrected but trailed off. There could be no after for them. When they lived through this, he would be in prison and she would face the Jedi Council.

"If we don't live through this," Axel said, "I hope my ghost haunts yours for eternity."

"We don't believe in ghosts."

"Leave it to me," he said, "to fall for a humorless Jedi."

She didn't want to hear those words. Not from him. As Axel slumped to the floor, unconscious, Gella shut her eyes and did her best to clear her mind, to find the strength through the Force. *I have every bit of faith in you,* he'd said to her before he shoved her into that pit. Gella Nattai trusted in the Force, in herself. She always landed on solid ground, and this time could be no different. Slowly, it worked. The weight loosened with every piece being moved through the Force.

"The Force is with me," she whispered, imagining every piece of wreckage that was trying to bury them alive. "And I am one with the Force."

She spoke the words, again and again until she and Axel lay atop a heap of rubble. The waves were so high, she could feel the spray of surf.

The *Paxion* was gone, but a cluster of Eirami starfighters returned to the city, circling overhead. She was certain Xiri was leading the charge.

Pushing herself, Gella sat up.

"Don't go. Stay," Axel said, blinking awake. He rubbed at the scar over his heart.

"I can't," she said, and yet she lingered.

Gella brushed his hair back. There were fine cuts on his regal, bruised face. Perhaps Axel was right. It was impossible to regain something after it was broken. The scars would still be there. They served as memories so that it could never happen again. As she drew her hand away, and left to get help, Gella was certain she would always prefer to have the scar.

Chapter Thirty-four

ERASMUS CITY CENTER, EIRAM

The new dawn for Eiram and E'ronoh began the day after the wedding. Getting married would be the easy part. The destruction to Erasmus Capital City was worse than any during the five years of the Forever War. They always rebuilt. Always.

Now Xiri A'lbaran and Phan-tu Zenn had to unravel a secret of the galaxy—how do you make peace stay?

For them, it would start with each other, and follow with a formal treaty. But as the day grew long in Eiram's meeting hall, all parties had to agree on the location. There was talk of multiple treaties, one on each planet, the same way they had initially planned wedding ceremonies. Xiri loved her deserts and Phan-tu loved his oceans, and one day they would have more than a legal document to negotiate. They had to rebuild—both worlds and the trust of their people. They had to decide which planet they would live on, how to distribute the aid pouring in from planets formerly friends, now friends again. They promised, each other and the summit, that they would do it together.

"After everything that's happened," Xiri said, "if we are a symbol of peace for the galaxy, then the treaty should be signed outside of our system."

It was the first time that day that they all agreed.

This marriage, this peace they had brokered, was a tender thing to be nurtured like seedlings taking hold in solid ground, so deep not even future generations of Eiram or E'ronoh could uproot it.

Chancellor Mollo listened to Princess Xiri speak during the final summit. The choice, to Mollo, was obvious. But he did not rush to offer his suggestion, at first. The destruction of the *Paxion* had left him gutted. Many of his crew had survived, thanks to escape pods, but the galaxy had lost so much for Eiram and E'ronoh. He needed these worlds to understand the cost of what could happen, should words get broken, treaties breached. But he was getting ahead of himself. First, they needed a location, and, for the first time in years, he looked forward to returning to Coruscant.

He glanced at Chancellor Greylark with a great deal of sympathy, even though she'd displayed no emotion when she'd had Axel arrested for conspiracy, murder, and terrorism.

The two people not in attendance were Queen Adrialla and the queen consort, who were enjoying a retreat in the riviera. Because the queen had agreed to destroy all the remaining poison, and because so much of Eiram had been devastated by a son of the Republic, the royals of Eiram would not be charged. And yet, Mollo made a mental note that he and Kyong needed to monitor the situation, in particular Eiram's research facility.

"What about Coruscant?" Chancellor Mollo said.

The Monarch A'lbaran, predictably, rejected the idea. "We are *not* of the Republic. Lest we forget that."

"There are nearby worlds," Master Char-Ryl-Roy offered, "with Jedi temples that would be a welcome middle ground."

"What about Jedha?" Gella Nattai suggested. The intrepid Jedi who had arrested Axel Greylark hadn't spoken a word all day until that moment.

The Monarch pursed his lips again. "The *Jedi* world?"

"The moon of Jedha is sacred to many, including the Jedi," Master Sun said. "Much of our history is tied there, yes, but we have no claim over it."

"And it is already the natural home to many schools of thought," Gella added.

One by one, they cast their votes until it was unanimous.

After Eiram and E'ronoh stabilized their homes, they would prepare delegations and reconvene on the moon of Jedha.

As they parted ways, Chancellor Mollo and what was left of the *Paxion* crew boarded Kyong's Longbeam, the *Aurora Sun*.

It seemed they could not make the first hyperspace jump fast enough because they were halfway across the galaxy before Mollo had properly settled in. Kyong appeared at his door, and he naturally welcomed her in. AR-K4, who had survived the *Paxion* crash, busied herself with making the chancellors comfortable.

"You can take your time," Mollo told Kyong.

He'd known the woman to be stoic, but he'd never known her to be cold. "Time for what?"

He hesitated to speak Axel Greylark's name. *Axel Greylark.* He'd always known the boy had ambition for destruction, but he hadn't imagined it would lead to this.

"Phan-tu Zenn and Gella Nattai do attest that *he* helped save their lives on their journey. If you wanted to appeal for a reduced sentence."

Kyong sat forward, her elaborate hair twisted into a crown of black braids. Her narrow eyes sparkled with something dark. "I'm going to tell you this once and only once. I serve the Republic." But for a moment, her stoic mask fell. The lines around her regal face cracked and her bottom lip trembled. She breathed deeply.

They were already breaking protocol by being on the same ship; he might as well go another step further.

"You should have trusted me," he told her, pressing down on the bruise of her son. It was something he never would have done before, but back then, he'd seen her as infallible.

"I do trust you, Orlen." She was rarely so informal; his name sounded strange at first. Then she moved past it. "I wanted to trust Axel, too. He's always shown me who he is. I just didn't want to see it because it feels like admitting that I have made a mistake I can't fix."

Mollo didn't know what to say to that. For the first time he noticed Axel's repaired QN-1 droid, powered down, grasped in Kyong's hand.

Before he could offer sympathy, her composure returned and she sniffed her tea with distaste before setting it on the table without taking a sip. "Perhaps we both need to do things differently."

"Perhaps," he agreed. First, he was going to need a new ship.

Gella Nattai and the Jedi remained on Eiram for another week. They helped initiate cleanup of the many wreckages, including the destruction of the belt of debris in the corridor of space.

On the final day of her stay, Gella Nattai had one last dinner with friends. While Gella, Phan-tu, and Xiri never spoke his name, Axel Greylark's betrayal was a phantom limb among them. When they asked her to venture to Jedha for the peace treaty, Gella, who had never truly had friends before, let alone friends who weren't Jedi, had to decline.

"But it was your idea!" Xiri said over a plate of Eirami fried fish.

Gella smiled widely. "A good one, too."

"Pardon me, but you spent weeks saying how much you want to go there," Phan-tu reminded her, pausing to sip a glass from a cask of Alderaanian wine someone had gifted them for their wedding.

"I feel I am called elsewhere," she said. "But I hope my journey returns me here. I know that if anyone in the galaxy has a chance to forge something stronger, better, brighter than before—it is you two."

They did not say goodbye.

Later that night, Gella meditated with Master Creighton Sun on a pier behind the palace. The seas had calmed, which was fortunate as it would take several more days to rebuild all three of the towers.

"I have some news for you, Gella," Master Sun said, easing his posture slightly. She waited and felt a foreign knot at the pit of her stomach. "Before she left, Chancellor Greylark gifted you the *Eventide*."

"Axel's ship?" Gella frowned.

"Well, Phan-tu did not want it, and I sense the chancellor does not want it to go to one of her son's—more troubled friends."

It was as the Force willed it.

"Speaking of travel," Gella told him, "I would like to formally declare myself a Wayseeker, and plan my return to Coruscant to seek the permission of the Jedi Council."

Master Sun watched her for a long time before flashing a rare smile. "That is wonderful, Gella. I take it this means you won't join the summit on Jedha. Aida and I will be leaving soon, in advance of the peace talks."

"I'll get back there eventually." She inhaled the sea and watched the clouds roll in, bringing the scent of petrichor from the city streets.

"Why the change of heart?"

Gella did not have all the words to explain it, not yet, but she did the best she could. "While I was on E'ronoh, I felt like the more I learned, the more I understood my place in the Force. That I am not in a rush anymore. Or simply, the Force is calling me and I want to answer but I won't know until I get there."

Master Sun gently squeezed her shoulder. "I would be honored to support you on behalf of the Council."

"Thank you, Master Sun."

———

Gella Nattai was on her way. She heard the call of the Force. She'd heard it her entire life, but now it was sharper. It was the song of stars charting routes to new worlds. It was the sigh of an ancient mountain. It was the churn of a sea change. As she sat in the cockpit of the *Eventide,* she familiarized herself with every part of it before leaving the docking bay. The navicomputer was programmed with hundreds of coordinates, and she flew across realspace for hours before charting a destination. It was the galaxy calling her home.

Epilogue

PRISON BARGE CA73Z, REDACTED

Axel Greylark woke in the dark.

The cell was small. A narrow cot, a toilet, and three meals a day. The secure prison barge flew through the galaxy, and he had no idea where he was. When he tried to make small talk with the guards, they only grunted a response. He was convinced he would wear them down eventually.

Most days, he passed the time retraining his muscles to obey him. His body revolted too often. On those days, he sat naked under the shower until his skin was red and angry. In those lowest moments, he remembered hot days across E'ronoh's desert, falling through the skies, the poison that had burned through his veins. He almost considered begging the guards to let him send a holo to Phan-tu and Xiri. To his mother. But he always stopped himself.

No one came. Not for days or weeks. Had it been weeks? In a place where every surface was the same metal, the same recycled plastic and glass, it was impossible to get a sense of the passage of time.

When he was bored, he picked fights. He relished the pain that lanced through his septum when a mammoth Zygerrian broke his nose. How he'd howled in the, albeit rare, matches he lost. And he loved betting on himself when the guards joined the covert fight rings.

After a long time with no communication, he returned from the medbay to find a datapad sitting on the floor of his cell. It was broken, or frozen, rather, a single message emblazoned on it.

"Do you now see what comes of trusting Jedi? But I promise, I have not abandoned you, My Chaos."

Axel squeezed the datapad, pressing down on the crack until it snapped and glass splintered on his thumbs.

Perhaps he'd been right when he'd told Phan-tu he'd end up running the place. Perhaps that was where his mother should have let him thrive. Perhaps there, he could only hurt himself, and a few who might deserve it.

No one deserves that, Axel thought, and it sounded strangely like Gella.

He tried not to think of her. His Jedi Knight. He wrote her name in the indistinguishable mush he ate for food. He saw her face in the subtle patterns and textures of the walls. The condensation on his water tin. He felt her presence, late when the lights were out and all he had was himself and the memory of dancing with her on the last day he half considered he could be a good man. He'd done everything to prove to everyone, even himself, that he wasn't.

He tried to carve her out of his heart as she had done to him, but she was wedged inside like a splinter around which skin had grown.

One day he'd get rid of it.

Axel Greylark waited in his cell, ready to feed his chaos.

Acknowledgments

My life as a *Star Wars* fan stretches back so far, I've never truly been able to pinpoint its beginning. We were simply a *Star Wars* household. This universal story started with George Lucas and has now continued with a legacy of writers and creatives expanding the galaxy. It is an incredible honor to be part of this galaxy far, far away.

To Mike Siglain, the fearless leader and creative director at Lucasfilm Publishing. Thank you for your guidance and generous time with all things *Star Wars*. Thank you to the fab five, the original Lumineers: Claudia Gray, Justina Ireland, Daniel José Older, Cavan Scott, and Charles Soule. To the rest of the High Republic squad—Robert Simpson, Brett Rector, Lindsay Knight, and Jen Heddle. This wouldn't be possible without your brilliant minds.

To my editor and literary Jedi Master, Tom Hoeler. You completely saw my vision for *Convergence* and helped me wrangle my own chaotic thoughts and character arcs. To the rest of the Del Rey/Random House Worlds team—from editorial to production to the art department—but especially Lydia Estrada, Gabriella Muñoz, and Elizabeth Schaefer, and to Yiyhoung Li for bringing Gella to life on the *Convergence* cover art.

An enormous thank-you to Lucasfilm's Story Group for your thoughtful comments and world-solves—Pablo Hidalgo, Matt Martin, Kelsey Sharpe, and Emily Shkoukani.

To my fellow Phase II authors—Tessa Gratton, George Mann, and especially Lydia Kang for all our phone and text sessions. I can't wait for everyone to see what's in store for our Space Baes.

Over the years, I've been surrounded by friends who are my anchors in the publishing storm. Dhonielle Clayton, Adriana Medina, Sarah Elizabeth Younger, Natalie Horbachevsky, Natalie C. Parker, Gretchen McNeil, and Mark Oshiro. From pep talks to writing retreats to organizing my deadline-birthday-advent-calendar for my thirty-fifth birthday, thank you for reminding me to eat and drink water, and for taking care of me like the high-maintenance succulent that I am.

To Cassie and Josh—thank you for letting me draft part of this book in your murder barn. To Holly and Kelly for our writing sessions and much boba tea.

To my romance author support group chat—Mia Sosa, Sabrina Sol, Diana Muñoz Stewart, Priscilla Oliveras, Alexis Daria, and Adriana Herrera.

As always, my family and biggest supporters—you all know who you are, but with a special shout-out to my brother Danilo Córdova. Keep making good art.

Finally, to all the readers who've picked up this book. From my very first short story, you've welcomed me into the literary side of the galaxy. I can't thank you enough for your support.

May the Force be with you.

Love,
Zoraida

PHOTO: © MELANIE BARBOSA

ZORAIDA CÓRDOVA is the acclaimed author of more than two dozen novels and short stories, including the Brooklyn Brujas series, *Star Wars: Galaxy's Edge: A Crash of Fate,* and *The Inheritance of Orquídea Divina.* In addition to writing novels, she's the co-editor of the bestselling anthology *Vampires Never Get Old* and the co-host of the writing podcast *Deadline City.* She writes romance novels as Zoey Castile. Córdova was born in Guayaquil, Ecuador, and calls New York City home. When she's not working, she's roaming the world in search of magical stories.

zoraidacordova.com

Read on for an excerpt from

CATACLYSM

By Lydia Kang

Chapter One

Chancellor Kyong Greylark sat in her spacious chambers. She was facing away from her vast desk, looking out over the skyline. It was near twilight, and the sun's golden light reflected against the spires and domes of shining silver, making them appear gilded.

It was a time of day that usually brought her a sense of peace and calm. But much as she tried to relax, her hands still gripped the edges of her chair as if she were on her ship, the *Aurora Sun,* crashing. A shiver ran down her spine, and the headdress of jadeite—a family heirloom—made a twinkling sound.

A door opened to her chambers.

"Chancellor Greylark," her aide said. "A message is incoming—"

"News about Jedha?" Kyong said.

"No, Chancellor."

Kyong silenced her with an upraised hand. It was the one time today she could have peace. Or at least seek it out, even if it would not come when she beckoned.

"I told you I wanted no interruptions unless it was about the peace accords," Kyong said.

"But . . . it's Chancellor Mollo, on Eiram. It's about your son."

Kyong turned around in her chair, mouth in a fixed line, and nodded. This time, the carved jadeite drops dangling in parallel arches over her head made no noise. She pressed a button on her desk, and a holoimage of Chancellor Mollo appeared.

"Chancellor Greylark," he said in his baritone voice. The Quarren was situated in a room far less grand than hers. His chancellor's robes were dun-colored and edged in silver, and his facial tentacles swayed with expectation. "I trust you are well?"

"I am fine, Chancellor Mollo. Thank you." She allowed a small nod, but that was all. A smile would say that she was inappropriately well considering her only child was incarcerated and the Greylark family was an embarrassment to the whole Republic. A frown would mean that she was not handling the political fallout well. A chancellor with a murderous son? The truth was unfathomable, yet there it was. "How is everything faring on Eiram?"

"Not perfect, but well. There is a slight incident happening on the shared moon, Eirie. I only just heard about it. Something about a downed transport ship that needs repairs. Oh, and the plans for the rebuilding of the Erasmus Capital City are under way. Communications between Queen Adrialla and Monarch A'lbaran are ongoing. Stiff and uncomfortable, but happening, thanks to the newly wedded heirs. Xiri and Phan-tu are keeping the tensions down."

"As always," Kyong said with a slight bow, "I am grateful that you are doing so much outreach in the Outer Rim."

"And I, grateful that you tolerate the hunk of metal that is Coruscant, and the endless political complexities there. Any news about Jedha?" Mollo asked. "Our incoming messages from there suddenly stopped a little while ago. It's concerning."

"We await confirmation of the signing of the peace accords," Kyong said. "Any moment now."

Mollo nodded. "Good. It is a shame that our security wouldn't allow our attendance. Nevertheless, I look forward to celebrating here with both the queen and the Monarch in due time." He paused, tentacles twitching. "There is something else. I wanted to speak to you. About Axel. There's been a proposal passed about by several different members in our advisory committees regarding his incarceration."

Kyong's eyebrows twitched. She had heard of no such discussion regarding Axel. The sentencing had been done swiftly after his capture in Eiram and he had arrived weeks ago at the prison on distant Pipyyr, somewhere near Bakura, but within the Outer Rim. When she imagined him in a cell, she would stop breathing for several seconds, so she had fixed the problem by trying desperately to not think of him at all.

Mollo went on. "You haven't heard of it, because I specifically asked for commentary without your input, so as to gather unbiased opinions." Mollo's holoimage leaned in. "They have proposed lessening Axel's sentence and transferring him to a low-security facility where he can be rehabilitated."

"What?" Kyong was shocked out of her usual stiff and formal self.

"We all recognize the mistakes that Axel made. But he had done some good. He'd saved Phan-tu Zenn from assassins. He helped expose and destroy the vials of poison—"

"By devastating the Eirami capital," Kyong retorted. "He killed that prisoner. Lied to everyone and covered up his actions. He killed an innocent E'roni father. What's worse is he's only part of a bigger picture, and we still don't fully understand the depth of that design. These were no small mistakes of a foolish young person, and we both know it."

Mollo shook his head. "I find it odd that I am the one defending your son, and you are the one reluctant to give him a second chance."

"You are incorrect. I do want him to have a second chance. But wrongs must be paid for, even if he is my only child." Kyong leaned back in her chair. The sun had now set past the skyline, and a lavender-blue darkness began to spread. Kyong turned toward the window for a moment to calm her breathing. The less Mollo could see of her expression, the better. Her distress was becoming difficult to hide.

"The committees came to the conclusion that if, and only if, both of us agreed to his rehabilitation and release to a low-security situation, they would make it happen."

"Both of us?" Kyong repeated.

Mollo's tentacles waved, then were still. His voice softened as he spoke. "I think he should be given a second chance. My answer is yes. What say you, Kyong?"

It wasn't often that Mollo used her first name, and it wasn't lost on her. Kyong tented her fingers. She thought of Axel as a tiny infant. His shining dark eyes and the tuft of dark hair on his head. The purplish birthmark across his low back that would disappear as he grew into toddlerhood. The pure innocence that was in that first smile, so many years ago. She hadn't seen that smile since his father died. They both carried that loss like a never-healing wound.

"My answer is . . ." Her voice hitched in her throat, and she began again. "My answer is no."

Mollo's tentacles waved more vigorously. "How can you—Kyong— I thought . . ."

Chancellor Greylark's aide suddenly burst into her chambers, and both chancellors turned toward the disruption.

"Chancellor Greylark. Chancellor Mollo. I'm so sorry to interrupt!" The Twi'lek aide bowed quickly, her eyes wide and her hands trembling. "Jedha. The peace talks on Jedha have failed! The ambassador from E'ronoh is dead, and the ambassador from Eiram is being accused of treason. There was—"

A holo appeared next to Chancellor Mollo's image, from one of Kyong's high-ranking representatives near Jedha. "Chancellor! I apologize for the intrusion—there's been a riot on Jedha. The permanent cease-fire agreement has not been signed—"

An aide interrupted at Mollo's side, voice flustered and rushed. "Chancellor Mollo! We have urgent news. Both parties from Eiram and E'ronoh have fled Jedha. There are casualties—"

The cacophony of news overtook their conversation as more aides streamed in and urgent calls began piling up. The two chancellors took in what information they could before they quieted their respective rooms and were briefly again alone, both stunned into silence for several moments.

Orlen Mollo closed his eyes tightly, as if he'd swallowed a bitter medicine. His hand covered his forehead. "No. After everything we've done. After the wedding."

Casualties. Treason. A broken cease-fire. It sounded horrible, but Kyong knew from experience that the details to come would be infinitely worse. They always were.

"What will we do? Kyong?" Mollo said, shaking his head.

Kyong Greylark stood, the thought of Axel now pushed aside in her mind. There was work to be done, and this was far more comfortable for her than to think of the transgressions of her family. Sometimes war was infinitely more comfortable than peace.

She spoke to the aide with a sharp voice that made even Chancellor Mollo wince. "Alert the Jedi Council."

THE MOON BETWEEN EIRAM AND E'RONOH
ONE HOUR PRIOR

The moon hung like a dull pearl between the gravitational tensions of Eiram and E'ronoh. With no bounties of mine-worthy ore deposits, only vast quantities of salts, it was often a forgotten trinket of trifling concern, valued more for the crooning Eiram songs regarding its pull upon its tides. On E'ronoh, the sun boasted a monopoly on the people's lore; the moon was a minor counterpoint in myth, fondly referred to as their Timekeeper.

And so when the explosion had occurred on the moon—a tiny, brief spark on the salt-laden sphere—only Captain Plana Van had noticed.

She had been piloting her transport ship to Eiram, full of algae-processing units, when the flash of gold light burst into her field of vision.

"What in the cold moon was that?" she yelped. (Though oft forgotten, the moon came in handy for cursing.) Reflexively, she slowed her transport as two crewmembers ran into the cockpit.

"Did you see that?" said Otto, a young kid learning the business, eyes wide open like a new Sargassum anemone. His skin had brighter-green freckles compared with Plana's, since he'd been on Eiram up until a few months ago. Plana had been living on ships almost non-stop for the last five years, so busy with her work that she'd spent only a scant handful of days on Eiram in any given year. Her time away from the planet showed on her face. Without a regular algae-enriched Eiram diet, her green freckles had become very faint.

"I did."

"I thought the war was over," said Lunnto, her copilot, an older Ei-rami man. His rounded belly reminded Plana of a golden jellyfish, one of her favorite pets. He tended to speak before he thought, but he had good instincts.

"There is a cease-fire," Plana said. She shrugged, doubting the possibility of true peace, but afraid to jinx it nevertheless. "We aren't receiving any distress signals. And anyway, what on Eirie could possibly explode? The one waystation is hardly ever used."

The skies and space above both planets had been mercifully quiet for the last few weeks. And the quiet had been most disconcerting. Plana, like everyone on Eiram, was used to bursts and explosions near the hyperlane shared by the two planets. If you weren't being shot at by an E'roni military patrol, then you were avoiding the raiding pirates that seemed to be multiplying exponentially in this system. Or trying not to get stuck full of shrapnel from the massive belt of destroyed ships and other debris that hovered near the gravity wells of both planets.

Plana pushed her heavy braids past her shoulders and tied them with a cord, a movement she associated with a coming battle. An incoming alert from Eiram lit up her screen. Of course they must have picked up on the explosion, too.

"Captain Van, this is Erasmus port commander Ailee. Please report your status update."

"Captain Van here." Her voice immediately grew cool and robotic, an old habit from her early years in the Eirami military. Plana was now in the military reserves, since her work as a hauler had been important enough that she hadn't been pulled into active duty throughout the war. "We were on our way home. Cargo is as previously reported. Nothing out of the normal on our mission until . . ." Actually, up until recently, it was expected that something should go wrong. War and all. The entire mission had been too quiet. This felt more normal, to be honest.

"We just witnessed a small disturbance on the moon. A single explosion. No distress signals. Our ship is unaffected."

"Captain Van, be aware, you're in neutral territory. Are you prepared for combat?"

Plana stiffened. "Aren't we in a cease-fire?"

"Nevertheless. Be prepared, as you always should be."

"No one has fired on us. We have no information on what caused that explosion."

As if waiting for her words to leave her mouth, Otto nervously said, "Uh, I'm registering a starfighter from E'ronoh on the moon, by the way. May be the source of the explosion."

"Or the instigator," Plana said.

Lunnto turned to stare at Plana Van. "You know what this looks like. It stinks of piracy. I'll bet that E'roni fighter shot down one of our supply ships. Trying to clean up the mess now."

Plana sighed. This delivery was supposed to be a quick, easy, peacetime job. The communication to Commander Ailee was still open. They heard everything.

"Captain Van," Commander Ailee commed in. "I'm ordering you to land on the moon and check for casualties."

"But there's no evidence—" Plana began.

"Captain Van. You may be a hauler, but as reserve military, you still obey my orders as your port's commanding officer."

"Yes, Commander." Plana rolled her eyes. Oh, for this war to be truly over.

She turned to their tiny crew—Lunnto and Otto. Pell, the navigator, was sleeping in the back somewhere.

"Well. Here we go." Plana sped her ship toward Eirie. Soon, they were descending upon the only active area of the moon. A single way-station, a refueling stop, and a provisions shop. She now had a view of the E'roni ship Otto had picked up on the scanner. It was docked with another transport spewing tendrils of smoke from the engine—the source of the explosion. Not Eirami make, but not E'roni, either. Probably a hauler from another sector making money bringing goods to one of the planets.

Compared with their own transport, the devilfighter from E'ronoh was small, but it was made for speed and power. The injured transport ship was perhaps twice the size, but still quite small itself for anything carrying goods across this sector. The hull seemed intact, but scorch marks blossomed from an irregular hole in the smoking engine.

Plana cleared her throat, hailing the E'roni ship. "This is Captain Plana Van of Eiram. Please state your identification and intentions." Might as well start vague.

There was silence for more than a full minute before a voice commed in.

"This is Lieutenant Gunnaw of E'ronoh, Thylefire Squadron." There was another long pause. Plana imagined him snarling. "Under the terms of the cease-fire, that is all that I am required to say. However. We came across this transport headed toward Shuraden. It was adrift, and we brought it to the moon for repairs."

Plana frowned. "The waystation here isn't capable of handling extensive repairs."

"We are aware of that fact. The ship's crew—there are only two—stated they could repair it themselves if they could dock somewhere safely. They didn't believe the cease-fire was fully legal and requested to come to the moon."

Neutral territory. It made sense, but still.

"What were they transporting?"

"What does it matter? They were looted by pirates. Cargo is gone now. We went inside to do a search and verify the story."

"Can you explain the nature of the explosion while you were moonside?"

"The ship's remaining engine blew. Not our fault."

"And where are you headed?"

"Not your business."

"And the survivors? May we speak to them?"

"They don't want to speak to you."

Plana bristled. This was like arguing with a rock. She commed into Commander Ailee and gave them an update.

"Something isn't right," Commander Ailee said. Plana felt the same, but said nothing. "From a nonmilitary perspective, we have a right to attend to the survivors ourselves and conduct a safety evaluation of that downed ship."

Plana could feel her blood pressure rising with worry. The cease-fire felt so tenuous. Any moment now, the war would be officially over. Then why did it feel like it was an impossibility, even with the union between the two planets?

"I am ordering you to search that ship, Captain Van, and sending four crescent fighters as backup," Commander Ailee said. "Anything that affects the moon affects us, far more than E'ronoh."

"Yes, Commander." The people of Eiram had always felt that way. The moon exerted crucial tidal forces over Eiram. The creatures on their watery planet lived and bred and died by the tides, and by extension, the people of Eiram did as well. If E'ronoh did anything that affected the moon—moved it by a kilometer in some as-yet-impossible but terrifying way—it would destroy Eiram. No one ever considered it, but Plana did at this moment, and it frightened her.

The commander was right. That E'roni ship and the defunct ship were hiding something.

"Oh, and Captain Van?"

"Yes?"

"Make it quick. More E'roni ships will be here in minutes, the second they see ours are on the way. Fire no shots unless absolutely necessary. For all we know, our ambassadors have already signed a permanent peace agreement on Jedha."

Plana Van cracked her knuckles, a habit she had before work got messy. She turned to her crew. "Get on the duo-cannon, and wake up Pell," she said. The navigator's nap was over. "We're boarding that ship."

ORRA LAGOON, EIRAM

The Eirami lagoon was one of many in this region, only five kilometers from the capital city. It was one of the things Phan-tu Zenn most loved about Eiram. In any town or village, no matter how busy or crowded it got, you could go in any direction to find water. And quiet.

Phan-tu was helping with a traditional slek gathering—a water vegetable that was so tender and delectable that he would have traded a boat for a bushel when homesick for a traditional slek stew. It was a favorite of his mother and sister when he was a child, and his longing for it never went away. Now Queen Adrialla and the queen's consort, Odelia, loved it as much as he did, though the fondness existed well before they'd adopted him. Though he was fairly adept at handling the goings-on at the palace, he always sought an excuse to get away back to the water. He'd grown up along the Rayes Canal, and his boyhood would always set him slightly apart from his royal parents.

And yet this lagoon, like so many other areas in Eiram, no longer resembled the memories from his childhood. Lush waters filled with life, greenery growing like tangled jungle around its edges, beaches that glinted yellow and gold like precious metals. Now the sands were often stained with oil and fuel that had leaked from downed ships. The greenery in many places had been burned alive from explosions. And dwellings were in disrepair, with resources being scarce. Incoming ships with supplies were constantly being harassed and raided by pirates taking advantage of the chaos. Finding peace out here was hard with the evidence of war everywhere.

Knee-deep in the cool water of the lagoon, he reached for a tiny, rare tendril near his feet, pulled it gently, and put it into the basket at his waist. Something buzzed at his wrist, and he swatted at it, before he realized it wasn't a biting midge, but his communicator. It was his wife, Xiri.

Wife! The word still seemed so strange.

"Hello, Xee," Phan-tu said, laughing. "I almost mistook your call for a bug bite."

"Well, thanks!" She wasn't laughing. Oof. "Listen, something's happening on the Timekeeper moon."

Phan-tu stood up and grew very still. "The moon? Why would something be happening there?" He reflexively looked up in the sky. The moon was a quarter full just over the horizon. Though not uninhabitable, it wasn't settled by either planet. Eiram loved its plentiful azure waters, and E'ronoh loved its hot temperatures and bronzed landscape—none of which were to be found on the moon. The tiny lagoon waves connected to the Erasmus Sea, and the height of the water lapping against his legs was a result of the moon's pull on Eiram.

"I don't know what's going on, but apparently there are Eirami crescent fighters on their way and I heard we're deploying ships, too." Xiri sounded out of breath. "I was flying when I got the call. I'm on my way to speak to Father and find out more information. You need to come here. Right away."

"Come to E'ronoh? I'm . . ." *Well, I'm up to my knees in water,* Phan-tu wanted to say. Which was the truth, but what he really bristled slightly at was what sounded like orders. "I was on my way to the palace to see the queen and the queen consort. I think we might do more good trying to calm any incendiary feelings on our own planets right now."

"Okay," Xiri said. "The peace treaty will be signed any moment. We're so close, Phan-tu! We just have to keep it together until then."

"Of course. We'll talk soon."

"Phan-tu?"

"Yes?" He waited expectantly.

There was a long pause. "I miss you."

"I miss you, too, Xee. Goodbye."

Sometimes it was still stilted and weird, speaking to Xiri. They were married, yes, and they loved each other. But theirs was still a very young partnership. Half the time they were together, and half the time they were on their respective planets calming tensions during the cease-fire. Phan-tu had yet to feel like he was a prince of E'ronoh, and he knew Xiri felt the same about her relationship to Eiram. Plus, they were always being watched, royalty that they were. Phan-tu had yet to put his arm instinctively around his wife's shoulders. Navigating each other's space was still a new thing. And navigating life as representatives of both planets felt just as raw and new.

Phan-tu strode out of the water. Nearby, children with their bright smattering of green freckles bowed as he walked by. He wasn't born royalty, but was now. Some older teens looked on from afar, slightly mocking grins on their faces. Not everyone was so happy he was married to the princess of E'ronoh. Before their marriage, he had cared less about glances and whispers. There was a war to stop, after all. Now it was often all he noticed.

Phan-tu jumped onto a speeder bike and made his way to the palace. He entered one of the large sitting rooms on the north side, where

Queen Adrialla was seated with several of her counselors. Water surrounded the room in a flowing mini river set with floating, iridescent lilies.

"Ah, Phan-tu. We were just going to call for you." The queen waved him forward. She arose from her dais intricately carved of sea wood tree, and reached out a bronzed hand. He touched it to his forehead in respect, and straightened. She smiled at him, eyes crinkling at their edges. Silver hair glinted in the dark braids woven in and out of her crown. Together, they walked into a side room, her shimmersilk robes rustling quietly. The counselors sat on one side of a large teardrop-shaped table. The queen consort rose from her seat to kiss Phan-tu on the cheek, her veil fluttering.

"And not a moment too soon. We need a cool head in this room," Odelia whispered, sitting to Queen Adrialla's right.

He noticed that the counselors were polite, but a subtle coldness had entered their interactions—a new behavior that began the day it was announced he would marry Xiri. He remembered words spoken to him by his guard Vigo, before the wedding. *Half of you belongs to E'ronoh now. How do we know you will love your people as much as you always have?*

It still stung him.

"What news?" the queen asked.

"An incoming transport ship of ours happened to see an explosion on the moon. Our sensors verified it. A small E'roni military vessel is in the area where a trade ship exploded while it was being repaired there."

"On Eirie? Our moon? How odd," one of the counselors said.

Our moon. Phan-tu felt possessive of it in a way he hadn't before. Likely all in the room felt the same way.

One of the counselors leaned in. "Commander Ailee wants the passengers to be questioned."

"The E'roni won't like it," said another counselor—the eldest, sporting a white beard down to his knees.

"No," said the queen. "But in good faith, they ought to allow it, if they have nothing to hide. We cannot do anything that will jeopardize this pending peace accord. We can only wait patiently for news that all has gone well on Jedha."

The counselors shifted in their seats. The planet had been at war for so many years, they appeared awfully uncomfortable with the idea of playing nice with the people that had been shooting down their ships, littering space with metal. And the dead.

Phan-tu looked at the console before him. "We have an incoming transmission. Speak, Commander Ailee." His wrist communicator buzzed as well. Xiri. He put his hands beneath the table and ignored it.

"Our pilot is boarding the ship."

"On whose authority?" the queen asked.

"Mine. There could be Eirami citizens on board. They're in neutral territory."

Phan-tu turned the volume down on his comm and raised it casually to his ear, pretending to scratch his head.

"Tell them not to board that ship!" Xiri said. "Phan-tu? Can you hear me? It's a breach of trust! Tell them—"

The queen gave him a sidelong glance. She couldn't hear what Xiri was saying, but she could tell when Phan-tu was keeping something from her. He put his hand down quickly.

"This is a time to build trust. I think it's unwise to board the ship without explicit permission from E'ronoh," Phan-tu said.

"Of course you do. Or is that your wife who thinks so?" the elder counselor said.

"She does," Phan-tu replied. "But that's beside the point. Both sides carry years of deep war wounds and fear. Working together is the only way to go forward."

Commander Ailee's voice came through the console. "Captain Van has boarded the ship."

Phan-tu's heart sank. It was too late.

THE MOON BETWEEN EIRAM AND E'RONOH

Binnot Ullo straightened up and dusted off his cargo uniform. Goi Ganok stood at his side, hands clasped tightly.

A middle-aged human woman, tall and muscular, entered. She wore a dark blue flight uniform with the water insignia of Eiram on her upper arm. Civilian, but holding herself like she was military. She was armed, as was her companion—an Eirami male who looked far younger, with deep greenish-blue freckles. He seemed about as nervous as Goi was. Just outside the door, the E'ronoh pilot, Lieutenant Gunnaw, frowned and waited.

"I'm Captain Plana Van, of Eiram. State your name, your home territory, and your mission."

"Binnot Ullo." Binnot bowed slightly. He had no interest in using a fake name. Neither he nor Goi was known widely outside of the Path. This would change soon. At least for Binnot. He lightly kicked Goi, who bowed like a squeaky droid that needed oiling.

"Goi Ganok. We're merely shipping folk." He smiled too widely, showing rows of minuscule teeth.

"Originally from Mirial and Roona, obviously," Binnot added. "We were on our way to Shuraden, from our station near Skye."

Captain Van narrowed her eyes. "Strange that you should travel near the Eiram system to do so. Most shippers avoid us because of our junk belt."

"It was faster this way," Binnot said.

"Not by much," Captain Van said. "I understand you were attacked by pirates and came to the moon for repairs. Did your attackers identify themselves?"

Binnot gave her a condescending glare. "They were *pirates*. Of course they didn't identify themselves."

"And your cargo? What were you hauling?"

"Protein concentrates. But the barrels were all taken." Binnot gestured to the empty compartment around him. He watched as the captain and her colleague circled the room. It was about twelve meters long and slightly less wide and tall, taking up the bulk of the small ship's volume. She sniffed the air once, then sniffed again.

The young Eirami man sniffed, too.

Captain Van turned to him. "You smell that, Otto?" She brushed past Binnot, her footsteps making dull thumping sounds as she crossed the storage area. Her steps suddenly sounded sonorous and hollow. She knelt and took a knife from her belt, wedging it against the edge of a flat metal section of flooring underfoot. It lifted, and she pulled it up, hard. She threw the square of metal away and it crashed against the wall.

The hidden floor compartment was full of sealed vats, a window on each showing they were filled to the brim with an inky liquid. They smelled like nothing to Binnot, perhaps faintly briny, but the odor clearly rankled the Eiram captain and her companion. Her nostrils flared and she grimaced, staggering back.

"That's klytobacter." She stared at Binnot. "What are you doing with this?"

Binnot shook his head, as did Goi, a little too energetically. "What's klytobacter?" Goi asked, trying to keep his face benign.

"One dry summer when I was a kid," Captain Van began, "it bloomed on the north shore of my home island on Eiram. Killed the fish, the sea vegetables, birds . . . everything. For years, we couldn't swim in or touch the water." Her eyes were full of accusations. "What are you doing with this?"

"We didn't know it was here! We didn't smell anything odd," Binnot said, his hands up in surrender. "We were only paid to bring the protein concentrates to Shuraden."

Captain Van put her hand on her blaster at her side. "You purposely crossed the Eiram system when you could have easily avoided it and now you have a biological weapon that could spell disaster for my planet?"

The Eirami man at her side's fists were clenched as he blurted out, "Are you working for E'ronoh?"

"Choose your words carefully!" Lieutenant Gunnaw had stepped into the room, seeing the tanks and staring hard at Binnot, then Otto.

"Otto!" Captain Van said, silencing him with a glare.

Goi actually looked angry, and blurted out, "No!"

Binnot hit him so hard in the shoulder that Goi lost his footing and shuffled sideways, growling at the cuff.

"This ship is going nowhere." Captain Van touched a communicator on her wrist. "Commander Ailee. They have a biological weapon on board. Klytobacter."

While Captain Van spoke to her commanding officer, Lieutenant Gunnaw was also speaking quickly into his wrist communicator. Goi was dripping with nervousness to the point that half his jacket was darkened with moisture. Binnot held a hand out to him, and Goi met his eyes. Binnot leaned closer and whispered.

"Remember, Goi. This is what we want. Isn't it?"

Goi barely nodded an assent.

When she finished her report, Captain Van and Otto quickly backed out of the storage compartment.

"This ship and you two are never leaving this moon if I have anything to do with it," Captain Van said just before the door to the storage area slid shut. Binnot and Goi heard it lock from the other side. Lieutenant Gunnaw could be heard arguing with Captain Van on the other side.

Oh I'm getting off this moon. Just watch me. But Binnot was satisfied. The Mother would be happy. Binnot will have ensured that this time, the war would rage with plenty of fuel. If there was any wonder if Eiram and E'ronoh should go back to the negotiation table, the klytobacter would destroy that prospect. Just as it would dissolve any goodwill that Xiri A'lbaran and Phan-tu Zenn's marriage ridiculousness ever conjured.

"Hey!" The E'roni pilot commed into the ship's speakers. "Eirami ships are all over the airspace above this waystation. What were you doing with that klytobacter?"

Binnot said, smoothly as possible, "They're lying. We have nothing. You saw it yourself!"

"Hold tight," the pilot said. "We have E'roni backup on the way. In fact . . . they're here."

They heard the low rumble of other craft nearby.

"Oh," Goi said. He put his hands over his earholes. "Here we go."

ERASMUS CITY CENTER, EIRAM

Phan-tu listened in shock as Commander Ailee gave her updated report. A bioweapon? His queen bristled at the word. She, too, had been guilty of gathering a poison to defend her people, only weeks ago. A terrible, desperate misstep. Now she looked at Phan-tu, not with worry, but with a slight self-satisfied expression, as if to say, *See, Phan-tu? Was I not justified for trying to do exactly as the E'roni were to do?*

But they had conceded it was a misstep, and now this was a step toward playing dirty in an already filthy war. Horrifying tactics like using drill ships were old news now. Killing had become sophisticated and brutal. Now klytobacter? Poisons killed warmongers. Klytobacter, however, would kill entire species and delicately balanced ecosystems. Klytobacter was a planet killer. This was too much. This was an escalation, plain and simple.

"How do we know it's really klytobacter?" he asked.

The elder counselor leaned forward. "We all know what it smells like. Like death."

Phan-tu could feel the room buzzing with rising fury. The queen's consort, Odelia, looked like her fists were on the cusp of breaking the table they grasped. He raised his hand to rub his forehead, whispering.

"Xiri? Klytobacter? Is it true?"

Xiri's voice came buzzing back quickly. "We have nothing to do with that! You have to believe me. I know your people might think it could be a response to Queen Adrialla manufacturing poison to use against E'ronoh. We've got to settle everyone down, and figure this out."

Queen Adrialla raised her hands, bracelets jangling. "This doesn't make sense. We are a breath away from an everlasting peace."

"Xiri is saying they have nothing to do with that klytobacter," Phan-tu said.

"She stood by me when I made my own mistakes trying to protect Eiram. I said I would protect the future of these two worlds. I believe Xiri. We need to discuss this, not act hastily," Queen Adrialla said firmly.

The elder counselor stood. "Princess Xiri means well. But Xiri is not E'ronoh, and E'ronoh is not Xiri. Some parts of E'ronoh will never stop trying to hurt us. Think of Viceroy Ferrol and his son. They tried to kill their own princess because of her ties to Eiram! We have to protect ourselves." He turned to the table of counselors and the royal family. "Since the wedding, we have all agreed to decide action by majority decision after Queen Adrialla's regrettable actions. What say you all to a maneuver that shows strength in responding to this klytobacter threat?"

Of the nine people at the table, six of them placed fists toward the center of the table—a vote of yes. Only the queen, her consort, and Phan-tu left their hands flat on the table indicating disagreement.

Queen Adrialla looked at her son helplessly. "We have no choice."

The eldest held out his hand. "For Eiram."

"For Eiram," they all spoke in unison. Except for Phan-tu, who felt like the ground was collapsing beneath his feet. All he and Xiri had been working toward. It was slipping away.

He could hear Xiri's tiny voice coming from his wrist. Though the sound was extremely faint, it was as good as a scream right in his ear. Answering would do no good.

"Tell them not to fire, please! Phan-tu, can you hear me? *Phan-tu!*"

THE MOON BETWEEN EIRAM AND E'RONOH

Captain Plana Van, back on her ship, hovered above the waystation where the transport ship full of klytobacter was docked. Two crescent ships flanked them, but she'd prefer if they were up front. Since she had last reported to Commander Ailee, two devilfighters from E'ronoh had shown up to join Lieutenant Gunnaw's ship and now faced them at too close a distance to be comfortable. Their transport ship wouldn't take more than a hit or two before it fell to pieces. No, wait. Now there were four devilfighters in sight. Things had heated up quickly.

Commander Ailee commed in. "You have it on my authority to fire on that cargo ship. It's carrying an outlawed bioweapon. E'ronoh has broken the pact of the cease-fire."

"But we can't know for sure that E'ronoh owns those tanks of klytobacter. The pilot said—"

Captain Van couldn't get another word out before multiple transmissions came in at once. Five, to be exact. One from an Eirami crescent ship nearby, three from the communications buoy just beyond the moon, and one directly from Eiram's central council.

"What in the cold moon is going on?" She hit them one by one.

"Urgent transmission in. The peace talks on Jedha have failed!"

"Ambassador Tintak from E'ronoh has been killed. It's off. Everything's off—"

"It was a fiasco. Eiram walked into a trap. The city of Jedha is in flames, there are casualty reports—"

Plana Van's hands shook as she stared out the viewport. They needed to fire. They had every right to, now that the cease-fire was dead. But Plana couldn't move. Stepping back into war was the last thing she truly wanted. Was she so sure the klytobacter was E'ronoh's fault? Did she have all the facts? But her gut said to defend her home planet, and the klytobacter terrified her. That was all that mattered. She took an enormous breath.

"On my command," she said. "Fire—"

But before she could even finish, explosions lit up her view. One of the crescent fighters had shot at Lieutenant Gunnaw's devilfighter, hovering above the waystation, while the other crescent fighter targeted the incapacitated transport ship full of lethal cargo still docked far below. Gunnaw's fighter exploded immediately, and the ship with Binnot and Goi was now smoking. Captain Van saw the two running away from the wreckage, looking for cover, feeling both relief and surprise at their escape. But Lieutenant Gunnaw was dead. Plana squeezed her eyes shut for a terrible moment.

"Get those survivors. We need to know where that bioweapon was made, and how to destroy the source," Commander Ailee ordered.

The ships scattered, with the two Eirami crescent fighters evading the two E'roni devilfighters. Hoping that no one would pursue her very obviously nonmilitary ship, Plana began to descend to the moon's surface to try to capture Binnot and Goi.

Her hope lasted all of five seconds. A devilfighter peeled away from chasing the crescent ships and began to close the distance. Plana made a sharp turn, veering away from the moon.

"We have to head back to Eiram," Plana said to her copilot, Lunnto. "We won't survive a fight with these devilfighters."

Captain Ailee commed in to all the Eirami ships in the area. "E'ronoh is sending out a distress call to their out-of-sector pilots. Both planets sent a large contingent to Jedha, but we're having trouble contacting ours. If those E'roni reinforcements come in—we'll be inundated. We have to stop the message."

"How many ships?" Plana's ship shook—they'd been hit. They stopped accelerating. Lunnto scrambled to bypass a leaking engine drive line. "Fix that! Now!" she hissed.

"What do you think I'm doing?" Lunnto yelled back, scrambling out of the cockpit to head to the engines.

"Captain Van! All pilots! Do you hear me? Destroy those communications buoys or we'll have more E'roni ships flooding in than we can handle!"

Plana growled. She couldn't fight a fleet of E'roni ships, but her little duo-cannon could take out a buoy.

"Leave that to me," she said. "Let's get out of here. The five buoys that serve these planets are C-12, C-13, A-01 through A-03. We have enough fuel and firepower to take them out."

The ship's engines suddenly hummed optimistically. Lunnto had fixed the drive line. As they accelerated toward the first communications buoy, an E'roni devilfighter followed close behind. But it only took one shot for the small buoy to explode in a sunburst of sparks.

Lunnto had returned to the cockpit, his face smudged with grease. "Are you sure we need to blow these up? What if we need them to talk to other sectors?" he asked, hitting buttons so fast his fingers were a blur.

No, I'm not sure, Plana thought, but they needed a leader right now. She spoke, more to herself than to Lunnto. "Why? No one has been helping us," Plana said. "The Republic says it wants to help, but we're not part of the Republic, and the chancellor's own son destroyed Erasmus City. The Jedi were supposed to help with the peace talks, and now that's been blown to smithereens. We're on our own, Lunnto." She frowned deeply. "That klytobacter came from somewhere. If E'ronoh is getting help from the outside, it's time to stop that. Let's hit that buoy next." She accelerated, leaving the other fighting ships behind them.

A bright light and a crash sent Plana flying from her captain's chair onto the floor, alarms beeping loudly. Her navigator, Pell, walked almost drunkenly into the cockpit, scratching his bluish beard and blinking slowly.

"Hey, I think someone's shooting at us!" Pell said, voice croaky.

Plana rolled her eyes. That was some nap. She scrambled back into her pilot's chair. She patted the console affectionately.

"Show me your stuff," she muttered, maximizing their acceleration. The devilfighter kept firing on them before an Eirami crescent ship finally cut them off. Plana's transport had only enough shield power for a few more hits.

Another buoy sizzled and died. Plana was a good pilot, but in her youth, she was an excellent shot. Some things, you don't forget. The other buoy was on the far side of Eiram, but they didn't even have to go there.

"Captain Van. The last communications buoy has been destroyed."

"Excellent!" Plana yelled, and her crew cheered. "Which of us got it?"

Commander Ailee sounded exhausted, and they'd only been in battle for minutes. "Hard to tell. E'roni ships fired simultaneously. Looks like they were thinking the same thing."

Plana's skin prickled as she decelerated and turned. From afar, the dark space surrounding Eiric was alight with explosions. Ships from E'ronoh and Eiram alike were being shot down. People were dying again. She thought of all the other planets and people out in the vast galaxy—so many who had come to the enormous wedding celebration only weeks ago. Now they were cut off from help. She thought of all those new communications buoys placed by countless hyperspace prospectors these last several years. They'd connected these two planets to the rest of the galaxy. In a wink, they were gone.

Alone. And once again, at war.